A DOCTOR BY DAY...

&

TAMED BY
THE RENEGADE

BY
EMILY FORBES

MILLS
BOON

A DOCTOR BY DAY…

BY
EMILY FORBES

MILLS & BOON

Published in Great Britain 2014
by Mills & Boon, an imprint of Harlequin (UK) Limited,
Eton House, 18-24 Paradise Road, Richmond, Surrey, TW9 1SR

© 2014 Emily Forbes

ISBN: 978-0-263-90800-8

Harlequin (UK) Limited's policy is to use papers that are natural, renewable and recyclable products and made from wood grown in sustainable forests. The logging and manufacturing processes conform to the legal environmental regulations of the country of origin.

Printed and bound in Spain
by Blackprint CPI, Barcelona

Dear Reader

I'd like to introduce you to the Anderson sisters—Scarlett, Ruby and Rose—and their search for a happily-ever-after. Scarlett doesn't think she needs one, Ruby doesn't think she deserves one, and Rose looks as if she might not get one. But all that is about to change…

In A DOCTOR BY DAY… Scarlett—the rational, clever, eldest sister—is swept off her feet by Jake, a sexy younger man with an unconventional part-time job who upends her orderly world and steals her heart. And in TAMED BY THE RENEGADE Ruby, the rebellious middle sister, falls in love for the first time when gorgeous Noah gets under her defences and teaches her how to love and accept—not only him, but also herself.

These two Anderson sisters might not have a lot in common, but I discovered they both have a thing for good-looking bare-chested men and, as usual, I had fun creating the heroes for my heroines. Jake and Noah are strong and loyal, smart and sexy, with slight non-conformist streaks—perfect for Scarlett and Ruby, even if they take some convincing.

I hope you enjoy these first two stories. I haven't decided if I'll give Rose her own story yet—she's putting up a good case for it in my imagination, but I'm tempted to let you decide. If you'd like to read about Rose I'd love to hear from you. Drop me a line at emilyforbes@internode.on.net

Until then, happy reading

Emily

Emily Forbes won a
2013 Australian Romantic Book of the Year Award
for her title
SYDNEY HARBOUR HOSPITAL: BELLA'S WISHLIST

Dedication

For romance readers everywhere,
this book is written as a thank-you to anyone
who has ever read one of my stories.

I started writing this story just after
I won the Australian Romantic Book of the Year award for
SYDNEY HARBOUR HOSPITAL: BELLA'S WISHLIST.

I was thrilled and honoured to win a RuBY,
which is a reader-voted award,
and I definitely couldn't have done it without your support.

I hope you enjoy this book too, and in particular Jake.
He is my gift to you!

Love, Emily

CHAPTER ONE

'LET ME GET this straight. Richard proposed and you turned him down?'

Scarlett turned and leant in close to her friend's ear, taking care to avoid the spiky tips of Mel's short pixie haircut. 'Shh,' she whispered. 'I don't want everyone to know and I'm sure Richard doesn't either.'

Mel's voice hadn't been overly loud but this wasn't a conversation Scarlett wanted the rest of the girls in their party to hear. She worked with most of them and she didn't want to be the subject of rampant hospital gossip and she certainly didn't want to be the one to start a tale.

She flicked a glance over their group but most of the girls seemed to be more focused on getting inside the club than listening to her and Mel. Candice, the bride-to-be, was at the front of the line, the long white veil she wore making it obvious she was the hen on the hen's night. The veil was longer than her dress and Scarlett thought she looked ridiculous but what would she know, hen's nights were not really her thing.

Neither was fashion, she thought as she wriggled her toes, trying to encourage some circulation into her extremities. Her feet were killing her. She'd borrowed a pair of platform stilettos to team with her simple black

dress. The shoes and her make-up were the only con-
cessions she'd made to dressing up for the night out but
the strappy sandals were proving to be a big mistake.

Scarlett's taste in clothing tended towards timeless
classics, she wasn't a trend follower. It was a waste of
good money, in her opinion, and her feet were now reminding her of her momentary lapse of reason. She
couldn't wait to get inside and sit down. The short walk
from the restaurant in Leigh Street to the Hindley Street
club was about her limit in five-inch heels.

She couldn't believe she was keen to get into the
club. Spending an evening at a male revue, especially
one called The Coop, wasn't something she had ever
done before and she could only imagine what the experience would be like—although if the guy on the door
was any example she wasn't going to need to rely on
her imagination.

Candice's name was on the door, allowing them to
bypass the queue and giving them free entry. Apparently Candice knew someone who worked here and
Scarlett wondered where on earth you'd meet someone
who worked in a strip club, but as the cute young shirtless guy on the door ushered them inside she decided
she didn't care, all she wanted was to sit down.

'I want to hear all about it once we're inside,' Mel
said, as another buffed and shirtless male greeted them
and led them to their table. The club was dimly lit and it
took Scarlett's eyes some time to adjust to the lighting.
A T-shaped stage jutted out into the centre of the club,
the catwalk stretching into the tables that were clustered
around the stage. A mirrored bar lined the far wall and
a dance floor hugged the back wall and was already
packed with young women dancing and singing. The

noise level was high and almost unpleasant, but Scarlett hoped that might work in her favour. Perhaps the noise would make any sort of conversation impossible.

She followed the girls to their table, which was front and centre at the end of the catwalk, and sank into a chair. Jugs of bright green cocktails were delivered, promptly poured into glasses and passed around, and Mel waited only until everyone had a drink before she continued her interrogation.

'So Richard was lying in his hospital bed, recovering from heart surgery, working up the nerve to propose, and then you knocked him back?' she asked, as she sipped her drink. It seemed Scarlett wasn't going to get out of this.

'It wasn't like that,' Scarlett protested. Surely Mel couldn't believe she'd be that heartless.

'Don't tell me he was down on one knee beside his bed?'

'No.' Scarlett shook her head. 'He was out of hospital.'

'Well, that makes all the difference,' Mel teased. 'How did he take it when you said no?'

Scarlett could tell Mel was enjoying her discomfort but she had made her decision for what she knew were perfectly valid reasons and she wasn't going to marry the guy just because he'd had a mid-life revelation.

'He was okay. What other choice did he have really? It was my decision. He can't change my mind. I think marriage is overrated and it's not for me.'

'Don't let Candice hear you.'

'She already knows. Richard showed her the ring he bought me, he wanted her opinion.'

'He bought you a ring!?'

Scarlett nodded.

'What was it like?' Mel's curiosity took another turn.

'Gorgeous,' she admitted. And it had been. A square-cut solitaire, over one carat in size, set in platinum. It was in a traditional setting and was exactly right for her, classic and expensive. 'Almost gorgeous enough that I wanted to accept his proposal.'

'So why did you say no?'

'I was thinking about saying yes but then he started talking about having kids and I freaked out. I don't want kids.'

'Really? How come I never knew that?'

Scarlett and Mel had been friends for years, since meeting on the first day of med school, but Scarlett hadn't realised she'd never shared her feelings about children. She supposed the topic had never come up before now.

'Kids are a huge sacrifice. Believe me, I should know. I've seen what my mother gave up to raise me and my sisters. I've worked really hard to get to this point in my career and I'm not done yet. I'm not going to give it all up to raise a family.'

Scarlett could feel the effects of the cocktails they'd been drinking on top of the wine she'd had at dinner. She could hear her words weren't as crisp as usual, a bit blurred around the edges, a bit of a lisp on the essess. She knew the alcohol had loosened her tongue too. She wasn't normally so forthcoming about her personal life but she and Mel had shared a lot over the years since they'd been paired as lab partners on their first day at uni. They had been the only two who hadn't already known someone—Mel had moved to Adelaide from Tasmania and Scarlett had been a mature entrant.

She'd felt years older than everyone else and hadn't been used to the social nuances of teenagers, even though she'd only just been out of her teens herself. Their isolation had been the only thing they'd had in common initially but they'd both recognised that it hadn't mattered. Over the years their friendship had grown until Mel felt, in a lot of ways, like another one of Scarlett's sisters, only a lot less trouble.

'But you don't have to have kids right now,' Mel countered. 'It could wait until you've finished your final exams.'

'I'd still need to establish myself in anaesthetics before I could take time off and Richard doesn't want to wait. He's forty-three and he's just had a major health scare. It's made him reassess his future.' Richard's recent heart attack and minor surgery had been a big shock to him at a relatively young age and Scarlett knew that coming face to face with his own mortality had been the trigger for his proposal and his reassessment of his priorities.

'You could get a nanny. And a housekeeper. The two of you could afford to pay for whatever help you want.'

'So I get married, have babies and then hire a nanny and a housekeeper.'

'Sounds all right to me.' Mel grinned.

Scarlett shook her head. 'Having or not having kids wasn't my only reason for turning him down. It just didn't feel right. It was more than just his desire to have a family. When he proposed it should have felt like a moment I'd been waiting for my whole life, but I remembered being more excited about getting accepted into my anaesthetics specialty than receiving a marriage proposal, and surely that's wrong. My heart was racing, but not with excitement, I think it was panic. There was no impending sense that this was the next stage of my life and I couldn't wait for it to get started. I could have married him but it would have been for the wrong reasons. At the end of the day, I didn't love him enough.'

She also knew that she'd been scared. Terrified even. She didn't want to have children with someone so much older and who had heart problems. What if he died and left her a single mother? That was exactly what had happened to her own mother and it was not what she wanted in her own future. She didn't love Richard enough to take that chance. It was easier to let him go.

She had thought Richard would be a safe choice, she'd thought he wanted the same things as her. She'd thought his focus was on his career and that because he was already in his forties he wouldn't want children. Wouldn't he have had them by now if that was the case? But when things had turned out differently from what she'd expected, she'd discovered that she didn't love him enough to change her mind. She didn't love him enough to risk everything she'd worked for.

'So that's it. All over?'

'It's the right decision. I know it is. I'm not even sure he loves me either. I think a lot of his plan for the future was driven by timing and circumstances and not so much by his love for me. He had never mentioned wanting children before his heart attack. I think he'd be marrying me for the wrong reasons too.'

Scarlett picked up her cocktail glass. The wait staff was well trained and had obviously been told to make the most of the break in the entertainment to keep the drinks coming. No sooner had one jug been emptied than another was delivered. Scarlett sipped her drink.

She didn't really need more but she wanted to let the alcohol numb her a little bit. She didn't want to spend the night thinking about Richard. That chapter of her life was over and she wasn't planning on having any regrets.

She'd been working and studying hard since she was sixteen and she had a few more years to go. She wanted to finish her studies and she wanted time to enjoy the fruits of her labour. She didn't want to be tied down at the moment. Surely that was a sign she wasn't ready for marriage. Surely that was a sign that it was time to have some fun.

'Let's talk about something else. I'm moving forward with my life, starting tonight.'

She looked around at all the women who were getting into the spirit of the evening, not just at Candice's table but throughout the room. She got the feeling she could let her hair down and not be judged. There was a sense of *what happened in the strip club stayed in the strip club* feel to the night. Maybe it was the effect of the green cocktails but Scarlett decided it was time to join the party.

Another round of cocktails had just been brought to their table and this time it was Scarlett who refilled their glasses before she turned her attention to the entertainment. Another set had just begun and the stripper on stage was young and athletic and, in her uneducated opinion, very good at his job. She felt slightly uncomfortable appreciating the 'talent' of the much younger men on stage but considering she was hardly the oldest female in the room, and she was certainly not the loudest in voicing her appreciation, she decided she would be rude not to enjoy the show.

By the time the set came to a close the green hue of

the drink was starting to make her feel a bit nauseous. She wasn't used to drinking much, her job didn't really allow for it, and she knew if she didn't make sure to drink some water she'd regret it in the morning.

'I think I need something other than alcohol,' she told Mel. 'I'm going to the bar. Do you want anything?'

Mel shook her head as Scarlett pushed her chair back and stood up, pleased to find she could feel her toes again after resting her feet. She picked her way through the tables, dodging the good-looking, scantily clad waiting staff. She didn't want to make eye contact with them but there didn't seem to be any other polite place to look as she made her way across the room.

The bar staff was all cut from the same cloth as the waiters. They were all men, all shirtless and all cute. Not one of them had any chest hair or any body fat. They were all waxed and tanned and gorgeous and Scarlett gave them each a quick once-over before they had time to notice her.

The barman closest to her was slicing lemons. He was about three feet away and standing in profile to her. He had a sculpted jaw, small ears and brown hair, cut shorter at the sides and longer on top, that he'd obviously run some product through with his fingers to keep it spiked up. The deejay was playing a faster-tempo dance number now and all the barmen were moving to the music. Nothing choreographed, their movements looked natural and Scarlett wondered if they even knew they were dancing. She watched his hips as he kept time to the beat. His abdominal muscles flexed as he twisted to reach another lemon, drawing her attention away from his butt. His skin was smooth and tanned and his triceps tensed as he slid the knife through the flesh.

He finished dissecting the last lemon and scraped the slices into a bowl, using the back of the knife. He slid the cutting board into a sink as he twirled the knife through his fingers. Scarlett held her breath and watched as the light reflected off the blade. She gasped as he lost control of the knife and it left his hand and spun through the air. She watched it fall and waited for it to hit the floor, waited for it to stab into something it shouldn't.

It landed on the floor behind the barman, where it lay innocuously on the rubber matting. No harm, no foul, but he'd heard her gasp and before he retrieved the knife he turned to look at her. He grinned. A cheeky, quick smile that lit up his face and made Scarlett think he made a habit of mucking around and that he didn't mind getting caught.

He held her gaze and winked at her. Scarlett blushed and quickly broke eye contact but when, out of the corner of her eye, she saw him turn around to pick up the knife she automatically went back for a second look. His jeans had stretched firmly across his butt and Scarlett couldn't help but admire him. His buttocks were round and firm and the denim of his pants moulded perfectly to his backside.

She was still looking as he stood up and turned to face her, catching her by surprise. Her blush deepened and she couldn't pretend she hadn't been checking him out but luckily he didn't seem offended if his broad grin was anything to go by. He didn't seem to mind being stared at but, then, why should he? He was gorgeous and probably very used to it. She didn't imagine she was the first woman to have been caught perving on him.

He ran the knife under hot water and put it to one

side. He grabbed a tea towel to dry his hands and then tucked the towel into the waistband of his jeans. Scarlett's eyes followed his movements. His jeans were loose at his hips and as he shoved the tea towel under his waistband the movement pushed his jeans even lower, giving her a glimpse of the diagonal line of his inguinal ligament. When she realised what she was doing she quickly raised her eyes, only to find he was still watching her.

He took three steps and came to a stop in front of her. He was still grinning and Scarlett was flustered, unsettled and unsure where to look.

'What can I get you?' he asked.

His voice was deep but quiet and she found herself leaning towards him as she tried to hear what he was saying. They were separated only by a few inches now and his features came into sharp relief, almost as though he'd been projected onto a glass pane in front of her. His green eyes were deep set and as he looked at her it seemed he could see what she was thinking.

His bottom lip was full even while he was smiling and his nose was perfectly straight, flaring slightly at the bottom into a small triangle. His chin and jaw were shaped like the bottom of a flawlessly proportioned pentagon and the angles of his face gave him an almost perfectly symmetrical appearance. His tanned shoulders were dusted with freckles and his jaw was lightly stubbled, and at close range he looked older than she'd first thought. But he was still young, mid-twenties maybe, definitely younger than her. Not that his age mattered. Sure, he was cute and his body was divine and he certainly looked like he would know how to show a woman a good time, but it was irrelevant to her.

Sexy young strip-club barmen were not her thing, even if they did have the ability to disconnect her brain and make her struggle to speak. He was waiting patiently for her answer and if he could read her thoughts, as she suspected, he was no doubt amused by her lack of reply.

'May I have a glass of water, please?' she managed to ask, just as if it looked like he was about to repeat his question.

Her words sounded strange and she could feel her tongue sticking to the roof of her mouth but she wasn't a hundred per cent sure it was from the alcohol. It could also be because of the half-naked man standing in front of her. She'd seen plenty of naked or semi-naked bodies before but it wasn't every day that one as fine as this appeared before her. Was it any wonder she was struggling to think clearly, let alone speak?

He turned and scooped ice into a glass with his left hand and Scarlett caught a glimpse of a tattoo on the inside of his left biceps, several inky black marks making a dark impression against his skin. He turned to pick up a slice of lemon from the bowl he'd just filled, obscuring his tattoo from view. He dropped the lemon onto the ice and grinned at her as it hit the cubes. His hips kept time with the music as he filled the glass with water and Scarlett's stomach did a peculiar flip as she watched. He looked completely comfortable in his skin and there was something very sensual about his movements.

'Anything else I can do for you?' he asked, as he placed the glass on the bar. His eyes swept over her face, from her eyes to her lips and down to her chest as he spoke to her. Scarlett knew the neck on her dress was high enough that there was no hint of cleavage but she blushed as if she was the one standing there half-naked, not him. His swift gaze was practised, she had no doubt he had plenty of experience at giving women a quick once over, but even she could see the appreciation in his eyes. She could feel her pulse beating between her thighs, and she could feel it getting stronger as the heat in his gaze intensified.

She swallowed and reached for the glass, only to find he hadn't let go of it yet. Her fingers touched his and a surge of electricity shot through her. She snatched her hand back as if the glass was hot instead of filled with ice-cold water.

He was smiling at her again as he pushed the glass closer before removing his hand. His green eyes laughed at her but not unkindly as he asked, 'First time?'

She looked at him in mute surprise. There was no room in her head for conversation as unfamiliar hormones ran rampant through her bloodstream.

'I'd remember if I'd seen you before,' he added, and Scarlett wondered if the bar staff relied on tips. That would explain why he was being so friendly.

But water was free, wasn't it? There was no need to tip and, therefore, no need for him to flirt with her. She'd never had a stranger flirt with her. She wasn't really the type. She knew it was because she never encouraged eye contact, she didn't have the knack of catching or holding someone's attention. She knew the barman had only noticed her because she'd gasped when he'd dropped the knife and she was positive he was only flirting with her out of habit.

She glanced around, partly to confirm that he was actually talking to her and partly to see if anyone was paying them any attention. The bar area wasn't busy; most of the women seemed happy to utilise the club's table service and let the shirtless waiters come to them. The focus of the room was the stage and the tables were set facing that way, which meant most of the women had their backs to the bar. No one was looking at her. No one except the hot barman.

She wasn't sure what she should do in this situation but, since no one was watching her and to ignore him would be rude, she smiled back. 'You have women who come here often enough that you can recognise them?'

'Believe it or not, we get a lot of regulars. Birthday parties and hen's nights are good for repeat business. We've even had repeat customers who hold divorce parties.'

'Divorce parties?'

'The club owner thinks divorcees are an untapped market. Cashed-up women looking for some fun.' He shrugged his smooth, sculpted shoulders. 'He's right and they do seem to enjoy themselves but I take it that's not why you're here?'

She shook her head and replied. 'Hen's night.'

Her eyes flicked across the room to the group she'd come with. No one seemed to have missed her and while she felt as though time was standing still she'd probably only been gone from the table for a few minutes.

As she scanned the room the stage lights came on and started pulsating. The deejay started spinning a eighties disco number and the dance floor cleared as everyone made their way back to their seats and focussed their attention on the front of the room as the next act, an athletic stripper in a sailor's outfit, took to the stage. Scarlett could see the stage from the bar. It was in the club's interest to make sure all patrons had a good view, but she wasn't in any hurry to return to her seat, she was more than happy with the view she had here. She checked again but it seemed as though her absence wasn't being noted. She guessed her company couldn't compete with a semi-naked man gyrating on a stage.

'You're with Candice?' he asked. Apparently he had followed her line of sight.

Scarlett's eyes shot back. 'You know her?' she asked, as she remembered that Candice had known someone who worked here. Was this him?

'We're old family friends,' he explained. He pulled the tea towel from the waistband of his jeans and began wiping the bar. It was already spotless and Scarlett wondered if it was a delaying tactic. Was he delaying so he could talk to her? A warm glow spread through her. She couldn't deny she was enjoying the attention. 'Do the two of you work together?' he asked.

Scarlett nodded.

'Are you a nurse too?'

She shook her head. 'I'm a doctor.'

Her answer surprised him. He'd thought he was a good judge of character and while he didn't think she looked like a nurse she looked even less like a doctor. Her neck was long and slender, her face a perfect oval. Her lips were full and pouty, shiny with a pale pink gloss. In contrast, her eyes were dark and mesmerising. Outlined with kohl, the lids dusted with dark eye shadow and her lashes coated with mascara, her eyes looked as though they could have a thousand secrets hidden in their depths.

Her hair, a brown so deep it was almost black, was

thick and she'd pulled it back into a bun at the nape of her neck. His fingers itched to reach across the bar and pull the pins out, to let her hair cascade over her shoulders.

He realised it was the bun that had thrown his judgement off. It was far too severe for her stunning features and gave her the appearance of someone who worked in administration. All she needed to complete the look was a pair of glasses.

On the surface she looked like organised efficiency but his imagination suggested that underneath the surface was a different story. Perhaps he'd been working at the club for too long, he thought as his mind wandered. Maybe he was having difficulty separating fact from fiction, reality from fantasy.

'What's so funny?' she asked.

He shook his head as he realised he was smiling. 'Nothing.' She was a doctor who worked with Candice. It wasn't funny, it was perfect, but the story would keep for another day. 'I'd better get back to work. Tell Candice I'll come over later and say hi.'

He watched as she left the bar and crossed the room to return to her table. He wasn't in a hurry to get back to work—checking her out was far more interesting. Her body was smoking hot. She had poured it into a simple black dress—round neck, sleeveless, zipped down the back. He wondered if she was trying to disguise her assets, but the sway of her hips drew his attention to her narrow waist and round bottom. He was enjoying watching her walk away.

Her dress stopped just above her knees and his eyes travelled lower. Her legs were bare, no stockings, and her calves were pale, her ankles slender. She was wearing heels, ridiculously high heels, which might explain the sexy sway of her hips. He just had time to notice her shoes had a leopardskin pattern before she slid into her seat at the end of the catwalk and the stage hid her legs from view.

He was fascinated. Her swollen lips, mysterious eyes, generous D bust and her unexpected shoes all contrasted sharply with her no-nonsense hairstyle and plain dress. She was a bombshell disguised as a secretary. Which part of her was real? Was she even aware of the bombshell? Was her outfit smoke and mirrors or did she really not know how hot she was? Did she ever let the bombshell out and how could he arrange to be there if she did?

By the time she sat down at her table, Evan, the sailor stripper, had been replaced by Caesar, a muscular man of Fijian descent, who was clad only in a loincloth. The guys were warming the crowd up again with their routines. As Jake mixed a fresh batch of cocktails Caesar backflipped off the catwalk and began dancing through the crowd, looking for a willing participant for his act. Jake watched Candice's friend as he measured and poured. He could see she was trying to avoid eye contact with Caesar, desperate not to be picked and dragged into the spotlight. Just watching her made him grin. She was definitely a club virgin.

He watched as she dipped her head to the side, bringing him into her line of sight. She saw him watching her, a reversal of their earlier roles, but not one to be embarrassed at being caught out, he gave her another wink.

Scarlett felt herself blush again. What was wrong with her? Why couldn't she keep her eyes to herself? Why did she keep seeking him out? She'd just turned down a marriage proposal and yet her head was full of lustful thoughts about a complete stranger.

She tried to focus instead on the dancer, *stripper*—she wasn't sure what they called themselves—only to find that his act was finishing and his spot was being taken by another man, slightly older than the others but just as buff and tanned, who wore tight black leather pants and nothing else. He held a microphone and greeted the audience in a loud, showman's voice, 'Good evening, chicks, and welcome to The Coop.'

'Good evening, Rooster!' A chorus of women's voices split the air as the majority of the audience called out a greeting in return.

'Listen up, ladies, the Himbo Limbo is about to begin. Choose your competitor and send them to me,' he said, as he spread his arms wide in an expansive, all-encompassing gesture that made the muscles on his chest and arms ripple.

'I nominate Scarlett!' Candice shouted, as she bounced in her chair.

Scarlett frowned. She had no idea who this Rooster character was or what he was talking about. 'What on earth is a Himbo Limbo?' she asked.

CHAPTER TWO

'IT'S JUST A limbo competition,' Candice told her, 'with a twist.'

Scarlett felt her antennae twitch. She could sense a disaster in the making or at the very least some embarrassment. 'What sort of twist?'

'The "Himbo" part refers to two strippers. Instead of using poles, the Himbos hold the rope,' Candice explained.

That didn't sound nearly as risqué as Scarlett's imagination had led her to envisage but she couldn't understand why Candice was sending her up if it was all so tame. 'Why don't you do it?' she asked, as Rooster called for the nominated hens or chicks to come forward.

'You do yoga, you should be flexible,' Candice replied, 'and, besides, I can't limbo in this skirt, it doesn't leave much to the imagination when I'm standing up straight, let alone if I'm horizontal.'

Scarlett couldn't argue with that, Candice's skirt was incredibly short. She didn't know if she was any more suitably attired, her little black dress was hardly limbo-appropriate, but regular yoga classes meant she was reasonably flexible so maybe it wouldn't be all bad. She hadn't expected games but it was highly likely there would be more embarrassing contests to come and this sounded like it could be one of the lesser evils.

She glanced around the room. Most of the tables seemed to be nominating a participant, although the majority seemed to be brides-to-be, not 'chicks'. She finally clicked why the club was named The Coop— it was full of hens and chicks and one very loud and proud Rooster.

'C'mon, Scarlett, do it for me, it'll be fun,' Candice pleaded.

Scarlett thought it would be about as much fun as getting her legs waxed but she wasn't sure how she could get out of it. It was unlike her to put herself in the spotlight but as the girls continued to egg her on she found herself giving in. Maybe she'd had one too many cocktails, she thought as she said, 'All right, I'll do it.'

Just as she stood up the two 'Himbos' appeared front and centre on the floor beside the catwalk. Scarlett breathed a sigh of relief. At least it seemed as though she wouldn't have to actually get up on the stage. The men were both very toned, no surprises there, and dressed in what could only be described as very tiny, very snug leather shorts. Scarlett thought one of the men was the stripper who had just finished his routine. He had swapped his loincloth for white shorts, which were a sharp contrast to his dark skin but left nothing to the imagination.

The other 'Himbo' was in a pair of slightly more respectable black leather shorts. Scarlett had never thought she'd consider men wearing tiny leather shorts 'respectable' but it seemed as though there was a fair bit about tonight that was going to challenge her traditional and conservative views.

Just when she thought it was safe to join in, the Himbos sprang up onto the stage and Rooster called to the girls, 'Okay, hens and chicks, make your way up to me.'

A spotlight swept the room and came to rest on the gaggle of women gathered by the stage before it moved to illuminate a short flight of stairs leading up onto the catwalk. Scarlett was horrified to realise they were expected on the stage after all but slightly mollified by the sight of the stairs. It was a relief to know they weren't expected to spring onto the stage in the Himbos' footsteps—she certainly wouldn't be springing anywhere in her borrowed platform heels.

The women made a beeline for the steps, eager to get the competition under way, as Scarlett held back. The steps had no railing and she didn't want to get jostled and go sprawling up the stairs in front of everyone. She was going to be embarrassed soon enough just doing the limbo, she didn't need to start by making a complete fool out of herself.

The women clustered around the Himbos as the deejay played dance music. The women and the Himbos were all dancing, with the exception of Scarlett, who tried her best to blend into the background behind the others, although that was hard to do given she was almost five feet eleven inches tall in her five-inch heels. Fortunately Rooster began to introduce the Himbos to the audience, which Scarlett took to mean that the contest would be starting soon and she wouldn't have to be embarrassed for too much longer. The Fijian stripper in the short white shorts, Caesar, was introduced first, followed by Rico, who was introduced as the 'Italian

Stallion'. The audience cheered and clapped as the Himbos took their places.

'And now I'd like to introduce our judge for this evening,' Rooster crowed, somehow managing, through sheer force of personality, to keep the attention on himself. 'A favourite among the chicks, our very own Judge Jake.'

The cheers of the audience turned into wolf whistles and the noise in the club reached maximum volume as Candice's friend, the barman Scarlett had been talking to earlier, came up onto the stage. It seemed she wasn't the only one who thought he was delicious.

He had changed his outfit but Scarlett was happy to see he wasn't wearing leather pants—she'd seen enough leather pants tonight to last her a lifetime. He'd changed from regular denim jeans into a black pair, which hugged his thighs. His chest was still bare and he had a length of rope looped over one shoulder and slung across his torso. He jogged across the stage, moving lightly and waving to his adoring audience, and Scarlett's level of embarrassment increased with every step he took towards her. It was too late to back out now but she wished the stage would open up and swallow her. She tried in vain to hide, even though she knew it was futile. He was going to see her standing there sooner or later.

Caesar and Rico had stepped in front of the women, creating some space, and Jake passed them each a black strap, which they fixed around their chests. At the front of the strap, positioned over their sternums, was a hook that looked like a mountaineering karabiner. Jake hoisted the rope from his shoulder and handed it to the Himbos. At each end of the rope was a small metal loop, which Caesar and Rico clipped into the karabiners.

Scarlett's eyes widened in surprise. She hadn't expected the rope to be tied around their chests, she'd expected them to hold it, stretched out between them. That would have given the competitors plenty of space to move but once the rope was tied around their chests and clipped into the karabiners it was quite short and didn't leave a lot of room to manoeuvre. Not, Scarlett thought, that most of the girls would mind, but she had no intention of brushing against half-naked strangers any more than she had to.

Jake waited until the limbo rope was in position before taking the microphone from Rooster and taking over the contest. The girls were asked to line up and after much jostling Scarlett found herself third in line behind two hens, one rather large one and one with an exceptionally long veil. Judge Jake approached each competitor in turn and asked them their name. He showed no surprise when he got to Scarlett and she knew then he'd already seen her on the stage. She just hoped he didn't think she'd volunteered.

Even in her heels she was still an inch or two shorter than him, and she had to look up slightly when she told him her name. Up close she could see that his green eyes were ringed with brown and he winked at her as he repeated her name and Scarlett felt her cheeks redden. She hoped the tell-tale blush wouldn't be noticeable but she suspected the spotlight would only serve to enhance the colour in her face.

With much cheering and clapping from the audience Jake got the contest under way. The plump hen went first and she could almost walk under the rope without

ducking, she was so short. The next hen, the one with
the long veil, wasn't so lucky. She trod on her veil as she
tipped her head backwards to duck under the rope. This
pulled her up short and made her fall and she landed
hard on her backside. Her faux pas was greeted with
laughter from the audience, though not cruel or nasty
laughter. Scarlett knew most of them would be laughing with relief that they weren't the ones lying flat on
their backs in front of a crowd.

She couldn't work out how the hen had managed to
trip herself up but as she was sprawled on the floor and
Jake was reaching for her hand to help her to her feet
Scarlett just prayed that she wouldn't be as unlucky or
as ungainly. She was next in line.

'How confident are you?' Jake asked her, as she
moved a step closer.

Scarlett looked at the girls around her, including the
one already disqualified. 'I've done a few limbos in
my time,' she fibbed. 'I think I can take this one.' Her
knees felt weak and she wondered how she was going to
manage to limbo on wobbly legs but her voice sounded
surprisingly normal and strong.

She wasn't sure why she'd chosen to announce her
lies to the room; she could only assume it had something to do with the challenge in Jake's eyes. She didn't
want to look like a complete klutz in front of him but
neither did she want to appear timid and pathetic. She
didn't normally think of herself as a competitive, win-
at-all-costs type of person but she didn't like to fail at
anything. She had high expectations of herself and she
certainly didn't want to be beaten by these women.

Jake laughed and announced, 'Scarlett Take-No-

Prisoners, who is standing in for her hen, Candice, let's see what you've got.'

The girls on her table whooped and cheered as Scarlett easily limboed under the rope and popped up on the other side.

After Scarlett were another six competitors, four hens, one with a rather heavy, awkward-looking tiara holding her veil in place, and two chicks. Two more fell on the first attempt and Scarlett thought the success rate was probably indirectly proportionate to the amount each 'chick' had had to drink.

As the contest continued and the number of competitors dropped, so did the height of the rope. As the rope descended the Himbos shortened it too, bringing them even closer together and giving the chicks less margin for error. Another two stumbled and were eliminated as the rope was lowered to the bottom of the Himbos' rib cages.

The girls were being urged on by their friends but despite the encouragement all but two were out of the competition after attempting to limbo under the rope when it was level with the Himbos' waists. By the time the rope was moved further south to their hips Scarlett's until-now-unknown competitive streak had well and truly emerged and she had no intention of losing tonight. It was now a two-chick race between her and a girl named Tracey and it was Scarlett's turn.

Scarlett sized up the competition. Tracey was several inches shorter than her so Scarlett slid her platform heels from her feet to level the playing field. The rope was very low now and she didn't need to make this any harder than it already was.

'Watch out, Tracey.' Jake laughed. 'The competition

is getting serious, clothing is being shed. What else is coming off, Scarlett?'

His green eyes were challenging her again and something in his expression made her want to challenge him back. 'Nothing yet,' she quipped, and was rewarded with a brief spark of something—maybe attraction, maybe anticipation, she wasn't sure—but there was definitely a light in his eyes. She turned her back, wanting to leave him hanging, and shimmied under the rope. She just managed to scrape under without over-balancing.

Jake had stepped around to the other side of the Himbos and was there to take her hand as she straightened. He kept his elbow bent, which kept her close, and his hand warmed her skin where it wrapped around her fingers. He smelt clean, as if he was freshly showered but she knew that couldn't be the case. He smelt good.

She could feel the heat coming off his half-naked body and she knew the skin on his chest would feel as warm and soft as his hand. Scarlett's stomach trembled as Jake continued to hold her hand as they waited for Tracey to take her turn at the limbo. Her body was tingling as Jake's touch awakened her senses and she could feel the pulse low in her belly starting to beat a little bit faster.

Scarlett knew she could pull her hand out of Jake's grasp but she didn't want to. This connection would be severed soon enough and she wanted to enjoy it while it lasted. They watched as Tracey almost made it under the rope before falling at the last hurdle, putting her hand on the ground just before she was ready to stand and thereby disqualifying herself.

Jake let go of Scarlett to help Tracey to her feet. 'I'm sorry, Tracey, you almost did it,' he said as he helped her up, before turning back to Scarlett. 'That makes you our winner tonight.' His smile lit up his green eyes as he added, 'Would you like to see how low you can go?'

Scarlett watched as Caesar and Rico moved the rope down another couple of inches until it was sitting across their groins. She looked back at Jake. He was now grinning mischievously and she knew he was waiting to see if she was up to the next challenge. She shook her head. She'd let him win this round. 'I'm done.'

'All right, here's your prize.' Jake reached his left hand behind him and when he brought it forward again he had a handful of fake money that he must have had stashed in his pocket. Scarlett frowned. What was she supposed to do with fake dollar bills?

He held the notes up in the air and Scarlett got another glimpse of the tattoo on the soft side of his arm. At close range she could see that the inky black marks were stars, five of them in total, their arrangement making a pattern that was familiar to every Australian. He had the Southern Cross constellation tattooed on his skin.

Jake kept his arm held high as he turned through one hundred and eighty degrees, showing the fake money to the crowd, who cheered as he called out, 'Tipping dollars!'

'Tipping dollars?' Scarlett repeated. She had no idea what he was talking about.

Jake lowered the microphone and leant in close as he pressed the fake banknotes into her hand. 'It's to tip the dancers,' he explained. 'Tuck some into the guys' shorts before you leave the stage and share the rest with your group for them to use later.'

The crowd applauded and cheered again as she tipped the Himbos while Jake escorted Tracey from the stage, but before she could follow the crowd began to chant, 'Jake, Jake, Jake!' and she knew she was expected to tip him too. She wasn't certain but she thought Candice might have been leading the call.

Jake was back by her side again. He didn't seem surprised or reticent and she suspected he loved the attention. She'd bet his star sign was Leo. They loved the limelight. She tucked a few notes into his waistband and as her fingers brushed against his hipbone she found herself searching his skin for more tattoos. But the skin of his torso and waist was smooth, tanned and ink-free. Her heart was hammering in her chest and she could feel a blush stealing across her cheeks. Somehow touching Jake felt a lot more personal than when she'd been tipping Caesar and Rico.

With shaky hands she picked up her shoes and fled the stage, retreating to the relative safety of her table.

'That was a side of you I hadn't seen before,' Mel said as she sat down.

'And don't expect to see it again any time soon,' Scarlett replied. Her heart was still racing, making her sound breathless. She hoped everyone would think it was from the exertion of the limbo, although she knew it was a reaction to Jake.

Performing in front of a crowd was completely out of character for her but part of her had enjoyed the chance to pretend to be someone else, someone less worried about behaving appropriately and less concerned about being who people expected her to be. Perhaps it was a case of 'anything goes' tonight or maybe normal inappropriate behaviour was considered appropriate within the four walls of The Coop, but she didn't have time to consider it any further as Mel interrupted her musings.

'I thought it was rather entertaining. But, tell me, who is Judge Jake and how does he know Candice?' Mel asked, as Scarlett handed the remaining tipping dollars to Candice.

'We're old family friends,' Candice interrupted. 'He's coming over now, I'll introduce you.'

Scarlett turned her head. Sure enough, Jake was approaching their table. He was no longer bare-chested, he'd put on a black T-shirt and a black leather jacket but, if anything, he looked even better. No, not better, she thought, but just as good.

Candice made quick introductions before Jake grabbed an empty chair from the table beside theirs. He flipped it around with a practised move and wedged it in between Scarlett and Mel before straddling it backwards. His long legs stuck out sideways and brushed against Scarlett's thigh.

'So you do own a shirt,' Scarlett said, as her eyes raked his torso.

'And a jacket,' he teased.

He was leaning forward over the back of the chair, his arms crossed. The teasing note in his voice and the gleam in his eye made her feel bold. She reached out and ran her hand down his sleeve. 'There's a definite leather theme going on in this place.'

'Hey,' he said, as he sat up straight in the chair, held the jacket on each side of the zip and lifted it slightly, adjusting it on his shoulders, 'this is mine.'

'It's nice.' It was. She could smell the leathery fragrance. She hadn't noticed a leather smell on the Himbos, not that she'd got that close to their shorts.

'Yeah?'

She grinned, feeling more at ease. It was much less

stressful now she was out of the spotlight and off the stage. 'Much better than leather pants.'

'Have you ever worn leather pants?'

Scarlett shook her head.

'Well, you should give them a go, you might be surprised at how comfortable they are.'

'You have leather pants too?'

He raised one hand. 'Guilty as charged. Call it part of our uniform. But you might be pleased to know I don't own leather shorts.'

'That's a relief,' she said, but, as much as she thought leather was being worn a little too often around the club, she suspected he would look rather good in leather pants. She suspected he'd look good in anything.

He shifted in his seat and his thigh brushed against hers for the second time. Her nerve endings sparked and it felt as if all the cells in her thigh muscles were straining to get closer to him, as though they were trying to leap out of her skin. She moved her leg away from his before she could be tempted to lean into him instead.

The alcohol she'd drunk tonight had most certainly reduced her inhibitions. Not only had she voluntarily got up on stage, she was now having lustful thoughts about a complete stranger. She was planning on having fun but she wasn't sure if her courage stretched far enough to include Jake. She should go home before she did something even more out of character. Before she could be tempted by a cute young barman who might, or might not, be flirting with her. There was no way she was going to make a move on him, well, not the first move anyway. She needed to get out of here. If he wanted to come with her that was his choice. If he chose to stay behind then she'd assume she'd read the signals wrong. There was a good possibility of that, she thought. She was hardly the most experienced woman at the table.

She'd done her duty to Candice. Surely she could leave now without appearing rude. She leant across the table to speak to Candice, ready to make her excuses. 'I think I might head off, if you don't mind. I had a really busy night on call before working today.'

'How are you getting home?'

'I'll take a cab.'

'Do you want me to come with you?' Mel asked. 'You shouldn't go on your own.' Hindley Street was not the street you wanted to walk down alone.

'I'll wait with you, if you like,' Jake said to her. 'I've finished my shift and was about to go anyway.'

'Perfect! Thanks, Jake.' Candice agreed on Scarlett's behalf without any hesitation. 'That way, Mel can stay and enjoy the rest of the evening. You don't mind, do you?' Candice asked, as she looked at her.

Scarlett didn't want to be accused of breaking up the party so she did what came naturally to her and agreed. 'Sure,' she replied. She'd had a lifetime of experience at being the one to keep the peace, being the one to do what everyone expected of her while her sisters did as they pleased, so of course she agreed, but it didn't hurt that she was more than happy for Jake to keep her company. She knew then that his touch had been deliberate and the thought sent a frisson of excitement through her body.

'Jake is one of the good guys, you can trust him,' Candice added, before she turned to Mel and whispered with a chuckle, 'I'm not denying he could charm a nun out of her habit but that's Scarlett's good fortune.'

As Scarlett ducked her head under the table to put her shoes back on and search for her handbag she heard Candice say something about charm but she couldn't catch the whole sentence. She thought about asking her to repeat her comment but when she found her handbag and looked up she saw that Jake was standing, ready to pull out her chair for her. Not wanting to keep him waiting, she decided that if what Candice had said was important she'd find out some other time.

She followed Jake from the club, aware of several women checking him out as he passed their tables, but their attention was short-lived as another dancer was on the stage and now that Jake was fully clothed there were obviously more interesting things to look at elsewhere. Scarlett didn't mind, she was happy to have him all to herself.

There was a taxi rank opposite the club but the queue was horrendously long, stretching for half a block. Knowing it could take for ever for her turn to come, she released Jake from his obligation. 'It's going to take ages, you don't need to wait,' she said, as they joined the end of the queue.

'I promised Candice I'd look after you.'

'That's okay, I won't tell her.' She smiled. 'Thank you for offering but it's busy enough. I'll be all right,' she said, as she slipped her shoes off. Her feet had had enough and she couldn't stand the thought of another minute standing in uncomfortable high heels. The concrete pavement was rough but cool under her skin and was soothing in an unexpected way. She glanced down the line and saw she wasn't the only one who'd divested herself of her footwear.

'Come on, I'll give you a lift,' he said, looking at her bare feet.

'It's fine, really,' Scarlett insisted. 'I'm just not used to wearing high heels.'

'I'm not going to leave you here and I think we've both got better things to do than stand on the street for an hour.'

His tone wasn't impatient. Maybe she was reading things into his words but the depth of his voice and the low volume made it sound as though the better things he had in mind involved them both and she was tempted to dive in, recklessly, heedlessly, and accept his offer. But her natural inclination not to cause trouble made her ask, 'What if I live miles away?'

'Then that's my problem. I'm not going to retract my offer. I'd look like a jerk.'

She looked up at him. Barefoot, she was now several inches shorter than he was. 'I'd hate to have that hanging over my head.'

'So, can I drop you home?' He grinned and all her objections, few though they were, vanished. She nodded and slipped her sandals back on before following him as he retraced their footsteps.

He led her to an alleyway behind The Coop and Scarlett followed blindly. She knew she would feel unsafe if he wasn't beside her but even though he was virtually a stranger she trusted him. It was an odd situation to be in, she wasn't normally a trusting person, particularly not when it came to men, but she only got good vibes from Jake and he wasn't really a stranger, was he? He knew Candice.

He stopped beside a dark green convertible that had been parked behind a dumpster, which kept it partially shielded from view. The roof was down and there was a cumbersome, heavy steering lock clamped to the wheel.

Jake opened the passenger door and shrugged out of his leather jacket. 'Here,' he said, as he held it out to her. 'It might be a bit cool with the top down but it's a bit temperamental and it'll be quicker and warmer if you wear this.'

Scarlett slipped her arms into the sleeves as Jake held it for her. His fingers brushed her neck as he turned up the collar. The jacket was much too large for her but it was warm and smelt divine, a heady combination of leather and clean male. She didn't bother to zip it, just pulled it close, wrapping it around her like a cocoon.

She sank into the low seat as Jake stowed the steering lock behind them and started the engine. The sound was low and throaty and reminded her of his voice. Scarlett relaxed. She closed her eyes and let the warmth and scent of the leather of the seats and Jake's jacket seduce her. It was nice to have someone else make a decision for her. Not being required to think was a novelty. All her life she had been the one people turned to for advice. She had been the one who everyone relied on to be sensible, responsible, to make the hard decisions, and Scarlett's natural tendency was to carefully consider all angles before making an informed and logical choice.

Letting a stranger give her a lift home was not the sort of thing she did. She wasn't a spontaneous sort of person. Every decision she made was carefully measured, considered and weighed before she acted on it. She was used to being in control. Of her life and of her actions.

Going home with someone she'd just met was the sort of thing her sister Ruby would do. Ruby would have set her sights on a guy the minute she walked into The Coop and wouldn't have thought twice about letting them give her a lift home. Even their younger sister, Rose, was more outgoing than she herself was. She would have walked into The Coop, tossed her blond hair, batted her long eyelashes and her big blue eyes and within minutes she would have had men falling at her feet. She would have flirted expertly and at the end of the night she would have been spoilt for choice if she wanted a lift home.

Scarlett didn't know if she could ever be as confident or as fearless as her sisters but it was kind of nice to step out of her comfort zone for a change. But she knew the only reason she felt safe to do that was because there was a connection with Jake. She wasn't thinking about the physical or chemical connection she felt but rather the safer, more reliable one that was their common friend, Candice. Scarlett knew that no matter how gorgeous and charming a man was, she would never let a complete stranger give her a lift home. She just didn't do things like that.

'Scarlett?'

She jumped as she felt Jake's hand on her knee. She opened her eyes to find they had left Hindley Street behind. The little green car was on the bridge over the River Torrens as Jake headed up Montefiore Hill.

'Are you okay?' he asked, and she realised he must have been speaking to her while she was daydreaming.

'Yes. I'm fine.'

Jake flicked the indicator on to turn at the lookout at the top of the hill. She tried not to notice the cars parked there, certain that the occupants were up to no good as they looked across the city lights. She had never fooled around in the backseat of a car but sitting here with Jake's hand still resting on her knee she could almost imagine what it would be like. But he removed his hand to negotiate the corner, leaving a cold circle the size of his palm on her skin. He drove past the old cathedral and up towards O'Connell Street.

'Are you hungry?' he asked, as the car idled at the next set of traffic lights.

'I am,' she said, as she rubbed at the cold spot on her knee. She was a little surprised to find she was hungry but dinner seemed like hours ago.

'My favourite late-night take-away is just up here. We can grab something to eat there, if you like?'

'Sure.' She thought it was probably a good idea to eat something else and soak up the rest of the alcohol she'd consumed but where they ate was another decision she was happy to let Jake make.

Jake slowed his sports car as they approached the café strip and he searched for a parking space. A car was pulling out from the kerb and he waited, taking the spot in front of a café with distinctive blue-and-white signage. She recognised the café; she'd walked past it plenty of times but had never been inside, but it seemed that Jake knew it well.

'Jake, how's it going?' The guy behind the counter greeted him as they walked in. 'What'll you have, the usual?'

'Sounds good,' he said, before explaining to Scarlett, 'You can't go past George's lamb yiros,' he told her.

There was a huge selection of dishes written on the blackboard above the counter but Scarlett could see the lamb revolving slowly on the enormous spit, cooking as it turned, and the smell carried to her. It smelt fantastic.

She'd never tried a yiros before but it was an easy decision. She nodded. 'Make that two,' she told George.

'You want garlic sauce with that?' George asked.

That sounded rather potent and Scarlett wasn't at all familiar with yiros etiquette. Jake was watching her, his head tipped to one side, waiting for her answer. She didn't want to be in close proximity to him if she had garlic sauce and he didn't. Even in a convertible she suspected it could be unpleasant.

'Is that how you usually have it?' she asked Jake.

'Yep.'

'Okay, then.' Scarlett watched as George expertly carved slices of lamb as it rotated on the spit and piled it onto flatbreads and garnished it with garlic sauce and salad before wrapping each yiros in wax paper and handing them over the counter. She followed Jake to a table tucked into the back corner of the café. All around them other patrons were devouring their yiros but from what she could see it was almost impossible to eat daintily. Worried about making a mess of Jake's jacket, she slipped it off and hung it over the back of her chair.

'Do you want to take your shoes off too?' Jake was smiling at her.

She shook her head. 'Not in here.'

'You could take them off on the street, why not in here?' he said, as he tore the wax paper to expose the top half of his yiros.

'We're in a restaurant. Earlier I couldn't face the thought of standing any longer but I'm okay as long as I'm sitting down,' Scarlett said, copying his actions.

'I've never understood why women insist on buying uncomfortable shoes—although they do look great on you.'

'Thank you.' The compliment almost made the pain worthwhile. 'But they're not mine and I didn't realise they were so uncomfortable. I borrowed them,' she admitted. 'Strip clubs aren't really my scene and I don't own anything suitable to wear to one.' She took a bite of the warm flatbread. The lamb was tender and juicy, perfectly complemented by the sauce.

'Going to the club doesn't mean you need to dress like a stripper.' He laughed.

She stuck one foot out from underneath the table, pointing her toes and swinging her foot from side to side. 'You think these look like stripper shoes?'

Jake raised one eyebrow and grinned. 'That wasn't what I meant,' he protested.

'I wonder what my sister would have to say about that!'

Scarlett smiled back before taking another bite of her yiros, only to discover a fraction too late why she should have said no to the garlic sauce as it squirted out of the bread and ran down the side of her hand. She was holding the yiros with two hands, trying to stop it from falling apart, and there was nothing she could do about the sauce that was now running over her wrist and heading for her elbow.

Jake reached across and ran his finger along her forearm, wiping the sauce from her skin. He was watching her as he put his finger in his mouth and sucked the sauce from it and Scarlett felt as though he'd run his tongue along her bare skin. She could see the heat in his eyes and could still feel the heat from his finger as it sent a current shooting through her.

'You've got sauce just here too,' Jake said, and Scarlett held her breath as he stretched his hand out and wiped the side of her cheek. His thumb grazed the corner of her lip and Scarlett couldn't help it—her lips parted under his touch and it was all she could do not to capture his thumb with her mouth. She inhaled deeply as Jake removed his hand and this time wiped his fingers on his serviette.

Despite the fact that they were sitting in a busy café, surrounded by other people, she was aware only of Jake. She ate the rest of her yiros in silence, acutely aware of him sitting opposite her, but somehow she managed to finish eating without any further mishap.

She felt the first wave of fatigue roll over her as she wiped a serviette over her lips and stifled a yawn.

'Are you ready to go?' Jake asked.

She was tired but in no hurry to get home. She was quite happy to sit for a bit longer in his company but she had no reason to delay. She stood as Jake picked his jacket up from her chair and slung it around her shoulders. He left his hand around her back, holding the jacket in place as he walked her to his car. Scarlett had to squeeze in close to him to manoeuvre between the tables and chairs and she could feel the length of his body where he pressed against her. The night air was cool on her skin when he released her to open the car door and she pulled his jacket more tightly around her to make up for the loss of warmth.

Within minutes she had directed Jake to her house. The night was over.

Almost.

Jake was out of the car and was walking her to her door.

'Thanks for the lift,' Scarlett said, as she unlocked her front door.

'It was my pleasure.' He was leaning on the door-jamb, watching her quietly.

'And for supper,' she added, reluctant for the evening to end.

Light spilled from the hallway and fell on Jake, illuminating him where he stood. She was in shadow but she could see Jake's hand reaching towards her shoulder.

'What are you doing?'

'Something I've been wanting to do all night.'

He was leaning forward. Was he going to kiss her? His head was next to hers, his lips beside her ear, and his voice was quiet and deep. She could feel the gentle puff of his breath on her skin as he spoke and then she could feel his fingers in her hair as he pulled the end of her ponytail and untucked her hair from its bun. He pulled her hair forward and loosened it over her shoulders and his hands brushed her skin.

'That's much better.'

Scarlett turned her head and lifted it, just slightly, less than an inch, to look at him. He was still watching her and the way he looked at her made the heat pool low in her belly. She could feel a fluttering of nerves, a tremble in her stomach, but the nerves were anticipatory, not anxious. Jake's green eyes were shining emerald in the light. His lips were millimetres from hers. He dipped his head into the shadow and closed the gap. His lips were warm and hungry, soft yet demanding. His body was lean and hard and his hands on her arms were firm but gentle. Scarlett pressed herself into him as two of them became one.

His hands slid behind her, cupping her bottom, holding her to him.

She wound her hands behind his head as her lips parted in response to the pressure of his tongue.

She was standing on her front porch, kissing a stranger, but he didn't feel like a stranger. Scarlett felt as though she belonged with him, as though she'd known him always. Every cell in her body responded to his touch. Every part of her recognised him, as though they'd met before, and as she kissed him she felt as if she was reuniting with a lover, not making out with a stranger.

She brought her hands to his chest and placed them flat against his pectoral muscles. She grabbed a fistful of his T-shirt, bunching the fabric up in her palms, and dragged him out of the doorway and into her hall.

She should be saying good-night. She should be thanking him for the lift and saying goodbye but the look in his eye and the taste of his mouth had disengaged her brain and she couldn't let him go. Not yet. She knew their first kiss was only a taste of what was to come.

She stepped to her right, towards her bedroom door, and her lips left Jake's mouth. He was watching her closely, his green eyes intense, and she knew he was waiting to see what she would do next. She knew it was her decision now.

She pushed the front door closed and stepped backwards into her bedroom.

Jake didn't wait for an invitation. He stepped towards her, following her lead. His hands were behind her back and she felt him slide the zip on the back of her dress down and her dress fell at her feet. She stepped out of it, naked except for her underwear and her borrowed heels.

The light from the hallway penetrated the darkness

of her room. Scarlett stood still as Jake ran his gaze over her. He dropped his head and kissed her neck. Scarlett arched her back as his fingers trailed after his mouth.

Jake whipped his T-shirt over his head and suddenly there was bare skin on bare skin.

He scooped her up and laid her on her bed.

She bent her knee and slipped a finger under the strap at the back of her sandal.

Jake felt her movement, sensed what she was doing. 'Leave them on.'

Scarlett dropped her hand and let her knee fall as Jake ran his fingers from the inside of her ankle, up her calf to the inside of her knee. His fingers left a line of heat behind and Scarlett felt herself melt at his touch. Her eyes drifted closed.

'Scarlett?'

She opened her eyes. 'Hmm?'

'How much have you had to drink?'

His question startled her. 'Why?'

'I want to be sure I'm not taking advantage of you,' he said, as his hand continued to move higher, to the soft, warm junction at the top of her thigh. He was watching her, waiting for her to stop him, but she couldn't. She was melting in a pool of desire.

'You're not,' she told him. 'I know what I'm doing.'

She actually had no idea what she was doing—this was completely out of character for her—but he didn't know that. He didn't know the real Scarlett. He didn't know that she was normally in control of her actions and emotions. As far as he knew, she went out every weekend and drank cocktails and danced until dawn. For once, maybe it would be fun to be that girl. She wasn't hurting anybody and she could use some fun.

She wanted to lose herself in his touch. She wanted to lose herself in his embrace. She didn't want to think, she didn't want to make decisions. She wanted Jake to take her away from reality. She would worry about tomorrow another day.

Tonight she intended to take what she wanted and tonight she wanted Jake.

CHAPTER THREE

SCARLETT STRUGGLED OUT of bed on Monday morning. She felt unaccustomedly lazy after an indulgent and unusual weekend and it took twenty minutes of yoga and two cups of coffee before she was ready to face the day. Her stint in Emergency was still ongoing and she knew she needed to be focused and sharp while working there, but she was having trouble keeping her attention on what had to be done. Her mind kept wandering off to relive the events of Saturday night.

If she closed her eyes she could picture Jake lying naked and almost exhausted in her bed. They may have only spent a few hours together but she knew she'd always be able to recall the ridges of his abdominal muscles and how they'd felt under her fingers, how his green eyes had lit up when he'd laughed and how it had felt making love to a fit, young and flexible male. It had been quite an experience.

She'd never slept with anyone with a tattoo before; she'd never slept with anyone she'd just met before and never on a first date. They hadn't even had a date—she couldn't count the late-night yiros stop at the café. She still couldn't believe she'd slept with him.

She grabbed a third coffee from the kiosk on her way

into the hospital, wondering if she'd have time to drink it and knowing she probably shouldn't. Two cups was probably enough for now. The triage nurse solved her dilemma for her.

'Can you go straight into treatment room three?' she said, as she confiscated Scarlett's coffee and waited for her to sign in for her shift. 'We have a fresh lot of med students and one of them has asked for an anaesthetic consult.'

All day yesterday she'd imagined being someone else, someone more like Ruby, someone who acted spontaneously and did crazy things without regard for others. But one night of rebellion did not make her Ruby. Ruby was the fun sister, Rose was the pretty one, Scarlett was the clever one, and that was the way it had always been. And now she was a doctor and with that hard-earned qualification came certain responsibilities, which included an ability to focus and concentrate. She took a deep breath and shook her head to clear the last of the weekend cobwebs from her mind as she pulled back the curtain and stepped into the treatment room.

There were three people in the cubicle. A blond-haired, angelic-looking toddler, about two years old, was sitting on her mother's lap, cradled in her arms. The mother's face was white, the daughter's face was tear-streaked, and sterile dressings had been draped over her left hand.

The doctor sat opposite the pair and looked up as Scarlett stepped into the space. As their eyes met Scarlett felt as though all the air in her lungs had been knocked out of her. The doctor was the spitting image of Jake. The same green eyes, the same chiselled jaw. The similarity was uncanny.

She knew she was staring but she couldn't seem to stop.

'Hello, Scarlett.' It was the same voice. The same cheeky grin.

'Jake?' There was a stethoscope poking out of his coat pocket, a white doctor's coat. None of this made sense. 'What are you doing here?'

'I'm here on a uni placement.'

'You're a med student?'

'Yep. And this is Margie and her daughter, Skye.' With those few words Jake got Scarlett's attention back on track. She had a job to do, she'd have to deal with the issue of his appearance later.

'Skye managed to grab hold of some exposed live wires on the back of an old electric heater this morning. Luckily she was wearing sheepskin slippers with rubber soles but she sustained third-degree burns to several fingers. She's going to need surgery but I need an opinion as to whether a wrist or arm block would suffice or whether she'll need a GA.'

'How old is Skye?' Scarlett asked Margie, as she took two steps across the room to the basin to wash her hands.

'Twenty-six months.'

'And has she ever had an anaesthetic before?'

'No.' Margie shook her head.

'Let me see the extent of what we're dealing with.' Now that Jake had told her what had happened Scarlett was aware of the odour of burnt flesh but she still wasn't prepared for the state of Skye's fingers.

Jake lifted the dressings and Scarlett noted that he only lifted the side closest to her, keeping the injury shielded from Margie and Skye. The skin on Skye's middle, ring and little fingers was badly burnt. Charred and black, and Scarlett wondered if they'd be able to save them.

'The flesh will need debriding at the very least and most likely she will need plastic surgery. She'll need to be kept very still and that would be an impossibility for a two-year-old, so she'll need a general. I'll book a theatre.'

Scarlett was in a hurry to escape the cubicle. The space was far too small for her and Jake. She couldn't breathe and she knew it wasn't the smell of burnt flesh that was affecting her. It was Jake.

She knew she needed to ignore him. She knew it was better to treat Saturday night exactly as what it had been—a once-in-a-lifetime abjuration of character. It wasn't something she planned to make a habit of and while she couldn't deny she'd enjoyed the experience, a man like Jake didn't fit into her plans. Not even short term. He wasn't her type. He was sexy and fun and she knew she wasn't either of those things.

She gave instructions to the triage nurse and went to change. She was pleased she was going to be busy. She'd worry about Jake later.

She hurried into Theatre, pulling up short when she saw a familiar figure fiddling with the MP3 dock in the corner. Richard was back at work.

Damn. How on earth could she have forgotten his sick leave was finished and that he was returning today?

She knew it was because her head had been filled with thoughts of Jake, so much so that everything else had been wiped from her mind. Added to that, the surprise of seeing Jake again this morning had completely obliterated any chance of her remembering anything else. Guilt burned inside her as she waited for Richard to turn around. She could feel her cheeks flush and her palms were damp with sweat.

Why did it have to be today? She wasn't prepared for this, not now.

She took a few deep breaths as she tried to quell her guilty feelings. She hadn't done anything wrong, and there was no reason to feel guilty. Her business was no longer Richard's business and there was no need for him to know what she'd been up to.

He turned around as their patient was wheeled into Theatre and Scarlett's heart sank as she saw Candice and Mel on either side of the barouche. She prayed they would keep tight-lipped about the events of Saturday night.

The usual flurry of activity—transferring the patient to the operating table and beginning sedation as Mel, who was a plastics registrar, discussed the surgery with Richard—meant there was no time for idle conversation, but as soon as everything was set Candice's first question let Scarlett know she wasn't going to be so lucky.

'Did you get home all right on Saturday?' Candice asked, as she covered their patient with sterile drapes. The tone of her voice made Scarlett suspect she knew more than she was letting on but, judging by the expression on her face, she didn't seem to be hiding anything, although Scarlett was terrified that Candice was going to say more. Candice was an experienced nurse and she was quite capable of continuing a lengthy and detailed conversation while she worked.

'Yes.' She kept her answer short. She didn't want to get into this in front of Richard.

'What did you do on Saturday?' Richard asked, as he prepared to begin putting their patient back together.

'It was my hen's night,' Candice replied.

Scarlett did not want to open a discussion about Saturday night's activities so before Richard could ask any more questions she tried to steer the conversation towards Richard's health instead. He had been off work for several weeks and it would be rude of them not to enquire as to how he was feeling. She glanced at Mel, hoping she would pick up the conversation.

Scarlett felt like a wanton woman. Her behaviour on Saturday night had been completely out of character and even though no one in the room had actually witnessed it, she still felt like everyone could see on her face what she'd been up to. She'd had casual sex with a stranger or, at best, a new acquaintance, only weeks after dumping her boyfriend, who had wanted to become her fiancé and was now standing two feet from her across an operating table. Even though she was entitled to behave as she pleased, the guilt she was experiencing only emphasised the fact she was ill equipped to be acting so out of character. She was far better suited to being responsible and careful and considerate. Being spontaneous might be all right for Ruby but it obviously didn't suit her nature. She needed to remember that.

She let her thoughts drift as she heard Mel take over the conversation. Richard's MP3 was playing in the background. He liked to listen to instrumental versions of bands like Dire Straits and The Police and today it was the Adelaide Symphony's performance of Queen's songs. Scarlett would normally hum along but her mind was elsewhere.

She'd made a mistake. But she'd learn from that. She didn't plan on repeating her error.

She knew she couldn't do casual. She couldn't live in the moment. The moments always seemed to follow her. She didn't know how Ruby did it. How did she go from one man to the next without blinking an eye?

She herself had a tendency to dwell on things, which was why she tried to do the right thing in the first place. She hated feeling guilty or feeling like she'd done wrong, which was exactly how she felt right now, not because she hadn't enjoyed herself but simply because it was so out of character for her. She wasn't like Ruby and she wasn't like her youngest sister Rose either, where she could breeze through life without a care in the world, not minding what other people thought of her. Scarlett didn't want to be judged unless she knew she was going to be judged favourably and she doubted that would be the case if people knew about Jake.

The sounds of Theatre continued to flow around her as she monitored her patient's condition until finally the surgery was finished. Scarlett reversed the anaesthetic and left the patient to be taken through to Recovery.

'Is everything all right?' Candice had followed Scarlett into the scrub room. Scarlett thought about asking her why she hadn't mentioned that Jake would be turning up at work today but she thought better of it. She didn't want to invite questions.

'Of course,' she replied, as she threw her gloves, cap and mask into the rubbish. 'Why?'

'You barely said a word during the whole procedure. Is Richard making things awkward for you?'

'No.' Scarlett shook her head and it was only then that she realised Richard had barely spoken to her. Had he been giving her the cold shoulder or had he been concentrating on the surgery? She had no idea. But she realised she didn't care. Not at all. Working in silence was preferable to making idle conversation at the moment. She had a terrible poker face and she didn't trust herself not to give away her guilty feelings. 'I'd forgotten Richard was coming back to work today. I hadn't prepared myself for that and it threw me off a little.'

It wasn't completely true. Seeing Richard had thrown her but not because he was back at work—it had only bothered her because of her guilt but she wasn't about to air her dirty laundry here. The fewer people who knew about her indiscretion the better. 'I need a coffee,' she told Candice. 'Are you coming?'

Candice shook her head. 'Not yet. I need to go into Recovery first.'

Scarlett was relieved. She didn't want company, she needed a moment of solitude. She walked through Emergency. The department was busy. Most of the curtains were pulled and people hurried to and fro. Scarlett was grateful to find the tearoom empty. She made another coffee and grabbed a biscuit. She stood by the window with her back to the door. She really needed something more substantial to eat. Her stomach was in turmoil; all the coffee was making her edgy and her nerves were already fraught, but the solitude of the tearoom was more appealing at the moment than braving the cafeteria crowds.

She heard the door open and she half turned her head, more a reflex than anything, to see who was interrupting her peace and quiet. She hoped it wasn't someone who felt like talking. The door opened fully and Jake walked in.

He winked at her. She couldn't believe how confident and cheeky he was, but the combination obviously served him well—it had worked on her. Her knees were shaking and she leant against the window, gripping the ledge with one hand to stop herself from collapsing to the floor. She wanted to touch him, to make sure he was real. She desperately needed to find some self-control. If she wasn't holding on to the window sill she knew she'd probably be halfway across the room by now.

She *never* reacted like this and her reaction irritated her and made her cranky. 'Have you come to tell me why you kept this news to yourself?'

'What news?' he asked, still grinning. 'That I was a med student or that I was coming here?'

'Either. Both.' She couldn't think straight.

'Would it have mattered?'

'Yes.' There was no way she would have jumped into bed with someone who would be turning up at her workplace virtually the next day.

'You never asked what I did.'

'I assumed you worked in a bar.' Scarlett was unsettled.

'You thought that was *all* I did?'

Scarlett shrugged. 'I guess.' He was right. She hadn't asked if he did anything else. She hadn't actually given it much thought. She hadn't wanted to know too much about him. She'd wanted it to be anonymous but she was annoyed with him for saying nothing. Confusion and guilt were making her short-tempered. 'You knew I worked here, you obviously knew on Saturday night that you'd be here today, and you still said nothing.' She felt as though he'd tricked her.

'I didn't think it mattered.'

'It matters to me.'

She felt like a fool. This was why she should never make spur-of-the-moment decisions.

Why hadn't he told her? Why hadn't *Candice* told her?

'Did Candice know you were going to be doing a placement with us?' she asked.

'Yep.'

'Why didn't she tell me?'

'Why would she think you cared?'

He had a point. And Scarlett didn't have an answer.

'What is the problem?'

Where did she start? How did she explain it? Would he understand that Saturday night had been completely out of character for her? Would he understand that her lapse in judgement had risked everything she'd worked so hard for?

It was unlikely. She couldn't expect him to understand.

He crossed the room, coming to stand beside her. She glanced nervously at the door. There was no telling how long their privacy would last. 'This isn't the place for this conversation.'

'No, I suppose it's not. It wasn't my intention to make things awkward, so for that I apologise. Why don't we have a drink together tonight and you can tell me why it matters and I can apologise properly?'

She didn't care about an apology. What she did care about was her reputation. And sleeping with a tattooed med student who worked in a strip club was not the way to get ahead in her career. It was not the way she wanted to catch people's attention. No matter how sexy he was.

Now that she'd recovered from the shock of seeing

him, she was able to study him more closely. He was clean-shaven today. His face was all smooth angles and his green eyes had a look of amused interest. He was wearing a crisp white shirt under his white coat and he looked, and smelt, clean and fresh. And young.

He dipped his hand into the pocket of his coat and pulled out a container of breath mints. He offered them to her and when she shook her head he tipped a couple into his hand. Scarlett followed his movements. The mints were tiny against his large palm but it was his long, delicate fingers that caught her attention. She could remember how they had felt on her skin. The pleasure he'd brought her with his touch. It was a shame to think that one night was all she could have but there was no alternative. She had plans that didn't include sexy young male students.

'How about The Botanic at eight?' he suggested. Apparently his plans differed from hers.

'No.' Scarlett gave a slight shake of her head. The Botanic was much too close to the hospital, they would have no privacy there. There were plenty of other pubs in the two kilometres between the hospital and her house and any number of bars in Rundle Street.

Why was she even considering other pubs? Her response simply should have been 'No' and that was that. She could think of half a dozen reasons why she shouldn't meet him but only one why she should. And that reason was enough to have her thinking of alternatives. She needed a chance to make her position clear. He was likely to be on placement in her hospital for the next month and she needed to lay down some ground rules.

The door to the tearoom was opening again and

Scarlett had to make a quick decision if she didn't want to risk being overheard. 'How about The Queen's Head?' she proposed, just as Candice appeared.

'Jake! You're here.' Candice bounced over and hugged him and Scarlett took the opportunity to escape from the tearoom while Jake was otherwise occupied. But before she could leave he held up eight fingers—*eight o'clock*—behind Candice's back and nodded at her in silent confirmation of their date.

Only it wasn't a date and Scarlett chose her outfit very carefully to ensure there would be no way Jake could misconstrue the purpose of their meeting. She chose a navy suit jacket and matching pencil skirt. She put a simple white silk camisole under the jacket and pulled out court shoes with a small heel, nothing as ridiculous as the platform sandals she had worn the night she'd met him, and redid her hair, pulling her thick curls into a tight bun. She needed a barrier of power dressing; she hoped it would combat their chemistry.

She spotted him the moment she walked through the front door into the bar. He was in the room to her right, leaning against the bar, keeping an eye on the entrance, waiting for her. God, he was gorgeous.

She was right on time; he'd obviously got there early. She wondered if he'd done it deliberately. And, if so, had it been so she didn't have the upper hand or was he just being chivalrous, not wanting her to wait alone at a bar?

He was wearing jeans and a white T-shirt with a green surf logo on the front that matched his eyes. The stark contrast in the formality of their outfits didn't go unnoticed by Scarlett and she was struck again by their age difference. But it wasn't enough to wipe out the instant surge of attraction she felt when their eyes met. She was aware of other women casting their eye over him as well. He exuded sex appeal and she wasn't the only one to notice, although he seemed completely unaware of the attention.

He straightened up and took two steps across the room, meeting her halfway. He leant towards her and kissed her cheek.

A surge of desire and adrenalin rushed through her and her body threatened to betray her. This was going to be harder than she'd anticipated.

'You came,' he said, as he let go of her hand and straightened up.

Scarlett wondered if he'd really doubted her. She'd bet he'd never been stood up by a woman.

'What would you like to drink?' he asked, as she resisted the urge to put her fingers over the spot on her cheek where she could still feel the imprint of his lips.

'A glass of wine, please.'

'Shall we share a bottle?'

She shook her head and reminded herself to be strong, decisive. *Remember, he must only be about twenty-three*, she told herself. *Just deal with him the same way you deal with Ruby and Rose. Firmly and decisively.* Scarlett was used to dictating the rules. They had to be able to work together.

'I'm not planning on being here very long,' she said. Firm and decisive.

'Ouch.' But he didn't seem to be offended. He was smiling, obviously not taking her seriously despite her outfit and her no-nonsense tone. 'What about something to eat?' he asked. 'Have you had dinner?'

'I'm fine.'

She waited as he ordered their drinks and a serve of

beef sliders with fries. He handed her a glass of wine and led her to a table in the corner. It was hot in the pub and Scarlett could feel herself starting to perspire. The back of her neck was damp under her bun. The heat was making breathing difficult, or maybe it was Jake's proximity—he had chosen the chair at right angles to hers, not opposite, and his knee brushed against hers as he sat. She slipped her jacket off, deciding that if he wasn't going to heed her power-dressing message she may as well be comfortable, but she sat, upright, tense and stiff on her chair.

'You can relax,' he told her. 'I can be trusted to keep my hands to myself, much as I would like to do otherwise.' His gaze ran down the length of her arm, from her bare shoulder to her wrist, and Scarlett imagined she could feel a trail of heat on her skin. She shifted in her chair, hoping that another inch of space would break the sensation.

Jake was still smiling. He sipped his beer and said, 'I apologise if my being at the hospital makes you uncomfortable but the fact of the matter is I'm there for the next four weeks so we're going to come into contact with each other. Why is that a problem for you?'

'It's not, as long as we agree to forget about Saturday night. I don't want anyone to know about that.'

'I don't think I can forget about it but I guess I can refrain from mentioning it, but only if you give me a good reason.'

'There're a dozen reasons why. You're a med student. I'm a registrar. I've worked really hard to get to where I am and I don't want to give people a reason to take it away from me.'

'What reason could this give them?'

But Scarlett didn't answer that question as something else occurred to her. 'Is that why you slept with me? Because we were going to be working together? Were you hoping it was going to work in your favour somehow?'

'You asked me in. Remember? Actually, dragged me in might be a better description.' He grinned.

She couldn't remember exactly how he'd ended up inside her house but she did know she hadn't wanted him to leave. But her final choice may have been different if she'd known what the future held. 'I never would have slept with you if I'd known you were going to turn up at my work.'

'So I just have to wait until my placement is finished and then you'll date me.'

'I don't want to date you,' she said.

'I think you do.'

He was smiling again and his smile went deep to her core, stoking the fire that smouldered in her belly just waiting for his touch. She should have ordered a soft drink, not wine, she thought as her resolve weakened with every glance.

'No, I don't,' she said, trying to find that firm, decisive tone she desperately needed. 'I want to pretend that Saturday night never happened and hope that people don't find out. I've worked hard to get where I am. I have a plan and I don't want to jeopardise it by having people look at me differently. I don't have any intention of telling anyone about Saturday night. One-night stands are not my thing.'

Jake took a draught of his beer. She could see him trying to hide a smile.

'Why are you still smiling?'

'Because if one-night hook-ups are out of character

for you then maybe I'm in with a chance of getting you to make it two.'

'You could have any woman you wanted. Why me?'

'You have that super-sexy secretary thing going on.'

'You think I look like a secretary?'

'Maybe not so much a secretary, maybe more a high-school principal,' he said. 'When you're dressed all neat and businesslike in your suit and your tidy hair and sitting there bossing me around, I feel like I'm back in the principal's office.'

The picture he painted made her laugh. She'd suspected he had a bit of a rebellious streak. 'Good. That should stop you from wanting to ask me out.'

Jake grinned. 'I dunno, she was pretty hot. And now that I know what happens when you strip back the layers and let your hair down...' He raised an eyebrow and shrugged. 'I had a really good time on Saturday night and, yes, I'd like to do it again,' he said simply, as the waitress placed his meal on the table. 'If I'm prepared to wait until I finish my placement, tell me why I shouldn't ask you out on a proper date.'

'You really want to take me out on a date?'

He nodded.

'But I'm not your type.'

'What is my type?'

'Someone more your own age.'

'How old do you think I am?'

She let her eyes travel over his face. Along the sharp edges of his jaw, across the smooth skin of his cheekbones, blemish- and wrinkle-free, the only lines on his face were smile lines. Her eyes met his. He was watching her just as intently. She reached across the table and pinched a few chips from his plate just to break eye contact as she answered, 'Twenty-three.'

'I'm twenty-six,' he said. 'I had a circuitous path to med school,' he explained, 'but that must put us close enough in age. So now will you date me?'

Scarlett shook her head. 'No. I'm still not your type.'

'And what makes you think you know what my type is?'

'I imagine it would be someone who is used to going clubbing, partying until the early morning.'

'That sounds like you.'

'If I'm out at two in the morning it's because I've been at work. Going clubbing is not my thing.'

'What is your thing?'

The rest of the bar receded into the distance as Jake looked at her. He leant towards her and Scarlett could feel herself being drawn in. He really was far too cute and she was struggling to remember what her thing was. She could feel herself growing warm under his gaze, her skin was burning but she'd already taken her jacket off and she had no more clothing to shed.

'I'm not sure but it's not going home with men who I meet in strip clubs.'

'I beg to differ.'

'I'm not going to date you.' She shook her head again, trying to convince herself as much as him that she meant every word.

'We'll see,' he said.

'You're not listening to me,' she replied, as she reached for her glass of wine. Jake reached for the salt at the same time and his hand brushed her forearm. Scarlett froze, immobilised by the current that raced up her arm. Her gaze dropped to his hand as he lightly curled his fingers around her arm and ran them along the sensitive skin to her wrist. She held her breath, waiting for him to stop touching her but hoping he wouldn't. She was a mess of contradictions. Her body wanted him; it felt as though every cell was straining towards him and clearly ignoring what her mind dictated and Scarlett wasn't sure whether her mind was strong enough to counteract the physical pull.

Jake was watching her watching him, as his fingers came to rest on her skin. 'I am listening,' he said. 'I hear what you're saying and I know you were intent on putting me straight tonight. I've heard what you've said and I see what you're wearing. Don't think I haven't noticed you've ditched your stripper heels in favour of something more demure, but I can also see your reaction to me and your body language is telling me something completely different.'

'That's just chemistry. A physical reaction.'

'And it should be celebrated. We both enjoyed Saturday night—why deny yourself pleasure?'

'But that's my point. Everything about Saturday night was completely out of character for me.'

'You don't like having a good time?'

'I'm not denying I had fun but it was only ever meant to be one night. I didn't think I'd ever see you again.'

'But that's what I don't understand. Why can't we do this again?'

'Because I have a plan.' Scarlett took a deep breath. She had one chance to convince him that getting involved would be a mistake. She had to convince him because by doing so she hoped she would convince herself. She moved her arm, removing herself from his touch as she sorted through her words. 'Usually I make carefully considered decisions. Usually I think about the consequences. Saturday night was just a lapse of control and I'm putting it down to a stressful week and one too many cocktails.'

'It was consensual, wasn't it? You told me you knew what you were doing.'

Scarlett nodded. 'I knew exactly what I was doing,' she admitted, 'but my point is I only intended to do it once.'

'That's a pity. Life should be fun.'

But in Scarlett's opinion life was meant to be taken seriously. That was the way to keep control. She wasn't young and irresponsible like Rose, she had never been like that, and she wasn't carefree and spontaneous like Ruby.

She stood and collected her jacket. She took a ten-dollar note from her purse and left it on the table to pay for her drink. She didn't want to be indebted to Jake.

'I'm sorry,' she told him. 'I have a plan and you don't fit into it.'

Firm and decisive.

And miserable.

But it was for the best.

CHAPTER FOUR

JAKE HAD EVERY intention of respecting Scarlett's wishes. As much as he didn't like, or even agree with, her decision he wasn't going to make her life difficult by making a nuisance of himself. If she didn't want to have anything to do with him he had to respect that. He had been raised to respect women and that included respecting their decisions.

He didn't need to be dating. His final year of studies and his part-time job at The Coop kept him busy enough. University life was almost over and he had to make sure he graduated well if he wanted to be accepted into the hospital of his choice for his intern year. Scarlett was right—scandal was best avoided. He didn't want to jeopardise his career chances any more than she did.

He decided he would respect her conditions for now and he wouldn't ask her out again while they were working together, but once his placement was finished he would see how things lay between them then. Their chemistry had been too good to just let her go without a little bit of a fight.

It would be easy to find things to occupy his time for the remainder of the placement, especially if the last few days were anything to go by. Their paths had barely crossed so his resolve wasn't tested.

Three more weeks, he told himself. He could wait that long, he thought as he glanced at the file in his hand. A twenty-nine-year-old female had presented to Emergency with abdominal pain. He pulled back the curtain and ducked inside the treatment cubicle. The busier he was the faster time would pass.

The woman lay on the bed, curled on her side, with her anxious-looking partner sitting beside her. He stood as soon as Jake drew the curtain behind him but his movement was restricted by his partner, who kept a tense grip on his hand.

'Doctor, you have to do something, my wife is in terrible pain.' He didn't wait for Jake to introduce himself.

'Is it the baby?' the woman asked. She was the same age as Scarlett and she also had thick, dark hair, but the similarities ended there. Her face was pinched with pain and the knuckles on her right hand were white as she squeezed her partner's fingers.

'You're pregnant?' Jake hadn't noticed that on the file but he hadn't had much chance to look at it.

The woman nodded.

'How many weeks?' She was several kilograms overweight so it was difficult to judge.

'Six.' So her extra weight wasn't all pregnancy-related and there was a chance that she may have been mistaken with dates, one way or the other.

'Have you had the pregnancy confirmed?'

'We did a home test yesterday. It was positive,' the husband replied.

A positive home pregnancy test at this early stage was an indicator but not, in Jake's opinion, full confirmation. He knew he had to treat that news as an unconfirmed pregnancy until he had a chance to do more tests. But an ectopic pregnancy could be the cause of her symptoms and he would need to keep that in mind, although he couldn't afford to rule out appendicitis or other abdominal disorders. He couldn't be influenced by the couple's suppositions. He needed to confirm a diagnosis, not play guessing games, and to do that he needed more information.

'I'm a final-year medical student—'

'My wife is pregnant and she's bleeding,' the husband interrupted Jake. 'We want to see a *doctor*.'

'The doctors are all busy,' Jake said, concentrating hard to keep his tone even. He addressed his next sentence to the wife. 'You're welcome to wait until one is available but I can't tell you how long that will be.' He suspected she wouldn't want to wait. 'I need to get some details and then I'll call a doctor when we know what is happening,' he explained. 'I can get started with your medical history and the physical exam and a doctor will join us when one becomes available.'

The look of nervousness he had seen earlier in the wife's eyes disappeared. She was in pain and he knew she wouldn't want to wait. A final-year medical student was close enough to the real thing for her. 'Okay,' she replied. Jake could almost see the husband deflate as his wife's agreement took the puff out of him.

Jake called for a nurse. He recorded the details of Angela's symptoms, their onset and severity, her menstrual history and her activities over the past twenty-four hours. He got the nurse to collect a urine sample so he could run a pregnancy test and then he began the physical exam. The medical history he'd taken made him suspect that an ectopic pregnancy was likely to be the cause of her pain but he wanted more confirmation.

'We need a pelvic ultrasound,' he told the nurse.

Sally ducked out of the cubicle to organise the equipment but she couldn't have been more than a few steps away when Angela cried out. She clutched her stomach and bent her knees to her chest. Jake looked at her in alarm. Her face was completely white and beads of perspiration had broken out across her forehead and upper lip.

A ruptured fallopian tube or burst appendix raced to the top of the list of possible diagnoses. The quickest way to find out the answer now was to open her up.

'Sally!' he called out. The nurse stuck her head back in and Jake tried to disguise the note of panic he suspected was evident in his voice as he told her, 'I need a gynae consult. Right now.'

Scarlett checked over her equipment, ready to anaesthetise her patient as soon as Diana, the gynaecologist, was ready. Their patient, a twenty-nine-year-old woman, was about to undergo surgery for a ruptured Fallopian tube. Apparently she had presented to Emergency with abdominal pain from an ectopic pregnancy and things had gone downhill from there. The general consensus was she was lucky that she'd already been in the hospital and therefore only minutes from help.

She turned her head as she heard the sucking sound of the theatre door as it was opened. Her heart tumbled in her chest as she saw Diana walk in, followed by Jake. He was looking straight at her, his green eyes clear and confident. He was tying his mask and the bottom half of his face was obscured but she didn't need to see all of his features. She'd recognise his green eyes anywhere; the corners crinkled as he smiled at her. She nodded a greeting in return. Her face seemed to have frozen—surprise had taken away her ability to smile.

His mask was green and matched his eyes perfectly. She wondered if he had chosen it deliberately but then she doubted he would have thought of that. While he was gorgeous looking with a body to match she couldn't accuse him of being vain.

He had short-sleeved scrubs on and Scarlett could see the bottom three stars of the tattoo on the inside of his left triceps. It gave her a little thrill to know the reason behind the tattoo. Having that knowledge seemed like such a personal thing and he had shared it with her on the night they had made love. He'd had the Southern Cross constellation tattooed on his arm before he'd taken off overseas for a gap year after finishing school to remind him of where he came from and to remind him that he always planned to come home.

They had lain together in her bed after making love. Jake had wrapped his right arm around her shoulders as she'd lain with her head on his chest and let her fingers trail over the ridges of his stomach muscles. His left hand had been tucked behind his head, in much the same position as it was now, and Scarlett had lifted her hand from his abdominals to run her fingers over each little star. She'd expected the stars to feel bumpy and raised but they had been smooth and flat on his skin. Just the memory of it now made her heartbeat quicken.

He tied the mask easily. He looked perfectly at home in Theatre. He didn't look like a student. He looked comfortable, he looked like he belonged. But Scarlett suspected he wasn't the type of person who would feel uncomfortable anywhere. He'd certainly seemed at home half-naked on a stage in front of a crowd of women so she supposed this setting would be a piece of cake. Two female doctors, two female nurses and Jake—it would be nothing out of the ordinary for him.

Scarlett finally recovered control of her facial muscles and was able to murmur a greeting as Diana introduced Jake and explained that he had been doing the consult when Angela's fallopian tube had ruptured and Diana had invited him to observe Theatre.

'If you stand just to my left you should get a good view of the surgery,' Diana told him.

Scarlett focussed on putting Angela to sleep as she tried to block out the picture of Diana and Jake standing shoulder to shoulder and tried to ignore the tightening of her stomach that she recognised as jealousy. She knew she was being ridiculous. They were only standing together and she had no right to be jealous but Diana was making her a bit crazy. Diana had a reputation as a serial dater around the hospital and Scarlett could imagine her wanting a taste of Jake, but surely not even Diana would sleep with a student?

Diana had made an incision into Angela's abdomen and confirmed what Jake had suspected. Angela had an ectopic pregnancy that had ruptured her fallopian tube.

'This was her first pregnancy, is that right?' she asked Jake.

'Yes. She and her husband said they'd been trying for a while.'

'I think I can repair the tube. I'm going to try,' she said, and explained her reasoning. 'Having one ectopic pregnancy increases her chances of having subsequent ectopic pregnancies. She won't thank me if I don't try to save the tube if it's at all possible. I can't afford to be careless with another woman's fertility.'

Scarlett couldn't fault Diana's skills as a doctor or surgeon but she couldn't help feeling her blood boil as she watched the surgery. As she watched Diana's arm brush against Jake's as she repaired and stitched. But Scarlett knew this was her issue, not Diana's.

Jake was paying close attention to the surgery, asking questions as he looked over Diana's shoulder. Scarlett imagined that Diana could feel Jake's breath on her cheek, just like she had on Saturday night, and she knew she wanted to be the one whose arm was brushing against his.

He hadn't spoken to her. He hadn't looked at her and Scarlett suspected that maybe he was deliberately avoiding her. She didn't want to be ignored. She wasn't sure what she wanted but it wasn't that. Not wanting to show that she was bothered by the lack of attention, she pretended to adjust her equipment but in reality everything was going smoothly with the sedation and there was no need for her to do anything other than monitor the machine.

'Right, that's looking good. I'm really pleased with that outcome.' Diana had managed to repair the tube and was sewing up the incision. There was a noticeable decrease in the tension in Theatre as Diana announced success.

'Scarlett, now the crisis is over there's something I wanted to speak to you about,' Diana said as she snipped a thread. 'I was thinking of asking Richard if he wanted to come with me to Candice's wedding but I wanted to make sure I wasn't stepping on your toes. It is over between the two of you, isn't it?'

Scarlett was mortified. She could feel her cheeks flushing and she was glad her face was half-hidden behind a mask. She would love to have some of Diana's confidence, even ten per cent would be good. She could never imagine announcing her dating plans to a room full of colleagues. But that wasn't the only difference between the two of them.

She had to answer Diana. She couldn't pretend she hadn't spoken directly to her. She looked up and her gaze landed on Jake first. He was watching her from behind Diana's shoulder.

Now he watched her!

Immediately she could feel heat flooding through her. She hated having such primeval reactions to him when he seemed quite unflustered but it reinforced her feeling that she had made the right decision by staying away from him. Nothing good could come from any involvement. She knew there was a good chance she would lose control.

She quickly averted her gaze, looking at Diana instead. She was a few years older than Scarlett, somewhere in her early thirties. Scarlett wondered if she knew Richard's biological clock was ticking but it wasn't up to her to tell her. Diana might well be hearing the same ticking as Richard. It wasn't Scarlett's business anymore.

'As far as I'm concerned, Richard is a free agent,' she told Diana. 'But I know he's already accepted an invitation to Candice's wedding and I'm pretty sure he'll still be planning to attend. Were you going to ask him as your date?'

'Not yet. I know he's already going but I thought it was a good opportunity to go together without any pressure.'

Scarlett thought inviting someone to a wedding as a first date, even an unofficial one, was buried in pressure. It was a gutsy move but she was actually relieved that Diana had set her sights on Richard as it meant Jake was safe. If Scarlett couldn't have him she didn't want anyone else to either.

'I'm sure he'd be flattered by your attention,' Scarlett said. She could feel Jake watching her still but she avoided his gaze by keeping her eyes glued to her monitors until it was time to reverse the anaesthetic.

But Jake followed her out of Theatre.

'Diana was talking about Richard Thomas, the plastic surgeon, wasn't she?' he asked, as they stripped off their masks and caps.

Scarlett looked down at her hands as she peeled off her gloves. She didn't need to see what she was doing but it allowed her to avoid eye contact. She threw her gloves in the bin as she replied, 'Yes.'

'You could date Richard but not me?' Jake kept the volume of his words low but Scarlett could hear the irritation in his voice. 'Don't you think that's a bit hypocritical?'

'Richard is a senior consultant, no one thinks there's anything wrong with a registrar dating a senior.'

'You don't think people might think you're sleeping your way to the top?'

Scarlett was about to deny his ridiculous accusation but then hesitated. Would people have thought that? Maybe. Not that she would admit he might be right.

Although she had to admit that she'd known dating

Richard wouldn't hurt her career prospects so perhaps she was guilty as charged.

She could feel her temper rising. Jake could certainly push her buttons and it annoyed her that he could make her second-guess herself. But she knew it was more than that. All her reactions to him were extreme and she hated losing control but that seemed to be a permanent hazard when she was around him. Extreme irritation. Extreme arousal. Extreme attraction. Extreme awareness. Every reaction, every one of her senses, became heightened in response to him.

'If a registrar can date a senior, why can't a registrar date an intern?' he asked.

'I'm sure they do but you're not an intern. You're still a student.'

'I won't always be. When I'm a registrar and you're a consultant, what will your excuse be then? Is this about me or you?'

She was normally calm, collected and controlled but she seemed to have trouble keeping a lid on her emotions around Jake. She shouldn't be having this conversation with him. She should just walk away but she couldn't make her feet move. She was attracted to him, she wasn't denying that, but once again it was her issue. She had a plan, she was determined to qualify as an anaesthesiologist and she wasn't going to be distracted by an emotion as basic as lust. Not when it could cost her her career.

'This is about both of us. I'm sure we'd be violating all sorts of workplace policies by dating and I for one don't want to be accused of sexual harassment. I am not prepared to jeopardise my career. No matter how tempted I am, nothing is worth that.'

'How about if we keep it low key? Take a leaf out of Diana's book and go to Candice's wedding together. As colleagues. Nothing more.'

'Richard hasn't accepted Diana's invitation yet,' Scarlett was quick to point out.

'Fair enough, but there's no reason to think he won't. She's a good-looking woman, smart, single, he's got no reason not to accept.'

Scarlett felt her stomach clench with another burst of jealousy. Not over the idea of Richard and Diana but because Jake had called her good looking.

'I don't need a lift, thank you, I'm going with my sister Ruby. She used to work with Candice and she's coming to town for the wedding.'

'Is she the one who owns the sexy shoes?'

He was smiling at her, his cheeky grin lighting up his eyes, seemingly unbothered by her rejection of his offer. Did nothing faze him? Was he always so relaxed and easygoing?

She shook her head. 'No, those were Rose's.'

'Another sister? How many do you have?'

'Only two.'

Talking about Ruby made her realise she would provide the perfect distraction. She decided she would focus on Ruby's visit. Ruby always blew into town like a mini-tornado and her sister's presence should be enough to keep her occupied *and* keep her mind off Jake. Ruby would give her enough to worry about and leave no time for sexy med students. Ruby was the perfect solution to her dilemma.

CHAPTER FIVE

SCARLETT SCANNED THE crowd as the passengers disembarked from the plane and were disgorged up the ramp and into the terminal. She hadn't seen Ruby for several months and although they kept in regular contact with phone calls and social media it wasn't the same as seeing each other in person. Scarlett paced impatiently. She was dying to give Ruby a big hug and to immerse herself in her sister's latest news. She always had a story to tell.

Ruby was the middle of the three Anderson sisters. Rose was the baby of the family and Scarlett the sensible, oldest sister. Ruby was the wild child, the sister who tried whatever she liked and did whatever she pleased. Scarlett used to wish she was that brave but the fact of the matter was she wasn't brave or rebellious or foolhardy. She was cautious, pragmatic and reliable, and she'd had to decide long ago to let Ruby have the adventures. And Ruby did. There was no denying that Ruby lived her life fully and Scarlett always enjoyed spending time with her, even though it could be exhausting. Ruby was more than a breath of fresh air in Scarlett's world, she was a whirlwind.

The two of them hadn't always been close and there

had been plenty of differences of opinion as they'd been growing up. Ruby had caused their mother plenty of headaches and to compensate for Ruby's headstrong behaviour Scarlett had always tried to do the right thing to avoid causing any further stress. She knew that sometimes she'd resented Ruby and her carefree and occasionally selfish attitude but as she'd matured, as they'd both matured, their differences had diminished. When Ruby had left home ten years ago, at the age of sixteen, Scarlett had missed her terribly. And although Ruby had come and gone, she'd never officially returned to South Australia and now Scarlett made sure to make the most of their time together.

A tall, thin woman with shoulder-length platinum-blond curls was walking briskly along the edge of the ramp, dodging fellow passengers and waving. It took Scarlett a moment to realise it was Ruby. Last time she had been home her natural strawberry blond locks had been dyed a dark red but the platinum shade was just as striking and probably better suited to her fair colouring.

Scarlett waved back and took in Ruby's outfit as she waited for her to reach the end of the ramp. Ruby's fashion choices were always interesting and today was no exception. The majority of Ruby's clothes came from markets and second-hand stores and Byron Bay, her current home town, had no shortage of either. Scarlett was constantly amazed that she chose to buy her clothes this way. After wearing second-hand clothes for most of their childhood, Scarlett had vowed she would always have new clothes and the more expensive the better. She chose to save her money and buy a few classic pieces each season, but not Ruby. Ruby was migratory and whenever she moved she'd leave most of her wardrobe behind, donated back to the second-hand clothes stores where it had come from, and pick up thrift-shop clothes that blended into her new environment when she relocated.

Today she was wearing a floaty, ankle-length, tie-dyed skirt with a tight black T-shirt emblazoned with what looked like a movie poster but it wasn't a movie Scarlett recognised. She looked like a stereotypical Byron Bay hippie. A multitude of different-coloured bangles adorned her wrists and ankles and her toenails were painted a bright tangerine. In contrast to her toenails, her fingernails were short, clean and unpainted—nurse's fingernails.

Despite her mismatched outfit she looked clean and fresh. Her hair was newly washed, her face make-up free. Her pale, flawless skin didn't need any help other than a lick of mascara for her eyelashes. Ruby looked like her father's side of the family. There were physical similarities to Rose, particularly now that Ruby's hair was blond, but Scarlett knew that she and Ruby looked nothing alike. And it wasn't just their taste in clothes.

Scarlett hugged her the minute she stepped off the ramp. She was skin and bone.

'You're so thin.'

'I've been too busy to eat.' Ruby grinned as Scarlett released her.

Scarlett recognised that look. 'You know you can stop having sex to eat,' she teased. 'Who is he?'

'Who *was* he, you mean.'

Ruby's relationships never lasted very long and it was almost always Ruby who did the leaving.

'Okay. I'll bite. Who was he?' Scarlett amended as she led the way to her car.

'He was a movie director.'

'You haven't taken up acting now, have you?'

While Ruby chopped and changed hairstyles, addresses and boyfriends almost as often as she changed her underwear, the one thing that had been constant in her life had been her job. Ruby was a nurse, and had nursed with Candice in Melbourne, hence the invitation to the wedding, and it was something that Scarlett thought she loved. While many other things about Ruby wouldn't surprise her, finding out she'd quit nursing would be unexpected.

'No, no.' Ruby laughed. 'He was directing a small-budget indie flick that was being filmed on the Central Coast, in and around Byron Bay.'

'How on earth did you meet him?' Scarlett asked, as Ruby threw her duffel bag into the car. Scarlett eyed the bag suspiciously. She couldn't imagine what Ruby had packed in there to wear to Candice's wedding. Whatever it was would surely be creased beyond recognition.

'There was an accident on set. Rohan brought the injured actor into the hospital.'

Scarlett was amazed at the different types of men Ruby had dated. In recent memory there had been a pharmacist, a guy who ran a surf school, a teacher and now a movie director, which probably explained Ruby's T-shirt, but Scarlett couldn't work out what they could possibly have in common.

'So what attracted you to him?' Scarlett asked, as she started the car and drove out of the car park.

'He was interesting. They all are. I like a guy who can give me new experiences. Not just in the bedroom,' she said in response to Scarlett's silent smirk, 'although I'm not opposed to that either, but I like seeing the world through different eyes. I guess, most importantly, there's always a connection, some chemistry. And that's hard to resist. When that happens I know I just have to give him a try. If they're good in bed, I'll keep them around for a bit. If they're not...*sayonara*.'

Scarlett thought she understood that feeling now. It was how she felt about Jake and that just served to confirm her idea that he was okay for a fling. Ruby's relationships never lasted long. Obviously chemistry was enough to sustain a short-term fling but did something that burned so brightly fizzle out just as rapidly? It certainly seemed to be the case for Ruby. Jake was sexy and fun but a very unlikely match for herself. She knew someone like Richard, someone meticulous and serious, would be a far better fit for her. If Jake was going to be anything to her it could only be temporary.

'What happened to this one?'

Ruby shrugged. 'They finished filming.'

'Did he break your heart?'

Ruby laughed. 'No. It was fun while it lasted but if he hadn't had to pack up and move on I would have moved on anyway. I was getting bored.'

'At least it means you have time to eat again,' Scarlett told her as she parked the car in front of her house. 'Which is good because we're having lunch with Mum.'

'Really?'

Scarlett could hear the note of trepidation in Ruby's voice. Ruby had a volatile relationship with their mother, which had become strained when Ruby had been a teenager and they had never recovered an easy camaraderie. Scarlett knew Ruby felt as though her mother was constantly disappointed in her. She felt their mother judged her sister and found her lacking.

And despite the fact that Ruby had straightened out her life, more or less, she never believed Scarlett when she tried to tell her that their mother loved her and just wanted to feel included in Ruby's life.

Ruby's unpredictable relationship with their mother was one reason she usually crashed at Scarlett's place when she visited. It was always better if Ruby and Lucy had their own space.

'We'll just have a quick lunch and then we'll come back here to get ready for the wedding. Have you got something to wear in there?' Scarlett asked, as Ruby dumped her duffel bag in the spare bedroom.

'Of course. I might even have something to lend to you.'

Scarlett raised her eyebrows. She couldn't imagine that she'd be able to fit into anything of Ruby's. While they were a similar height, Ruby's stick-thin figure was quite the opposite of Scarlett's curves.

'What time is Richard picking us up for the wedding?' Ruby wanted to know.

'He's not. Mel is going to swing past in a cab for us just before four.'

Ruby was frowning. 'Is Richard working?'

'No. We're not together anymore.'

'You're kidding.' Ruby plopped herself on the bed. 'What happened?'

Scarlett hadn't intended to tell Ruby about breaking up with Richard right at this minute, she'd planned to ease into that conversation, but there was no way to avoid the question now.

'Is he still planning on going to the wedding?' Ruby asked when Scarlett had finished giving her the abbreviated version of events. 'Is it going to be awkward?'

'It'll be fine.' Scarlett didn't bother to explain that Richard had accepted Diana's invitation and would be accompanying her to the wedding. That wouldn't matter to Ruby.

'I asked Candice to put me with some hot single guys,' Ruby announced. 'Maybe she's put us together.'

Scarlett immediately wondered if Candice might have put her on the same table as Jake. It had been at least twenty minutes since she'd last thought of him—that had to be counted as progress.

'We can find ourselves a couple of eligible bachelors and organise a double date.' Ruby immediately started thinking about picking up guys at the wedding, which was why Scarlett hadn't intended to say anything about Richard. She'd had some disastrous dating experiences with Ruby in the past. Their taste in men was about as different as their taste in clothes. Conservative and sensible was Scarlett's motto, which was why Jake was so not her type, and she didn't think she'd ever heard Ruby even *use* the word 'conservative', except maybe to describe Scarlett.

'Or do you already have another beau waiting in the wings?' Ruby asked, when Scarlett didn't reply.

She shook her head. 'I'm not like you. I can't just go from one man to the next.' She wished she could. She wished she didn't have her goals set. She wished she could just be with Jake, even temporarily, without worrying about the consequences. Even though she'd been the one to lay down the rules she had struggled to put him out of her thoughts. He had kept his part of the bargain and had kept his distance around the hospital, but she had been aware of him watching her and she could always tell the exact moment he was anywhere in her vicinity. Her body seemed attuned to his presence; it seemed to pick up his frequency before her brain had registered it. The more she told herself to ignore him the more often she noticed him.

She kept up a constant stream of questions to Ruby as she drove to their mother's house, hoping that listening to Ruby chatter would keep thoughts of Jake at bay. It worked, sort of. And whatever part of her brain wasn't taken up with Ruby's conversation was soon occupied with concern for their mother, who seemed to age noticeably every time Scarlett saw her.

Lucy was only forty-seven but could have been mistaken for someone five, if not ten years older. She was an older, more tired version of Scarlett. They had the same thick chestnut hair but while Scarlett's was still dark, her mother's was streaked with grey. They shared the same dark eyes but Lucy's were underscored with deep shadows and Scarlett knew that her mother's figure had once looked like hers but three pregnancies and years of shiftwork and irregular meals as a nurse had combined to sap Lucy's vitality.

This was what Scarlett feared her own future would look like if she succumbed and travelled down the marriage and babies path. In her opinion and experience there wasn't much to recommend it.

The conversation started with the usual discussion about their various careers but Scarlett knew she was on tenterhooks, waiting for something to be said that would set the cat among the pigeons.

It wasn't long before Lucy changed the topic. 'So you haven't settled down yet, Ruby?'

Scarlett held her breath as she wished, not for the first time, that Ruby drank alcohol. She was sure a glass of wine would help to mellow the different personalities and ease the tension but she knew Ruby had perfectly valid reasons for her abstinence and Scarlett couldn't argue with those. She waited for Ruby's response.

'Mum, I'm twenty-six, settling down is the last thing on my mind. I'm in the prime of my life and I intend to have fun while I can. Scarlett is the one you need to talk to. Do you know she's broken up with Richard?'

Scarlett had expected to hear Ruby's usual announcement that she was far too young to even think about settling down but she hadn't expected her to deflect attention from herself by announcing Scarlett's own news.

'Scarlett? When did that happen? Why didn't you tell me?'

Ruby's tactic seemed to have worked. Lucy forgot her usual retort, which went along the lines of the fact that she'd had three children by the time she was twenty-six, which then inevitably led to the argument that only one of those pregnancies had actually been planned and Ruby didn't intend to follow that path. Ruby had a point but although Lucy may not have been terribly successful in either her family planning or in choosing the fathers of her children, she had done her best to raise her daughters. Scarlett knew it had never been Lucy's intention to have three children by three different men but it was the way things had worked out.

Lucy had been a single parent for most of Scarlett's twenty-nine years. She had given birth to Scarlett just after her eighteenth birthday and Scarlett had always felt an obligation to protect her mother as much as possible. Lucy had been unlucky in love and Scarlett also knew that Ruby and Rose, to a lesser degree, had tested Lucy's patience and therefore Scarlett had tried not to add to her mother's burden. She hadn't told her mother about the break-up because she didn't want Lucy worrying about her.

'Are you okay?' Lucy asked, when Scarlett wasn't quick enough with an explanation.

'I'm fine. It was my decision.'

'But why? What went wrong? I thought Richard was what you wanted.'

Richard might have been what she wanted but it had turned out he hadn't been *who* she wanted. If she'd had a checklist she would have put plenty of ticks beside his name, beginning with the fact that he was older than her, settled in his career and didn't want children. She didn't really have an aversion to having a family but she was terrified of being left to raise them alone, like her mother had been. If she was ever going to have kids she'd make damn sure it was with someone who loved her. And there was no guarantee that even that would be enough. Therefore it was safer not to reproduce. In her mind it was safer not to put herself in that situation, although if Richard hadn't changed his mind she may well have stayed with him. She'd even thought she loved him.

Until she'd met Jake.

Whether or not it was simply a matter of timing or circumstances, she hadn't been able to resist Jake. Which meant she couldn't have been in love with Richard, could she? Not when she'd been so quick to fall for Jake's charms and jump into his bed. Ruby bed-hopped but to her credit she had never professed or even pretended to be in love. Scarlett knew now that she had been pretending with Richard.

'I didn't love him.' That was the simplest explanation and the one that would lead to the least amount of questioning.

Scarlett knew her mother had been not so secretly hoping she would marry Richard. Or someone like him. Someone who could take care of her financially and give her the security she had never had. Scarlett had to admit that security was something she craved too but she intended to rely on herself, not another person, for that security. If she was going to get married it would be because she needed something only that other person could give her. It wouldn't be for something she could provide for herself. Her mother had lost one partner to illness, one had simply left and the other had been booted out. Through her mother's misfortunes Scarlett had learnt not to rely on anyone but herself.

Scarlett looked at Lucy. She was so afraid of ending up like her, old and alone. But as much as she didn't want to be alone, she was more afraid of being left. And Richard's heart attack had given her a glimpse of the future and that terrified her.

Somehow both she and Ruby managed to get through lunch relatively unscathed but Scarlett was relieved to get home and focus on getting ready for Candice's wedding.

She got out of the shower and stuck her head into the spare bedroom to see what Ruby was wearing. Ruby had dried her hair and had swept it to one side before tucking the end up so it curled and sat just below her jawline. But that was all she'd done. She was still wrapped in her towel.

'Not dressed yet?' Scarlett asked.

In answer, Ruby pulled a slim parcel, wrapped in

tissue paper, from her duffel bag. She unwrapped it to reveal a royal blue silk tank-top, heavily embroidered from the shoulders to the waist. Embroidery was another fashion trend that was loved in Byron Bay but at least this garment actually looked new and wasn't tie-dyed, Scarlett thought as Ruby dropped her towel, pulled on some knickers and shimmied into the top.

She didn't bother with a bra; she didn't need one. The top hung loosely from her shoulders and fell just a few inches below her butt. Scarlett waited to see what pants Ruby was going to wear but she just slipped her feet into a pair of strappy silver heels and appeared to be done.

Scarlett raised her eyebrows. 'Is that what you're wearing?'

'What's wrong?' Ruby looked down at her feet. She pulled out another pair of shoes. Neutral peeptoe wedges with an ankle strap. 'These are the only other shoes I have. I think the silver ones go best with the dress.'

So it *was* a dress. 'I wasn't talking about the shoes.'

'What's the matter, then? Don't I look all right?'

Actually, she looked amazing. The 'dress' skimmed perfectly over her long, lean figure and she could get away with the short length as she had fantastic legs. Good legs, courtesy of their mother, were probably the one thing she and Ruby and Rose did have in common, that and the same shoe size. Scarlett couldn't fault Ruby for having the confidence to wear the outfit. Not when she looked so gorgeous. 'You look fabulous.'

'Thanks,' Ruby said, as she twirled in front of the mirror. She was a girl who was used to receiving compliments and she wasn't really looking for approval. 'Now it's your turn. What are you wearing?'

Ruby followed Scarlett into her room and waited as Scarlett pulled her dress from the wardrobe. It was a simple sleeveless shift dress, knee-length and panelled. The centre panel had a floral pattern and the sides were black and cut in at the waist to take the emphasis away from the hips and draw the eye in.

'You can't wear that,' Ruby said.

'Why not?'

'It's okay for an office party or a lunch but it's too casual for an evening wedding and it'll make you look old. I'll find you something else.' Ruby pulled no punches as she began to rummage through the wardrobe. Scarlett had thought the floral fabric gave the dress a fun, celebratory air but Ruby obviously thought otherwise.

'What about this?' Ruby was holding up a silk shirt dress that Scarlett had bought to wear as a top. It had a boat neck, a gathered waist and loose, elbow-length sleeves. In keeping with the sixties style, the fabric was printed with a paisley pattern in pale pink, cream and green.

'I don't know. I haven't got the right pants to wear with it.' Scarlett had intended to wear it with skinny satin pants but all she had were black ones and they had looked wrong against the colour and pattern of the top and she hadn't managed to find the right alternative colour yet.

'Pants! Who said anything about pants?' Ruby cried. 'This is a dress. Put it on, let's have a look.'

Scarlett found her underwear, there was no chance of going braless with DD breasts, and then pulled the dress over her head. It fell to mid-thigh and was much shorter than anything she would normally wear but still several inches longer than the dress Ruby had on.

Ruby was searching the bottom of the wardrobe for shoes. Scarlett would have to remind her not to bend over at the wedding unless she wanted to give all the other guests a glimpse of her undies. She pulled out a pair of neutral pumps and held them out in front of her, her head turned to one side as she looked at them with the dress. She screwed up her nose. The shoes were obviously not to her liking.

'Do you have anything else in this colour?'

Scarlett shook her head.

'That's okay, I'll lend you mine.'

Scarlett smiled to herself; Jake was going to think she didn't own any shoes of her own. *Stop it. Stop thinking about him.*

Ruby disappeared to her room and came back with her nude wedges. 'These will be better.'

Scarlett slipped them on. They were a good choice, the right colour and a better fit stylewise, plus they made her legs look exceptionally long. The floaty sleeves and the neckline preserved enough of her modesty to ensure that overall the outfit wasn't too revealing. It was a win-win.

'Perfect,' Ruby declared. 'Now for hair and make-up. Sit on the bed and I'll fix you up.'

Ruby might not believe in make-up for herself but she had a natural flair for colour and for the dramatic and by the time she'd finished Scarlett felt pretty enough, even if she didn't quite look like herself. But that was okay, she could think of her make-up as war paint. Ruby's ministrations had bolstered her confidence and prepared her for seeing Jake.

* * *

Candice and Ewan's wedding was being held in the garden of the National Wine Centre and as Scarlett made her way through the vines to the chairs placed alongside them she was glad she was wearing wedges. She and Ruby had only just found a seat when Candice's sister, who was the matron of honour, started down the aisle that had been constructed between two rows of vines.

She was accompanied by two angelic-looking children, a flower girl and page boy. Scarlett knew they weren't Candice's niece and nephew and she wondered briefly who they belonged to before her attention was diverted by the bride, who was being walked down the aisle by her father.

The ceremony was lovely, simple and straightforward but heartfelt. Scarlett always loved a good wedding, even if she couldn't quite dismiss the feeling that disaster beckoned. She crossed her fingers, hoping for the best for Candice and Ewan.

As the ceremony ended and she rose from her seat to follow the other guests back to the function centre, she searched the faces for Jake. She lost sight of Ruby as she melted into the crowd that had gathered on the outdoor terrace for pre-dinner drinks, but Scarlett didn't worry. Ruby knew a few of Candice's friends and she'd be fine. She was no shrinking violet. Scarlett had too many nerves of her own in anticipation of seeing Jake to worry about Ruby. Despite their differences, she hadn't been able to stop thinking about him. She hadn't yet found the secret to letting the idea of him go.

She finally found him. He was talking to an attractive couple who appeared to be the parents of the flower girl and page boy. He kissed the woman on the cheek.

There was something familiar about her but Scarlett couldn't work out if she knew her. Jake squatted down to talk to the children. He was too far away for Scarlett to hear what he said, but his comments made them both laugh. He ruffled the boy's hair as he stood up and his movements brought Scarlett into his line of sight.

He didn't take his eyes off her and she could read his lips as he excused himself and began to walk towards her. He was wearing a light grey suit and Scarlett had a fleeting thought that this was the most dressed she'd seen him. He had a white shirt under his suit jacket and a green tie that matched his eyes. Even fully dressed, he looked gorgeous.

His walk was fluid and graceful as he crossed the terrace, collecting two glasses of champagne from a waiter as he made his way to her. Scarlett hadn't moved since their eyes had met. She was frozen to the spot, fixed in place by his eye contact, totally under his spell.

CHAPTER SIX

HE FLASHED HIS cheeky smile at her as he reached her side and that was enough to break the spell and allow her to breathe again.

'You look gorgeous.' He ran his eyes over her and Scarlett felt herself grow warm with his attention. Her make-over, courtesy of Ruby, had bolstered her confidence but not enough to prevent her from dissolving into a mass of nerves under his gaze. The make-up and hairstyle—Ruby had held her hair back with a hairband and teased it behind the band into a sixties style, letting the weight of it fall down Scarlett's back—were not protection enough against the surge of attraction she felt the moment she saw him.

'Champagne?'

Her hand shook as she accepted the glass and a shiver of excitement ran through her as his fingers brushed hers.

'Are you cold?' he asked. 'Shall we move into the sun?'

It was late afternoon and the sun was getting low in the sky, the heat losing its intensity as the day drew to an end. They were standing on the terrace in the shade of the building and Jake moved a few steps into the sunshine. Scarlett followed automatically. Her feet didn't wait for any conscious instruction—it seemed she was programmed to his frequency and she couldn't override her reaction.

'How was your day?' he asked.

Scarlett sipped her champagne as she filled him in on her day's activities and was surprised to find she'd drunk half her glass by the time she'd finished talking.

'So it's been a family affair for both of us today.'

Of course, he'd been talking to his sister—that was why the woman had looked familiar. Their faces were a similar shape, although his sister's was more heart-shaped, less of a pentagon, less angular than Jake's.

'That was your sister you were talking to earlier? Were the flower girl and page boy your niece and nephew?'

Jake nodded. 'That's Mary and her husband, Ted.'

'Are the rest of your family here?'

'Evangeline is. My brothers aren't and my other sister, Ruth, lives in the States. Her first baby is due any day now and my parents have gone over to help her.'

'That's a big family. What number are you?'

'Two older brothers, three older sisters, then me.'

Scarlett smiled as aspects of Jake's personality fell into place. 'That's why you're so relaxed, you're the baby. I bet there was always someone looking out for you and you've never had to worry about anything.'

'And I bet you're the eldest sibling.' Jake grinned. There was no malice in his voice, just laughter. His green eyes sparkled and Scarlett basked in his attention. 'You would always be complaining that the rest never had it as tough as you and that the younger ones all got away with murder.'

In Scarlett's case it was true. She wondered if the lack of responsibility her sisters seemed to feel was due simply to their personalities or also to their birth order. She knew of several studies that indicated that birth order had a lot of influence over personality and she didn't begrudge her sisters, but sometimes she wished she could experience what it felt like to be carefree, instead of constantly thinking about her responsibilities and worrying about doing the right thing. But she knew Jake's comment had been made in jest. As accurate as he was, she was sure he wouldn't really want to know how tough her childhood and her early years in particular had been.

'So you're number one and Ruby is number two?' he asked, and when Scarlett nodded he added, 'Which one is she?' But before she could answer he changed his mind. 'No, don't tell me, I'll see if I can guess.'

'Good luck.' Scarlett laughed.

'I assume by that you mean you don't look alike?'

The champagne had taken the edge off her nerves and she laughed and raised one eyebrow and replied, 'I'll let you be the judge of that.'

'If I guess right, what will you give me?'

She had no idea and when he looked at her as though he wanted to devour her she was too scared to ask what he wanted.

'Can't decide?' Jake grinned, laughing at her with his green eyes and making her stomach flutter. 'Don't worry, I'll think of something.'

His cheeky bravado made her accept his challenge, confident he'd never be able to pick out Ruby. With a tilt of her head and a slight smirk she agreed. 'Okay, go for it.'

He scanned the crowd, commenting on the different women and why they couldn't be Ruby. He had a practised eye but his comments weren't offensive, they were simply entertaining.

'You're supposed to be telling me which one *is* Ruby, not which ones aren't,' Scarlett teased.

'She's the blonde over there, wearing the blue top and no bottoms.' Jake nodded towards Ruby, picking her out without hesitation.

Scarlett laughed at his description, it was exactly what she would have said, but she was amazed that he'd got it right. 'How did you know?'

'I could tell by her legs.' He looked back at Scarlett before lowering his eyes and running his gaze down her bare legs. The heat in his gaze stirred the pool of desire in her belly and she could feel it spread through her. 'You have the same legs,' he told her.

Self-consciously Scarlett tugged at the hem of her dress, trying desperately to make it longer as she fought the tide of desire.

'Don't,' he remonstrated. 'You have fabulous legs, you should show them off.'

Scarlett blushed, wondering if he could see the effect he had on her or whether the make-up hid her discomfort. His green gaze held hers and his cheeky smile curled the corners of his mouth. She had to look away before she gave in to a crazy notion and leant forward to taste his lips. She looked across the terrace, away from temptation, and her gaze met Ruby's.

Ruby's ears must have been burning. She was looking directly at them and was now coming their way. Scarlett felt a flutter of panic. She didn't want to introduce them. She didn't want Jake to fancy Ruby and in her experience men always did. She didn't want Jake to be like all the others. She knew she was being hypocritical and selfish and she also knew that if Ruby wanted Jake there'd be precious little she could do to stop her, but she wasn't going to stand by and facilitate a meeting. She needed to keep them apart for as long as possible.

As she was deciding on a course of action the flower girl came running up to them, crashing into Jake's knees and distracting Scarlett.

'Papa is coming to pick us up, I have to say goodbye,' she said, as Jake swung her up to sit on his hip.

While he was busy with his niece Scarlett saw the perfect opportunity to make an escape and headed Ruby off at the pass. She touched Jake's shoulder. 'I'll catch up with you later,' she said, knowing he was too busy to stop her.

She intercepted Ruby halfway across the terrace. She tucked her arm into her sister's and guided her over to a drinks waiter.

'Hot guy. Who is he?' Ruby said, as she glanced back to where Jake was still conversing with his niece.

'He's a friend of Candice's.'

'I don't remember her having friends like that when we worked together.'

'He's from Adelaide.'

'That's okay.' She shrugged. 'Is he single?'

'As far as I know.'

'I might have to meet him later.'

Scarlett knew her little interception wouldn't be enough to stop Ruby. Ruby wouldn't wait for an introduction, she'd introduce herself. It was yet another difference between them. She needed to go to the bathroom but she didn't dare leave Ruby alone. She knew the first thing she'd do would be to head for Jake. Scarlett lifted a glass of champagne and a non-alcoholic cider from the waiter's tray before steering Ruby towards Mel. She'd make her keep an eye on Ruby for the time being.

She handed them each a glass, champagne for Mel and cider for Ruby, and said, 'I'm just going to the loo.' She ducked inside the restaurant and almost knocked over the seating plan that was displayed on a board by the main doors. She looked it over quickly. She found her name on table six. Ruby's name was there too. And so was Jake's.

She scanned the room for table six and when she found it she detoured past to check the place settings on her way to the bathroom. She circled the table, looking for her name. She found Ruby's first. To her left was Jake. To Jake's left was her own name.

Candice had put Jake between her and Ruby.

She couldn't think of a worse situation. She couldn't possibly sit next to him all through dinner but she didn't want Ruby next to him either. She picked up her name card before putting it back down. Who should she move? She couldn't move both of them so which one should it be?

Her nerves wouldn't stand being seated next to Jake. She'd have to move herself. She picked up her place card again and switched it with that of another girl at the table, a nurse from the hospital, who she knew was single. Maybe *she* could distract Jake from Ruby.

Scarlett was trying to relax and make the best of the situation she'd created when she'd moved her place setting. Her manoeuvring had resulted in her sitting between one of the groom's friends, Simon, and Jake's brother-in-law, Ted. While both men seemed perfectly nice, and Scarlett knew this would be a good opportunity to pump Ted for information about Jake, she was having huge trouble concentrating on their conversation. Her meddling had positioned her opposite Jake and now she had a bird's-eye view of Jake and Ruby. They were deep in discussion, a discussion she was desperate to overhear, but the noise level in the room meant that was impossible.

She realised too late that what she should have done was switch Jake's name card. That way neither she nor Ruby would have been sitting next to him and she still would have only moved one person. But that hadn't occurred to her until now and what's done was done. She would just have to live with the consequences.

From what she could see, Ruby and Jake appeared to be getting on famously. It was what she had been afraid of and it wasn't surprising. Ruby had a lot of her father in her—he was extremely charismatic and was always the life of the party—but she would hate to know that her sister was comparing her to him because he was also a liar and a cheat, two things Ruby definitely wasn't.

Maybe Ruby was more Jake's type, Scarlett thought. She definitely danced to the beat of her own drum and did whatever she pleased, creating her own fun, much like Scarlett suspected Jake did. She sighed and let Ted refill her glass as she resigned herself to the fact that she couldn't control the world and she definitely couldn't control Jake and Ruby. If they were kindred spirits she should be wishing them luck.

She turned her head and tried her best to ignore Jake as she made an effort to engage Simon in conversation

while she picked at her dinner. The food looked delicious and she was almost certain it was, but seeing Ruby
and Jake together had ruined her appetite.

By the time her main-course plate had been cleared
away Candice and Ewan were on the dance floor, dancing their version of the bridal waltz. Slowly the guests
began to join the bride and groom. From the corner of
her eye Scarlett saw Jake rising from his seat. Involun-
tarily, she turned her head, expecting to see him ask
Ruby to dance, but his eyes were fixed on hers as he
made his way around their table to her side.

'Dance with me?' His voice poured over her, soften-
ing her resistance with its treacle tones. His green eyes
had her fixed in his sights, making her forget where they
were and who he was. She couldn't concentrate when
he looked at her like that, as if he wanted to consume
her, as if she was the only woman in the room. Just a
look from him now and she was ready to self-combust.
Just a look and she could recall the touch of his fingers
on her skin, the warmth of his lips on hers, the weight
of his body between her thighs. Her body responded
to his gaze and she felt the heat pooling in her groin.

As if he could read her thoughts, the corners of his
mouth lifted into a smile that was just for her. He was
holding out one hand to help her from her seat. It was
hard to resist and automatically she put her hand in his.
Her skin came alive as his fingers closed around hers.
The heat in her belly raced through her and joined with
the fire in her fingertips and her heartbeat quickened
as her body came to life.

But as her body woke up, so did her brain. Touching him was enough to make her come to her senses.

'No.' She snatched her hand back, as though she'd been burnt. 'I can't.'

She couldn't imagine being held in his arms while everyone else watched. She couldn't imagine being able to keep her feelings under control while his hands were on her skin, while she could feel his breath on her cheek, while they danced in front of a crowd. It was too dangerous. She'd almost made a big mistake.

'I'll dance with you.'

Scarlett's heart lodged in her throat as she heard Ruby's invitation and Jake's acceptance and it stayed there, making breathing almost impossible as she had to sit and watch and smile while Jake danced with Ruby. While he held Ruby in his arms.

Her hand shook as she poured herself a glass of water and lifted it to her lips. She swallowed hard, forcing the liquid past the lump in her throat. She needed to get a grip on her emotions. She couldn't let him affect her like this. Why did he upset her equilibrium so massively? This reaction was so unlike her. She wanted him but she knew she couldn't have him. She needed to forget about Jake. He could dance with whoever he pleased, it couldn't matter to her.

But she still wished it didn't have to be Ruby.

Ruby had been waiting to get Jake alone and out of earshot of the rest of the table. There were things she needed to ask him. Like what was going on between him and Scarlett. He'd told her he was a med student and that he was doing a placement in Emergency with Scarlett, a rather interesting piece of information that Scarlett had neglected to tell her, and Ruby wanted to know why. She had seen them on the terrace during the pre-dinner drinks and she remembered Scarlett's expression. It had been clear to her that Scarlett only had eyes for Jake—she had been completely unaware of anyone else but him.

She had baited Scarlett earlier, teasing her about meeting Jake, wanting to see if Scarlett let any info slip, but she played her cards close to her chest, just as she'd always done. But it was obvious to Ruby that Scarlett liked Jake and she wanted to know if her sister's feelings were reciprocated.

Jake held her right hand in his left and she could feel his right palm pressing into the small of her back. The pressure was firm enough just to let her know that he knew what he was doing. He had nice strong arms and a good frame and she relaxed and let him lead her around the dance floor.

'Now that we're alone, are you going to tell me what's going on between you and my sister?'

'I don't know what you're talking about.' He avoided her gaze as he spun her out of the way of another couple who looked fairly clueless.

'I'm talking about the fact that neither of you could keep your eyes off each other all through dinner yet you behaved as though you were strangers. Why didn't you move around the table and talk to her? Why were you ignoring her?'

'Because she wants me to.' His gaze was direct this time.

'How do you know?'

'I asked Candice to put Scarlett next to me at the table,' Jake told her, 'and I assume she did, there was no reason not to, yet Scarlett was sitting opposite me. She must have moved place settings to avoid me.'

'Why would she do that? What have you done to her?'

'Nothing. But I think I make her uncomfortable.'

'Because she likes you?'

'Yes,' he admitted. 'But not enough.'

'You should ask her out.' Ruby could never see the point of hanging back. If she wanted something she went and got it, and she figured more people should live by that philosophy.

'I have.'

'Really?'

'Yep.'

'And…?'

'She turned me down. She says she can't date a student. Apparently it's unethical.'

'She's probably right,' Ruby said. 'She's a bit of a stickler for the rules. But surely she's allowed to dance with you tonight?'

'I believe she is.'

'So why isn't she?'

'She doesn't know what to do with me. I don't think I fit into any of her neat little boxes. I suspect she feels I might cause chaos in her orderly world.'

'So what are your plans? You obviously like her too. Are you just going to keep ignoring her or are you going to ask her out again?'

Jake was laughing.

'What?'

'I feel like I'm dancing with one of my sisters. They like to boss me around as well.'

'Well, it sounds as though you need it.'

'Then you'll be pleased to know that I do have a plan. I thought I'd let her have a few more glasses of champagne before I ask her to dance again. She likes me better when she's had a few drinks,' he explained.

'Is that so?'

'Yep. I'll wait for her to relax a bit more and then hopefully she'll be up for some fun.'

'Can I give you some advice?' she asked.

'About Scarlett?'

Ruby nodded.

'Sure.'

'She's not really about having fun. She takes life very seriously.'

'I've learnt that but I'd like to see if I can change her mind. Show her how to have a good time.'

Ruby grinned at him. She suspected that would be something he'd be very good at but she thought it only fair to warn him. 'You'll need to take things slowly. She's not very good at letting people into her world. She's cautious. She expects people to let her down, men in particular. She doesn't like to rely on anyone but herself. For anything.'

'That's okay, I'm not in any hurry. I can do slow.'

Scarlett felt as though she'd been watching Jake dance for hours. He was a good dancer and watching him was certainly no hardship, but watching the succession of partners was becoming tedious.

She wished she hadn't felt so self-conscious, she wished she could trust herself to keep her emotions in check, she wished she could have danced with him. The dance floor was crowded now; she was probably more conspicuous sitting alone at the table than she would be if she was in Jake's arms. He danced confidently. He was light on his feet and had good rhythm.

He'd looked like he didn't have a care in the world as he'd danced with Ruby, his sisters, Mel, several of the nurses, Candice—she'd been keeping a mental tally—and now with Diana.

He had removed his suit jacket and she could see the muscles in his butt, back and shoulders flex and relax as he guided Diana around the floor. If he asked her to dance again she'd say yes, she decided. Surely one dance couldn't hurt.

She followed his path around the dance floor, her eyes glued to the crisp brightness of his white shirt, her eyes straining as she tried to see if his tattoo was visible through the thin fabric. He hadn't so much as glanced her way since he'd taken to the dance floor and she felt safe to study him, knowing he was unlikely to catch her out.

She found his tattoo fascinating. She felt as if it was their secret, even though she knew any number of other women had probably seen it but she refused to let her mind dwell on that. She wanted to feel as though they had shared something special. She knew they weren't likely to share anything else, but she could still close her eyes and recall tracing her fingers over the tattooed stars. It would be her memory. One no one could take away.

He lifted his left arm and spun Diana under and away from him and Scarlett's eyes immediately flicked to the inside of his upper arm, to the junction of his biceps and triceps muscles, to see if she could spy the stars. As she searched for the shadow of the Southern Cross she heard someone pull out the chair next to her and guiltily she looked away from Jake to find Richard sitting down beside her.

'Richard! How are you feeling?'

'Surprisingly fit and well. I really feel as though I have a new lease of life.'

She studied him properly for the first time in weeks. He'd aged in that time but it wasn't all that surprising. He'd lost weight but he didn't look too thin, and the fact that he'd lost his tan after stopping his weekly golf game was probably to blame. He was a good-looking man, she acknowledged, but he certainly didn't take her breath away and make her insides go all gooey like Jake did. She realised now she had never had that same intensity of reaction to Richard. Had he ever turned her knees to jelly? She didn't think so. But she'd been happy. Or maybe just not *unhappy*.

'I came over to apologise. Diana told me you knew she was going to invite me to come to the wedding with her but I hope it hasn't put you on the spot. It wasn't my intention to make you feel uncomfortable in any way by accompanying Diana today.'

'It's not a problem,' Scarlett reassured him. 'I was happy for her to ask you.' It was far better than the alternative—that Diana had wanted to ask Jake. 'I want you to have everything you wish for and I'm sorry I couldn't give you what you wanted.' Scarlett didn't bear Richard any ill will. They weren't compatible, and maybe he could be happy with Diana.

Now that he had unburdened himself, his gaze sought out his date. 'Diana doesn't seem to be in any hurry to get off the dance floor.'

Why would she be? Scarlett thought. She was dancing with Jake.

'Shall we join them?' Richard asked.

'Are you up to it?'

'Most definitely.'

She might as well be dancing instead of sitting alone at the table. She took Richard's hand and was curious to discover that she felt nothing. There was no rush of desire, no overreacting nerve endings, no breathlessness. She fought to pay attention to Richard as he guided her around the dance floor but her body had a mind of its own and her eyes kept seeking Jake.

If she had any doubts about her decision not to marry Richard she had her answer now as her eyes found Jake. Even if she could count on Richard to be dependable and committed she knew she could never go back. Their relationship had been convenient and safe, but it had never been exciting. Jake was like a drug and she knew she could easily become addicted to the buzz she got when she was with him, to the surge of attraction and the adrenalin, and that was what she wanted now. She wanted excitement.

She kept her eyes on Jake. While she couldn't imagine being with him long term she knew what she wanted now. Adventure. Excitement. Pleasure. Richard was a good man but she wanted more than that. There was no harm in wanting, was there?

Jake and Diana were getting closer. Scarlett remembered why she didn't like dancing with a partner—men got to call the shots. Richard was guiding her around the dance floor and she had no control over where they went. Jake and Diana were right beside them now and there was nothing she could do about it.

'Shall we swap partners?' Jake asked, directing his question to Diana. Richard and Diana didn't even argue. As if the move had been rehearsed, Jake let go of Diana and she stepped into Richard's arms. Their timing gave

Scarlett no option. If she hadn't let Jake take hold of her she would have been stranded in the middle of the dance floor. But as she felt his hand close over hers and the familiar flutter in her belly she thought perhaps she should have escaped while she'd had the chance. But Jake wasn't letting her go.

'I've been waiting all night to dance with you. Just one dance, can you give me that?' he asked, as if he knew she was deliberating over her options.

The band was playing a slower number now and Jake slid his hand further around her back, pulling her in close. His hand was warm against the small of her back and he positioned her so that one of her legs was tucked between his thighs and he was able to control her movements with slight pressure of his hands, his fingers and his thighs. But Scarlett didn't feel trapped or controlled. She felt like part of him. He was light on his feet and she relaxed and let him take over. She'd been wishing she could have just one dance, and this was her chance.

Her breasts were pressed against his chest and she could feel the heat of his body through his shirt. His body was hard and strong against hers. She turned her head to the right and breathed in his scent. He smelt like a summer day, fresh and warm. His left arm was outstretched and she could see the dark shadow of his tattoo through the sleeve of his shirt. She focused on the stars. She didn't need to concentrate on dancing, her body followed Jake's rhythm effortlessly. She wanted to rest her head against him and close her eyes and imagine they were alone but she had to resist and remember where they were. She forced herself to make conversation.

'Where did you learn to dance?'

'I spent years being dragged along to my sisters' ballet classes. When I wouldn't sit still and started complaining, Mum enrolled me in classes too. Not ballet—jazz and contemporary mainly. I loved it and I've never stopped. When I was in high school it was a good way to get the girls—girls love a boy who can dance. And it comes in handy now for my job.'

Scarlett frowned. 'For medicine?' That made no sense and she wondered if she'd drifted off and had missed part of his answer.

He shook his head and his lips lifted in a smile as he laughed. 'No, The Coop.'

'You need to be able to dance to work behind the bar?' She remembered him moving to the music but his movements had looked completely natural, albeit totally hot, but they certainly hadn't looked choreographed.

'I'm not just a barman,' he said, as he tipped her backwards into a dip and then lifted her upright again before she had a chance to complain that she was too heavy. She knew she wasn't, she knew he had total control, he was ninety per cent sexy, muscled hunk and ten per cent cheek, although she admitted she should allocate some percentage for intelligence as well.

'Sure, there's judging the contests too,' she said, once she'd recovered her equilibrium.

'Everyone at The Coop does a bit of everything.'

He paused and Scarlett wondered what he was waiting for. He had tilted his head to the side as he watched her and once again she had the sense she'd missed something but she had no idea what.

He was smiling at her as he said, 'You do realise I'm a stripper?'

'What?' Scarlett frowned, not sure if she'd heard correctly.

'A stripper,' he repeated. 'Someone who gets paid to take their clothes off in public.'

CHAPTER SEVEN

SCARLETT STOPPED DEAD in the middle of the dance floor, almost causing a collision.

'I know what a stripper is,' she said, although she still wasn't quite sure that she believed her own ears. But even while she thought her ears were deceiving her, her imagination was taking flight. Her initial reaction was completely visual. She could picture him playing the part. An image of him semi-naked, bare-footed, bare-chested and wearing only jeans was imprinted on her brain from the time they'd first met. If she closed her eyes she could picture the muscle definition of his ab-dominals, the smoothness of his tanned chest and the perfectly shaped stars of his tattoo. She could imagine him on stage wearing nothing but a cheeky grin and tiny leather shorts, lapping up the attention.

Her heart was racing at the mental picture she had created until she suddenly wondered if he was pulling her leg. She searched his face, looking for a tell-tale grin. She narrowed her eyes and watched him carefully as she asked, 'Is that really what you do?'

'Of course.' She could see no sign of a smirk accom-panying his reply. 'What did you think I did there?' he asked as he steered her to the side of the dance floor, making sure they weren't going to get trampled.

'I thought you worked behind the bar.'

'I do but we're jacks of all trades. We're bar staff, waiters, strippers.'

He really wasn't kidding and she had no idea what to do with this new information. She wasn't sure if she should be shocked or intrigued, horrified or excited.

'You really didn't know?' he asked.

Gradually she became aware that they were still standing on the edge of the dance floor. She took his arm and almost dragged him outside to the terrace. She was not going to have this conversation around other people. How would she ever explain sleeping with a student *and* a stripper? She breathed a sigh of relief as he followed her outdoors.

Thank God no one knows we slept together, she thought, and she intended to keep it that way.

'Of course I didn't know,' she told him, as she checked their surroundings to make sure they were alone. 'Do you think I would have slept with you if I'd known?'

'You tell me. You didn't seem to have too many reservations. You didn't seem that interested in the finer details.'

She knew he was right. She'd wanted to do something out of character and she hadn't seen any reason to find out too much about him. She'd simply been looking for a physical connection, not a deep and meaningful conversation. In fact, she'd deliberately avoided any personal discussion. She'd been tempted by a hot stranger and she'd been more than happy to let him scratch an itch for her.

Her anger, which she knew stemmed from surprise and embarrassment, subsided. It was hardly his fault that she was naïve. It was hardly his fault she hadn't asked any questions, let alone the right ones.

'You're right. I'm sorry,' she apologised. 'I didn't stop to think. I didn't want to know anything about you really, other than what I could see. I wanted to pretend I was someone else, someone who was used to having a good time.'

'Well, that's my job. To make sure people have a good time.'

Just how good a time was he talking about? Was that what he'd been doing for her? And how many women had been there before her? She felt a blush steal across her throat and embarrassment made her words stick to the roof of her mouth. 'Do you—? Are you—?'

Jake shook his head. He obviously got the gist of her half-asked question. 'No. My job stops when I leave The Coop. Anything after that is my choice, my time.'

'But you must have picked up other girls in The Coop?'

'Actually, I haven't. I make a point not to. Most of the girls in The Coop are not at their best. Drunk and loud isn't really my type.'

She wondered if she should admit to having been slightly more intoxicated than she was used to but while she'd certainly had more to drink than was usual she knew she'd been in full control. She remembered every blissful minute of that night.

'I noticed you because you were different from the usual clients but I didn't intend to sleep with you.'

'You didn't?' Scarlett blushed. Had she made a complete idiot of herself by kissing him back, inviting him in and then almost begging him to sleep with her?

'Well, not that night anyway.' He grinned and Scarlett relaxed very slightly. 'You were a friend of a friend, I was being nice, offering to walk you to your taxi, but then...' He shrugged.

'So you take your clothes off in front of complete strangers for a living but you don't use your job to pick up women?'

'I do have some morals and it's not all my clothes. It's no different to being a life model for an art class or a patient for the surface anatomy viva in our exams. I keep more clothes on than they do and I'm paid better and it's fun. There's no harm in it. It's not illegal.'

'I couldn't do it.' Scarlett hadn't had a chance to work out what she thought about Jake being a stripper but she knew it was not something she could ever imagine doing.

He laughed and the sound lifted her spirits. She supposed in the grand scheme of things that finding out he was a stripper was hardly the worst thing that had ever happened.

'No one is asking you to,' he said. 'You were happy to join in at The Coop, though. You have to admit it's good entertainment.'

'I hated it. I was so far out of my comfort zone.'

'What did you hate? The show? The music? The atmosphere? Me?'

'No.' Definitely not him. 'Being on the stage. I had to pretend I was someone else up there. The girl you met at The Coop wasn't me.'

'The girl I met at The Coop came from somewhere.'

'I was pretending I was Ruby,' she admitted. 'I'm the

nerdy, shy, clever sister who behaved completely out of character that night. You should be dancing with Ruby, I'm sure the two of you have far more in common.'

Now more than ever, Scarlett wished she was more like Ruby. Surely Jake would rather be with someone who didn't take life so seriously? She was no match for him.

'And I'd rather be out here with you,' he said, as he ran one finger along the bare skin of her forearm, leaving a trail of heat from her elbow to her wrist. Scarlett could feel her nipples tauten in response to his touch and she couldn't think of anywhere else she'd rather be either.

'It's you I want to get to know,' he told her. 'Not Ruby or anyone else.'

'Why?' Scarlett knew exactly why she had slept with Jake but she couldn't understand why he'd want to be with her.

'When I first saw you I thought you were gorgeous and sexy and then I found out you were intelligent and fun as well. I think you're fascinating and I want to see all your different layers. Not just the person you want everyone to see. Do you remember the children's party game Pass the Parcel?'

Scarlett nodded. She knew the game but she didn't have the words to tell Jake that she hadn't gone to parties when she was little. She used to be invited to them but she never told her mother because she knew they didn't have the money for a present and she didn't have a party dress. She didn't want Jake feeling sorry for her. Those days were well and truly behind her, there was no point in bringing up the past.

'You remind me of the parcel.'

She frowned. 'How?'

'You seem to have lots of different layers and I want to unwrap each one and find out what's underneath.'

'I don't have different layers. What you see is what you get. I'm not complicated or interesting. All my life I've been the responsible one, the one who doesn't cause any problems, the one who does the right thing, who worries about what other people think.'

'I disagree. The girl on stage doing the limbo, she's inside you somewhere, underneath that responsible exterior.'

Scarlett shook her head. 'I was pretending. I'm not sure I really know how to be that person and I'm not sure if I want to be. I'm not Ruby and while I admit there are times I envy her I'm not sure that I really want to be her.'

'Are you and Ruby really so different?'

'Ruby is the wild one of our family. She's the fun, outgoing one, the one who has the adventures, the one who doesn't care what people think. If that's what you want, I'm not that person. I've always chosen studying over partying. I'm not a party girl.'

'And I'm not saying you should be. I'm only saying I think there's more to you than you want people to see and I find you fascinating. I want to get to know you. The real you. The complete you. I think we'd have fun together.'

Scarlett couldn't deny that she had fun with Jake but she couldn't imagine it continuing. 'I think you'll be disappointed. I don't think we have anything in common.'

'I disagree.'

Scarlett held up one finger and proceeded to straighten her adjacent fingers as she counted off their differences. 'You work in a strip club. As a stripper. Something I was naively unaware of. You're a student at my hospital. You have a tattoo.'

Jake laughed. 'Well, I happen to think we have plenty in common.'

He gently flexed her index finger, returning it to her palm. 'We're following the same career path. We're at the wedding of a mutual friend,' he said, as the next finger went down, followed by her third finger. 'I have a very small tattoo in a very discreet spot and I seem to remember you rather liked it. And...' he grinned as he closed her fist and finished negating her argument '...you can't hold my part-time profession against me, not when you've only known about it for five minutes, and especially not when you've already slept with me.'

'But I wouldn't have slept with you if I'd known.'

'Liar.' He was leaning in close. His lips brushed her ear and his words were soft puffs of air on the sensitive skin of her neck. 'You might not have slept with me if you'd known I was a med student but you know you wanted me as much that night as I wanted you and, stripper or not, you would have had your way with me.' His hand was on her waist and he slid it around to cup her bottom, pulling her in against him so her belly was pressed into his groin. There was no need to guess what was on his mind. Her nipples hardened in response to his physical reaction, pushing against the soft silk of her underwear, and she knew he'd be able to feel them jutting into his chest. His next words confirmed her thoughts. 'You want me now, too.'

She should have been cross with him. She should have found his arrogance infuriating but she couldn't deny he was right. She did want him. More now than she had on that first night. Now that she knew how her body responded to his touch she thought there would probably always be a part of her that would want him but that didn't make it right. And it had nothing to do with him being a stripper. She just knew they were an incompatible combination. He was too different. But she couldn't deny she was drawn to him. But that just made him different and dangerous.

'Don't be mad, dance with me,' he said.

The music from the band floated through the open doors onto the terrace. They were standing behind a potted tree, partially shielded from view of the guests inside, and Scarlett knew it would be difficult to see them due to the shadows. They were alone but she had no idea how long their solitude would last. She didn't want to have any more missed opportunities tonight. She let the music wash over her as she relaxed against him and let him take control.

He kept his hand on her bottom and held her close against his body. She rested her cheek on his chest. His heart was a steady, soothing beat under her ear. She could have stayed like that for hours but the evening was nearly over. She wished she hadn't been so stubborn, she wished she had danced with him earlier. She could have spent the night in his arms instead of watching all the other women enjoying his company.

She closed her eyes as she dreamed about what might have been.

It had taken him all evening but now he had her right where he wanted her to be—in his arms. He finally had her undivided attention. They were alone, without interruptions. He was convinced he could get her to relax if he had the time. If they had no other distractions and no observers.

He had been aware of her watching him dance for most of the evening. Once again her words had contrasted with her actions. Her dark eyes with their hidden secrets had followed him around the dance floor. He shouldn't find that enticing, he should find it frustrating, but it seemed that every time she contradicted herself it only made him more interested.

He'd meant it when he'd said he found her fascinating. He'd known since the moment he'd laid eyes on her that she was a bundle of contradictions. The serious hairstyle and simple black dress paired with her sexy hip-swivelling walk and the sky-high heels. She was an intriguing mix of sexy and smart.

It had been the contrasts in her that had hooked him from that first glance. Her pouty lips were the type that should be painted red but hers had been slick with a pale pink gloss. Her full lips had promised forbidden delights but had framed a smile that had been hesitant and unsure.

She was an interesting but possibly dangerous package, just waiting for the right spark to set her off. Her performance on stage had hinted at what could be but she had confirmed his expectation later that night when she'd taken him to her bed and he'd been lost in the promise and mystery of her ever since.

He wanted to strip away her layers and discover what was hidden at each level. He had never been so quickly and utterly captivated before. Her contrasts appeared limitless and he was desperate to discover them all. He had never thought that contrariness could be so interesting.

The music stopped, although it took them both a few seconds to notice. It wasn't until they were interrupted by the sound of the emcee announcing it was time to farewell the bride and groom that they realised the band had fallen silent.

Scarlett stayed in his arms. She seemed in no hurry to move and he was more than happy for her to stay right where she was. 'I'm not ready for the night to end.'

'It doesn't have to end yet,' he said. 'Let me take you home.' As he uttered the words he remembered Ruby's cautionary advice to take it slowly.

'And then what? We both know where that would lead.'

'Would that be so terrible?' He'd forgotten his vow to stay away. He'd forgotten he'd agreed to avoid scandal. He was completely under her spell and all he could think of was getting her out of her dress and having her long legs wrapped around him again while he tasted and explored her and learnt her secrets.

'Just think of all the fun we can have.'

'Do you have any idea how much trouble I would be in if anyone found out I was sleeping with a student?'

'It's not the first time.'

'I know. That makes it worse. Last time I could plead ignorance. What's my excuse this time?'

'My irresistible charm,' he whispered in her ear. His lips brushed against her earlobe and he could have sworn he could feel her resistance start to cave. 'I thought you wanted adventure?' he said, as he ducked his head lower and let his lips graze the edge of her jaw. 'You don't need to leave all the adventures for Ruby. I can be your adventure. The first student you seduced. The first stripper you took to your bed.'

'Seducing students and strippers isn't the sort of adventure I had in mind.' She was panting now, her words breathless.

'It's our secret. No one else needs to know.' His fingers brushed her breast, skimming across her nipple as he kissed the hollow at the base of her throat, and Scarlett moaned softly.

She tipped her head back to speak but ended up offering him her throat and he pressed his lips under her jaw over the pulse of her heart, and Scarlett only just managed to get her words out. 'You've only got two more weeks on placement. Can we wait until then?'

'Nine days.'

'What?'

'I've actually only got nine more days, not counting the weekend,' he said, as he ran his hand down her arm and hooked his fingers around hers. 'I guess I can wait that long.'

'Really?'

'Yes, really.' The way he was grinning at her made her think he'd just got what he wanted but she had no idea what that was. 'I was always prepared to wait until the end of my placement. Two more weeks of platonic friendship won't kill me. Especially if you're the prize at the end of it.'

Scarlett woke up with a start just as she felt Jake's fingers brush over her breast and trail across her stomach. Her eyes flew open and she was surprised to find herself alone in her bed. She would have sworn she wasn't dreaming. Even now her breasts ached with longing and her groin throbbed as her body refused to give up on the idea that Jake was sharing her bed.

Last night when he'd kissed the hollow at the base of her throat it had sent a spear of longing shooting from her belly to her groin and despite her concerns she'd been tempted, oh, so tempted to give in right then and there. But she'd resisted and now she was paying the price—an overactive imagination that refused to accept that Jake wasn't in her bed.

She closed her eyes as she ran her hands over her breasts. Her nipples puckered as she imagined Jake's fingers on her skin and she squeezed her knees together as the nerve centres in her erogenous zones sprang to life. Her fantasy had left her on edge. She needed release but unless she took matters into her own hands she wasn't going to get it. Doing it herself wasn't nearly as much fun. She swung her legs out of bed, deciding to head for the shower instead.

When she emerged from the shower, marginally less frustrated, she was surprised to find Ruby in the kitchen, pouring a glass of orange juice.

'You're up early,' Scarlett said.

'I promised Rose I'd go with her to check out the vintage clothes market. Do you want to come with us?'

Ruby knew of Scarlett's aversion to second-hand clothes. Vintage in her opinion was just another word for second-hand, but she was tempted to go anyway. It wasn't often she got a chance to spend time with both her sisters at once. And going with them didn't mean she had to buy clothes herself.

Before she could answer there was a knock on the front door. 'Is that Rose?' she asked.

Ruby shook her head. 'Too early.'

Scarlett frowned and went to open the front door.

Jake was waiting there, lounging casually against the veranda post as if he popped past every Sunday morning.

'What are you doing here?'

'I came to collect on our bet.'

Scarlett frowned. 'We didn't have a bet.'

'Yes, we did. Yesterday. At Candice's wedding. And I won. I correctly identified Ruby.'

'Oh,' Scarlett said, as she remembered how confident she'd been when she'd agreed to the bet. 'What's your prize?'

He said nothing further. Just smiled his sexy smile and Scarlett had a feeling she knew what he wanted. She held her breath.

'You and I are going to spend the day together.'

She exhaled. She had the perfect excuse. 'I can't. I'm going shopping with Ruby and Rose.'

'Tell them you've had a better offer.' He was still smiling at her.

He had an unfair advantage. Did he know what his smile did to her? She suspected he did. 'I thought we agreed to wait for two weeks?'

'This isn't a date. It's just two friends, hanging out. If it makes it any better we're going out of town. It's highly unlikely we'll bump into anyone who knows us and we're not doing anything wrong.'

When Scarlett still hesitated he added, 'You can trust me. I agreed to wait until I finished my placement before I let you seduce me again. No matter how much you beg I'm not going to let you take advantage of me. Today we are purely platonic. But before you accept my invitation I have a couple of questions for you, in the interests of full disclosure. Do you get motion sickness?'

'No.'

'Do you have a fear of roller-coasters?'

Scarlett frowned. As far as she knew, there were no roller-coasters in South Australia. Where was he planning on taking her? 'No.'

'What about confined spaces?'

She shook her head. She was afraid of being abandoned, of being unwanted, but she didn't have any, or almost any, of the usual phobias. 'Only spiders.'

'Good.'

'Where are we going?'

'Mallala.'

'Mallala?' Scarlett couldn't imagine what a small country town, an hour north of Adelaide, had that could possibly be of interest to her. 'What are we doing there?'

'You'll find out soon enough. We'll have fun, trust me.'

Her curiosity was piqued. 'Can you wait here?' she asked. 'I'll see if Ruby lets me make an excuse.' She didn't want Jake to come in as she suspected he and Ruby would gang up on her and make her go. If she tackled them individually she might at least feel as though she was still in charge of the decision.

'Who was it?' Ruby asked.

'Jake. He's invited me to spend the day with him. He has some secret activity planned.'

'I bet he does.' Ruby's eyes were sparkling as she laughed.

'What's so funny?'

'Nothing, I'm just imagining the activity and I'm amazed either of you have lasted this long. There were enough sparks between you and Jake last night to start a bushfire. The pair of you couldn't keep your eyes off each other. I'm surprised you didn't go home with him after the wedding. You should definitely go.'

Scarlett knew what Ruby was picturing but she also knew she was wrong. Jake had promised a platonic activity and Scarlett believed him. There was no reason not to. For a start, there'd be no reason to drive to Mallala if he wanted to spend the day in bed.

'I'm not sure it's a good idea,' she said.

'Are you kidding me?' Ruby replied. 'It's a terrific idea. He's cute and hot and fun and he likes you.'

'He's also a student.'

'Pah! It's easy enough to sneak around and not get caught if you want something badly enough. If you want *him* badly enough, which I think you do.'

'We've discussed it.'

'Discussed it? What are you wasting your time talking for? Get his gear off.'

'Shh,' Scarlett said. She was very much aware of the fact that Jake was still by the open front door and could probably hear their conversation if he listened hard enough. 'You know me, I like to play by the rules and I like to have a plan.'

'Okay, let's hear this plan of yours.' Ruby was still laughing.

'We're keeping things platonic until he finishes his placement in two weeks' time.'

'Are you sure you can wait that long?'

'We'll have to.'

'And what if his next placement is back in your hospital?'

Scarlett shook her head. 'He wants to do obstetrics and everyone wants to be sent to the city because it's convenient, but it's rare that students get two plum placements in a row.'

'Two weeks is a long time.'

'For you maybe. It will give me time to work out if I really want to do this.'

'Why wouldn't you? He's sexy and cute and smart. Have some fun.'

'I'm not sure I can handle it, handle him,' Scarlett admitted. 'He's so different from my usual type.'

'He's asked you to spend a day with him, not the rest of your life,' Ruby argued. 'Maybe it's time you tried something different.'

'You don't get much more different than a stripper.'

'What?' Ruby inhaled some orange juice and then coughed, sending a spray of juice onto the kitchen bench.

'He has a part-time job at a male revue as a stripper,' Scarlett told her, enjoying the fact that she'd been able to shock Ruby for once. It wasn't often she had that opportunity.

Ruby didn't stay shocked for long. She burst into hysterical laughter. 'I knew I liked him. A naughty streak gets me every time. Have you seen his show?'

Scarlett could feel herself blushing. 'I've seen all I need to see. Thank God no one knows I slept with him.'

'You slept with him? When?'

'The night we met. Before I knew he was a med student.'

'Well, it seems you're already experiencing different as far as he's concerned. That changes everything.'

'I'd forgotten I hadn't told you and it doesn't change anything.'

'What else haven't you told me?'

'Nothing. That's it.'

'Well, that's plenty. Now, stop arguing and go and get ready before he changes his mind. I'm not leaving till tomorrow, we can have dinner with Rose tonight.'

An hour later Scarlett slid the hair elastic down her ponytail, letting it sit lower at the base of her neck to accommodate the helmet that she was about to pull on. She wriggled it into place. It was a snug fit but not uncomfortable and the padding muffled the sounds of their surroundings. Jake adjusted the chin strap and Scarlett caught her breath as his fingers brushed the soft skin of her throat.

'You're good to go.' He grinned at her as he pulled his own helmet on.

Jake had brought her to a race circuit in the middle of dry dusty paddocks, and she was about to climb into a V8 racing car for a hot lap. The car was emblazoned with advertising and even though she knew it was the same model as hundreds of family sedans that filled the roads every day it looked fast and dangerous. She wasn't convinced this was a good idea but she didn't want to back out now. She was determined to be brave. Jake had arranged this for her and she was determined to enjoy herself. She had to trust Jake not to hurt her, to keep her safe, but even she could see the irony in that.

He opened the passenger door for her and helped to strap her into the racing harness.

'Sit right back, as flat as you can against the seat,' he said, as he tightened the straps. His hands brushed across her chest as he adjusted the harness and even though she was fully clothed in a fire-retardant racing suit she would swear she could feel the heat of his hands.

Jake slid through a back window into the seat behind her as Sean, their racing driver, double-checked the harness. Scarlett wasn't surprised to find she had no reaction whatsoever to Sean's touch.

Scarlett nervously checked her surroundings. The interior of the car looked familiar, more like the family sedans she was used to, with the exception of the steering-wheel, extra roll bars, the harnesses in place of seat belts and the fire extinguisher that was positioned between her and the driver's seat. On the dashboard in front of her, in place of the glove box, was a horizontal handle. Now that she thought about it, not much was actually that familiar. She took a deep breath and steeled her nerves as Sean climbed into the driver's seat.

The V8 engine growled as he pushed the start button and the car throbbed under her. Sean gave them both a thumbs-up before pulling out of the pits and onto a start line. Scarlett could see the bank of lights at the end of the straight and Sean revved the engine as he waited for the all-clear. He was giving them the full experience. The light changed to green and Sean pushed his foot to the floor and the car shot off down the track. The power of the engine forced Scarlett back into her seat. She didn't think it was possible to sit further back, the harness was so tight to begin with, but she was definitely flattened against the backrest.

She could hear Sean changing gear as they approached the first turn. She was sure he was taking the corner too fast and she grabbed the handle in front of her with both hands, clinging on tightly—at least now she knew what the handle was for—but before she could say anything they had rounded the corner and were flying along the back straight.

Her knuckles were white and she was sure her face was too. It was terrifying. She wasn't sure yet whether it was also fun. She would reserve judgement on that.

As they approached another hairpin turn and the barrier fence loomed large in the windscreen she squeezed her eyes shut.

'It's more fun if you open your eyes.' She could hear Jake's voice and she realised the helmets must have an inbuilt communications system.

'I'm trying to keep them open but they're refusing,' she replied.

She felt the car change direction and forced her eyes open as Sean put his foot to the floor and they flew past the pits.

'Haven't we finished?' she said, as the pit buildings went by in a blur.

'Not yet. We're doing three laps.'

Another two laps! She wasn't sure she could take it. Her eyes flicked across to the dashboard as Sean came out of the hairpin at the end of the pit straight and hit the gas. She could see the speedometer—did it really read two hundred and sixty kilometres per hour?

She held on tight to the handle in front of her and concentrated on being brave. It would only be a few more minutes. She could manage.

Three minutes later she climbed out of the car on shaky legs. Jake hauled himself out through the rear window, a wide grin on his face.

'Did you enjoy that?' he asked, as he pulled his helmet off before helping her to undo hers.

'I think so.' That had been so far out of her comfort

zone she wasn't sure what to think. She was normally so cautious she still wasn't sure what had convinced her to take the challenge and get into a racing car, but looking at Jake, so calm and confident, she knew it was he who had made her feel brave. He made her feel as though she could take on the world and if anything bad happened he'd be there to pick up the pieces. He was teaching her to live in the moment, not worry about the future.

'There's more to come,' he said.

'I'm not sure my heart can take more.' Scarlett wasn't just talking about the racing. Jake had tucked his helmet under his arm and he looked every inch the sexy race-car driver. How was it that he always looked to have everything under control? The wilder things got, the happier he seemed.

'Sean's going to take you out on the skid pan. And this time you get to drive.'

'What?' Scarlett turned to Sean. 'You're going to let *me* drive your racing car?'

'Don't worry, it's insured.' Sean laughed. 'And there's nothing to hit out there. Just flat dirt.'

For the next half an hour Scarlett was let loose on the skid pan. Sean taught her how to deliberately lose control. Deliberating losing control of anything, let alone a moving vehicle, was extremely difficult for her. Her natural impulse was to hit the brakes the moment she felt the rear of the car start to slide out but when she eventually managed to follow Sean's instructions and let the car slide he then taught her to steer into the skid. Eventually she could feel the car straighten and she was able to drive out of trouble. Once she'd mastered the skid pan she felt as if she'd been given the moon.

The minute she pulled the car to a stop in front of

Jake she leapt out and ran over to the fence to hug him. 'I did it! I did it! Did you see me?'

'I did. You were brilliant.' He hugged her tight and Scarlett thought this might just be the best day she'd ever had.

'That was so much fun. Thank you.' In the end she'd actually enjoyed losing control. There had been no time to worry about anything, she'd had to use all her energy to control the car and concentrate on doing what Sean told her. There'd been no time to be frightened. 'If that's what adventure is like, I'm a fan.'

'That's adrenalin.' He removed her helmet for her. 'Come on, I think you've earned a drink.' He took her hand as she thanked Sean and walked with her back to the pit buildings, only letting go of her hand to allow her to change out of her racing suit. He was waiting for her when she emerged from the change room and he handed her a soft drink before leading her to a viewing area overlooking the race track. They finished their drinks as they watched other people's laps. It looked just as fast as it had felt.

'I can't believe I actually did that,' Scarlett mused as cars flew past them. 'How on earth did you get into this?'

'My godfather was into car racing. He started in the Car Club and I used to come out here on weekends with him. He was a doctor, a surgeon, but car racing was his passion. He taught me to give everything one hundred per cent.'

'Your car belonged to him, didn't it?' Scarlett remembered Jake telling her that on the night they'd met. The first night he'd driven her home. When Jake nodded, she added, 'Do you ever race your car?'

'No, it's not certified for racing but I still try to make it out here for car club meetings a couple of times a year. MG owners are a rather passionate, eclectic bunch. It's good fun.'

She had to agree—it *was* fun. But the best part had been spending time with Jake. He'd chosen the perfect activity. Away from the pressure of work and people they knew, taking her some place where she couldn't possibly focus on anything other than the matter at hand. There'd been no time to even think about whether spending time with him was the right or wrong thing to do. All she knew was that it felt right. Whenever she was with him she felt as though she was where she was supposed to be.

He was different but Ruby was right. Perhaps different was good. He made her happy and that certainly felt good. She was content just being in the moment when she was with him. It was unusual for her not to be worrying about work or finances or what other people expected of her. It was nice to feel relaxed.

Maybe this was how life was supposed to feel. Maybe she could be relaxed and happy and a little bit adventurous if she was with the right person. Was Jake the right person for her? Could he be?

She glanced over at him as he watched the cars zip by. He was leaning on a railing inside the protective fence and she let her eyes run over the curve of his backside. He was wearing a simple T-shirt and jeans, quite a contrast to the elegance of the suit he'd worn to the wedding and she couldn't decide how she preferred him. In a suit, in scrubs, casually outfitted or naked in her bed? He looked good in anything. And better in nothing.

She was just about to thank him again for the

day when her fantasies were interrupted by terrified screams. The screams weren't coming from the race-track but from behind them. Scarlett whipped around. The screams imparted a sense of urgency, and she saw several car tyres roll from behind one of the pit build-ings and go bouncing along the ground.

Jake took off at a run and Scarlett was close be-hind him.

CHAPTER EIGHT

THEY ROUNDED THE corner of the building. A pile of old car tyres, which Scarlett suspected had once been neatly stacked, had collapsed, sending tyres rolling in all directions. A woman and two children were frantically tugging at what remained of the stack.

'What are you doing?'

'What's happened?' They spoke together.

'My son,' the woman panted. 'He's under here.'

Jake looked at Scarlett but only fleetingly. Before Scarlett could process what had happened Jake was hauling the tyres from the pile and tossing them to one side.

Watching Jake kicked Scarlett into action too.

'Are these also your children?' she asked the woman.

'Yes.'

'Take them around the front, into the building.' Scarlett could only imagine what grisly scene they might be about to uncover. It was better if the children were somewhere else. 'Find someone to keep an eye on them,' she told the mother, as more people arrived on the scene. Jake quickly issued instructions to the newcomers as the woman shepherded her other children out of sight but not without an anxious backward glance and Scarlett knew she'd be back as soon as possible.

Just as the on-site paramedics arrived and the boy's mother returned, Jake pulled another tyre from the stack to finally reveal the unmoving figure of a young boy. He was unnervingly still, there was not even a slight rise and fall of his chest, and Scarlett feared the worst. She introduced herself to the paramedics and gave them Jake's background as Jake bent his head to check the boy's breathing and simultaneously felt for a pulse.

'Unconscious and in respiratory arrest but he has a pulse,' Jake told the paramedics as he started mouth-to-mouth, breathing for the boy.

Who knew what other injuries he had sustained? Scarlett knew the list could be long. He could have spinal fractures, a head injury, rib fractures, a pneumothorax, just to name a few, but the priority was establishing an airway and getting oxygen into his lungs. They worked frantically for the next few minutes.

Scarlett inserted an endotracheal tube into the boy's trachea to establish an artificial airway and once one of the paramedics was squeezing the ambu bag, forcing air into the boy's lungs, Jake and Scarlett helped to fit a cervical collar around his neck before transferring him onto a spinal board then a stretcher and then into the ambulance. Somehow, in the middle of the frenetic activity, Jake managed to keep chatting to the boy's mother, keeping her informed.

Scarlett breathed a sigh of relief as the ambulance raced away, lights and sirens at full strength. They had done their bit, and had done it well. Now it was up to the paramedics and the trauma team at the receiving hospital. Now that the crisis was over Scarlett found her hands were shaking. By comparison, Jake appeared remarkably unflustered if somewhat filthy from the physical exertion.

'You were unbelievably calm,' Scarlett commented, as she rubbed her hands on her arms to try to disguise her rattled nerves.

'I've been in worse situations,' he replied.

'Really? When?' Despite her recent weeks in the Emergency department Scarlett had never felt under the same sort of pressure that she had been under just then. Working in the middle of nowhere with very limited resources was an entirely new experience for her. When would Jake have experienced worse?

'I spent some time travelling around Asia during my gap year. I was travelling from Vietnam to Thailand when Cyclone Nargis hit Myanmar. The whole area became the true definition of a disaster zone. I volunteered with a charity and what I experienced there was life-changing. I had put med school on hold while I travelled and while I wasn't qualified to give any medical care I volunteered to help in the hospital.

'There were plenty of jobs assisting the medicos for anyone who wasn't squeamish and there were plenty of emergencies and terrible injuries. It was tragic and truly dreadful but any little thing anyone could do could make a difference so it was hugely rewarding at the same time, and it confirmed for me that medicine was what I wanted to do.'

Jake was constantly surprising her. He was far more mature and multi-faceted than she had given him credit for, which made him even more intriguing.

'I had no idea,' she said, but her teeth were chattering and her words weren't very clear. She rubbed her arms again, trying to stop the shaking.

Jake wrapped an arm around her shoulders. 'Come on, let's get you warm and home.' She knew the shivering was an after-effect of the adrenalin but she kept quiet. She didn't want to give Jake a reason to remove his arm. It was comforting. It was perfect. 'There won't be any more racing happening while the ambulance is gone.'

Jake opened the boot of his car, pulled out his leather jacket and helped her into it. He glanced down at his filthy T-shirt. 'This has seen better days,' he said. He whipped it off, treating Scarlett to one of her favourite views—his naked torso, abdominal muscles and tattoo. A familiar surge of longing rushed through her and she wasn't surprised to find that the heat of her reaction counteracted the adrenalin and she stopped shaking.

She was tempted to break her agreement. She was tempted to throw herself at him right then and there, but unfortunately Jake swapped the dirty T-shirt for a clean hoodie that he found in the boot and removed temptation from under her nose.

Disappointed, she climbed into his car. The end of his placement couldn't come soon enough for Scarlett.

One more day.

Less than twelve hours really until she and Jake would be free.

For the past eight days he had been leaving little notes for her, counting down the days. Yesterday he'd managed to tape an envelope to her locker. Inside had been a note that had simply said: *One more day.* The day before that she'd found a sticky note inside a patient's file that had read: *Two days to go.* Today she'd gone into the operating theatre and found an invitation on the whiteboard.

> *Med students dinner tonight, 7.30, Casa Barce-lona. All invited.*

Underneath it was a postscript that read: *Only twelve more hours*. She recognised the handwriting and she knew Jake had been in early and left the note for her. She wiped the postscript off before anyone else saw it but she was smiling and his note put her in a good mood that lasted all day.

One more day had become twelve more hours, which had now become a matter of minutes.

Scarlett checked the clock on the theatre wall as she hummed along to Richard's MP3. The final surgery for her shift was almost finished and even the nasty injury sustained by the victim of a dog attack couldn't dampen her enthusiasm and love of life today.

She hadn't wanted to go to the dinner, she'd had other plans for Jake, but he'd talked her round and she smiled as she walked through the restaurant doors as she remembered what he'd said earlier in the day. 'You need to eat, you'll need your strength.'

They'd ordered shared platters from the tapas menu for the group, and although the food was still coming Scarlett had eaten enough. She was getting edgy. She'd done the right thing, joined in the end-of-placement celebration but now she wanted to get on with the rest of the evening. Jake was sitting beside her on the long wooden bench, his thigh was pressed against hers, and she could feel the heat coming off his body and smell his freshly showered scent. She'd had enough of sitting there politely, pretending to be interested in the conversation and trying to ignore her raging hormones. She wanted to take Jake home, strip him of his clothes and take him to her bed.

She was wondering how she could suggest to him that it was time to leave without being overheard when talk moved onto the students' next placements. They had been informed of their next hospitals just that afternoon and despite her plans she was keen to hear where they were all going.

'You're doing obstetrics, Jake?' someone asked. 'Where are you going?'

'Mount Gambier.'

Scarlett's heart dropped in her chest. He was going to the country.

He must have seen her expression because he stood up from the table without adding anything further. He turned to her and held out his hand as the band started to play. 'Time for dancing,' he said.

She stood too, accepting his invitation. This would give them a chance to talk in private.

'Mount Gambier! That's five hours away,' she said as soon as they were on the dance floor. 'Couldn't you have got somewhere closer?'

'It's a great placement and I'll be the only obstetric student so I should get to do more deliveries than if I was sharing the load with other students,' he said, and she knew she was being selfish. He was right, the placement was important and a good hospital would make all the difference. 'I hear that Annie runs a really good programme,' he added, as he dipped her.

'Annie?'

'Dr Annie Simpson. She's the ob-gyn.' He was grinning at her now. 'There's no need to be jealous, she's way too old for me.'

'How old?'

'Early thirties.'

'Hey, I'm almost thirty.'

'I know,' he said, as he spun her away from him. 'I'm just stirring you. I have everything I want right here,' he said, as he pulled her back into his arms.

Scarlett had no idea what dance they were doing but she didn't care. She didn't need to worry about the steps, she just had to follow Jake's lead.

'I know this isn't what we were hoping for,' he told her, 'but we've got a couple of days before I go so I suggest we make the most of our time and get out of here.'

'You want to leave together?'

'I thought that was the general idea. Tell you what, why don't I leave? Everyone will assume I'm going to work at The Coop. I'll grab a taxi and meet you out the front in ten minutes. You can make an excuse and join me. Okay?'

Scarlett nodded. 'That's a better plan.'

'You're not the only one with a plan,' he said, with a grin that melted her insides.

Scarlett rolled over in bed and stretched. She was still half-asleep and she could have quite happily stayed in bed for the day if she didn't have to go to work. The pillow next to her still had an indentation from Jake's head, from where he'd lain beside her for the night. She buried her face in the pillow and breathed in his scent.

She lifted her head when she heard him come into the room. He was freshly showered but only half-dressed.

He had his pants on but she was treated to a fine view
of his lean, well-defined torso, his ripped abdominals
and a glimpse of his tattoo as he put a cup of coffee on
her bedside table. He bent a little further and kissed her
on the lips before reaching for his shirt and pulling it
over his head. He grabbed his car keys and tossed them
in the air, then caught them again. It seemed as though
his good mood was a match for hers.

'I won't be able to see you tonight, I have a late lecture and then I have to work at The Coop,' he said as
he slipped his feet into his shoes.

'You could come past after work,' she suggested.

'It'll be late.'

'That's okay. You can wake me up when you get
here.'

'Sounds good,' he said, as he flashed his cheeky grin.
His green eyes were alight as he leant over and kissed
her a second time before ducking out of the door. She
heard the front door open and then close.

In two days he'd be leaving for Blue Lake Hospital
in Mt Gambier and she wanted to make the most of the
little time they had together before he left. She smiled as
she thought about last night. Their time together might
be limited for the next month but if last night was anything to go by, they would be able to make the most
of any spare moments. She stretched again and sat up,
reaching for her coffee cup.

The sudden movement made her feel a little light-
headed and a wave of nausea hit her as she inhaled the
strong odour of the coffee. She put the coffee back on
the table, deciding to leave it until after her shower.
She spent far too long in the shower, leaving herself no
time for breakfast, and she left for work with the coffee

sitting untouched by her bed. She grabbed a take-away coffee and a cinnamon scroll from the cafeteria but her stomach protested over that combination of flavours too.

She put her breakfast down on a bench in the change room as she prepared to get changed into her scrubs.

She looked up as the door swung open to admit Mel.

'Are you all right?' Mel asked, as she took one look at her.

'Yep, just tired, I think. It's making me feel a little off.'

'You look dreadful. Are you hungover?'

'No.' She wasn't hungover, she'd barely touched any alcohol last night—she hadn't needed to. She'd got by on pure adrenalin. The excitement of being able to go home with Jake without feeling guilty, even if they still didn't tell anyone else what they were doing, had been enough of a buzz. She hadn't needed to drink, not when she'd had Jake.

Scarlett hadn't said anything to Mel about Jake yet. It was early days and she wanted to keep whatever happened under wraps for now, just between the two of them for a little longer. 'I think it must be something I ate last night.'

'Are you going to eat that?' Mel nodded at Scarlett's coffee and scroll, which were on the bench beside her.

Scarlett looked at her breakfast. She'd taken the scroll out of its bag but even the thought of eating or drinking anything was enough to make her feel ill. She shook her head. 'No. It's all yours.'

She bent forward to step into a pair of surgical trousers as Mel picked up the scroll and bit into it. The smell of cinnamon wafted over Scarlett. She wasn't sure if it was the smell or the position she was in but she felt decidedly woozy. She straightened up, hoping that would clear her head. 'I'm not feeling—'

Scarlett looked around her. The room looked different but it took her a moment to realise it was because she was lying on the floor. The cinnamon scroll was next to her with a bite out of it. She frowned. She didn't remember eating the scroll. And what was she doing on the floor?

'Scarlett? Can you hear me?'

She turned her head and winced as a stabbing pain shot from the back of her head into her eye socket. Mel was kneeling on the floor beside her. 'What happened?'

'You fainted.'

She frowned. 'But I never faint.'

'Okay, you passed out. Are you hurt?'

'I don't think so.'

She struggled to sit up but Mel put a hand out to stop her.

'Stay there. If you're not hurt I still want to take your BP before you go anywhere.'

Mel ducked out of the change room and came back seconds later with a sphygmomanometer. She wrapped the cuff around Scarlett's arm before inflating it. 'Ninety over sixty. What is it normally?'

'One-ten on eighty,' Scarlett replied. 'I'm fine.'

'You need to eat something.'

They both looked at the cinnamon scroll lying on the floor. 'Not that.' Mel laughed.

'Eating is what got me into this state,' Scarlett told her. 'I think if I eat anything I'll throw up.'

'Shall I run a drip for you instead?'

Scarlett shook her head, wincing again as the movement made her head throb. 'I'm not hungover and I haven't been vomiting. I don't think I'm dehydrated. I just feel off. I'm sure it's just a slight dose of food poisoning or maybe a food allergy of some sort.'

'Could be gastro. Are you having any stomach cramps?' Mel asked, as she took Scarlett's temperature. 'Your temperature's normal. No headaches?'

'I have one now,' Scarlett said as she gingerly touched the bump on the back of her head. 'But I didn't have one before.'

Mel shrugged. 'Okay, you can skip the drip and get up, but only if you agree to go straight home and have plenty of fluids when you get there and something to eat when you can.'

'Just give me a minute, I'll be fine.'

'You need to go home in case it develops into something that could be contagious.'

'I'm sure it's just something I ate,' she protested.

'Maybe. But you did just faint. You shouldn't be at work.'

'Fine.' She felt too drained to argue and the bump on her head was throbbing.

'I'll call past after work and see how you are.'

Scarlett couldn't remember the last time she'd spent the day on the couch. She had an afternoon sleep and woke up feeling like her old self, other than the lump on the back of her head. She put the whole episode down to a lack of sleep, a chilli overload with the tapas menu and no breakfast. Thinking of food made her realise she was actually hungry. She put some bread into the toaster and flicked the kettle on for a cup of tea, thinking it still might be advisable to steer clear of coffee for a little longer.

Mel arrived as she was finishing off the first piece of toast.

'Good, you're eating. Are you feeling better?'

'I'm almost back to normal. I told you it was just something I ate.'

'I know you did but I checked and no one else who was at the restaurant last night is sick,' Mel said, as she dumped her handbag on the kitchen table and rummaged through it. 'I brought you something,' she said, pulling something from her bag.

In her hand she held a pregnancy test kit.

Scarlett stared at the box. 'Why on earth would I be pregnant?'

'You're probably not but you don't have a hangover, you didn't have a temperature or a headache or stomach pain and no one else has been sick. You're just feeling a little off and you haven't been eating.'

'I'm eating now.'

'Have you had a coffee today?'

Scarlett shook her head. 'I've made a couple but I can't stand the smell.'

'When was your last period?'

'Jeez, would you give it a rest?' Scarlett was getting nervous now.

'Well? Do you remember?'

'I'd have to check my diary.'

Mel handed her the test kit. 'Just do me a favour. Take the test and then we can cross that off the list as well.'

Scarlett sighed and snatched the kit from Mel before storming off to the bathroom. There must be a dozen different ailments she could have. Why on earth would she be pregnant? *How* could she be pregnant?

She opened the box and checked the instructions before weeing on the stick. She sat on the toilet and waited, calculating dates in her head while she waited for the time to elapse. She didn't need to check her diary. Her last period had been due on the day of Candice's wedding ten days ago and she realised now that it hadn't come. She'd been too busy at work, too busy thinking about Jake, to notice.

What if Mel was right?

She felt her stomach start to heave and knew she wasn't going to be able to keep the toast down. She stood up from the toilet, flipped open the lid and vomited into the bowl until her stomach was empty.

She rinsed her mouth and spat into the basin. The stick was sitting on the edge of the basin, daring her to pick it up.

Her hand shook as she lifted it from the sink and took it out to Mel.

She nodded at Mel's handbag. 'Do you have another one of these in there?'

'Why? Didn't it work?'

'I hope not. It's positive.'

'Oh, my God. You're pregnant!' Mel jumped out of her chair.

'No. I can't be.' Scarlett shook her head. 'That's why I need to do another test.'

Mel held her hand out. 'Let me see.' She looked at the window and Scarlett knew what she'd see. Two pink lines. 'You really are pregnant.'

Scarlett collapsed onto the couch. She'd been hoping that Mel would tell her she was seeing things. Seeing pink lines that weren't really there. 'What am I going to do? I don't want a baby.'

If she didn't want children that were planned, what on earth was she supposed to do with an unexpected baby?

'Richard will be over the moon. You don't have to worry about doing this on your own.'

'I doubt that very much.'

'You told me he wants kids. You told me that's why you broke up.'

'It might not be his.'

'What?' Mel's expression would have been funny if the situation wasn't so dire. 'Whose could it be?' she asked.

Scarlett buried her face in her hands. 'God, what a bloody mess.' She took a deep breath. 'I slept with Jake.'

'Oh, my God. When?'

'Candice's hen's night.' She wasn't about to admit to last night's dalliance as well. 'Before I knew who he was. Well, before I knew he was a med student.'

'Oh, my God!' Mel repeated. 'What happened?'

'Remember he offered to walk me to the taxi? When we got to the street there was a huge queue for cabs so he offered to give me a lift home. One thing led to another.'

'Jeez, that was fast work. Candice was right when she said he was a charmer. Didn't you practise safe sex?'

'Of course we did. But something must have gone wrong.'

'So when you said you "can't" be pregnant, you actually could be, you just don't want to be?'

'There's no way I'm having kids, especially not on my own. And I can't imagine that Jake would want to be a father at this point in time either.'

'It doesn't have to be his, does it?'

'What do you mean?

'Is there a chance it could Richard's?'

Scarlett shook her head. 'No.' She was almost certain it wasn't Richard's.

'Well, there's always more than one option but you don't have to work it all out tonight. It's still very early days and anything could happen. If you really don't want it, maybe that's what you should hope for.'

Scarlett didn't know if she could wish for it all to go away. Not if she really was pregnant. But Mel was right, it was early days and she needed more confirmation than a home pregnancy test. The best she could hope for was that this was a mistake and all she was really suffering from was a bad case of gastro.

'Are you going to be okay? Would you like me to stay the night?' Mel asked.

'No. I'll be fine.'

Scarlett doubted she'd be fine but she'd got herself into this mess and she didn't expect Mel to have to help her sort it out. She'd figure it out one way or another but she needed a bit of time to process what had just happened. She sent Jake a quick message saying she wasn't feeling well and not to come past tonight. She hated to put him off but she needed time and space. She couldn't deal with seeing him just yet.

She was mortified. She had always tried to do the right thing, always tried to behave and avoid trouble. Her sisters constantly did as they pleased while she tried not to cause anyone grief. Most of the time her sisters got away with their behaviour and it was typical of her luck that the one time she did something out of character, the one time she was spontaneous or, dare she say irresponsible, she got into trouble.

She was always the one who helped others. Was she now going to be the one in need of help? And who would she turn to? Her mother? Jake?

If she was pregnant, she was ninety-nine per cent certain it was Jake's. But expecting support from him wasn't fair, he hadn't asked to be a father. Oh, why couldn't the baby be Richard's? At least then she would know the father wanted to be involved, but of course it couldn't be that simple.

She pulled her diary from her bag and double-checked her dates. As she'd suspected, her last period had started four weeks *before* Candice's wedding. Almost six weeks ago. She was ten days late. She was never late.

She hadn't slept with Richard since well before that but she'd slept with Jake almost four weeks ago. It had to be his.

Mel was hovering outside Emergency the next morning, waiting for Scarlett when she arrived at work. 'How are you feeling?'

'I'm okay.'

'Have you eaten?'

Scarlett nodded. She'd swapped coffee for tea and a piece of buttered toast and so far she'd managed to keep her breakfast down.

'Have you worked out what you're going to do?' Mel asked. 'What you're going to tell Jake?'

'Nothing yet. I want to get the test confirmed first. It still could be a mistake.'

'You mean to tell me you haven't done another home pregnancy test just to see?'

'Of course I have.' She'd gone to the pharmacy last

night after Mel had left and bought three more tests, all different brands, hoping one of them would give her a different answer.

'And?'

'They were all positive.' It was starting to look like she was going to have to deal with it.

'You know as well as I do that any official test is just a variation on weeing on the stick at this stage,' Mel said, effectively negating Scarlett's reasoning for wanting to take a fifth, if somewhat more official, test. 'I think you need to move past denial and work out what you're going to do. You need to talk to Jake. Have you got plans to see him before he goes to the country?'

Scarlett nodded. 'We're having breakfast in the morning.'

'Isn't he leaving tomorrow?'

She nodded again. 'He's driving down with a couple of other med students who are on different rotations. They're leaving at lunchtime.'

'You can't tell him minutes before he gets in the car,' Mel protested. 'Not when he's got a four-and-a-half-hour drive in front of him. That's not fair. Why are you waiting until the last minute?'

'I'm working all day today and he's working at The Coop tonight. Tomorrow is the only chance I've got.'

She was still getting used to the idea that she *might* be pregnant and she and Jake had both been flat out with other commitments over the past two days. She could think of half a dozen reasons why she hadn't said anything, half a dozen excuses for why she'd kept quiet, but she knew in reality she'd been stalling.

'You can't pretend this isn't happening.'

'Why not?' Might be pregnant was a whole different ballgame to definitely pregnant. Definitely pregnant meant having a baby and she wasn't sure she was ready to deal with that. Might be pregnant was working for her at the moment. She was hoping it was all a big mistake and that if she wished hard enough it would go away and she wouldn't have to say anything.

'Because eventually it's going to be obvious,' Mel said.

'If it's true,' Scarlett answered, but even as she uttered the words she knew that all the wishing in the world wasn't going to change the fact that she *was* pregnant. Four different tests had confirmed it, plus her period still hadn't come and the nausea hadn't gone away, neither had her aversion to coffee. Even her boobs were tender and she could swear they were already bigger. People *were* going to notice something, she couldn't keep denying it.

'Don't you think Jake deserves to hear it from you before other people find out?'

Mel was right. Jake would be in the country for the next month. She couldn't delay for much longer. 'Might be pregnant' was rapidly becoming 'time to face reality' and she couldn't risk him finding out some other way. She needed to tell him. She nodded.

'You'll have to go to The Coop tonight, then. I think you might need more than just an hour over breakfast to work this out. I'll come with you.'

'What for?'

'To make sure you don't chicken out.'

Scarlett had spent ages choosing an outfit. She knew she should be spending her time working out what she was going to say to Jake but sorting through her wardrobe was marginally less stressful and also managed to distract her from the thought of the dreaded conversation.

She didn't want to look like she was going into a business meeting, neither did she want to look like she was planning on clubbing until the wee hours of the morning, and eventually she settled on a wrap dress made of black jersey. Unfortunately the wrap style highlighted her breasts but she didn't have anything else suitable. She didn't think her boobs could get bigger than their normal DD but it seemed she was wrong and the black fabric wasn't enough to disguise her new dimensions. She'd decided to leave her hair loose, partly to try to soften her look and partly in an attempt to hide her boobs.

She'd also ditched the five-inch heels she'd borrowed last time in favour of pointy-toed black patent leather boots with a two-inch heel. The boots were smart enough but far more comfortable and less stripper-like than the sandals and she thought far more suited to a pregnant woman, even if she did feel knocked up as opposed to pregnant.

But when Mel arrived to collect her Scarlett immediately felt mumsy by comparison, despite her kick-ass, pointy-toed boots. Mel was wearing a very short sequin tank dress with spaghetti straps, and she'd spiked up her short pixie hair and she looked edgy, like someone who belonged in the club. Scarlett's outfit could only be described as conservative next to Mel's.

Scarlett clutched her hands around her small handbag, holding it protectively in front of her as she looked around the club. Looking at the other patrons, she knew she'd be the least likely to be picked as the girl who'd have a one-night stand, let alone get pregnant, but that's was what she was. And even though their 'liaison' had turned into more than a one-night stand she was under no illusion that she and Jake had the sort of relationship that could handle having a baby together. Not yet. And probably not ever.

If ever there was a case of wrong place, wrong time, Scarlett thought this was it. She couldn't begin to imagine telling Jake her news in the club.

She scanned the room, aware that her heart was racing. She was terrified of telling Jake but Mel was right, he had a right to know. But she was still pinning her hopes on him not wanting the baby either. He was young and still studying. It was hardly good timing for him. He'd probably be scared too. Maybe they had other options.

But then she remembered how he interacted with his niece and that he was contemplating doing paediatrics or obstetrics as his specialty, and she *knew* he would want the baby. Now she had to tell him about the baby *and* tell him *she* didn't want it.

Her eyes flicked over to the bar but she couldn't see Jake. Maybe he wasn't at work, maybe she'd got her wires crossed, maybe she could just go home. She was about to plead her case to Mel when the music started pumping and Mel nudged her in the ribs.

'There he is.'

Scarlett looked to the front of the room where three spotlights illuminated the catwalk. She could see Caesar and Rico and centre stage was Jake. All three of them were dressed alike in white T-shirts that hugged their chests and tight jeans that hugged their thighs, but Scarlett only had eyes for Jake.

The contrast between the three of them—Caesar

bulky and dark, Rico lithe and serious and Jake ripped and cheeky—was interesting but Scarlett couldn't tear her eyes away from Jake. Their routine was well choreographed and well-rehearsed. Their movements were in perfect harmony as they played to the appreciative crowd but as Jake strutted down the catwalk she couldn't even pretend to be interested in anything or anyone but him.

As he gyrated his hips and winked at the women she hoped she was blending into the crowd. Jake in performance mode, even while fully clothed, was mesmerising and she wanted to enjoy the show anonymously.

The lyrics were familiar and she found herself moving to the beat of the song.

Jake's hands were at the neck of his T-shirt and she watched in fascination as he ripped his shirt in one smooth movement, tearing it down the middle to expose his chest.

Heat pooled low in her belly as he threw his shirt to one side before running his hands over his chest and along the ridge of his abdominals and down to his groin. She could feel the heat spreading from her stomach to her thighs and she was embarrassed by her lack of self-control.

Jake lifted his hands from his groin and linked his fingers behind his head, and his tattoo pulsed as his muscles flexed. His abdominal muscles rippled as he fell to his knees and women started shoving fistfuls of tipping dollars into his waistband as he winked and bestowed his cheeky grin on them. His star sign was most definitely a Leo.

Scarlett's mouth went dry as she watched the women go wild for Jake and suddenly, seeing him on stage performing for the adoring masses, wasn't so appealing. As he got to his feet he had his hands on his jeans and she knew what was coming next. She didn't need to see this. She didn't need to be reminded that she'd got herself knocked up by a stripper, even one as sexy and as intelligent as Jake. Could tonight get any worse?

CHAPTER NINE

SCARLETT WAS MORTIFIED. Her stomach heaved as she watched Jake, Caesar and Rico fall into position for the finale. She couldn't face what was coming next. She turned and fled to the ladies' room before Jake could rip his pants off and stand semi-naked in front of a room full of screaming women.

She was aware of Mel following her as she almost ran to the bathroom. Thank goodness the room was empty—everyone else was enjoying the show.

She got as far as the basins before she lost the contents of her stomach. Mel held her hair out of the way as she waited for her to finish vomiting.

'Wait here,' Mel told her when her stomach was finally empty, and Scarlett rinsed her mouth with tap water. 'I'll bring you a glass of water for a proper drink.'

When Mel came back Scarlett was sitting on a toilet seat with her head in her hands. 'I'm pregnant to a stripper,' she said, as Mel handed her the glass.

'It could be worse,' Mel replied.

'How could it possibly be worse?'

'It's not as if taking his clothes off is all he's good at. He's going to be a doctor, he's also a nice guy, cute, intelligent and, as an added bonus, all his bits appear to be in good working order.'

Scarlett groaned in response before rinsing her mouth again with the last of the water. 'I can't possibly talk to him now. I need to go home.'

'Give me a minute,' Mel said, as she took the glass and ducked out of the bathroom.

'I've left a message with Rooster,' she told Scarlett when she returned a few minutes later. 'I've asked Jake to call past your place when he knocks off. I've said it's urgent so now we can go home.'

It was late before Jake arrived but Mel had waited and she let him in before leaving.

He had stopped at the Blue and White Café. Scarlett could smell the yiros and recognised the wrapping.

'Are you hungry?' he asked as he bent to kiss her, before offering her one of the packets.

Scarlett held up one hand, refusing the wrap, and covered her mouth and nose with her other hand. The smell of the roast meat and garlic sauce made the bile rise in her throat.

'What's wrong? Are you sick?'

She shook her head. Her eyes were underlined with dark shadows and she knew she looked pale and tired, especially compared to Jake, who looked fantastically fit and healthy.

'I'm not sick,' she said, as she tugged on his hand, pulling him down to sit beside her. 'I'm pregnant.'

'Pregnant? Are you sure?'

She nodded. She knew she had to accept the facts. She couldn't deny it for ever.

'Shit. Pregnant? How many weeks are you?'

'Six, I think. It could only have happened that first time.'

'But we used protection.'

'Condoms are only ninety-eight per cent effective. Someone has to fall into the two per cent, and apparently it's us.'

'Have you had it confirmed?'

'There's no need. I've missed a period, I'm nauseous, I can't stand the smell of coffee or raw meat or apparently...' she waved her hand at his yiros '...garlic sauce. I've bought every home pregnancy test the pharmacy sells and they all came back positive. And my boobs are bigger.'

Jake smiled.

She stared at him as tears welled in her eyes. She felt like crying and he was smiling? What was the matter with him? She swallowed, fighting not to lose control. 'You think this is funny?'

'No, I know it's not,' he said, as he took one of her hands in his. Her hand felt cold against his warm palm. 'But I must say this isn't one of the first conversations I imagined us having when we moved on from our platonic status. I thought we might start with dinner and a movie. I was looking forward to getting to know you better, not choosing colours for a nursery.'

'Stop it.' Her voice caught as she fought back the tears. She couldn't believe he could see humour in their situation.

She shook her hand free from his hold but he wasn't going to let her go easily. He wrapped one arm around her shoulders and pulled her into him, resting her head against his chest as he kissed her forehead.

'Sorry. In our family we use humour when we're out of our depth. Somehow it helps make a crazy situation seem not so bad. In a family our size there's always someone with a bigger problem.'

'I'm not sure that it gets bigger than this.' Her voice was muffled against his body.

'Sure it does. People have been having children for thousands of years and plenty of them weren't planned. Other people cope. We'll manage too.'

'But I don't want children.'

He sat back, putting some distance between them so he could see her face. 'What do you mean, you don't want children?'

His tone suggested he'd never heard anything so ridiculous. Did he expect, just because she had a womb, that she had a desperate desire to reproduce? That one of her life's ambitions was to be a mother? He was about to learn a lot more about her than he'd bargained for.

'I didn't think you would want them either,' she said.

'Someday, in the future, definitely.'

'This isn't the future. This is happening now.'

He took hold of both her hands and fixed her in place with his green eyes. 'And so we will deal with it now. We can handle this.' His gaze was unwavering and she wanted to believe him. She almost did. Almost.

But she was scared.

'I'm not sure that I can.'

'Why not?'

'Because I don't want to. It's typical of my luck that the one time I do something out of character, something unplanned, I get into trouble. This wasn't ever something I wanted. This is why Richard and I broke up. He wanted children and I didn't. I wasn't prepared to give

up my life to marry him and become a mother and I
definitely don't want to be a single mother.'

'You don't have to go through this on your own, you
know. It's my responsibility too.'

Scarlett shook her head. 'You can't promise that.'

'I can promise whatever I like.'

'There's nothing stopping you from walking away.'

'Nothing except my sense of duty and responsibility and family.'

'But you didn't ask for this any more than I did, and
when it all gets too much? What then?'

He didn't answer immediately and Scarlett began
to worry about what he was going to say. His answer
surprised her.

'What is this really about?' he asked. 'I haven't said
or done anything to make you think that when I give
you my word I can't be trusted. What is bugging you?'

'Apart from the fact that I'm pregnant?' She managed a half smile, although she suspected it looked more
like a grimace.

'Apart from that,' he agreed.

'I've seen how hard it is to raise a family, especially
as a single mother. My mum had me when she was eighteen and I have never met my father. Mum struggled
constantly to provide for my sisters and me and I have
seen the sacrifices she had to make, and while I appreciate what she has done for me, for all of us, I don't
want to be like her.'

'You've never met your father? But what about Ruby
and Rose?'

She knew what he was asking. 'We're half-sisters.
We all have different fathers. Our mother had three children by three different men. My father left before I was

born. Ruby's father was a liar and adulterer. He had a whole other family in Melbourne that Mum didn't know about until she fell pregnant with Ruby. He was quite happy cheating on his wife but when Mum fell pregnant he got scared and went running back to Melbourne.'

'And what about Rose's dad?'

'He was lovely.'

'Was?'

Scarlett nodded. 'He married Mum when I was eight. That was the happiest time for all of us. We still didn't have much money but we were a family. But he died when I was sixteen.'

'What happened?'

'He was much older than Mum and he died suddenly of a heart attack. Mum has been on her own ever since.'

'Does your father know about you?'

Scarlett nodded. 'He knew Mum was pregnant. Mum told him. That's only right, isn't it? The father should know?' she asked, seeking confirmation from him.

'Most definitely. Do you know where your father is?'

She shook her head. 'No.'

'Have you tried to track him down?'

'I figure he doesn't want to see me. He could have looked for me. He could have looked for my mother. He knew where to start at least. But this isn't about my father. This is about me. I've watched my mother struggle as a single mum. I've seen what she gave up to raise me and my sisters. I've lived it and I don't want to battle for the rest of my life. I know what it's like to be poor, to wear second-hand clothes, to share a bed with my siblings, to say no to birthday parties because we couldn't afford to buy a present, and I can't consider putting my career on hold to raise a child. I've worked hard to make something of my life and I'm not done yet. I don't want to give it up now.'

'Why would you have to give it up?' he asked. 'You don't need to worry. You didn't get into this situation on your own. It's my responsibility too and I won't let you down. I know you're scared but I'm not going to abandon you. We are in this together.'

He was handling the news far better than she'd expected, far better than she was, but she wasn't sure if she could believe him.

'How can you be so sure? This has come completely out of the blue. We might end up hating each other,' she said, but she was thinking, *You'll end up leaving me.*

'Whatever happens, it will still be my child.'

'Are you saying you really *want* to be a father now?' She had assumed he wouldn't want a baby either at this point in his life.

'I'm saying I don't like the alternatives and you can trust me to do the right thing.'

Trusting men to keep their word wasn't something she was very good at, particularly when they were promising to stay. She appreciated the sentiment but she wasn't convinced she believed it and she was too tired to give it the consideration she needed to. She couldn't think about it any more tonight. The sun would be up in a few hours and she needed some sleep and so did he.

'I need some time to think about this.'

He didn't push her. He just nodded. 'Do you want me to delay the drive tomorrow? I can leave later.'

'No. We need more than a couple of hours to think this over.'

'All right. But don't make any big decisions without talking to me first, okay?'

'Okay.'

Jake kissed her gently on the lips, his touch light and soft and warm. Scarlett closed her eyes, savouring his taste. He rested his hand on her stomach, deliberately or not, she wasn't sure, but her belly fluttered under his fingers. She knew it was just her normal reaction to his touch but part of her imagined it was the fluttering of a tiny baby. 'Look after yourself. I'll talk to you soon,' he said. And then he was gone and she was alone.

She knew it wasn't his fault, she knew he had to go, but she couldn't help but feel he was already leaving her.

He was almost home. It had been a long first week on his country placement. The hours in Obstetrics were always erratic and often long but it was the additional stress of Scarlett's unexpected pregnancy that had pushed the limits of his endurance. He knew Scarlett was worried about him managing the long drive at the end of a working week and even though he'd told her he was fine, that he was used to long hours, he felt tired and he knew apprehension was contributing to his fatigue.

When he had spoken to Scarlett during the week he'd heard the consternation in her voice and he knew she was still undecided about the pregnancy. He couldn't admit to himself that she was undecided about the baby. Their baby, his baby. His child.

Even though the timing wasn't perfect he was excited about the news, but Scarlett's hesitancy was certainly spoiling the moment. He could understand how their very different upbringings were causing conflicting emotions for them both but he hadn't expected her to be so set against the pregnancy. He'd meant it when he'd said he'd be there for her. He would support her in any way she wanted, but his child came first and he knew he would fight for his unborn child with every cell in his body until he took his last breath.

He had spent almost every spare minute of the past week looking at his options and getting the finer details from his brother-in-law, Ted, who was a family lawyer. But what Ted had told him hadn't eased his mind or solved his dilemma.

According to Ted, and in Australian law, a father had no rights over an unborn child. If Scarlett didn't want this baby apparently there wasn't much he could do about it, but he refused to accept that as final.

He drummed his fingers on the steering-wheel as he waited for the traffic lights at the bottom of the freeway to turn green. Fifteen more minutes and he hoped he'd start to get some answers.

It didn't go quite as he planned. With Scarlett, nothing ever went as planned.

He had imagined presenting a reasonable, logical and rational argument to convince Scarlett to have their baby, but all sensible thought evaporated as soon as he saw her.

She greeted him at the door wearing a silk robe, which was loosely tied at her waist, and he knew that with one tug the robe would fall away and that underneath she'd be naked.

He managed to resist until she had closed the front door and then he reached for her. His mouth covered hers as his fingers undid her robe. Scarlett moaned as his fingers brushed her bare skin as he pushed the robe from her shoulders. It fell to the floor with a soft rustle as he scooped her up and carried her into her bedroom, and all arguments were forgotten as they made up for the week apart.

The good mood lasted until they were both spent and satisfied. Until he had showered and they were sitting in the kitchen, sharing a midnight supper of scrambled eggs.

'I've been thinking about our situation. I think we should get married,' he said.

'What on earth for?'

'I know you're scared. I thought if we were married it would give you security. I want to raise our baby together, as a family.' Jake had thought he had worked out where her reluctance was coming from. She wanted financial security but he suspected she also wanted emotional security, and he was prepared to offer her that.

'We both know that being married is no guarantee that a relationship will last,' she argued. 'It's no guarantee of anything and it's not the 1960s. I don't want to get married because I'm pregnant. I don't even want to be pregnant.'

Had he misread her story so badly? He had tried to see things from her perspective but had he still got it completely wrong?'

'This could be the adventure you're supposed to have.'

'This is not my idea of an adventure.'

She obviously hadn't changed her mind over the past week. He was prepared to do the right thing, he was prepared to support her in any way she wanted, but his child had to be his priority. He moved to Plan B.

'Scarlett, I want this baby. I want our baby. I know you're worried about doing this on your own but I want to be part of this. If I have to I will raise our baby alone but I need one thing from you, I need you to stay pregnant. I'm begging you, please, don't do anything rash.'

'You work in a strip club. How on earth are you going to have time to raise a baby?'

'You and I both know I won't be working there for ever. At the end of the year I'll be a doctor. I'll be an intern. I won't be working in the bar and I will have a decent income.'

'And then you want to specialise. You'll be studying for years to come. You can't take time off to care for a baby and neither can I. The future doesn't take care of itself.'

'I have money saved, I own my apartment, I can provide for my child.'

'I appreciate you want to do this but in my experience men don't stick around. What happens when you're working eighty-hour weeks as an intern? What happens when you want to travel back to Asia? What happens when you start to feel trapped? I'll end up alone with the baby, a single mother.'

'Have I told you about the programme at Blue Lake Hospital?' he asked. 'Annie Simpson, the obstetrician who is supervising me, runs a programme for teenage mothers in conjunction with the high school to help the girls to finish school and keep their babies. If teenagers can do it, you can too.'

'This isn't part of my plan.'

'We can make a new plan. We can work this out. Together. You're strong and smart and you're not going to have to do this alone.'

'I'm not strong enough. I'm not like my mother.'

'You don't have to be. I will be there for you.' But

it was obvious to him now that Scarlett didn't think he would be enough. 'What has your mum said?' he asked. Maybe someone else's opinion would help her to see sense.

Scarlett didn't reply, she just shook her head.

'Have you told your mum about the baby? Have you told Ruby?'

'No. I don't want to tell anyone. I don't want it to be real.'

'Why haven't you said anything?'

'I'm worried that Mum will be disappointed in me.'

'Your mother raised three daughters on her own. If anyone will understand, she will.'

'I don't want to repeat her mistakes.'

'Has she ever told you that you were a mistake?'

'I know I was.'

'You were unplanned but she chose to have you. Do you think she'd want you to make a different choice? You have a career, you have my support. You're in a much better position than she was. Has she ever complained about the sacrifices she made? Has she ever told you she didn't want you?'

'No.'

'I think you should talk to her. You can't make decisions based on your mother's experiences. Especially if you don't really know what her experience was. You are in a very different position. Can I ask you, please, before you make a decision, will you do me a favour and talk to your mum?'

It took all weekend but Jake finally thought he'd managed to convince Scarlett to at least talk to her mother. He knew that conversation could go one of two ways but he hoped it would persuade her to keep the baby. He was prepared to raise a child, his child, alone if he had to. He had no doubt he could but he'd prefer to do it with Scarlett. He knew they could do it together, he just had to convince her to trust him and that was the difficult part. He wasn't sure how he was going to achieve that but he wasn't going to give up yet.

CHAPTER TEN

SCARLETT SAT ON the couch opposite her mother. Her heart was racing and her hands were shaking so badly she had to lace her fingers together and hold her hands in her lap to disguise the tremor. She was more nervous now than she'd been when she'd told Jake the news. She was only here because Jake had asked her to let her mother know. He had been so supportive she felt she owed him this at least.

Jake made her feel good about herself but she wasn't feeling so good at the moment. She felt like she was letting him down. She wasn't being the person she knew he wanted her to be. She wasn't sure if she *could* be that person. Was he asking too much or was she being unfair?

She sat quietly, waiting while her mother poured their tea. Her mother always insisted on making tea properly, in a warmed teapot and using fine bone-china cups. Scarlett normally found the routine soothing and had asked for tea specifically for that purpose, but today nothing was comforting.

'What's the matter, darling?' Lucy asked, as she passed Scarlett her cup and saucer. 'Nothing's so terrible that you can't tell me about it.'

'How do you know something's wrong?'

'I'm your mother, I can tell when something is troubling you.'

She took a deep breath. 'I'm pregnant.'

'Oh, thank God.' Lucy moved seats, coming to sit beside Scarlett as she hugged her. 'I'm so pleased.'

'You are?'

'Yes. You look exhausted and you look like you've lost weight. I thought you were going to tell me you were sick. But pregnant! That's exciting.'

Scarlett hadn't expected that. 'Is it? I thought you'd think I was crazy.'

'Why?'

Scarlett shrugged. 'Another Anderson female getting knocked up while single.'

'It's hardly the worst thing that can happen,' Lucy replied matter-of-factly, 'but you don't sound thrilled with your news. Are you having doubts?'

Scarlett nodded. 'I don't want to be pregnant. It's really not part of my plan, short term or long term. I broke up with Richard because he wanted kids. His heart attack was the catalyst for his change of mind but it scared me. I was terrified I'd end up alone, raising his family, and that was not what I wanted for my future.'

'Is Richard the father?'

Scarlett shook her head. 'No. It's more complicated than that.'

'What are you going to do?'

'I don't know yet. Do you ever think of how different your life would have been if you hadn't fallen pregnant with me? Did you ever think of not having me?'

'No.' Lucy shook her head. 'Not once. My life would

certainly have been different but it couldn't have been any better. I wouldn't want to change a thing.'

'But I saw how hard your life was. I've lived through the struggle.'

'I'm not pretending that being a single mother is easy but you're in a much better position than I was. You're twelve years older than I was when I fell pregnant, that puts a completely different spin on things, and you have a career. A very good career.'

'I always thought Ruby would be the one to make a mistake. I would have placed money on Ruby being in this situation before me.'

Lucy smiled but refrained from commenting. She never compared her girls. 'Don't think of your pregnancy as a mistake,' she said. 'A baby is a gift. I know you want a different life to the one I've had. I want that for you too. But if I had to choose between having you girls or having an easy life I would do it all again, exactly the same. I love you more than anything in the world.

'I know it hasn't always been easy but the best things in life are often the things worth fighting for. Not everything in life works out exactly how you'd like it to or planned for. But some of life's surprises can be the best things that ever happen to you. Sometimes they can take you on an adventure you never expected.'

Scarlett wondered why everyone kept talking about adventure. What were they seeing that she wasn't?

'I don't know if I have the courage to be a single mother.'

'You'll find the strength if you need to. Trust me, once this baby is born there is nothing you won't do for him or her. I know you've worked hard at your studies but that just means that you will be financially secure. You can raise a baby. You'll be surprised at how your priorities will change. I know you—once you hold that baby in your arms you will do anything to protect him or her. A mother's love is like no other. You'll wonder how you ever doubted yourself.'

Lucy sipped her tea before asking, 'But why are you assuming you'll be a single mother? What about the baby's father? Does he know? How does he feel?'

'He wants the baby. He wants to be involved.' Scarlett didn't tell her mother that Jake had offered to raise the baby on his own if need be. She wasn't sure how she felt about that yet.

'Is it serious between you?'

'I don't know. I thought it could be but it's only early days. I was looking forward to seeing how things developed between us but being pregnant is a complicating factor I wasn't expecting and I'm not sure now if we've missed our opportunity. If I have the baby nothing will be the same again but if I choose *not* to have the baby that will change everything anyway.'

'Are you considering a termination?'

'I don't think I'm brave enough to go through with it. And Jake wants the baby. Knowing that, I don't think I could do it. It doesn't seem right. None of this seems right.'

'I've always been a big believer in the saying that things happen for a reason. Do you love Jake?'

'I don't know that either. When I'm with him everything feels right, as if my world is in balance. I'm not aware of anything else when he's beside me. He calms me and excites me at the same time. I feel alive. I feel happy. I feel like I'm the person I'm supposed to be.'

'That's how I felt about your father.'

'Really?'

Lucy nodded. 'I loved your father. We might have been young but nothing was as important to me as he was until you came along.'

'What happened to you both? Why wasn't he around?'

'I thought he would be. I thought we were going to raise you together but his family had other plans. They didn't want him throwing his future away by becoming a teenage father. His family moved interstate, they deliberately took him away and they paid for me to terminate the pregnancy.'

'You were going to have a termination?' Scarlett's stomach dropped. She'd had no idea her mother had considered not having her. She was horrified to think she might not have existed and she knew then that as much as she wished not to be pregnant, there had never really been any question that she wouldn't keep the baby.

'Obviously I couldn't do it. I had to keep you.'

Scarlett had always believed her father knew about her. What if that wasn't the case? What if he thought the pregnancy had been terminated? 'Does my father know you kept me? Did you tell him?'

'Yes, of course. Your grandparents made sure of it. But I never heard anything from him.'

'And you never tried to find him?'

'No.' Lucy shook her head. 'I always hoped he'd come looking for us but he never did. He broke my heart and I was angry and afraid, but I recovered once I had you. I had to. I poured all that love into you and tried not to think about your father.'

'Are you sorry about how things worked out?'

'I have no regrets. I've been lucky in so many ways. I got something wonderful from our relationship. I got you. Love is a gamble. A risk. You can't make someone love you but you have to be prepared to take the chance that they will. But the one thing you don't have to gamble on is the love you will feel for a child of your own.'

Her mother's words resonated with her. It was time to stop wishing for a father she'd never known, for a father who had never wanted to know her. She couldn't change the past and she'd wasted many years wishing for something she wasn't going to get. He didn't deserve her time. She didn't owe him anything. She owed her mother and now she owed it to her unborn child to look after him or her. She had other priorities. She put her hand over her stomach. She could feel a mother's love already.

She saw her mother notice her gesture. 'Sometimes you have to trust in yourself and sometimes you have to learn to trust other people,' Lucy told her. 'You have one life to live and this is it. Nothing matters except this baby. You'll realise that soon enough. You'll work out what the right thing is to do.'

Scarlett had the opportunity to give her own child the very thing she herself had wanted. Her own child had a father who wanted her and she couldn't deny her child that right. She had to do her best for her own baby and that included giving it a chance to know Jake.

Scarlett slowed her car as she approached the outskirts of Penola. She was almost there. Another forty minutes and she would be with Jake.

The countryside was getting prettier. This was wine

country, the famous Coonawarra district, and rows of grapevines ran in perfectly straight lines out into the distance on both sides of the road, their symmetry only broken by the occasional enormous old gum tree or small creek or picturesque stone building. Many of the numerous wineries had modern cellar door and visitor facilities but the town itself looked as though it hadn't changed for a hundred years. She stopped to buy a cold drink and stretch her legs but didn't want to waste precious minutes dawdling here when she could be on her way to Jake.

She got back on the road and her mind wandered as she drove out of town. She wondered if they'd have a chance over the weekend to come back here for a meal as most of the wineries appeared to have a restaurant, or maybe they could just browse in some of the shops.

The road veered to the right around a blind corner and Scarlett eased her foot off the accelerator, her unfamiliarity with the highway making her cautious.

She rounded the corner and was shocked to find herself face to face with a wine tanker that was halfway across the road and taking up most of her lane. Desperate to get out of its way, she yanked on the steering-wheel and was relieved when the truck missed the side of her car by inches. But her relief was short-lived.

Her evasive action had forced her partially off the road and before she could correct her drift her car was hit by the airstream from the moving truck and forced further sideways. She felt herself losing control of the car as her outside tyres lost traction on the loose stones at the roadside. Her speed and momentum took over and carried her car completely off the road.

The car was skidding across the dirt but somehow she managed to resist the temptation to hit the brakes and instead remembered what Sean had taught her on the skid pan. *Steer into the skid.*

It had seemed strange then and it seemed even stranger now, but she tried to do what she'd been taught. She turned the car into the skid.

But she was still sliding. She hoped the car wasn't going to roll.

She waited, fighting to get the wheels aligned. Her knuckles were white as she gripped the steering-wheel and waited for the car to straighten. She knew she was supposed to wait until the moment the wheels were aligned again before she accelerated out of the skid. Were they aligned yet? She didn't know.

She was aware of a scraping sound and an occasional thwack of branches as the car careered through the scrubby bush. This was a totally different experience to the skid pan. On the skid pan there'd been no outside interference, nothing to interrupt her concentration and nothing that had really been a threat to her safety. Looming in the passenger window was a tree, more than one, actually. There certainly hadn't been any trees in the middle of the skid pan.

She had no clue what to do now. If she did nothing, she was going to hit a tree.

Were her wheels aligned yet? She had no idea.

Her survival instinct took over. She took a chance and touched her foot to the accelerator pedal, hoping her wheels were aligned, hoping and praying she could now drive out of the skid. The car surged forward as she depressed the pedal but she didn't have full control and she felt the back of the car slide sideways again.

The car was fighting her. There was nothing she could do.

She heard the crunch of metal, a thud and her world went dark.

'Jake, we've got a consult in Emergency. MVA with a pregnant woman.'

Jake's eyes flicked to the clock on the wall. He hadn't heard from Scarlett yet, he'd expected her in the last half hour. His gut contracted so violently he thought he was going to throw up. He felt the blood rush from his head and he gripped the counter at the nurses' station as he tried to steady himself.

'Jake?' He felt Annie's hand on his shoulder. 'Are you okay?' Her words were jumbled, the sound of the blood rushing from his head loud enough to partially drown out her voice.

'Scarlett.' His voice caught in his throat and sounded husky and hoarse. 'Did they give you a name?'

'No.' Annie shook her head. 'But whoever it is, she's alive. Let's get down there and we'll find out.'

There was an ambulance in the bay. The doors were open and the paramedics were unloading a stretcher. Jake caught a glimpse of raven hair and he took off, sprinting past Thang, the doctor on duty.

'Jake! What are you doing?'

'That's my—' What was she? Girlfriend, partner, mother of my child? How did he describe her?

She was his everything.

He loved every contrary and complex thing about her and he wasn't going to let anything bad happen to her. He'd promised to take care of her and that started now.

Seeing her lying pale and still on the stretcher with

her dark hair spread around her she looked like Sleeping Beauty, except for the bloody gash at her temple. His heart beat a loud and angry tattoo in his chest. She was injured. But how badly?

He was by her side and his hand sought hers. 'Scarlett?'

Her eyelids flickered open and he could see her searching for him. Her eyes darted from side to side. Her neck was immobilised in a cervical collar and she couldn't turn her head. He hoped the collar was only a precaution. 'Jake?' He leant over the stretcher as the paramedics wheeled her inside.

'I'm here.' He squeezed her fingers gently and relief flooded through him as he felt her squeeze his fingers in return.

'The baby?'

'Let's get you into an exam room. Everything will be okay.' He hoped he was right.

He ran his eyes over her as they rushed her inside the hospital. She was covered with a dusting of fine white powder from the airbag but apart from the gash at her temple he couldn't see any other external signs of injury.

She was taken straight into a treatment room. Jake followed but Thang stopped him just inside. 'We need to do a general exam,' he told him, and Jake knew Thang meant him to wait outside.

'I'm fine. I want you to check the baby first.' Scarlett lifted one hand from the stretcher, holding it up to stop Thang. Jake saw her wince with the movement but she didn't back down. 'I'm a doctor too, I know I don't have any life-threatening injuries.' She looked at Jake, her dark eyes pleading with him. 'Don't you think I'd tell you if there was anything serious, anything that could harm the baby?'

A week ago he wasn't sure if he could have given her the answer she wanted but looking at her now he knew her concern for their child was genuine. Something had happened in the last week that had made her certain about this baby. Something had made her become the mother he knew she could be.

His heart swelled with love. For Scarlett and their baby. He smiled and nodded. 'Scarlett's right,' he told Thang. 'Let's check the baby first.'

'Are you really okay?' he asked once Thang had agreed with the order of examination and Scarlett had been transferred from the stretcher to a bed.

Scarlett nodded. 'I'm fine, thanks to you.'

'Me?'

'I think if you hadn't taken me on that skid-pan exercise, things might have been a lot worse. That might have saved my life but I'm still worried the baby—'

'All right, that's my cue,' Annie interrupted. 'I'm Annie Simpson, the ob-gyn. Let's have a look at this baby, shall we? How many weeks are you?'

'I think maybe eight.'

'Have you had any prenatal appointments?' Annie asked as she took control of the situation.

'No.'

'Any unusual symptoms—spotting, cramping, pain?'

'Now or before?'

'Before today.'

'Just morning sickness but I've got pain here now.' She lifted her shirt and ran her hand lightly across her lower abdomen.

The nurse wrapped a blood-pressure cuff around

Scarlett's arm and slipped an oxygen monitor onto her finger, while Annie flicked the ultrasound monitor on and squeezed gel onto the transducer head of the ultrasound. 'If you're eight-weeks gestation, an abdominal ultrasound will tell us what we need to know. This gel will be a little cold, I haven't had time to warm it up,' Annie said, as she squeezed a little onto Scarlett's stomach.

Jake pulled a chair beside the bed and held Scarlett's hand. Annie adjusted the angle of the monitor so everyone could see and then began to sweep the ultrasound head across Scarlett's belly. A black-and-white image appeared on the screen. They all knew what they were looking for.

A black pocket appeared on the screen. Scarlett's uterus. Inside the pocket was a tiny figure, shaped like a jelly baby.

'Oh.' Scarlett lifted her hand and reached for the screen, almost as though she wanted to hold the baby.

Annie moved the ultrasound head slowly. 'There's a good strong heartbeat.' They could see a tiny flicker of a pulse on the screen. 'That's a good sign.'

A tear rolled down Scarlett's cheek. Jake leant over and gently kissed it away. 'It's all fine,' he told her. 'We're all going to be fine.'

Annie pushed a few buttons and took some measurements. 'Your baby seems perfectly okay and I'd say you're pretty spot on with your dates. It all looks about right for eight weeks. You can see the limb buds, the arms and legs just here.' She pushed another button and printed a picture. She handed it to Scarlett. 'Congratulations, the first picture for your album.'

'Can you believe it?' Scarlett said, as they stared at the picture. 'It's really happening.'

'I wish I could give you some time together but Thang will want to come in and examine Scarlett now,' Annie told them.

Jake nodded. He intended to stay with Scarlett but Thang banned him from the exam room.

'I should be in there with her,' he said to Annie, as he paced nervously outside.

'Let Thang do his job,' Annie told him. 'He doesn't need you hovering over his shoulder. The baby is fine and Scarlett seems okay too. You can relax.'

But he couldn't relax. Not until he knew the state of affairs.

Thang reappeared from the exam room. He pulled off his gloves as he delivered a reassuring summary. 'Soft-tissue injuries in the main. Whiplash, mild concussion, some bruising from the seat belt and possibly a cracked rib, but overall it seems as though she was very lucky. No apparent liver, kidney or spleen injuries. She's refusing any pain relief so she really just needs rest. You can go back in now.'

'Can I take her home?' Jake looked at both Annie and Thang.

Thang nodded while Annie replied, 'Ordinarily I'd keep her in for observation—'

'I promise not to let her out of my sight.'

'All right. I'll arrange for someone to collect her things from her car. It'll be towed into town, but she'll need a few things in the meantime, some clothes and toiletries and the like. Why don't you organise that and then you can come back and pick her up?'

Jake hadn't considered the practicalities. All he

wanted was to get Scarlett out of here and into the five-star accommodation he'd booked for them for the weekend. It had been a far better option than taking her to the hospital accommodation he was sharing with two other med students but Annie's suggestion made sense and the sooner he followed her instructions the sooner he'd have Scarlett to himself.

'Are you in pain?' Jake asked her.

'No. Well, yes, but I'm okay.' Talking was painful. *Breathing* was painful but Scarlett wasn't going to complain. She was lucky to still be doing those things.

She lay in the warm bath that Jake had drawn for her and she felt good, battered and bruised but good. The accommodation was gorgeous. The marble bathroom was huge and luxurious and their room had a soft king-sized bed, a log fire and French doors that opened onto a private patio area overlooking the expansive grounds of the rural resort. It was a room made for champagne and romance but she'd have to make do with the romance. Surrounded by bubbles of a different kind, cocooned in the warm water and drinking a hot chocolate while candles flickered on the basin edge, she felt quite decadent. 'I can put up with some discomfort now that I know the baby is okay.'

'You sound far more positive than you did a week ago. I was worried you weren't going to have the baby. What's changed?'

Jake was sitting at the end of the bath. He was wearing jeans but his chest and feet were bare. This was one of her favourite Jakes. She ran her eyes over his naked torso. 'Why don't you join me in here and I'll tell you.'

'I don't think there's room for me.'

'I'll make room.' She smiled and slid forward in the bath. She watched as Jake stood and unbuttoned his jeans, dropping them to the floor along with his underwear. Just a glimpse of him naked was enough to elevate her pulse.

He slipped into the bath behind her, pulling her back to nestle between his thighs. Scarlett could feel his arousal and she was tempted to take advantage of it but she knew she needed to tell him what she was thinking, and if she didn't take the opportunity now who knew when she'd have another one?

'You were right,' she said, as he wrapped his arms around her. 'I had a few things to sort out but Mum and I had a big talk, like you asked, and she made me realise some things about myself and my life.

'Growing up, I always wished I had a father. I wanted to be like the other girls at school. I used to make up stories about why my dad wasn't around. I think my favourite was when I told everyone he was a spy, and when I was older and Mum married Rose's dad I claimed him as my own and said he'd just returned from a secret mission. Rose's dad was lovely and he treated me like I was his own daughter. I don't think I would have been any happier with my own father, but part of me always felt as though something was missing.

'Mum has only just told me that my father's family wanted her to terminate the pregnancy, terminate me, which was something I never knew. When Mum told me I realised I could never do that and was never thinking that way. I was just wishing I wasn't pregnant, which isn't the same thing as not wanting the baby. Accepting I was pregnant was my major hurdle.

'I spent years wishing I had a father when I should

have been grateful that I had a mother who loved me and chose to keep me. Knowing how much easier things would have been for her if she had terminated the pregnancy made me realise that I am in the same situation and I am choosing to make the same decision she did. All I wanted was a father of my own and I want to be able to give my own child the chance I never had. It wouldn't be fair of me to take that away from the baby or from you.

'But I should warn you. Trust is difficult for me. Because Mum's relationships didn't last I expected the same from mine, and I know I often don't give anyone a chance. I expect them to leave. My mother and my sisters have been my roots. They keep me anchored to the ground and I've always worried that if I give myself to someone else they might rip me from the roots and then discard me. I felt I might disintegrate and disappear like the seeds of a dandelion blown by the wind. But the past is just that, and it's Mum's past, not mine. I need to take a chance.'

Jake kissed the side of her neck, just at the point where it joined her shoulder. 'I will be your shelter,' he said. 'I will protect you and any little seeds that fall from you. Those seeds are the beginnings of a new family, our family, and I will protect you all and be there always. I promise you. Will you do this with me?'

Scarlett nodded. 'I want to see whether we can build a relationship. I was worried that this pregnancy had ruined any chance we had but then I realised it was me who was jeopardising that. If you're prepared to trust in us then so am I.'

'Do you want to look for your father?'

'No. I've thought about this a lot this week. Why

I've never gone looking for him myself when I've had years when I could have searched for him. But I know it was because I was scared to. I didn't want him to reject me. I don't know if I never want to find him but that is a question for another day.

'What I do know is that I want my own child to know you. That's what's important now. I need to build my own future, our future, and to do that I need to trust in you and believe that we can make this work or at least be prepared to give it our best shot. I can't continue to make assumptions about my life based on the past. I need to look to the future and I want you to be a part of that. Starting now.

'I am going to focus on you, me and our baby. On seeing if we have a relationship that can work. You were right. Things haven't worked out exactly as I planned but they may turn out to be better. This will be the biggest adventure of my life and if you are prepared to go on it with me I think I might just survive.'

They had made love in the enormous bed. Scarlett had insisted she was fine and he'd been unable to resist, although they had taken it slowly, carefully and tenderly. She was propped up in bed, her dark eyes enormous in her pale face, but despite her pallor he thought she'd never looked more beautiful.

He had drawn the curtains and lit the gas log fire and the room was illuminated only by the soft light of the flames. Now was the perfect time to give Scarlett his present.

He reached into the drawer of the bedside table where he had hidden the package earlier. 'I have something for you,' he said, as he handed her a gift bag.

Scarlett peeked inside and pulled out a wooden matryoshka doll.

'She's beautiful. What is she for?'

'For you. She reminds me of you.'

Scarlett frowned. 'She does?'

'Yes. Remember when I described you as the parcel in the pass-the-parcel game?'

Scarlett laughed. 'Yes. Not the most flattering description.'

'I agree, and I've decided that you're still layered but perhaps you're more like one of these dolls. Complex but within every layer is something else equally as interesting and equally as valuable.'

'Where on earth did you find her?' Scarlett asked. 'She even looks a bit like me,' she said, as she studied her closely. The first doll was a woman with her dark hair pulled into a bun and with an intricately detailed face, dark eyes and full lips, dressed in a white doctor's coat with a stethoscope around her neck.

'I had her made for you. There's a local artist who makes these to order. This is you in all your different complexities. The doctor,' he said as Scarlett separated the first doll to reveal one wearing a replica of the paisley dress she'd worn to Candice's wedding. 'The party you.' Next was Scarlett the sister. The artist had painted tiny images of Ruby and Rose on either side of her, and then there was Scarlett dressed in white, a lace veil covering her dark hair.

'Is this a wedding dress?'

Jake nodded as Scarlett shook the doll. Something rattled inside.

She looked at him, her dark eyes wide. 'I'm not ready for marriage. It's not a ring, is it?'

'It's okay, open it.' He smiled.

Inside was another doll. Still Scarlett but this time dressed in a simple pale pink shirt. It still rattled.

'There's one more,' Jake said.

Nestled inside was a tiny doll.

Scarlett lifted it out. It was a dark-eyed baby wrapped in a swaddling cloth.

Jake picked up the final empty doll and pushed the two halves back together before cupping it in his hand. 'This doll is you, the mother, and this…' he rolled his finger over the baby '…is our baby. There's no ring. Not yet. I am going to marry you but only when you are ready. I believe we were meant to meet at this point in our lives. This baby is meant to be ours and we are meant to be together. Married or not, we're ready for this.' He kissed her gently before asking. 'Do you remember why I got my tattoo?'

Scarlett nodded. 'To remind you to always come home.'

'You and our baby are my home now. I will always be there for you. For both of you. I want to marry you because I love you.' He rested his hand over her belly. 'I love you both. Just tell me when you are ready.'

Scarlett closed her palm around the baby doll, cradling it in her hand. She slid her hand under Jake's and wrapped his fingers around hers, holding them together. 'I'm not ready yet but I know this is where I'm supposed to be. With you. I love you too.'

EPILOGUE

'CAN YOU BELIEVE it? In one week you'll be Mrs Chamberlain.'

Scarlett was in the kitchen, chopping vegetables for a salad, when Jake came up behind her and wrapped his arms around her swollen belly as he kissed her neck. It was ten days until Christmas and the temperature had been climbing steadily for weeks. Scarlett was feeling huge and uncomfortably pregnant but the touch of Jake's hand was enough to make her forget her discomfort.

'I can't wait to see you walk down the aisle.'

'Don't you mean waddle?' she said, as she turned her head and smiled at her fiancé.

'No. You look beautiful. This last trimester suits you,' he said, as he slipped his hand inside her loose camisole and cupped her breast.

Scarlett moaned as his fingers teased her nipple, sending shivers of longing through her. She didn't know about this last trimester suiting her but it had certainly fired up her libido. It seemed all Jake had to do was look at her and she felt like ripping all his clothes off. Hers too.

'I have something to show you,' Jake said. 'An early wedding present.'

'Ooh, what is it? You know I love presents.'

In reply Jake pulled his T-shirt over his head and the sight of his naked torso almost made Scarlett forget about the present. He was too gorgeous for words. He had finished his undergraduate medical degree and left his job at The Coop in order to spend more time with her before he started his internship, but he had kept up his exercise routine and still looked fabulous.

Scarlett ran her eyes over his body in appreciation and it was then she noticed a sterile dressing on his left upper arm.

Concern flooded through her. 'What happened to you?' she asked, reaching out one hand towards his arm.

Jake's fingers teased the edge of the dressing, pulling it from his skin where it had covered his tattoo.

'I got a new tattoo,' he told her.

He lifted his arm and Scarlett could see two new stars inked on his arm at a forty-five-degree angle to the Southern Cross.

'What are they?'

'Alpha and Beta Centauri, the Pointer Stars.' He pointed to the first star, furthest from the Southern Cross. 'This one is you and this one,' he said, pointing to the second new star, 'is our baby. The two of you will always guide me home. Every time you see these stars I want you to remember that you can depend on me. I love you and I can't wait to spend the rest of my life taking care of you.'

Scarlett linked her arms around his neck. 'I do know that. It's one of the reasons I agreed to marry you.'

'What were the others?'

'You make me feel safe, adored and happy. I love

you and if we didn't have to wait for all our siblings to get home I'd marry you tomorrow.'

'Haven't you learnt by now that I'm a patient man?'

'I have learnt that. It's another reason why I agreed to marry you. You waited so long for me to give you an answer I thought you deserved it to be yes.

'Five months was about my limit,' he teased. 'Any other reasons spring to mind?'

'Yes. I can't resist your tattoos.'

'You like these.' Jake grinned at her and flexed his biceps.

'I do.' She ran her fingers lightly up his arm and reached behind his head. She pulled his forward and kissed him hard on the mouth. 'Shall I show you just how much?' she whispered. She dropped her hands to the waistband of his shorts and discovered his reaction was as intense as hers. 'It looks like you're not that patient after all.' She laughed.

'There is only so much waiting I can do in one lifetime,' he said, as Scarlett divested him of the rest of his clothes. 'And it seems I've just run out of patience,' he added, as he scooped her into his arms and carried her off to bed.

* * * * *

TAMED BY
THE RENEGADE

BY
EMILY FORBES

Published in Great Britain 2014
by Mills & Boon, an imprint of Harlequin (UK) Limited,
Eton House, 18-24 Paradise Road, Richmond, Surrey, TW9 1SR

ISBN: 978-0-263-90800-8

Harlequin (UK) Limited's policy is to use papers that are natural,
renewable and recyclable products and made from wood grown in
sustainable forests. The logging and manufacturing processes conform
to the legal environmental regulations of the country of origin.

Printed and bound in Spain
by Blackprint CPI, Barcelona

Emily Forbes began her writing life as a partnership between two sisters who are both passionate bibliophiles. As a team, 'Emily' had ten books published. One of her proudest moments was winning the 2013 Australia Romantic Book of the Year Award for SYDNEY HARBOUR HOSPITAL: BELLA'S WISHLIST.

While Emily's love of writing remains as strong as ever, the demands of life with young families have recently made it difficult to work on stories together. But rather than give up her dream Emily now writes solo. The challenges may be different, but the reward of having a book published is still as sweet as ever.

Whether as a team or as an individual, Emily hopes to keep bringing stories to her readers. Her inspiration comes from everywhere, and stories she hears while travelling, at mothers' lunches, in the media and in her other career as a physiotherapist all get embellished with a large dose of imagination until they develop a life of their own.

If you would like to get in touch with Emily you can e-mail her at emilyforbes@internode.on.net

Recent titles by Emily Forbes:

THE HONOURABLE ARMY DOC
DARE SHE DATE THE CELEBRITY DOC?
BREAKING THE PLAYBOY'S RULES
SYDNEY HARBOUR HOSPITAL: BELLA'S WISHLIST*
GEORGIE'S BIG GREEK WEDDING?
BREAKING HER NO-DATES RULE
NAVY OFFICER TO FAMILY MAN
DR DROP-DEAD-GORGEOUS
THE PLAYBOY FIREFIGHTER'S PROPOSAL

Sydney Harbour Hospital

Dedication

For my fabulous brothers and sisters-in-law:
Andrew, Tim, Michelle, Brigid, Terry,
Rebecca, Nick, Alexandra, Duncan, Nick, Rachel,
Luke, Danielle, Ben and Kiera—with love.

PROLOGUE

Sunday, 14th December

RUBY HAD ALWAYS known she'd have to grow up one day but she'd suspected it would be a gradual process, like growing out a fringe or recovering from a broken heart. She never expected to have to grow up overnight.

A few hours earlier she'd been asleep in her bed. Now she was about to walk into an intensive care unit halfway across the country and she was terrified of what she would find. She didn't know if she was strong enough to deal with this crisis. She suspected she was a flight-not-fight type of personality. In fact, she knew she was. She'd always run away when the going had got tough.

Perhaps being able to cope with traumatic situations was a sure sign of maturation. The trouble was she was afraid of what she was about to see and afraid she wouldn't cope.

Maybe this disaster would be the catalyst that forced her to grow up. Maybe it would trigger her development into the sort of person others could depend on, but she really wasn't sure if she had that level of resolve.

She waited as her sister's fiancé keyed the security

code into the door and held it for her and then she trailed in Jake's footsteps as he crossed the room.

Ruby could see her sister, Scarlett, and their mother sitting side by side. Scarlett was holding their mother's hand and Ruby knew she was comforting Lucy, not the other way around. Scarlett had always looked after all of them, their mother included.

Seeing her family huddled together threatened to damage the wall around the well of emotion that she'd been trying to keep under control since she'd left Byron Bay in the early hours of the morning. Throughout the flight to Adelaide, and even on the short trip from the airport to the hospital, she'd fought to keep her emotions in check. She hadn't wanted to fall apart in front of a plane full of strangers or in front of her sister's fiancé—she didn't know him well enough yet and she couldn't let him see that she wasn't as brave or as strong as Scarlett was.

Scarlett stood up the moment she saw Ruby. She came towards her with her arms open and wrapped Ruby in her embrace. Ruby relaxed into her older sister's comforting hug. She could feel the tears welling in her eyes and gathering on her lashes ready to spill over as she soaked up Scarlett's reassurance.

She and Scarlett were of similar height but Ruby's skinny frame was always a sharp contrast to Scarlett's curves. Even more so today, thought Ruby as she felt Scarlett's rounded belly, firm and hard and stretched tight as a drum, pressing into her. Ruby stepped back out of Scarlett's embrace to take a proper look at her. Scarlett was into the final trimester of her pregnancy and it was the first time Ruby had seen her in several months, the first time she'd seen her looking pregnant. It suited her.

But seeing Scarlett's new curves served as another little push to Ruby's subconscious, another little hint that times were changing and she might have to change along with them. Scarlett had always been there for her. They'd always been close because Scarlett had made that her priority. Their relationship had been nurtured, and on occasion saved, by Scarlett's determination and perseverance. She'd been there for all of them at one time or another but now she had another person totally dependent on her. Her fiancé and their baby would be Scarlett's priorities now.

Ruby knew that didn't mean that Scarlett would abandon any of them. Not her, not their mother and certainly not Rose, their younger sister and the reason they were all here in the ICU, but Scarlett couldn't be expected to shoulder all their worries. Rose needed them and they needed to look out for her. *She* needed to look out for Rose.

She'd never really given much thought to how her family was faring. She'd chosen her own path at the age of sixteen and hadn't spent much time considering others. She realised now how selfish she'd been. It was time for her to step up.

She hugged her mother next. Anyone watching may have thought it strange that she greeted her sister before her mother but Ruby and Lucy didn't have an easy relationship. Ruby had always felt far more comfortable sharing her thoughts and feelings with her sister, but she recognised that the sometimes stilted relationship she had with her mother was her own fault. She'd always pushed her mother away. Ruby had always wanted to assert her independence and it had backfired on her in spectacular fashion during her teenage years but she'd been too proud then to admit her mistakes. She wasn't sure if she'd changed all that much in the ensuing years.

'It's good to have you home.' Lucy welcomed her with open arms.

Her mother would say she was home but Adelaide hadn't been home to Ruby for almost eleven years. She wasn't sure where she would say home was. But she wasn't going to argue over semantics now. It wasn't important. She was going to be mature and agreeable. Whether she called Adelaide home or not was irrelevant—she was here now. A week earlier than planned. She'd had flights booked for the end of the week, scheduled for Scarlett and Jake's wedding, she hadn't planned on making a middle of the night dash to the bedside of her critically ill little sister.

Ruby could hear the soft click and hiss of the ventilator behind her. So far she'd avoided looking at Rose and still she hesitated. She wasn't sure if she could handle seeing her younger sister lying in a hospital bed connected to machines.

She let go of her mother and asked, 'Have the doctors been back? Have they said anything more?' She asked the question even though she was unsure about whether she was ready to hear the answer.

She knew the question was just another delaying tactic. When Jake had met her at the airport he'd told her what they knew about Rose's condition so far. Which wasn't much and not nearly enough to thaw the icy fingers that had gripped her heart since Scarlett had phoned her in the middle of the night. She knew the doctors suspected meningitis and had put Rose into a medically induced coma and started her on a course of antibiotics, but Jake hadn't been able to tell her anything further.

She had directed her question at Scarlett and was struck again how she automatically turned to her sister and not their mother in a crisis. Scarlett, as the eldest of the Anderson sisters, had always been the level-headed one. The one who everyone in their scrambled family turned to in times of crisis, but Ruby had a premonition that this crisis might be too big for Scarlett to handle alone and she suspected she would have to be prepared to stand up and be counted too. The only issue was she didn't know if she was capable of that.

Up until now Ruby had done a very good job of avoiding major responsibility but it seemed times might be changing. She was going to have to be prepared to take some of the burden from Scarlett.

She'd had plenty of experience of her life changing around her without warning or consultation. It had been something that had shaped her into the woman she was today, one who wanted total control over her own life. One who didn't want to give anyone else an opportunity to upset her apple cart. Taking control hadn't always worked out so well for her but at least her mistakes, downfalls and dramas had been of her own making.

But even though recently she'd been doing a relatively good job of controlling her own little world she wasn't able to control the world that existed around her, and the wider world had a habit of intruding when she didn't want it to and throwing curve balls her way.

Scarlett shook her head in reply to Ruby's question. Jake and Scarlett were both doctors yet they had no more insight into Rose's situation and the lack of information frustrated Ruby.

Ruby herself wasn't a stranger to hospitals. All the sights and sounds and smells, which to many others would seem unfamiliar, were nothing unusual for her. She was a nurse, she'd had plenty of experience looking after patients and their families but she'd never been on the other side. She'd never had to sit by and watch while someone she loved was on life support and being cared for by a team of doctors and nurses. It was a very different situation and, for reasons she didn't fully understand yet, it made her uneasy. She knew it was, in part, due to exhaustion. She was tired and emotional but she had to face her fears. She'd been on the go since four this morning and lack of sleep wasn't making things any rosier.

Rose.

She needed to face her fears. She needed to see Rose.

She could feel anxiety gripping her chest, adding to the pressure of those icy fingers around her heart as she forced herself to look at her younger sister. She knew she was nervous, worried about the sight that was going to confront her. She turned to the bed.

Half a dozen various tubes and leads connected Rose to monitors and to life. Ruby tried to ignore the mechanical sounds of the ventilator as she focused on Rose. The pale skin of her arms was covered in a purple rash that was indicative of septicaemia but the rash didn't appear to have spread to her face. Ruby didn't know how she would have reacted to that. Rose had always been unbelievably pretty and Ruby didn't want to face such a stark and obvious sign of Rose's affliction. She looked as though she was sleeping and Ruby was grateful for small mercies.

But she still didn't understand why nothing was happening. Everyone was sitting around, waiting. If the doctors wanted to run more tests, where were they? Why wasn't someone doing something? What were they waiting for?

'Where are the doctors?' She turned away from Rose and, out of habit as much as anything else, once again directed her question to Scarlett. She forced herself to look at Lucy next. Forced herself to include her mother, but Lucy looked as though she was in shock and Ruby doubted she'd even heard her question.

Her mother looked tired. Lucy had always been beautiful. Scarlett had inherited her looks but although Lucy often looked tired, Ruby had never thought she looked older than her years. Until today.

Lucy had been only eighteen when Scarlett was born and they were often mistaken for sisters. But Ruby knew people wouldn't be making that mistake today. Sitting side by side, their similarities were still obvious but so was their age difference. Growing up, Ruby had longed for their colouring, longed for their dark hair, dark eyes and flawless fair skin. She had the fair skin but she'd hated her red hair, even though her mother had insisted it was strawberry blond, and the smattering of freckles that were strewn across the bridge of her nose.

Ruby could see some strands of grey in Lucy's dark hair, which she didn't remember seeing before. She knew she had caused some of the lines on her mother's face but there were more of those too than there used to be. Definitely more than there had been a few months ago when Ruby had last come back to Adelaide, and she suspected the events of the past twelve hours had put them there.

But this wasn't about her or her mother now. It was about Rose, and she needed to stay calm and positive. Biting back a scream of frustration, she looked back at Scarlett, wanting someone to answer her.

'They're waiting for the results of the blood tests,' Scarlett told her.

'I thought they'd diagnosed meningitis?'

Scarlett nodded. 'They're treating her for septicaemia and bacterial meningitis but they haven't identified the strain yet.'

Ruby knew that bacterial meningitis was more serious than the viral form and she also knew that the prognosis varied widely between the different strains of bacteria and between different people. What she didn't understand was how Rose could have caught the disease.

'How did this happen? How did Rose get sick?' As she asked yet another question she wondered if they should be talking in front of Rose. She believed that coma patients could hear conversations going on around them but she figured Rose had probably heard everything else that had been discussed so far this morning.

'No one can really say,' Jake answered, 'but the most likely scenario is that Rose picked it up at work in the after-school care facility. The bacteria can't live outside the body for long so people need to be in close contact.'

Rose was studying to be a primary school teacher and her practical work plus her part-time job in an after-school care facility would give her plenty of exposure to all manner of bugs.

'But it's also reasonably common in young adults aged between fifteen and twenty-four so it's almost

impossible to tell where she came into contact with it.'
Jake shrugged.

Rose was twenty-one, six years younger than Ruby,
and her age put her right inside the high-risk age bracket.

Ruby glanced at Scarlett as a realisation hit her. 'Is
it safe for you to be in here?' she asked. Scarlett's pregnancy was definitely showing but Ruby couldn't remember enough about the disease to know if Scarlett
was putting herself or her baby at risk.

Scarlett nodded in reply. 'I'm fine. It's passed
through sneezing and coughing via droplets in the air.'
They both looked at Rose. Attached to the ventilator,
she wasn't doing either of those things.

'Has anyone else from the school fallen ill?'

'We haven't been told but anyone she had contact
with at school will be given antibiotics as a precaution,
but there are other possibilities that complicate things
further in terms of treating other people but don't really affect Rose's treatment. What the doctors need to
do now is identify the strain of bacterium.'

'Rose was out at a lunch for a friend's birthday yesterday. She came home early and said she wasn't feeling well and went straight to bed.' Lucy added to Jake's
tale. 'We assume she was already infected when she
went to lunch but because there can be such a short period of time between becoming infected and presenting
with symptoms it's adding to the confusion. When she
came home she had a temperature and a headache but
it didn't seem anything out of the ordinary. She didn't
complain about a stiff or sore neck or a rash. I didn't
see any of the red flags for meningitis so I just assumed
it was a flu virus.'

Lucy was also a nurse but she worked in aged care, and meningitis wasn't something she saw much of.

'She got up to go to the bathroom around midnight and I heard her collapse. When I reached her she was having trouble breathing and that's when I noticed the rash. I rang the ambulance and even though they arrived quickly, by the time we got to the hospital she had gone downhill rapidly. She was in cardiac failure, her blood pressure was too low to register and she had no pulse. The rash on her body was spreading before my eyes. I just wish I'd suspected something more sinister than flu to begin with.'

'I'm not sure that anyone would have, Lucy. You know how variable the signs and symptoms can be and how often they're missed.'

Jake's words were meant to be reassuring but Ruby doubted anything would ease her mother's conscience. Not yet. Not until they knew Rose's prognosis and maybe not even then. But Ruby was grateful to Jake for being there to support them all. She knew Scarlett and Lucy would be struggling with the situation as much as she was and it wasn't fair to expect Scarlett to support them all. They couldn't expect Scarlett to have enough strength for all of them. Not always.

Ruby was pleased that Scarlett now had Jake to take care of her. No one was looking to lean on Ruby but neither was anyone offering a shoulder to support her. She had always rebuffed offers of help or support so she supposed no one thought she might need some now.

Before she could follow that train of thought any further they were interrupted by one of the ICU nurses and a trio of doctors.

'The doctors want to do a lumbar puncture,' the nurse explained.

Four pairs of eyes swivelled to the doctors.

'Now?' Lucy asked.

The doctors were nodding. Ruby wondered who they all were and what they did, but no one seemed to think it was important to introduce her.

'We really need to identify the bacterium responsible for the infection as the outcomes can be vastly different.' The doctor who spoke looked easily the more senior of the three. Balding and carrying some extra weight, Ruby assumed he was the specialist. 'There are increased mortality rates and poorer outcomes with the pneumococcal strain compared to meningococcal. It's fatal in about ten per cent of cases and one in seven will suffer a permanent disability.'

Ruby had heard enough now. She wished he'd stop talking.

'We don't know yet whether there's any permanent damage to her heart and some of her other major organs are showing signs of stress. We're hoping to minimise the damage to her vital organs and her extremities but we need to make a proper diagnosis in order to implement the right treatment.'

Ruby was feeling sick. She didn't want to think about the consequences of Rose's illness. She didn't want to think about what else could go wrong. She wanted to believe that Rose would get better and that everything would go back to normal.

So much for being positive and grown up.

'The next thirty-six to forty-eight hours are critical.'

And Ruby knew immediately what the doctor meant.

Rose had to get through the next two days if she was going to have any chance of surviving.

CHAPTER ONE

EVERYONE ELSE HEARD the unspoken words too and Ruby watched as Scarlett turned to Jake.

It seemed she was right, Scarlett couldn't be expected to support them all. This was one time when she needed someone to support her. Lucy wouldn't be able to lean on Scarlett, she had enough to deal with. Ruby might need to be the one to offer her mother comfort now.

As the medical team began to set up for the lumbar puncture Ruby found herself, along with the rest of her family, being ushered out of Rose's cubicle.

The ICU had suddenly become a hive of activity and Ruby had to stop and wait as another patient was wheeled in and she was separated from the others by the barouche. As the bed was pushed past her she caught a glimpse of a solidly built man and she immediately wondered what had happened to him.

What had brought him to the ICU? There were usually only a couple of reasons why young men ended up here—accidents, usually involving vehicles, or serious illness. She turned her head, watching as he went past. Despite the oxygen mask covering his face, he looked too well to be seriously ill. His face was tanned and his colour was good and the one arm that she could see poking out from under the blankets was also tanned and well muscled. He looked robust and healthy enough.

She could see the outline of a cradle that was keeping the weight of the blankets off his leg and was suggestive of a lower-limb fracture. A motorbike accident, she decided before she ducked around the end of his bed to catch up with Scarlett and their mother.

They were hovering in the corridor, looking lost. They looked unsure what to do as they waited for the doctors to finish with Rose. Ruby was exhausted. It had been a crazy day—emotional, upsetting and stressful. She didn't want to pace the hospital corridors, waiting for Rose's procedure to be completed, she needed a shower and some fresh air to give her some strength to face what was yet to come.

'Does anyone mind if I go and have a shower while the doctors are with Rose?' Ruby asked.

She knew Lucy would wait and she knew Scarlett wouldn't let her wait alone. Ruby also knew that she should offer to stay too. Hadn't she just told herself she would need to be the one to offer support to her mother? But she couldn't do it. She knew she'd go crazy with the tension of waiting and that would inevitably lead to her picking a fight with Lucy, something neither of them needed. She told herself it was best for everyone if she got away from the hospital and cleared her head before she exploded.

'I'll give you a lift to our place, if you like,' Jake offered, when no one insisted she stay.

'Don't you want to wait with Scarlett? There'd be a shower in the hospital I could use, surely?' She knew Scarlett would be able to organise a shower for her in the staff facilities at the hospital but she would prefer to get outside. She really wanted a chance to get some fresh air at the same time.

'It'll be nicer to shower at our house,' Scarlett replied.

'It's only five minutes to home and your bag is still in my car,' Jake said. The two of them were giving her permission to leave and she wasn't going to argue further.

'Are you sure you don't mind ferrying me around?' she asked him, as they left the hospital and returned to his car.

'Not at all. I'm just doing whatever needs to be done at the moment—chauffeur, cook, liaison person.'

'Liaison person?'

'Between your family and the medical team,' he explained. 'It's difficult for Scarlett and your mum to ask the right questions, they're too close. It seems to work best if I do it.'

'How can you do all that and go to work?'

'I was already on holidays leading up to the wedding. I've quit The Coop.'

'You've quit?'

Jake laughed. 'In case you haven't noticed, I'm about to become a husband and a father. I think my nights spent working in a strip club have been numbered for a while. It's time to move on to the more responsible stage of my life. I start my internship in three weeks. Quitting The Coop now was supposed to give us time for a honeymoon. So I am at your service. Anything you need, just ask.'

Ruby appreciated the offer. She had come to think of Jake as the brother she wished she had.

Jake was a good man. It was lucky for Scarlett that when Ruby had met Jake it had been clear he'd only had eyes for Scarlett, otherwise who knew what would have happened? Only Ruby did know, Jake was cute and smart but far too conventional for her. She smiled to herself, not quite believing she would ever describe someone who worked as stripper in a male revue club called The Coop as conventional! In fact, his gig as a stripper was far more in keeping with the type of man she usually looked for. Her men were always a little bit edgy. She needed the excitement. But despite his old job Jake was basically a good person. He wouldn't be able to handle someone like her.

Scarlett was perfect for him. As he was for her. Jake was cute and smart. Scarlett was clever and sensible and they made a good match. Plus it was obvious that he adored her and, most importantly, he allowed Scarlett to be herself instead of the person Scarlett thought she should be or the one she thought people wanted her to be. That had always been Scarlett's undoing. She always wanted to please everybody.

The same thing could definitely *not* be said about *her*.

Jake pulled to a stop in front of Scarlett's renovated cottage. Ruby grabbed her duffel bag from the boot of his dark green MG and followed him through the gate in the high brick wall and into the tiny front garden. She was travelling light, and hadn't had time to do more than throw a change of clothes into her bag before racing to the airport. She had known that the phone call in the early hours of the morning would only be bad news. A phone call in the blackest part of the night was only *ever* bad news.

Now that she was here, she had no recollection of what she'd actually packed. She hoped she had at least one change of clothes, although if she'd forgotten anything she'd borrow it from Scarlett. She had none of Scarlett's curves but, being summer, she'd get away with wearing her sister's clothes. It didn't matter if they were loose on her and in desperate times she knew Scarlett had several tops that could be worn as dresses.

Jake slid his key into the lock on the front door. A Christmas wreath decorated the door, jolting Ruby back to the present. Christmas was less than two weeks away but she had never felt in less of a festive mood.

'You know where everything is,' he said, as he held the door open for her. 'Make yourself at home.'

Ruby always stayed with Scarlett when she visited. It worked best if she and Lucy had their own space, but she hadn't thought about the ramifications of her earlier arrival. She'd originally planned to arrive two days before the wedding, timing her arrival with Jake's temporary move back to his parents' home, but now that she was here early she hadn't considered that a change of plan might be needed.

'Does it still suit you for me to stay? I'm not crowding you?' she asked.

'It's fine,' he assured her. 'The spare bedroom is still yours to use.'

'Are you sure? I can stay at Mum's.' She could manage a few days there if necessary.

'Ruby, don't worry about it. Have a shower and I'll be back to pick you up in about forty minutes, okay?'

She nodded and stopped arguing and pushed open the door to the spare bedroom. She upended her bag on the bed and rifled through the contents. There were a few T-shirts, a couple of skirts and a dress in various shades of the rainbow, plus an old pair of cut-off denim shorts. She'd make do for a few days. She turned to the wardrobe to grab a clothes hanger. Tucked in the corner beside the wardrobe was a white wooden baby's bassinette and hanging on the wardrobe doors were two long dresses in pale green silk. The bridesmaids' dresses, one for her and one for Rose.

She wondered what Scarlett and Jake would do about their wedding. So much had changed in just twenty-four hours. It was more than just Ruby's expectations of herself. Yesterday Scarlett and Jake had been counting down the days to their wedding and the birth of their first child. Now they were sitting at Rose's bedside, waiting and hoping for some good news.

A wedding and a baby. Ruby knew one could be postponed but not the other. She hoped the baby didn't decide to come early. They had enough going on at present.

She threw her clothes onto a couple of hangers and headed for the shower. She showered quickly and turned her back to the bathroom mirror as she dried herself. She hated looking at her reflection in the mirror. She disliked any form of self-examination or introspection.

She knew she wasn't particularly brilliant, like Scarlett. She was smart enough but didn't love studying and she wasn't pretty like Rose. Her face was too round, her nose was too small and she felt that her features still looked babyish despite the fact that she had just turned twenty-seven. At five feet nine inches she was tallish and model thin with no boobs to speak of. Her shoulder-length strawberry-blond locks were currently died platinum blonde, but despite regularly changing the colour of her hair she was yet to find a colour that she thought suited her. Her eyes were her best feature, large and an unusual shade of green. The colour of an emu's egg. The colour of the bridesmaids' dresses.

She wasn't dark and curvaceous like Scarlett or blonde, petite and beautiful like Rose. She didn't have Scarlett's lustrous mane of raven hair or accompanying thick dark eyelashes neither did she have Rose's perfectly proportioned heart-shaped face or dimples. She and Scarlett had their mother's long, lean legs but that was where the similarities ended.

Scarlett was the clever sister, Rose was the pretty one and Ruby was never really sure which sister she was. She knew others described her as the fun one but she also knew that she'd worked hard to cultivate that image. She wanted to be seen as the fun one, the extrovert, and she knew it was because she was scared that if she stopped and stood still she would disappear. In her mind, if people thought she was fun they would gravitate towards her and then she would know she existed and she wouldn't be lonely.

Ruby returned to her room and swapped the bath towel for a fresh singlet top and a long skirt made of a multitude of patchwork squares. It had been hot outside, the dry Adelaide summer heat was making the day almost unpleasant, and it had been warm in the ICU too.

Scarlett had left a pile of books stacked beside the bed. Ruby flicked through them as she waited for Jake. At the bottom of the pile was a Jane Austen novel, which Ruby recognised as one of Rose's favourites. She stashed it in her bag, deciding she'd take it to the hospital to read to Rose. It would help to pass the time.

As she followed Jake back into the ICU she couldn't help but notice that the new guy, the motorbike accident, had been put into the cubicle next to Rose. The nurses had removed his blankets—she obviously wasn't the only one who found ICU uncomfortably warm—and she ran her eyes over him appreciatively. His torso was bare but partly covered by his right arm, which was fixed across his chest in a blue orthopaedic sling. She could see the definition of his pectoral muscles above the sling and the ridges of his lower abdominal muscles below it. His chest was smooth and hairless and wonderfully masculine. She could feel her steps slowing as she gave herself time to appreciate his sculpted chest and arms. She couldn't blame the nurses for exposing him—something so gorgeous shouldn't be covered up.

His smooth, tanned skin was unmarked by any tattoos as far as she could see, but his youth, physique and the injuries she suspected he had still suggested a motorbike accident. Her eyes drifted up over the curve of his deltoid muscle to where his hair brushed his shoulder. His hair was long and brushed back from a strong forehead. The oxygen mask over his face had been replaced with tubing, exposing a square jaw and full lips. He reminded her of a fair-haired Greek god—dark blond and tanned and perfectly formed—but surely he had to be mortal. He'd been injured after all.

Too late she realised he was awake.

CHAPTER TWO

HE WAS AWAKE and he was watching her.

His eyes were bright blue and she could see him follow her path as she continued slowly past. Knowing she was in his sights made her blush but she managed to smile at him. There was nothing else to do. She'd been sprung admiring him. She knew it and so did he.

He grinned back, his smile full of mischief, and Ruby felt a warm glow suffuse her body and lift her spirits. She knew he'd only been in the ICU for an hour or two but already he looked far too healthy and vital for this room. Which made her wonder about his smile. She had probably imagined a connection—most likely he was still delirious and drugged and would smile at anyone.

She kept walking. Each bed was separated by a thin partition wall and at the foot of each bed was a curtain that could be pulled across for privacy. The cubicles were arranged around the outside of the room with a raised central station for the medical team. Ruby stepped into Rose's cubicle and her neighbour disappeared from view.

It felt like it had taken her several minutes to cross the room when in reality it had probably been seconds, but even though he was now out of sight his image was burnt on her retina—bright blue eyes, a tanned and ripped torso and a roguish smile. She knew the memory of his smile would get her through the rest of the day.

'How did the lumbar puncture go?' Jake asked, as he greeted Scarlett with a kiss.

'Fine, apparently. We're just waiting for the results.'

Ruby sighed. More waiting. Being impatient wasn't going to speed up the process but she didn't care, she wanted answers.

She offered to sit with Rose. She would read to her to pass the time while the others stretched their legs. As they left Ruby saw the swish of the curtain in the next cubicle as the nurse pulled it closed. Voices carried to her from the other side of the partition as she pulled the novel from her handbag.

'Is your pain relief working?' the nurse asked. 'You can top it up if you need to by pushing this button.'

'I can handle the pain,' he replied. 'What's the damage?'

His voice was deep and sent an unusual tremble through her chest. It reminded her of distant thunder as it rumbled through her. His voice matched his rugged, muscular and masculine physique perfectly.

'I need to know what injuries I sustained.'

'You have a broken collarbone, a fractured elbow and a couple of busted ribs.'

'No serious chest injuries?'

'No, but the list does go on. You also have a fractured femur.'

'Dammit.'

Ruby almost burst out laughing. She wasn't even

pretending to read as she smiled to herself and continued to eavesdrop on the conversation.

'What have they done with that?' he asked.

'It's been screwed and plated.'

'How long will I be in ICU?'

'You've only just got here. What's your hurry?'

Ruby caught herself frowning as she listened to the nurse's flirty tones.

'It will give me an idea how severe my injuries are.'

'I take it you're no stranger to hospitals?'

'I've been patched up a few times.'

Ruby would swear she could hear the smile in his voice and she could imagine his bright blue eyes sparkling with just a hint of recklessness.

'You lost a lot of blood and you've just undergone major surgery. Protocol dictates that we need to keep a close eye on you for the next twenty-four hours.'

'Whose protocol?' he challenged.

'The hospital's insurance company and your team's.'

'I thought as much.'

'ICU is not such a bad place to recuperate for a few days. It's much more secure than any of the other beds, including the private rooms on the general wards. I'm guessing there may be quite a bit of interest in your story and at least we can keep journalists at bay while you're with us.'

Ruby's curiosity was piqued. She had always been a sucker for anything with a hint of difference, be it a job, a situation or, more often than not, a man. She listened with interest, waiting for further details but was left disappointed.

'Fair enough. I won't make a fuss for a day or two but I'm not a great one for standing still.'

'I think you've managed to solve that problem for a while at least. You won't be going too far at all on that broken leg.'

It went quiet in the cubicle next door and Ruby saw the nurse move on to the patient on the other side. She opened the novel and started to read but she could hear her words weren't flowing. Her mind was distracted, fixated on the motorbike man. Who was he? And why would the media be interested in him?

She forced herself to keep reading. She couldn't worry about a stranger in the bed next door. She tried choosing some of her favourite scenes, ones that showed the heroine's sense of humour, but she found herself constantly looking at Rose, waiting for a response from her, expecting to see a smile or a hint of laughter but, of course, there was nothing. Unrealistically, she'd been hoping for a miracle, hoping the story would trigger a response, and it was difficult to continue without even a flicker of encouragement from Rose.

Ruby closed the book.

'Hello? Are you still there?'

Ruby frowned. She recognised the voice. Deep and quiet, it was the motorbike man. 'Are you talking to me?' she asked.

'Yes. Do you think you could keep reading?'

Her frown deepened. 'You want to listen to a romance novel written in the nineteenth century?'

'Romance? I thought it was a comedy.'

His comment made her smile. She'd always enjoyed the unexpected humour in this book too.

'But it's not the content...I like the sound of your voice,' he said simply. 'I could listen to you read the phone book.'

Ruby laughed and opened the book again. If the motorbike man could make her laugh when she really didn't feel like it, she figured he deserved a favour. 'If it's all the same, I'll stick with Jane Austen,' she said.

She picked up from where she'd stopped but this time the words flowed far more smoothly. She lost track of time as she turned the pages, only stopping when the nurse interrupted to do Rose's obs.

Ruby took a moment to stretch her legs. At least, that was what she told herself she was doing when she stood and wandered into the cubicle next door. She wanted to know why the motorbike man was in the ICU and she was going to ask him. He'd been very quiet while she'd been reading—she'd half expected some interruptions but she'd heard nothing from him—but now she saw why.

He was asleep.

Her eyes swept over his face. His cheekbones were wide and his nose was perfectly straight and narrow, flaring ever so slightly where it ended just above full lips. His eyebrows and lashes were a shade darker than his hair and she could see the beginnings of a darker beard on his jaw. A couple of little scars marked his face, one below his eye, another on his lip, but they did nothing to detract from his looks. His dark blond hair framed his face but one stray strand lay across his cheek. Ruby was tempted to reach out and brush it away but she was afraid of waking him. He looked like he was sleeping comfortably and she didn't want to disturb him.

He had a face she suspected she could look at for hours but she could hear the nurse's footsteps moving around Rose's bed. Ruby ducked out of the cubicle before she was caught being somewhere she had no business to be.

Monday, 15th December

Sitting by Rose's bed wasn't achieving anything. Ruby had spent the whole day in ICU and nothing had changed for the better.

The doctors had confirmed that Rose had pneumococcal meningitis but if anyone expected a diagnosis to make a difference they were disappointed. Rose's condition hadn't improved and the doctors were now worried about her declining kidney function as a result of the blood poisoning. Her condition and treatment remained the same and the family just sat and waited for a sign, for anything, to indicate that she was recovering.

Ruby had chatted to Scarlett, Jake and her mother when they'd all been at Rose's bedside and when she and Rose had been alone she'd read to her and kept one ear peeled for the sound of the voice of the motorbike man next door, the man with the devilish grin and the voice like distant thunder, but it seemed he wasn't in a talkative mood today.

There was a lot more activity in the ICU and Ruby knew that there wasn't a moment when they were alone but she was disappointed he hadn't even tried to strike up a conversation with her. By the end of the day she had learned nothing further about him. She still didn't know who he was and he'd had no visitors, not a single one. He'd had no one to talk to other than the doctors and nurses and Ruby hadn't learnt anything interesting from them.

Where was his family? Where were the people who cared about him?

She supposed she could have asked him, should have asked him, but whenever she had gone in or out of Rose's cubicle there had been one of the medical staff with him and she hadn't been able to do more than smile at him.

She should have tried harder. She should have worked on her timing but she was nervous, which was something quite out of character for her. Holding back was not in her nature. Normally, if she wanted something, whether it was information or an introduction, she would make it happen. But the butterflies that took flight in her stomach whenever they made eye contact were enough to make her hesitate.

If they'd been in a social setting she would have walked straight up to him so perhaps it was the fact that he was at a disadvantage physically that made her hesitant. He didn't know that she'd stood at his bedside the night before and watched him sleep. She thought that might freak him out so she was keeping her distance. He had no way of getting away from her if she encroached on his personal space. He wouldn't be able to avoid her and she hated to think that she wouldn't know if he was pleased with her attention or not. She didn't want him to feel obligated to be nice to her just because he was confined to a bed.

She didn't consider that he could easily be blunt and tell her to leave him alone—something about the way he smiled at her made her think he wouldn't be rude, but she didn't want to put him in an awkward position. So she said nothing.

* * *

By late afternoon she was tired of staring at the same four walls. Tired of pretending everything would be fine. Rose had made it through another twenty-four hours but that was all that had happened. She supposed that was better than the alternative but she had reached her limit of being cooped up. She knew she wasn't doing a very good job of being supportive but she couldn't stay inside the hospital for a minute longer.

Lucy was coming to take over the bedside vigil from her so Ruby arranged to meet her friend Candice for dinner. The last time she'd been back to Adelaide several months earlier had been for Candice's wedding. It was strange to think that had been when Jake had been persistently pursuing Scarlett and she'd been trying to fend off his advances but not doing so very successfully. Now, months later, it was hard to imagine them not together.

Ruby and Candice had nursed together in Melbourne but had both grown up in Adelaide. In typical Adelaide fashion there were only ever three degrees of separation. Ruby and Candice had worked together, now Candice worked as a theatre nurse for emergency surgery in this hospital, where Scarlett was an anaesthetist and Jake was about to be an intern, and Candice and Jake had grown up together as family friends. If anyone understood what Ruby and her family were going through at the moment, it was Candice.

As they selected their dishes from the Thai menu Ruby filled her friend in on Rose's status before Candice moved the conversation on to 'other business', as she called it.

'So, are you bringing a plus one to Scarlett's wedding?'

Ruby shook her head.

'Why not? I know you have one, you always have one. I used to wonder how you found so many.'

'You don't wonder any more?'

'Not now that I'm married.' Candice laughed. 'It doesn't bother me any longer that you seem to have more than your fair share of men. Now that I've taken myself out of the marketplace you can have as many as you want, but I do like to meet one of them every now and again. Who's the latest?'

Ruby paused. She didn't think there was actually that much to say but it would be nice to talk about the things they always used to discuss. It would be nice to get her mind off Rose's medical predicament for just a while.

'I'm not sure that there is a latest,' she admitted.

'You're between boyfriends?'

'I'm not sure exactly.'

'How can you not be sure? What's going on?'

'Mitch was asleep when Scarlett rang me about Rose in the middle of the night. The phone call didn't wake him. I left him a note.' Mitch was a musician, a drummer, and his band had been playing at one of the local pubs that night. He'd got home late and hadn't been asleep long when Scarlett's phone call had woken Ruby. But Mitch had slept through all of that and Ruby hadn't thought it necessary to wake him. It wasn't any of his business. She hadn't thought about Mitch since she'd walked out.

'You left him a note?' Candice's tone let Ruby know exactly what she thought about that. 'Have you spoken to him?'

Ruby shook her head. 'He hasn't called me either,'

she said defensively. 'We don't, didn't, have that sort of relationship.' They hadn't been like Scarlett and Jake. Or Candice and her husband, Ewan. They had both found the person they wanted to spend the rest of their life with. They had found the person who came first. Ruby had no idea what that was like.

'Well, if neither of you are prepared to pick up the phone, you're probably perfectly matched,' Candice decided, 'but it's kind of ironic 'cos now you'll never know.'

'It doesn't matter,' Ruby said with a shrug. 'I'd never planned to bring him home to meet my family and certainly not for Scarlett's wedding. We wouldn't have lasted much longer anyway. I'd been seeing him for almost two months.'

Two months was her self-imposed time limit on relationships. Any longer than that and there was the chance that one of them could start to think the relationship was serious and that was something Ruby had always taken pains to avoid. A serious relationship meant sharing bits of your soul with another person. Letting them see deep inside you. It meant taking things a step further than sharing a bed and your body. Sharing your mind was a far scarier proposition and not one that Ruby was particularly keen on.

In her experience people started to expect more from a relationship as it started to edge towards three months. Boyfriends wanted to know more about her. They would expect to be invited to an event as her plus one. Three months meant it was serious. It meant it would hurt if she was abandoned.

'Besides,' she added, 'worrying about a plus one to the wedding is irrelevant as I assume Scarlett and Jake will postpone it. I can't imagine Scarlett will want to get married while Rose is in hospital. She'll want to wait until Rose has recovered.' Ruby couldn't voice the alternative. That Rose might not get better.

'They haven't said what they're planning on doing?'

Ruby shook her head. 'No. It seems kind of an odd conversation to have in the ICU. We tend to talk about what the doctor's latest update means and what treatment Rose should have. I think everyone is just avoiding the topic of anything to do with the future. I don't think any of us can think more than a day ahead at this stage. So it means we sit there not really talking about much at all. It's no wonder the days seem interminably long in Intensive Care, but it's all we can do. Just be there for Rose.'

'Let's hope she's out of there soon and then a few more of us can split the shifts and visit her.'

Access to the ICU was restricted to family members only, and that reminded Ruby of the lonely motorbike man. She wondered why she hadn't thought to ask Candice for information. She might have even been working on the day he had been brought in. She might be the one person Ruby knew who would have the lowdown on him.

'Speaking of visiting, there's a guy in the bed next to Rose who hasn't had any visitors at all. He was brought into ICU yesterday. He looked as though he would have come through Emergency first. Were you working? Do you know anything about him?'

Candice grinned. 'I wasn't working but I heard about him. He's into motorsport apparently, a racing-car driver or something. By all reports, he'd done a fair bit of damage to himself but the girls were still very complimentary about him.' Her grin widened. 'It's not every day they get to see quite such a glorious naked man. Even if they did have to cover him with sterile drapes, they copped quite an eyeful in between times.'

Ruby's imagination quickly added what Candice was describing to what she'd already seen for herself and created a rather glorious picture. Almost real enough to make her blush. 'Do you know his name?' she asked.

'Neil? No, that's not right.' Candice shook her head. 'Noel maybe? Something starting with an N anyway. The girls weren't interested in his name.' She laughed. 'But I can find out if you like.'

'No, that's okay. I was just curious.' She should have checked his chart while he slept, just to find out his name, but that seemed like invading his privacy just a little too much.

'That would make you just one in a long line, from what I hear.'

Ruby was curious but she'd hoped Candice would have been able to give her a name or something to enable her to do some research when she got home. She didn't want to think of it as cyber-stalking but wasn't that one of the purposes of the internet? But she still didn't have enough to go on.

It was ridiculous. She was never going to find out anything about him. She rather liked the fantasy of the lonely bachelor that she'd built up around him but she knew it was probably a complete fallacy. She knew the simplest way to get some answers would be to strike up a conversation with him. If she wanted to know more, she was going to have to drum up some courage and ask him herself.

Normally she was up for a bit of fun, some harmless

flirtation, as much as the next person. All right, usually a bit more than the next person. A girl had to know how to have fun but even she wasn't sure that an intensive care unit was the appropriate place to attempt to pick up a man. She was sure it wouldn't make the list in a women's magazine when they printed their articles on the top ten places to meet men. Not unless you worked there and then it could technically come under the heading of a workplace.

And although Ruby couldn't be accused of being mainstream in her approach to dating, or even meeting men, even she wasn't convinced that having an eye on a man who was lying in an ICU, no matter how hot he looked, was acceptable in the dating jungle.

Tuesday, 16th December

But nothing ventured, nothing gained was her motto, and the next morning was as good a time as any to venture, she decided as she keyed in the code to open the door into the ICU. Now that she knew he wasn't an axe murderer or serial killer, she could relax. Her judgement had been known to let her down on occasion.

She summoned up her courage and pushed the door open. She'd check on Rose and then strike up a conversation. There'd be no harm in saying a simple 'Hello' as she walked past. She didn't need to crowd him. She could say hello and then the ball would be in his court. If he wanted to engage her in conversation she'd be a willing participant. He'd had no visitors, perhaps she could offer to help. There must be something he needed and, if not, at least she would have broken the ice.

She was all ready to flash him her best smile as she

made her way to Rose's cubicle but his bed was empty, stripped of its sheets, leaving the mattress exposed, the machines all neatly packed away. The bed looked as though it had never been occupied.

The adrenalin that had been coursing through her body clumped together to form a little ball of lead in her chest and plummeted to the pit of her stomach, leaving her feeling flat.

He was gone and she'd missed her chance.

She couldn't believe it.

It wasn't really in her nature to be hesitant and she couldn't explain why she'd held back. But she had and now she would never know anything more about him. Disappointment flooded her, joining the ball of lead in her gut.

She stepped past the empty bed and into Rose's cubicle. Seeing Rose still lying inert, her condition obviously unchanged, and hearing the mechanical suck and hiss of the ventilator didn't do anything to lift her spirits.

She leant over and squeezed Rose's hand in greeting before kissing her cheek. Even if Rose wasn't responding she had to let her sister know she was there. She kissed her mother next and then sank into a chair beside Lucy.

'Has there been any change?' she asked.

Lucy shook her head. 'No, but we've passed the forty-eight-hour mark.'

Ruby knew that was a big milestone but what she didn't know was how much that meant if Rose still hadn't shown any signs of improvement.

'Have the doctors seen her this morning?'

'Yes, and they seem to think it's a positive that Rose

hasn't declined any further.' Ruby could hear the hopeful note in her mum's voice, as if praying for Rose's recovery would be enough to make it happen. That might have worked if they'd been a religious family but they weren't. But, still, none of them were prepared to discuss anything other than the idea that Rose would recover, even though they all knew there were no guarantees. They only had their belief to get them through this. 'Will you be able to stay until she's better?' Lucy added.

Ruby nodded. She wouldn't leave while Rose was critically ill. She'd stay as long as she could and hopefully that would be long enough.

'What about work? Can you get extra time off?'

Ruby hadn't thought about work since she'd jumped on a plane before sunrise on Sunday and her mother's question made her realise she hadn't actually told work she was away. She'd been working as an agency nurse in Byron Bay. She'd been working as an agency nurse for years actually as the flexibility suited her. There was no commitment. She could almost come and go as she pleased, which she did on a fairly frequent basis. When she'd decided she'd had enough of one place she could up and leave without feeling like she was leaving an employer in the lurch.

Had she missed a shift? She couldn't remember. She certainly hadn't had a phone call telling her she'd forgotten to turn up. She did a quick calculation. Today was Monday, wasn't it? No, Tuesday. That was okay, her next shift wasn't until tomorrow. She had time to sort that out.

'Time off isn't a problem,' she told Lucy. 'I'll just tell the agency I'm unavailable.'

Getting days off wasn't difficult but losing the pay cheque would hurt. But there wasn't anything she could do about that. She wasn't leaving until Rose was out of the woods.

'Are you still working agency? You don't want something more permanent?'

Lucy had been working for the same aged care facility for ever. Ruby knew she was very attached to the residents but they didn't live forever. In normal nursing patients came and went and Ruby couldn't see what difference having a permanent job would make to her life when there was so much change anyway. Ruby didn't want to form attachments, it would make leaving difficult.

'It's just as well I'm doing agency work as it meant I could jump on a plane and come to Adelaide without letting anyone down,' she said, but she knew better than to expect that to be the end of the conversation. She waited for the inevitable question.

'You don't want to settle down?'

There it was. Their conversations always seemed to come back to that. No matter what they were discussing, her mother always seemed to be able to raise the topic of settling down.

By the age of twenty-six Lucy had been a mother of three but Ruby knew it hadn't all been by choice and she had no intention of making the same mistakes her mother had made. She chose to ignore the fact that not only had she made some of the same mistakes, she had also made other, different, ones and now she was trying just to get through life. She wanted company but she didn't want commitment. She didn't want to share her private thoughts or her history with anyone else.

She could feel her hackles rising.

She knew she should be mature enough not to fight with her mother, especially not at the moment next to her sister's ICU bed. Rose always tried to avoid confrontation and Ruby didn't want to get into a fight here in case Rose could hear them. She knew she wouldn't have given work a second thought if Lucy hadn't asked about it and that realisation put a match to her already short fuse. She needed to remove herself from the situation before Lucy could ask any more questions.

'Have you eaten today?' she asked. She needed some breathing space and a quick trip to the hospital kiosk would give her a chance to get it. 'I'm starving. I skipped breakfast so I might go and grab something to eat. Would you like something?' She couldn't remember when she'd last seen her mother eat and, as she expected, Lucy declined her offer.

As she left the ICU she couldn't help but look at the empty space in the cubicle beside Rose. She hoped the vacant bed meant he'd been moved because he was recovering well. She didn't want to think that things might have gone from bad to worse.

She kept her eyes peeled for him as she made her way along the hospital corridors but he was nowhere to be seen. It wasn't as though she'd really expected to bump into him but she still felt a frisson of disappointment as she stepped up to the counter of the hospital kiosk and placed her order.

She just wanted to see him once more. She needed to know he was okay.

She picked up her green tea and vegetarian wrap and turned from the counter and found the person she'd been

searching for. He was sitting on the opposite side of the
room, watching her with his bright blue eyes.

It had been twenty-four hours since she'd seen him
and she couldn't help but think what a difference a day
made. One day ago he'd been in an intensive care bed
and now he was dressed and sitting in the hospital kiosk.
Watching her.

Although he was on the far side of a crowded room
Ruby would have sworn they had the place to themselves. She certainly wasn't aware of anyone else. Not
while he was watching her. Even from a distance the
colour of his eyes was a vivid blue and somehow he had
become familiar to her despite the fact she still had no
idea who he was.

He smiled and her heart skipped a beat.

He didn't look surprised to see her. Neither did he
seem embarrassed to be caught watching her. If she
didn't know better she would think he'd been waiting
for her.

Her heart pounded in her chest as she walked towards him. She told herself she had to walk past him
to get out of the kiosk but there were actually several
different exits, she could have easily chosen a different route, but her feet were already moving in his direction. It was no use pretending she didn't want to see
him; for the past two days she'd thought of nothing else
except her sister and the stranger in the bed next to her.

She was three steps away when she discovered that
the path she'd taken was blocked by his wheelchair. She
hesitated and looked up, meeting his eyes, before continuing on another step.

'Hello.' His voice rumbled through her. It was deep
and strong but quiet. It sounded as though he was far

away but it was loud enough to bring her to a stop beside him. It was only one little word, two syllables, but to Ruby's ears it was so much more than a simple greeting. To Ruby it was the start of something more.

CHAPTER THREE

'HELLO,' SHE MANAGED in reply, before her words disappeared and she stood in front of him completely speechless. She wasn't normally tongue-tied and she knew she'd had a whole conversation planned for when she next saw him but that had been based on the expectation that he would still be in the ICU. Not sitting in the middle of a busy kiosk looking a picture of health.

Someone had washed his hair and Ruby could see now that it was more blond than brown. It swept back from his forehead in a widow's peak, exposing his strong brow and allowing his blue eyes to shine, and hung to his jaw line, framing and accentuating the oval shape of his face. Despite the length of his hair and the fullness of his lips his was a masculine face, and as if to reinforce the fact his jaw was darkened by the growth of a new beard. In contrast to his hair his three-day designer stubble was more brown than blond. His face was pleasant and friendly and his smile was brilliant.

Ruby's eyes dropped from his lips to his body. His right arm was tucked inside his T-shirt and she could see the tell-tale bumps and lumps from the sling, but his left arm was tanned and muscly, really muscly, and lightly dusted with fair hair.

He was wearing shorts and a hinged knee brace was fitted over his right leg. She remembered the list of injuries the nurse had rattled off. A fractured clavicle, ribs, elbow and femur. He'd certainly done a good job on himself. From the neck down he didn't really look in a fit state to be out of the ward, let alone left abandoned in the kiosk.

'Would you do me a favour?' he asked, as Ruby finished her inspection and lifted her eyes back up to his face. She blushed slightly. She'd been caught blatantly checking him out.

Anything, she thought, but she just nodded in reply, still unable to find her voice.

At least he seemed willing and able to carry on a conversation. 'Would you mind pushing me outside? I'd really love to get into the sunshine but I can't move this damn thing without help,' he said, as he used his head to gesture towards his chest and his arm where it lay trapped in the sling. 'Actually, that's not quite true,' he clarified. 'I can move but only if I'm happy to go round in circles.'

He smiled at her and Ruby's heart skipped another beat. His smile was full of cheek and made his blue eyes sparkle. She could feel herself being taken in by his charm. He was handsome and charismatic and in her experience that was a dangerous combination. And she'd always been a sucker for danger.

She tilted her head to one side as she studied him. 'How did you get down here?' she asked. Her voice was husky. That wasn't unusual but even to her ears it sounded huskier than normal, as if it had been days, not minutes, since she'd used it.

'I bribed a nurse,' he said with a wink.

Ruby felt the heat from his gaze course through her and she could just imagine the nurses falling over themselves to help him. She knew they'd normally be too busy to lend a hand—if a patient wanted to get outside they'd have to do so under their own steam—but seeing his smile and his automatic wink she knew just how that scene would have played out.

She raised one eyebrow. 'I bet it was a young nurse.'

He laughed, or rather he began to laugh before he stopped short and winced, and Ruby realised his broken ribs must have been protesting, but even so the brief sound of his laugh reverberated through her and made her smile along with him.

'It was,' he admitted. 'So, will you help me? I've had enough of being cooped up inside.'

She couldn't blame the nurse who'd fallen for his charms, she could see he'd be difficult to resist and she could well imagine how restless he was feeling. Despite the fact he was wheelchair-bound with a rather cumbersome-looking brace on his leg, he still looked too vital, too energetic to tolerate being stuck inside.

'Sure, but you'll have to hold this for me,' she said, as she handed him her lunch.

He took her food, balancing it in his lap along with his own cup and stabilising it all with his left hand and forearm.

Ruby bent down to release the wheelchair brakes, a co-conspirator to his escape. She could smell the coffee in his cup as she flicked off the right brake. As she leaned behind him and flicked off the left one her hair brushed over his shoulder—she was close enough now to smell him too. His hair smelt faintly of limes. He smelt fresh and far better than he should considering he'd spent the past couple of days in a hospital bed. Ruby knew from looking at his leg that he wouldn't have been able to shower himself and she wondered which nurse had volunteered to wash his hair and give him a sponge bath.

She felt her temperature rise as the thought of sponging him down took hold. She ran her eyes over the muscles in his left leg as her mind wandered. She forced herself to straighten up before she was tempted to reach out and run a hand down his thigh, only to find herself, once again, under the scrutiny of his blue-eyed gaze. She wondered if he could guess what she was thinking. She hoped not.

She stood behind him and gripped the handles of the wheelchair, glad of a reason to break eye contact. She gathered her errant thoughts together and pushed him out through the kiosk doors.

Outside several picnic tables and benches were scattered around a paved courtyard and shaded by a couple of large elm trees. It was late in the morning, well before a regular lunchtime, and the courtyard was virtually deserted. Ruby pushed the wheelchair towards a picnic bench.

'Where would you like me to put you?' she asked.

'Here's fine.' His back was towards the morning sun and Ruby could see the soft golden hairs on his forearm as the sunlight kissed his skin. 'Will you keep me company?' he asked, as she flicked the brakes on his wheelchair, locking him in position.

She hesitated. The old Ruby wouldn't have hesitated but she was making a conscious effort not to always put herself first but to consider other people's needs. Her family's, for instance. Would anyone miss her? Should she be at Rose's bedside?

'You'd be doing me a favour,' he added, as he waited for her reply. 'I'm tired of my own company. You could save me from sitting here and talking to myself.'

Rose had company, Ruby told herself. Lucy was with her and surely they could spare her while she ate her brunch.

'That doesn't sound very enticing, does it? It makes me sound boring. I'll admit to being bored but I hope I'm not boring,' he added, when she still didn't answer.

By way of an answer, Ruby sat on the bench in the shade of one of the elm trees. Her fair skin burnt easily and even though it wasn't yet midday she knew better than to expose herself to the summer sun. He smiled at her as she sat down and Ruby knew she'd made a good decision.

'I'm Noah,' he told her, as he handed her tea over.

Noah.

Not Noel. Not Neil. Noah. She liked Noah far better. His name suited him. He looked strong and capable. He looked like a man who would take charge. He looked like a man who could handle himself physically. A man who worked with his hands.

If he was into racing cars, as Candice had proposed, then she guessed he did all those things, just not in the way she'd first imagined. He would need physical strength in his job. Mental strength as well.

He was passing her the wrap. 'Do you have a name?'

Her fingers brushed his as she took the wrap and it took her a second or two to answer as her brain was busy trying to process his question and deal with the sensations running through her.

'Ruby.'

'That's a pretty name.'

'Do you say that to all the girls?'

'Only when it's true.'

He was watching her with his bright blue eyes and his attention sent a shiver of expectation through her that made her hands shake as she undid her wrap.

'You've coloured your hair,' he said, as he sipped his coffee.

Ruby self-consciously put a hand to her head.

'Your hair wasn't pink yesterday, was it?' he asked.

She shook her head. Her natural strawberry blond locks had been dyed platinum blond until earlier today when she'd updated her colour. Her hair was now pale pink and she was pleased with the result. 'I coloured it this morning.'

'Good. I recognised your voice but the colour of your hair confused me. I was worried my concussion had ruined either my eyesight or my memory or that the drugs they're giving me are way stronger than I need them to be.'

Ruby smiled. 'I did this for Rose.'

'She's your sister? In ICU?'

She nodded. 'I'm constantly changing the colour of my hair and when Rose and I speak on the phone she always wants to know what colour it is. Pink is her favourite. I thought maybe it would be enough to elicit a response.'

'And?'

Ruby shook her head. 'Nothing.'

She wasn't sure why she told Noah all that. She usually avoided talking about anything personal and she didn't want to talk about Rose. She'd rather talk about him.

'I heard you were in a car accident,' she said, swinging the conversation back to him. Talking about him seemed safer. It was far less emotional and there was less of a chance of her making an idiot of herself by bursting into tears.

'Who told you that?'

She smiled. 'I have friends in high places.'

He looked a little panicked and Ruby suddenly remembered the nurse talking about the media. She took pity on him. 'I'm a nurse, we talk.'

'You work here?'

'No. But I have friends who do. But don't worry, that's all I know. I didn't know your name until you told me. So, are you going to tell me what happened? I was sure you'd crashed a motorbike, not a car.'

'A motorbike? Why?'

Because she could picture him astride a motorbike. She could almost hear the deep throaty growl of the engine as it throbbed between his powerful thighs. She could see him push his hair back from his forehead as he removed his helmet. She could picture him placing it between his thighs and leaning forwards onto it as he invited her to go for a ride. She had several fantasies involving men on motorbikes and he fitted them perfectly but she couldn't tell him any of that.

She kept it simple. 'You look like a motorbike type of guy. Except for the lack of tattoos.'

He grinned and raised an eyebrow. 'You were looking for tattoos?'

She blushed and he chuckled.

'Motorbikes are far too dangerous,' he added.

'Says a man who races cars for a living.'

'I thought you didn't know anything about me?'

'I promise, that's it. What else should I know? Are you famous? The nurse was taking about the media not having access to the ICU. Should I recognise you?'

'You mean you don't?'

His voice was teasing. It was deep and throaty and she couldn't decide if it was more like the motorbike engine in her imagination or distant thunder, but the sound was soothing and she felt herself relax for the first time since she'd landed in Adelaide. She'd been wound up like a spring and she could feel herself unwinding as she sat in the company of this divine hunk of a man.

'Only from the ICU,' she told him.

'You don't read motoring magazines?'

'Not if I can help it.'

'That's right,' he said, 'romance novels are your thing. I'm sorry I didn't thank you for reading to me. I wasn't in a very sociable mood yesterday. I hate being out of action but I enjoyed listening to you, you have a very sexy voice.'

His comment flustered her. He was very direct. She was almost as uncomfortable with receiving a compliment as she was talking about herself so she changed the subject again.

'It was my pleasure but now you need to answer my question. Are you famous? Do we need to be worried about the paparazzi with long lenses?'

'No. My team put out a press release. The media have their story and it wasn't nearly as exciting as they would have liked.'

'Your team?'

'I drive V8 race cars. That's my job but I'm just part of a team. I crashed a car but it was only in testing.'

'Only?'

He nodded. 'It's far better to crash during testing than in a race. The team has more time to repair things but they still weren't very happy with me. I turned months of work into a mass of crumpled metal. Luckily, it turns out it wasn't my fault. It was a mechanical failure so now I'm back in their good books.'

'You think you're lucky it wasn't your fault. How about lucky you're still alive!'

He shrugged. 'It was no big deal. The media have their story. It was an engineering problem with the car, not driver error. It didn't happen during an event and I don't have any life-threatening injuries. It's not exciting enough for front-page news.'

It sounded exciting enough to Ruby.

'If it happened in a couple of months' time they'd be more interested,' he added.

'What happens in a couple of months?'

'The racing season would be about to start. The media will be looking for stories then.'

Ruby frowned. 'You're not planning on being ready to race in a few weeks, are you?'

'I'm going to give it my best shot. I have almost twelve weeks. I think I'm in with a chance.'

'Really? You have a busted arm, collarbone, leg and ribs and you think you'll be racing cars again in a few weeks?' From what Ruby could remember from her stints in orthopaedics, he'd be cutting it fine.

'Don't forget the concussion,' he said. 'But my leg has been pinned, my elbow is only cracked and my collarbone and ribs will heal in no time.'

Ruby raised her eyebrows but tried to keep quiet. It wasn't her place to make a judgement. Stranger things had happened and many times she'd seen how a positive mental attitude could overcome the most difficult physical problems. But even so…

'Even if you are healed, you'd have to be crazy to put yourself back in a car. The safety features must leave a lot to be desired if you've sustained these sorts of injuries.' She thought perhaps he was a little bit crazy but that wasn't all that surprising. You'd have to be a little bit mad to make your living from racing cars.

'It was the safety features that *gave* me some of these injuries. The harness broke a couple of my ribs and my helmet cracked my collarbone. But I've had worse.'

Definitely a little bit crazy, she decided.

'It's a challenge but I like a challenge.'

He was watching her closely as he said this and Ruby could see the challenge in his eyes. He was just her type—sexy, a little bit dangerous and a risk-taker. She was always attracted to men who were a little bit different. It kept life interesting.

He was rubbing his temple with his left hand, his biceps muscle flexing as he moved his hand to the other side of his head.

'Are you okay?' she asked.

'Bit of a headache.'

Great attention to detail, Rubes. Terrific nursing skills. He'd told her he had concussion and he was probably due some pain relief too.

'You probably shouldn't have been sitting in the sun,' she said. She stood up and collected their rubbish and threw it into the bin. 'Come on, I'll take you back inside.' It was time she got back to Rose anyway. She couldn't hide out here for ever, as tempting as that was. She needed to do her bit.

She stopped at a vending machine in the hospital entrance and bought a bottle of water.

'Here, I think you should rehydrate yourself,' she said as she handed him the bottle. He drank it as he directed her to one of the side rooms on the orthopaedic ward.

'Let me give you some money for the water,' he said as she wheeled him into his private room. He must have good health insurance but, then, she guessed he'd need it in his line of work.

'Don't worry about it. You can owe me.'

'As long as you make sure you come back to collect.'

'Oh, I will,' she said.

She was going to make sure she saw him again.

He could be a good distraction for her while Rose was in hospital. She could have a bit of company and a bit of fun. She didn't want to be a third wheel in Scarlett's relationship or in Candice's and she couldn't spend every minute with her mum. No matter how supportive she wanted to be, she knew that would end in tears and neither of them needed that stress.

In just a very short space of time Noah had cheered her up. There had been no awkwardness between them. Ruby had felt as though they were continuing a conversation they'd started before. It didn't feel as though she was making a new acquaintance but rather catching up with an old friend. It was weird but nice. Comforting. She had no idea if he'd felt the same but she figured she'd find out.

She returned to ICU feeling far more positive about the world. Seeing him had been a bright spot in her day.

The only bright spot.

And now that she knew where to find him she was determined to see him again.

Wednesday, 17th December

Noah had sweated through his morning exercise session with the physiotherapist. He always gave everything one hundred and ten per cent and his rehabilitation would be no exception. He knew he needed to be vigilant about his exercise programme if he had any hope of getting back behind the wheel of his race car in time for the opening event of the season, but he had additional motivation today. He'd pushed himself hard, hoping that exercise would provide a distraction from his constant thoughts about a slip of a girl with amazing legs and pink hair.

The physiotherapist had remonstrated with him a couple of times when he'd lost focus, when his mind had drifted off as he'd recalled the husky sound of her voice, the smattering of freckles that dusted her upturned nose and the smoothness of her thighs below the frayed hems of her tiny denim shorts. He liked her legs almost as much as he liked her voice.

But it had been her voice that had initially snookered him and he'd been thinking of her ever since he'd first heard her husky, throaty tones. He had been furious about the accident and irritated to find himself in ICU, but he'd resigned himself to the fact that he was stuck there for at least twenty-four hours when she had begun to read in her sexy, deep voice and he'd forgotten to be annoyed. He hadn't really paid much attention to the story but her voice had soothed him and excited him at the same time.

She had fascinated him from the moment she had started talking. She would make a good jazz singer. Her voice was smoky and sultry and listening to her had made ICU tolerable, and as much as he'd wanted to get out of there part of him had been sorry to go. He should have spoken to her when he'd had the chance but he'd been in too much pain. And that had been a mistake. Once he was transferred there was no guarantee he'd ever see her again.

And that was when he'd decided to work hard on his exercises and use his medication to control the pain. He would be a model patient. He knew the benefits that could bring, and he was certain that if he combined that with his infamous charm he should be able to persuade at least some of the nurses to help him out in his quest to track her down. Not that he intended to outline his exact plans to them, they didn't need to know all the details. And then, with relatively little effort, he'd found her.

She wasn't a blonde anymore but that was irrelevant. She still had the sexiest voice he'd ever heard and she'd promised to come back. Now he was just killing time while he waited.

He wasn't worried about her keeping her word. He knew when someone was interested and he was certain she was just as interested in him as he was in her. He hadn't been able to get Ruby out of his head.

He was contemplating doing a few more upper-limb exercises just to pass the time when a knock on his door distracted him. The medical staff never knocked and the cleaners had already been. He hoped it was Ruby, even though he knew it could just be the kitchen staff coming to collect his lunch tray.

The door opened and she appeared. Her hair was still

pink and there was a smile in her green eyes that made it feel like the sun had just been switched on.

'Good morning,' he said. 'Have you come to collect on that drink I owe you?'

'Yep. And I wondered if you felt like playing hooky?'

He grinned. His day had just improved considerably. 'Do I need to be over eighteen?'

'Slow down, Romeo. I might not be known for my athletic ability but at the moment I can outrun you so you'll have to behave. I thought you might like to get outside.'

'Sure.'

She stepped into his room. She was wearing a tiny pair of denim shorts, the same pair she'd worn yesterday if he remembered correctly, and he knew he wouldn't have forgotten. The shorts showed off her legs and he let his gaze run over them in appreciation. They were incredible. Long and lean and toned. Her toenails were bright purple and her hair was pink. She wore a green T-shirt that matched her eyes and hung loosely on her slim frame. She was a kaleidoscope of colour and she brightened his room and his mood.

She reached out and took the bread roll from his lunch tray, which was yet to be cleared.

'Are you hungry?' he asked.

'No. It's not for me. I had something a bit more adventurous than the kiosk courtyard in mind,' she said as she dropped the roll into her bag. 'I'm kidnapping you. Just for an hour or so. Is that okay?'

That was perfectly okay as far as he was concerned.

Her small cotton bag, heavily decorated with shiny bits, was slung across her body. She pulled a pair of sunglasses from the bag and handed them to him.

'What are these for?' he asked.

'I'm being a responsible kidnapper. I need to get out-side and I'm taking you with me but I don't want you to get another headache from the sun.'

He slipped the sunglasses on and looked into the mirror on the wall opposite his bed. He looked ridicu-lous. 'I think these might be the ugliest sunglasses I've ever seen.'

'Then you'd be wrong. They were actually the pick of the bunch in the hospital gift shop.'

He took the glasses off and stuck them on top of his head. 'You're kidding me.'

'Yep, but you'll have to suck it up, they're the best you've got.' She laughed. Her laugh was loud and con-tagious. She laughed like she really meant it, like she was really amused, and her laugh was infectious. She was grinning widely and he could see that her left eye tooth was a little crooked. She was adorable and he felt a hundred per cent better for her company.

'Where are you taking me?'

'Not far but I need to get away from the hospital for a bit. I need to clear my head.'

'What's happened? How are things with Rose?'

'Still the same and I can't spend all day sitting in ICU, I get too frustrated.'

'There's been no improvement?'

Ruby shook her head. 'No. And the doctors think that the longer she shows no sign of improvement the worse her prognosis is.'

'They could be wrong. I've known doctors to be wrong before.'

Ruby smiled but it wasn't the full-blown smile that lit up her face. It was a cautious half smile. 'I'm a nurse, don't forget. I've known them to be wrong before too, but I also know the odds for bacterial meningitis,' she said, as she fetched his wheelchair from the corner of the room. 'Do you mind if we don't talk about Rose? I just want to have some fun for a while. Do you need a hand to get into the chair?'

Noah shook his head. 'No. If you bring it closer I can manage.'

He took his wallet from the bedside cabinet and stood on his left leg while he stuffed the wallet into the front pocket of his shorts. She hovered over him as he transferred himself into the wheelchair. He was a tall man, almost six feet three inches, and Ruby's head was tucked underneath his chin. He could smell her hair. She smelt like a flower garden.

He swivelled around forty-five degrees and lowered himself into the chair. Sitting down brought his eyes in line with her thighs. Her legs looked smooth and soft and he was tempted to reach out and stroke her skin. But before he could move she had released his brakes and stepped in behind him. Her floral scent wafted over him again.

She pushed him out of his room and then parked him at the nurses' station, giving him instructions to tell the nurses he'd be back in an hour. While he was doing as he was told he saw her swipe a couple more bread rolls from the lunch trays that had been stacked into the catering trolleys and left in the corridor. These joined the one already in her bag and he wondered what on earth she planned to do with them.

Ruby paused out the front of the hospital and delved into her sequined bag. She pulled out a floppy hat and jammed it onto her head. She was starting to remind him of Mary Poppins and he wondered what else she had stashed in the bag. She looked fabulously quirky but her full lips, pert nose and round face, which was at odds with the slightness of her figure, combined together to make her look very young. He should find out how old she was. Being a nurse, she'd have to be at least twenty-one but she could have passed for seventeen.

'Sunglasses on,' she instructed, as her wide red mouth broke into a smile. She waited for him to put the hideous glasses on before she pushed him out onto North Terrace and turned left.

Noah was familiar with these streets. The hospital was close to the V8 street-racing circuit that ran through the eastern parklands of the city and along the nearby roads. Ruby pushed him east for a hundred metres before taking him through the ornate, wrought-iron gates of the Botanic Gardens. They meandered slowly along the paths past green lawns and towering trees. Noah had spent a lot of time in the city over the past few years but had never been into the gardens. Despite the fact that they were only a few hundred metres from the city traffic, he had an immediate sense of peace and tranquillity, which was a welcome change after the continuous noise and activity of the hospital.

Ruby turned off the main path and brought him to a stop next to a large lake. The moment they stopped, several curious ducks paddled over to inspect them. He watched as Ruby took a couple of the bread rolls from her bag and proceeded to break off small pieces and throw them into the lake, creating chaos amongst the ducks. Finally, he knew why she'd swiped the rolls.

Outside, surrounded by the foliage and greenery of the gardens, she looked even more vital. She was bright against the botanical backdrop and she looked perfectly at home. She reminded him of a flamingo, with her long legs and pink hair and the water of the lake behind her.

He knew that if he turned his head and looked back over his shoulder he would be able to see the tops of the hospital buildings poking above the trees but he didn't want to turn his head. He didn't want to look away from Ruby. He stayed still, happily content to sit and watch. It wasn't often that he got a chance to be quiet and still. While he loved his job, by definition it meant he was constantly on the go in a noisy environment. Peace and tranquillity were something he'd learnt to savour.

'This was a brilliant idea,' he told her.

'Oh, I'm full of good ideas,' she said as she turned and smiled at him and he had a sudden, overwhelming urge to pull her down to him and kiss her smiling mouth.

CHAPTER FOUR

HE WONDERED HOW she'd taste. Of strawberries, he imagined.

He wondered how she'd react.

'Here,' she said, as she put several pieces of torn-apart bread roll into his lap. 'It's your turn. Tell me,' she asked, as he attempted to throw bread to the ducks with his left hand, 'how does someone get a job as a racing-car driver?'

'I started like most kids, I guess,' he replied, as a turtle popped its head out of the lake and snagged a piece of bread before disappearing back into the murky depths. 'I grew up on a sheep station in western New South Wales and we used to ride around the farm on horses and motorbikes. That's how I know motorbikes are dangerous.

'Then I got into go-kart racing. It's quite competitive among the kids and we could race go-karts before we could get a normal driver's licence. There were plenty of regular competitions and if you're good enough, some-one takes notice and eventually offers you a drive in a real car. You work your way up through the different classes until you end up at the top. Which in Australia is either in championship cars or in V8s. Dad took me to watch the V8s racing at Bathurst when I was about thirteen and I've been hooked on them ever since.'

'So it's a real job?' she asked. 'What do you write when you have to fill in a form and there's a box marked "Occupation"?'

'Yes, it's a real job.' He laughed as he threw the last of the bread into the lake. 'I write "Professional Athlete" on the form.'

'Really? You call yourself an athlete?'

She was smiling at him, not taking either of them seriously.

'You might be surprised at how physically demanding it is.'

'I might indeed.' She grinned and he watched as she looked him over. He knew he was in good physical shape. He knew how much effort he put into staying fit and he was more than happy for her to give him the once-over. He just hoped she liked what she saw.

'And is your family still in country New South Wales? Is that why you haven't had many visitors?'

She had been paying attention. He nodded. 'Dad has just had a hip replacement so he can't travel and Mum is home with him. But I doubt they would have made the trip to see me even if they could.'

'Why not?'

'Because, in the scheme of things, my injuries are relatively minor. Getting injured goes hand in hand with racing. I can't expect them to drop everything whenever I crash a car.'

'Do you do it a lot?'

'No, thank goodness. But I've been racing professionally for eight years—I've had my share of accidents.'

'So who does look after you when you're injured?'

'No one.'

'No girlfriend? No wife?'

'Not any more.' Noah removed his sunglasses. They were sitting in the shade of a willow tree and if they were going to have this conversation he wanted to be able to see her clearly. 'I'm divorced.'

'Divorced?'

When he nodded she asked, 'What was her name?

'Steph.'

'Do you mind talking about her?'

Ruby had the most incredible enormous green eyes. They reminded him of the colour of the waterholes on the farm where the oil from the leaves of the overhanging eucalyptus turned the water green, and he knew that as long as he was looking into her eyes he'd tell her anything she wanted to know.

He shook his head. 'No. It was a long time ago.'

'Where did you meet her?'

'We grew up together. Steph was the daughter of the town vet. She spent a lot of time at our place and we went to school together.'

'You were friends?'

He nodded. 'And things would have been better all round if we'd left it that way.'

'What happened?'

'We were young. Our marriage was an impulse and when the dust settled she decided that real life with me didn't suit her. She didn't like living out of a suitcase. She wanted to settle down and have a family. Now she does.'

'And you're okay with that?'

'We got married for all the wrong reasons and there weren't enough other reasons to stay together. It's not really in my nature to give up but we should never have got married in the first place. People make mistakes. You learn from them and move on. Now, yesterday I insisted I wasn't boring but I'm starting to get bored with the sound of my own voice. It's time for me to listen to you. Tell me something I should know.'

'I can't think of anything.'

'I'll make it easy for you.' He picked up her left hand. Her hand was tiny and slight in his palm. There was no ring on her ring finger. 'No husband?' She shook her head as he turned her hand over. He was reluctant to let her go. Her hand fitted so perfectly into his. 'What about a boyfriend?'

'I'm not sure.'

'What does that mean?'

'I walked out four days ago when I got the phone call about Rose. I don't think I'll be going back.'

'You haven't seen him for four days?'

'No.'

'Have you spoken to him?'

She shook her head. 'I wouldn't know what to say. We didn't have the sort of relationship where we talked much.'

'Ah.' He grinned and raised an eyebrow.

'Stop it.' She laughed and pulled her hand from his. 'That's not what I meant.'

His comment had the desired effect. He'd wanted to lighten the tension.

'So, do you think he knows it's over?' he asked.

Noah liked this girl. She stirred all the right emotions in him. Physically he was attracted to her. He loved her voice, her laugh, her legs, the way her face came to life when something amused her, and he wanted to spend time getting to know her. She was adorable—cute, funny and sexy—but he wasn't going to make a move if she was already in a relationship. That never ended well for anyone.

Ruby shrugged. 'I don't expect he'll care. And chances are, by the time I get back to Byron Bay, he would have moved on. He's a drummer in a band. If they get a gig somewhere else they'll head off.'

That sounded to him like Ruby was single. He was going to assume as much anyway.

'You live in Byron Bay?'

'For the moment.'

He was beginning to think she was well named. Getting information out of her was like drawing blood out of a stone but he was determined to find out more about her.

'You're just down the road from me,' he told her. 'I live on the Sunshine Coast when I'm not travelling around the country.'

'So what are you doing here?'

It seemed she was done talking about herself. He'd noticed before that she changed the subject whenever he asked her a personal question and the first chance she got to turn the conversation back to him she took it. He wanted to know more about her but he didn't want to frighten her off so he went with the change of topic. He hoped there'd be time later to get to know her better but he was smart enough to realise that if he scared her now he'd be ruining those chances.

'The cars are built here. My mechanics were doing modifications and organised testing at a race track north of Adelaide. I go where I'm told. The first race of the season is here and it's often stinking hot. They wanted race conditions.'

'Do you spend a lot of time here?'

'I've been coming here since I was twenty-two, every year for the past eight years, to race but I don't get to see a lot. We fly in, spend four days at the race track and have one rest day before heading to the next spot.'

'What's your favourite place of anywhere you've been?'

'Home,' he said. 'I always look forward to going home to the Coast, probably because I don't get to spend enough time there, but here is pretty good too.'

'Adelaide?'

'No. Right here. With you. At the risk of sounding like a crazy stalker, I asked the nurses to leave me at the kiosk because I was hoping I'd see you there.'

She smiled and he thought she seemed pleased. 'And what were you planning on doing if I didn't turn up?'

'I thought about hanging around the ICU but I didn't want to look completely crazy or desperate.'

She laughed. 'Probably a wise decision.'

'What about you?' he asked. 'Where is your favourite place?'

Ruby had been leaning on the railing at the edge of the lake, facing him. He'd had trouble concentrating as her thighs were level with his eyes and were proving to be very distracting. She pushed herself off the railing as she said, 'Come on, I'll show you.'

He frowned. 'It's here?'

'Yep.'

The path she chose took them past a small kiosk at the northern end of the lake. Chairs and tables were shaded by umbrellas and there were signs advertising ice cream.

'Hang on,' he said, when he saw the signs. 'How about I buy you that drink I owe you?'

She detoured past the kiosk counter. 'I wouldn't say no to a strawberry gelato.'

Somehow he'd known she would taste like strawberries.

He ordered strawberry for her and a coffee gelato for him.

'More coffee?'

'One of my vices,' he admitted. It wasn't something he was supposed to drink a lot of. Large quantities were considered incompatible with his occupation but he'd never been able to give it up completely.

'What are your other vices?' she asked, as they waited for their order.

'Fast cars.'

He knew she was waiting for him to say more. Sometimes he would quip about fast women but he wanted Ruby to think favourably of him. There was something different about her, something special, and it made him chose his words carefully. He didn't want to come across as flippant or careless. He hadn't been able to get her out of his head and he wanted to create a good impression.

'Don't eat it yet,' she admonished, as he attempted to dip the spoon into the gelato. 'Save it for a moment.'

He was happy to follow her direction. He was naturally right-handed and tasks that he'd never thought about were proving rather challenging when he had to rely on his left hand. He was happy to let the gelato soften a little more.

She pushed him up an inclined path towards a spectacular building perched on top of a hill. It was made almost entirely of glass. The central section had a huge domed ceiling and glass wings extended from either side and ended in curved glass walls. The panes of glass were clear, with the exception of some at the very top of the walls that were stained a peacock blue. The building must have stretched for fifty metres, if not further, and the summer sunlight bouncing off the glass made it look like a massive diamond.

'What is this place?'

'This is my favourite place.' She stepped around in front of his chair and waved one arm expansively towards it. 'It's the Palm House. Isn't it gorgeous?'

'It is,' he agreed.

Ruby's face was alight with pleasure. Her green eyes shone and he wished he had a camera to capture her expression.

'It might be a tad warm inside but we'll just stay a little while. Just long enough to eat our gelato,' she said as she wheeled him inside.

The floor was tiled in an intricate pattern of black, ochre and cream, and ornate plaster garden beds followed the curves of the building. Ruby pushed him along the tiled floor to the far end of one of the wings and tucked his chair into a little alcove, turning him so he had a view back along the central pathway. The path was lined with lush palms and the afternoon sun streamed through the glass walls and was filtered through the palm fronds.

Ruby sat on the cream plaster wall of the garden bed beside him and took an enormous scoop of her gelato. She tipped her head back and looked up at the domed glass ceiling as she sucked the gelato off the spoon. Her long, slim neck was exposed and he had a strong urge to kiss her throat, and then her mouth closed around the spoon while she slowly pulled the spoon out through her lips and he forgot all about her throat. All he could think about now were her lips. He watched, fascinated, as she ate her gelato.

The scoop she'd taken had been too big to eat all in one mouthful and the gelato that remained on the spoon had been moulded to the shape of the inside of her mouth. She put the spoon back into her mouth and sucked the rest of the gelato off it. He'd never seen anyone eat an ice cream that sensually before.

He could imagine the warmth of her mouth on his flesh as her lips closed around him and he felt a stirring in his groin as he watched her lick the spoon clean with a pointed pink tongue. It was good to know that some important parts of his anatomy hadn't been damaged in the accident.

He needed to adjust himself but it was hard to do when he only had one functioning hand and it was busy holding a cup of gelato. Some distraction was needed and he hoped conversation would suffice.

'What appeals to you about the palm house?' he asked. He was curious to hear her answer. The plants weren't the prettiest in the gardens, there were plenty of palms and a lot of dry-climate plants, the type that would maybe flower once a year, but they certainly weren't as beautiful or as sweet-smelling as others, but the building was stunning. He could understand if the building itself resonated with her. Ruby wasn't terribly forthcoming about herself. Perhaps finding out what made this spot important to her would give him some more insight into what made her tick.

She should have expected the question but she was caught unprepared with an answer. Perhaps she'd made a mistake, bringing him here. She feared her impulsiveness might make things awkward.

The palm house had been built in Germany in the nineteenth century and shipped out to Australia in pieces, before being reassembled in Adelaide. The plants it housed were from Madagascar. Ruby had always felt it was an odd combination, a European building filled with African plants and transplanted into an Australian garden, but somehow it worked and it gave her hope that even though she often felt out of place, maybe one day she too would find a place to belong. But she wasn't prepared to share those thoughts with Noah. Not at this point in time and probably not ever.

But Australia was filled with buildings that had their origins in other countries and the others didn't affect her in the same way. There was something more about this one. There was another reason why this building touched her soul and this reason she could share without revealing anything as personal.

'I love the idea that something made of glass, something so fragile and beautiful, can be strong and protective too. I love how it offers shelter to everything within it. I'd like to be like that.'

'You're not?'

'No. This building reminds me of Scarlett. My other sister.'

'The dark-haired one?' he asked.

Ruby nodded as she finished her gelato. 'She's the

family protector. She's the one who always has our backs, she's the one we turn to in a crisis. I'd like to be strong like that but I'm not sure that I am.'

Noah was watching her closely. He didn't comment and she wondered if she'd made him feel uncomfortable, if she'd shared too much. She stood up from the wall. It was time to move on. If they were moving maybe neither of them would feel that they had to speak. She didn't want him to ask any questions that she couldn't answer. He had finished his ice cream and their hour was up. As much as she'd enjoyed their excursion, it was time to return him to the hospital before she gave away any more of her secrets.

Ruby was glad to have Rose to herself when she got back to the ICU. She needed some time to sort through what had just happened with Noah. For a big man there was a sense of calmness about him that lulled her into a state of peace and security, and his unwavering blue-eyed gaze and his quiet, deep voice made it seem as though he really was interested in her and what she had to say. She'd have to be careful. It was too easy to let her guard down around him.

He'd been able to make her laugh. He'd been able to make her forget about life's problems for a while. All she could think about when she was with him, all she wanted to think about, was how she could get him to smile for her. The only time she had laughed in the past four days had been when she had been with him.

It made no sense. To all intents and purposes he was a stranger but somehow she just knew he was going to be more than that. He was going to be important.

Ruby didn't bother picking up the novel from beside the bed. She had far better things to talk to Rose about today.

'I've just had the most amazing time,' she told her as she pushed the strands of blond hair from her sister's forehead and kissed her gently. 'Have you ever walked into a room and seen a man—he might not be the most handsome or the tallest or the best dressed—you know nothing about him, you don't know if he's nice or funny or smart because he's a complete stranger, but for some inexplicable reason your eyes meet and you are drawn together? There's an instant connection and you know he feels it too. How could he not?'

Ruby pulled a tube of hand cream from her bag and squeezed a dollop into her palm. She picked up Rose's hand and massaged the cream into her skin. It was a soothing gesture, one she hoped would calm Rose as much as it would her. Ruby had been running on adrenalin since meeting Noah. Her heart was still racing and she needed to stop and take a breath. She needed to stop and take stock of what had just happened.

'You know the expression "Their eyes met across a crowded room"?' she said, as she worked the cream into Rose's hand. 'I always thought that was just something people said, but it's true. We weren't exactly in a crowded room, not the first time, but the second time, in the hospital kiosk, it really felt as though we were the only two people there. It was incredible.

'I have no idea whether you've ever felt like that about someone, Rosie. I'm sorry I've never asked you but I hope, one day, you have this feeling too. This feeling that some things happen for a reason. Some things are just meant to be.'

It was easy to talk to Rose because she couldn't talk

back. She couldn't ask any difficult questions and Ruby didn't have to feel self-conscious about these unfamiliar feelings.

'His name is Noah,' she continued, 'and he is the most gorgeous man. Handsome and nice, with the sexiest voice and a taste for adventure that, I admit, I find irresistible. There's something about him, Rose, that I can't ignore.

'I know you'd say I get carried away every time I meet someone new but Noah is different.

'Or maybe I am.'

She pondered that thought for a moment as she moved around the bed and began to massage Rose's other hand.

'Maybe I'm looking for something different, something more, and seeing it in Noah when it might not be there. You'd probably say I'm projecting but I can't deny how I felt when he held my hand. His skin was warm and his touch made the butterflies in my stomach take flight. And his smile just makes everything seem brighter. And have I told you about his eyes? He's got the most incredible eyes. That's where the connection is. He just has to look at me and I want to melt.

'He's exciting, Rosie. He makes me excited. He just has to look at me and I want him. And I'm going to have him, too. I have to.'

Ruby closed her eyes as she pictured Noah taking her into her arms. She could imagine running her fingers through his hair and over the rough stubble of his beard and feeling his arms around her. Feeling the heat of his body against hers and the beating of his heart.

She had always loved new beginnings, new possibilities, and a new relationship was no exception. She loved the feeling of an initial attraction, the excitement and anticipation. It was like having a fresh, clean slate. Like the beach in the early morning after the tide had gone out and there wasn't a mark on the sand until someone took that first step.

At the beginning of a relationship Ruby always felt like the freshly washed sand. When the other person didn't know her very well she got a chance to create a new Ruby. She got a chance to draw lines in the sand until she had made the person she wanted someone else to see.

She loved the opportunity to start afresh. There was always the hope that if she got enough chances to re-invent herself then one day she just might get it right.

'Hi, Rubes. I'm glad you're here. Jake and I need to talk to you.'

Ruby opened her eyes as Scarlett's voice interrupted her daydreams.

'What's up?'

'We have to make a decision about the wedding,' Scarlett said, as she sank into the spare chair beside Rose's bed.

'What do you mean?'

'The wedding can't go ahead as we'd planned,' Jake explained. 'Rose won't be out of hospital by the week-end and if we're going to postpone the wedding I'll need to notify people and cancel the reception venue.'

'You're going to postpone it?'

'We're not sure. We can't decide.'

'That's why we thought we'd get your opinion. You can be the impartial umpire.'

Ruby wasn't sure she was up to that task. 'I don't know if I can make that call.'

'Just listen to the options and give us your opinion,' Scarlett asked her.

'I suggested that we have the ceremony here,' Jake told her.

'In the ICU?'

He nodded. 'With just the bare minimum of people. Us, you, your mum, Rose obviously and my parents. We can get married here and then have the reception as planned. The other guests can just join us for the party.'

Ruby couldn't see what was wrong with that plan if they were determined to get married, but from Scarlett's expression it seemed that plan wasn't her favourite. 'What do you think, Scarlett?' she asked her sister.

'I'm not really in the mood for a party and that's what the reception will be.'

'Okay, let's cancel the reception and just get married,' Jake suggested. 'Keep it simple.'

'I want to wait,' Scarlett told him. 'I want to marry you but I want both my sisters to be there when I do.'

'Rose *would* be there.'

Scarlett shook her head. 'I want her to be part of it. I want to give her a chance to get well. I don't care about a big white wedding, that's never been my dream, I would marry you in a registry office or in the hospital chapel, but I want Ruby and Rose standing beside me.'

Ruby wasn't sure why they needed her opinion. If someone wanted to wait, wasn't that what you did? But she could tell that Jake was worried about what would happen if Rose didn't make it and she knew that was why he didn't want to delay but, to his credit, he didn't voice that thought.

'What do you reckon, Rubes?' Scarlett asked.

She wanted to tell them they should get married and that Rose would understand but she couldn't do it. She didn't actually believe that. She took a deep breath.

'If I were in Rose's shoes I'd want you to wait. I'm sorry, I know that probably sounds selfish but that's my opinion. Rose has made it through four days, she *will* get better. We have to believe that. Can you wait? Just long enough to give her a chance to wake up?'

'Please, Jake.' Scarlett held his hands as she pleaded with him. 'As soon as she's awake we'll get married, I promise.'

Jake nodded and smiled. 'Okay, I'm not going to argue with two of you. You're right, we'll wait for Rose.'

Scarlett threw her arms around his neck and kissed him. 'Thank you. I love you.'

'I love you too. You know I just want you to have a perfect wedding.'

Ruby wondered what they would do if things didn't go according to plan but she figured Jake would work something out. He seemed to know how to handle Scarlett. She was obviously the most important person in his life and his mission seemed to be to take care of her and keep her happy and he was apparently doing a good job of both.

Ruby wished again that she had someone like Jake in her life. Someone who would put her first. Someone who she knew would always be there for her.

Thursday, 18th December

Thursday looked as though it was going to be a very ordinary day. Ruby had been so confident yesterday that things were improving for Rose. She'd been convinced that Rose had turned the corner. She'd made it through four days—surely that counted for something—but someone had apparently forgotten to tell the doctors the good news and they had a different perspective to Ruby and she didn't like what they told her. She had to admit it wasn't all *bad* news but what she didn't understand was why it couldn't be all *good* news.

She hated herself for not coping. She hated knowing she wasn't strong enough to deal with this but that didn't change the fact that it was true.

She had to get away from the ICU. She needed some time and space to work out why she was so upset.

She paced the hospital corridors until, once again, she found herself outside Noah's room. That was no surprise. For the past two days she had felt best when she'd been with him. She couldn't explain why that was, she still hadn't quite been able to work out what it was about him that made her feel better—all she knew was that he brightened her day.

Was it his rebellious streak, his taste for adventure that made her feel she could escape from the real world when she was with him?

Was it his sense of capability and control? He was gorgeous and big and she got a sense that he could and would protect her. Even though she knew that was a ridiculous notion at the moment, given that he was being held together by metal rods and slings and painkillers, but he still seemed capable of anything.

Was it the fact he was able to make her laugh, something she needed badly at this point in time?

Or was it his smile and his warm blue eyes that fixed her under his spell?

She pushed open his door, hoping her timing was good and he'd had his daily physio and would be happy for her company.

'Ruby!' His obvious pleasure turned to concern. 'What's wrong? Is it Rose?'

Maybe it was simply the sense that he knew her already? He'd taken one look at her and had somehow known she was upset. How did he know her so well? Did he feel that same connection?

Ruby could feel her emotions building. Tears were threatening but she couldn't have said whether they were being caused by Noah's concern or by her own concern for her sister. She nodded.

'What's happened? Is it bad news?'

'Not completely,' she sniffed, fighting back tears. 'She's responding to the antibiotics, the rash isn't spreading and the septicaemia is under control. They're going to lighten the sedation so she'll gradually wake up and be weaned off the life support.'

'That sounds like good news to me.'

'It's mostly good news but they are also talking about the possibility that they may have to amputate some of her toes and they're worried about her kidney function too.'

'So things aren't perfect but could they still be worse?'

'Yes, but I don't want them to be worse, I want them to be better.' She knew she sounded spoilt and self-indulgent but she couldn't help how she felt. She tried to explain her feelings more succinctly. 'You're right, things could be a lot worse, and I know I'm being silly, but all our lives we've been defined a certain way and I don't want things to change.'

'Defined how?'

'Scarlett is the clever one, Rose is the pretty one…'

'And you are?'

'I'm supposed to be the fun one. But I'm not feeling very fun today,' she admitted. Ruby did like to have fun. If people saw her having fun she thought they wouldn't notice that she was lonely. And by going out and having fun she made sure she had company. It was a win-win situation. 'And I don't want Rose to have scars.'

'You said she *may* need surgery so if, and I'll say it again, *if,* she needs that surgery, it's only toes, it won't change the way she looks. She'll still be pretty. I think you, on the other hand, need to get out of here and have some fun. I will take charge today, as long as you agree to push me wherever I decide to go. We need to get out into the real world. You need to be kept busy.'

Ruby was happy to let Noah take control. She didn't feel like being in charge today. He signed himself out and then directed her to the cosmopolitan hub of Rundle Street, one block to the south. A two-block strip of fashion boutiques, coffee shops and pubs, it was busy with the lunchtime crowd. The street was festooned with Christmas decorations and the boutique windows showcased a colourful display of party dresses for the festive season. Ruby had never felt less like celebrating Christmas and, once again, her circumstances meant that the holiday had completely slipped her mind.

'That would look nice on you.'

She paused in front of a shop window when Noah pointed out a stunning dress on the display. It was a simple black dress and she could imagine how it would look on her. She had very similar proportions to display mannequins, long, thin limbs and no boobs worth mentioning, but the dress had been cleverly, and heavily, beaded, which created the illusion of a figure that was far curvier than hers. The figure of a woman. Her fair skin was a good foil for black and Ruby thought Noah was right—the style probably would suit her—but she had never owned anything as beautiful as this and she couldn't imagine wearing it.

'Where would I ever wear it? It's not really the thing for Byron Bay, it's far too fancy.' Byron Bay wasn't known for its formality and Ruby didn't really enjoy shopping. She bought clothes from thrift shops, knowing that the money was going to a good cause, and when she moved, as she was often wont to do, she donated the clothes back. They were only clothes after all. She looked at the dress and knew it would cost more than her entire wardrobe put together. 'It's far too beautiful for me.'

'I disagree.'

Did he really think she was pretty enough to wear that dress? He was looking at her so intently that she almost believed him but his attention embarrassed her so she took off again, pushing him in front of her, avoiding his eyes as she searched for a table that could accommodate them for a coffee.

There were crowds of people sitting at sidewalk tables, enjoying a glass of wine with lunch or a beer at one of the several pubs in the street, but she continued past them all. Noah shouldn't drink in his condition so she didn't feel like she should offer to stop. The crowd sitting outside the Exeter Hotel was particularly boisterous and caught Noah's attention.

'Shall I buy you a drink?' he offered. 'Would a glass of wine be a good stress-reliever?'

Ruby shook her head. 'I don't drink alcohol,' she told him.

'You don't? Why not?' He sounded surprised but Ruby was used to that reaction.

'I don't like the way it makes me feel.' That was a half-truth. The rest of the story was that she'd made a few bad decisions when she'd been drinking, actually more than a few, but she wasn't going to elaborate. That was definitely not a conversation she planned on having with Noah. She parked him at the next empty café table they came across and went inside to order, hoping that would be enough to end the discussion.

'Are you feeling better yet?' Noah asked, as she poured herself a second cup of green tea from the pot.

'Not really.' She sighed. 'It's been a big twenty-four hours since I saw you yesterday.'

In just a couple of days spending time with Noah had become a good foil for the time spent in ICU. Time spent worrying about Rose, time spent getting nowhere, time spent on edge around her mother was counteracted by Noah's ability to relax her, to make her laugh and to let her think about other things, but he wasn't having his usual influence on her today.

'Something else is bothering you?' he asked.

Ruby knew she wasn't being great company and she owed it to Noah to explain why. 'Scarlett and Jake were supposed to be getting married this weekend but they've had to postpone the wedding.'

'Because of Rose?'

Ruby nodded.

'You don't agree with their decision?'

'No, I do. They want to wait until Rose is better, or at least conscious, which I think is the right thing to do… But it means that I will need to stay in Adelaide longer, which means I need to find somewhere to live.' That was the crux of the matter. It was another issue that she had to deal with but, once again, she didn't know where to start.

'I'm not following you. Where are you living now?'

'At Scarlett's, but I want to give them some privacy and I can't afford to stay in a hotel.'

'Why don't you stay with your mother?'

'I can't stay with Lucy, we clash too much, we always have, and it's not good for anyone and especially not at the moment. We're all under enough stress, without adding living arrangements into the mix.'

'What about a friend? You said you had friends who worked at the hospital.'

'I may have exaggerated a little.'

Noah smiled as Ruby continued.

'I left Adelaide when I was sixteen. I haven't lived here for ten years and I lost touch with my friends. I do have one friend who is a nurse at the hospital but she and her husband haven't been married all that long and that would make me feel more uncomfortable than staying with Scarlett.'

Ruby realised that for the first time since they'd met they had talked more about her than about him. She'd forgotten his talent for turning the conversation back to her and she'd forgotten to be careful. She still wasn't sure why she found herself telling him her story. She never talked about herself. Never. She'd only intended to tell him about the wedding and here she was, talking to him about her past.

Noah was silent for a little bit. He finished his coffee,

also in silence, and Ruby started to worry that she'd said too much.

'Can you cook?' he asked, as he put his cup down.

Ruby frowned. 'What?'

'Cooking—are you any good at it?'

'I'm okay.' Pasta and stir fries counted as cooking, didn't they?

'I have a suggestion for you, then.'

'Really?' Ruby couldn't imagine what he could suggest. Or what cooking had to do with anything.

'I need a nurse-cum-housekeeper.'

'You do? What on earth for?'

'My racing team have rented a furnished apartment, it was where I was staying before the accident put me in hospital. The hospital has agreed to discharge me, which means I can go back to the apartment, but I won't be able to manage on my own. I've got one good arm and it's my left one, which isn't particularly useful when I'm right-handed, and I've got one good leg. I won't be able to use crutches for a few weeks so I'm stuck in this chair. I need some help with general tasks, cooking and showering and the like, and it makes sense if I can have one person who can do it all. Craig, the team manager, was going to arrange some agency help but I'd prefer it if it was you.'

'Me?'

'It makes sense, doesn't it? I already know you and you're a nurse. The apartment has plenty of room. The team would pay you a wage and the arrangement would give you somewhere to live. If you don't mind being a nurse and cook. The apartment is on the other side of the south parklands, only a few minutes from the hospital. It would still be convenient for you in terms of visiting Rose as well.

'Why don't you think about it and let me know tomorrow? As soon as I've got some help organised, I can get out of here.'

She didn't need to think about it. If someone else got the job she wouldn't have any reason to see him again. He would be out of hospital and out of her life. And she didn't want that. There were probably half a dozen reasons why this was a bad idea but she couldn't think of any at present. All she could think of was one very good reason to do this—she would be able to keep seeing Noah.

'I'll do it.'

It was an easy decision. She just hoped it was the right one.

CHAPTER FIVE

Friday, 19th December

'YOU'RE DOING WHAT?'

Scarlett's reaction shouldn't have surprised Ruby. The role of sensible older sister, who looked out for everyone else, came naturally to her, but Ruby hadn't really expected her announcement to be a big deal. To Ruby the arrangement made perfect sense in every way.

'I'm going to be a live-in nurse.'

'For a man you've just met?'

'It's a job, Scarlett. I need somewhere to live and I need an income. This works for me.'

'But you don't know anything about him!'

'I know enough, as much as I would about any client. If he was eighty-five and infirm you wouldn't be carrying on like this, would you?'

'But he's not, is he?'

'No.' Ruby grinned. 'He's seriously hot. It's much more fun that way,' she teased.

Scarlett rolled her eyes and turned to Candice. 'Have you met him?' she asked.

'No, but all reports seem to agree with Ruby. Apparently he's gorgeous and he's loaded and he's nice.'

Candice shrugged. 'As a nurse, I can think of plenty of worse jobs than being Noah Christiansen's live-in carer.'

Ruby knew Scarlett had called in reinforcements to lend weight to her argument but it seemed as though her plan to invite Candice to join them for dinner might have backfired.

'But I don't understand why you have to live in.' Scarlett wasn't giving up easily. 'You can stay with us.'

'Scarlett, really, be logical. I appreciate the offer but I'm not going to stay with you. You're supposed to be on your honeymoon, you're seven and a half months pregnant and Jake is about to start his internship. You've got enough to deal with.'

'Well, if you need somewhere to live and someone to look after, you could move back in with Mum and Rose. I'm sure Mum could use some help.'

Ruby felt a little bit guilty. She had fully intended to pull her weight, to grow up and take some responsibility, and yet what was she doing? At the first opportunity she was bailing. 'You know how that would end,' she protested. 'I can't move back in with Mum. I left when I was sixteen and I'm not going back now. I can still help with Rose once she's out of hospital. I can take her to appointments or whatever, I'll just have to juggle things.'

Scarlett turned to Candice, who, in Ruby's opinion, seemed to have the good sense to stay out of the argument. 'You and Ewan have a spare room, don't you?'

'Scarlett, stop,' Ruby interrupted. 'I've made my decision.'

'You've got to stop running, Ruby.'

She knew she'd eventually have to learn to deal with things but she couldn't make herself do it just yet. It was much easier to run off with Noah. But at least she was planning on staying in town. 'I'm not running,' she argued. 'Noah will need help for a while and this gives me something to do and somewhere to stay while Rose recovers and until you and Jake can get married.'

Noah was her escape from the stress and drama of her family and, while she knew she was taking the easy option, she had no intention of changing her mind. But she was prepared to extend Scarlett an olive branch. 'If it will make you feel any better, you can meet him beforehand,' she offered, assuming that Scarlett would be too preoccupied with other matters to take her up on this suggestion.

Saturday, 20th December

'Noah?'

His hospital door opened and an attractive woman with dark hair stepped into his room. 'I'm—'

He had been expecting Ruby and this definitely wasn't her, but he recognised her anyway. 'Scarlett,' he interrupted.

A frown appeared between the woman's dark eyes. 'How do you know who I am?'

'I remember you from the ICU. It's a pleasure to meet you.'

'I wanted to talk to you—'

'About Ruby,' he interrupted again.

'Yes.'

Scarlett shut the door and Noah started to laugh.

'What's so funny?' she asked.

'Ruby warned me to expect you and I've been wondering how long it would take before you came to check me out and make sure I'm not a crazy serial killer. Even if I didn't remember you from the ICU, you're just like Ruby described. Am I right in assuming you want to know what my intentions are?'

Scarlett folded her arms and rested them on her pregnant belly. 'Something like that.'

'I promise everything is above board and totally legitimate. I've got some major rehab ahead of me if I want to get back to work in the foreseeable future. I'm not going to make it if I'm stuck in here for any length of time. Ruby told me you're a doctor, you know getting out of here will be the best thing for my recovery,' he said, hoping to appeal to her practical side, 'but in order to get discharged, I need some help. I'm not kidnapping Ruby, I'm not taking advantage of her, I'm not sleeping with her, I'm employing her. As my carer.'

'Does she know that?'

'Yes. This was her decision and she is an adult.'

'She doesn't always act like one.'

'Ruby told me she hasn't lived here for ten years. She must have managed to run her life without any help while she's been away.'

Scarlett's expression made Noah think that maybe that wasn't the case. He wondered what had gone wrong in the past. *Intriguing.*

He had seen Ruby retreat into her shell on several occasions but although he was gradually learning more about her it was all in bits and pieces and he had suspected she was deliberately withholding information. Scarlett's expression confirmed his suspicions and further piqued his curiosity.

He knew she didn't drink alcohol but she hadn't really explained why. Likewise, she'd told him she'd moved away at the age of sixteen but had told him nothing further. He'd have to remember to ask her where she'd gone when she'd left and find out what she'd been up to for the past ten years. Sixteen was young to move away, unless her whole family had gone, but he had the distinct impression that hadn't been the case.

He'd have plenty of opportunity to learn everything he could about her—they were about to spend a lot of time together. He was excited about that. She fascinated him.

'She's a bit vulnerable at the moment.' The warning note in Scarlett's words was evident. 'She doesn't cope well with stress.'

'And you're not sure that she's thinking clearly?' He agreed she was going through a stressful time but he thought she was coping remarkably well. Most people would find the week Ruby had just had stressful and it was his opinion that Ruby knew exactly what she was doing. He thought that she coped better with life than other people, for whatever reason, liked to believe.

'Don't you think it's strange that she's jumped at this chance when she knows nothing about you?'

'It's a job, nothing more,' he said, hoping he wouldn't be caught out in a lie, but at this stage that was all it was. Scarlett didn't need to know anything else, not yet. 'I can't manage on my own—I need someone to give me a hand and Ruby needs somewhere to stay. This made sense—to both of us.'

'She's doesn't need a place to stay,' Scarlett argued. 'She can stay with me.'

'She doesn't want to.' Noah wasn't about to back down, it wasn't in his nature. Scarlett might have her opinion but he had one too and he was never afraid of a challenge. 'She wants to give you some space, as I'm sure she's told you. I'm not denying it suits me to have Ruby look after me but it suits her too.'

Monday, 22nd December

It was the beginning of a new week and Ruby had a feeling things were going to improve. The doctors were beginning to wean Rose from the ventilator. Her sedation had been lightened gradually over the past few days and there had been definite signs she was waking up. Her blood gases were good and everyone, Ruby included, was feeling extremely optimistic and positive about the outcome, and when Ruby stopped into the ICU and saw Rose's eyes were open she knew she'd been right.

'Rose! You're awake!' She turned to Lucy, who was sitting beside Rose, holding her hand while the nurse recorded her obs. 'Why didn't anyone call me?'

'The doctors were just doing a trial to see if she could breathe on her own,' Lucy told her. 'She did so well they decided to take her off the ventilator but they've only just removed it. There hasn't been time to call anyone yet.'

'How are you feeling?' Ruby asked, as she bent over to kiss Rose.

'Weird.' Rose's voice was raspy.

'You sound like me.' Ruby smiled.

'I know I've been here a week and I can remember some things but I don't know what happened when. I remember you reading to me. I liked that.'

Ruby felt a twinge of guilt. The only reason she hadn't given up reading initially had been because Noah had asked her to continue. If he hadn't, she might have closed the book and left it at that, and Rose wouldn't have that memory.

'And I remember Noah.'

'You do?'

'You made him sound hard to forget.'

The nurse interrupted them as she spoke to Rose. 'Your respiratory muscles will get tired easily,' she said. 'I'd suggest you keep conversation to a minimum for today and just concentrate on breathing again. Your muscles need to become fit.'

'It's okay,' Ruby replied. 'I'll do the talking for us both.' Today was the day she was going to start her new job as Noah's carer. She was looking forward to it, probably far more than she ought to and certainly far more than she would admit to anyone, but she couldn't keep the note of excitement out of her voice as she filled Rose in on what she'd missed.

'He gets discharged soon,' she said, as she checked the time. 'And then it will be your turn next.' Ruby was convinced now that Rose would get out of here too. 'I'd better go but I'll see you later, okay?'

Ruby left Rose and Lucy and made her way down to Noah's ward. He was ready and waiting. She accompanied Noah, the nurse who was responsible for his discharge and Craig Bellamy, Noah's team manager, out of the hospital. It was quite a procession but in a few minutes Ruby and Noah would be on their own. Noah's discharge would be complete and Ruby would be responsible for his well-being. She was on an emotional high. Her day couldn't be going any better.

Craig had been busy organising all the things Ruby had thought she might need to manage Noah's care, including transport. 'The car is this way,' he said, as he led them through the car park.

Ruby's heart plummeted when Craig pushed the button to unlock the car and she heard the 'beep beep' and saw the corresponding flash of the indicator lights.

'No way! I can't drive a racing car!'

The car was completely covered in writing and company logos from the front fender to the back bumper bar. Ruby wasn't a particularly confident driver and this was definitely a 'look at me' type of car. There was no chance she could drive through the streets inconspicuously in this. She didn't want to draw attention to herself but there'd be no way to avoid it in this vehicle.

'It's just an ordinary car,' Noah replied. 'The paintwork is just part of our sponsorship deal, it's only advertising.'

'And you were worried about being seen in those sunglasses I bought you from the gift shop?' Ruby said, as she checked it out.

'I get paid to wear glasses from a certain designer. I was more worried that someone would recognise me and think the designer had lost his touch,' Noah explained with a smile, as Craig opened the passenger side door.

'Well, I'm not sure that having me behind the wheel is going to be good for your image or your sponsors either,' Ruby said, when she looked inside.

'Why not?'

'It's a manual.' She hadn't thought to ask for an automatic, she'd never imagined the car would have a manual gearbox.

'Can't you drive a manual?'

'I can but not very well. It's years since I've had to. I assumed it would be an automatic.'

'I can arrange something else but it will take a few hours,' Craig offered.

Ruby shrugged. Her day was going rapidly downhill but she wasn't going to let a few minor problems dampen her mood. She'd have to cope. 'It's all right, I'll give it a go.' She turned to Noah and added the proviso, 'As long as you're prepared to take the risk?'

'I make my living speeding around a race circuit with twenty other cars all travelling in excess of two hundred kilometres per hour and all jockeying for the same position. You can't be as dangerous as that!'

The sound of his laughter bolstered her enthusiasm and she grinned. 'You'd think not, so let's hope I don't surprise you.'

With the nurse's assistance Noah transferred from the hospital wheelchair into the car as Craig opened the boot and ran through some final details with Ruby.

'The electric wheelchair is disassembled and is in here. Will you be all right to put it together?'

'I should be able to work that out,' she said. She didn't want Craig to think she was completely useless, he might decide not to employ her. Noah had asked for an electric wheelchair and they'd decided that with left-hand controls he should be able to operate it and this would give him a bit of independence, at least around the apartment.

'Most of Noah's things are already there and I've had the rest of the equipment you requested delivered to the penthouse too. Here is a credit card for your use, the details are inside here, and these are the access cards for the apartment. I think that's it,' Craig said, as he handed her a large yellow envelope.

Ruby took a deep breath as she slid into the driver's seat. This was it. They were alone. For the next few weeks she and Noah would be almost inseparable. She was both eager and terrified. She was excited at the prospect but nervous that the experience wasn't going to live up to her expectations. She glanced across at Noah. He grinned at her, his blue eyes full of mischief, as she turned the key in the ignition. She relaxed. She was pretty sure she was going to enjoy the next month or two.

She put the car into gear and somehow managed not to stall the engine, but she didn't give the car quite enough fuel and she bunny-hopped out of the parking lot and around the East End, much to Noah's amusement.

She wasn't sure she liked the sound of his laugh quite so much when he was laughing at her expense. 'You might not be laughing after a few days of this,' she told him.

'You don't think you'll improve?'

'One can only hope,' she said, as she flicked the indicator on and turned left through the parklands. 'Oh, hell.'

'What's wrong?'

'I didn't mean to come this way. I've always hated this roundabout,' she said, as the notorious Britannia roundabout loomed ahead of them.

'Get in the right-hand lane and hug the roundabout,' he told her. 'That way it won't matter what the other cars do, you'll be out of their way.'

But even with the new dual roundabout system Ruby

made hard work of it. Another car cut across in front of her and she slammed on the brakes and just avoided stalling the engine. That rattled her and she almost missed the exit, but eventually she was through safely and in a couple of minutes Noah was directing her into the car park under the apartment block.

Ruby swiped the card that let them access the lift to the penthouse and tried, unsuccessfully, not to act like a country bumpkin when the doors slid open and she stepped straight into an apartment that could have come from the pages of a glossy high-end interiors magazine. Noah had already mastered control of the electric wheelchair and she let him go in front of her, glad he couldn't see the stunned expression on her face.

The apartment was superb. The polished floors of the foyer led into an open-plan kitchen, living and dining room. The kitchen was built for entertaining with a massive granite island bench, an industrial range hood, a double oven and a state-of-the-art coffee machine that Ruby suspected she'd never work out.

Modular leather lounges were clustered in front of floor-to-ceiling windows that looked out onto an enormous balcony with views from the hills to the city and out to the coast. The living and dining area were separated by a pod-shaped wood fire, which was suspended from the ceiling, and a baby grand piano was tucked into the corner of the room. Ruby had never seen anything quite like it before. The apartment was luxurious, expensive, modern and stunning.

Fortunately, it was single level, with the bedrooms positioned on the opposite side of the living room. The main bedroom had city views and a small en suite bathroom, which was not designed to accommodate Noah's chair. He insisted that Ruby take the main bedroom and he would take the room across the hall. Ruby quelled her disappointment at the idea of separate bedrooms. What had she expected? That he would want to jump straight into bed with her? He really wasn't in any state to be fooling around. Not yet. She tried to concentrate as they finished the tour and Noah gave her a lesson in how to work the coffee machine.

Once he'd had his caffeine fix he was ready to move on to other business. He took a whiteboard marker from one of the kitchen drawers and handed it to Ruby. 'Can I ask you to draw up a calendar on one of the windows?'

'A calendar?'

Noah nodded. 'I need somewhere to record my weekly goals and rehab plans, including my daily exercise routine and appointments.'

Ruby looked at the enormous, and spotlessly clean, window. He wanted her to write on that!? 'Why do you want to put it up here?' she asked. 'Why don't you just save all this into your phone? I can do that for you if you like.'

'I want a constant reminder of where I'm at and where I need to get to,' he explained. 'And if you have to drive me to my appointments it'll be easier if we can both see what's happening at a glance. I need you to write it because if I do it left-handed neither of us will be able to read it.'

Ruby shrugged and started drawing squares on the windows and writing the date in little numbers in the top left-hand corner of each.

He stopped her when she reached the fourteenth of February.

'Why are you finishing there?' She was positive

he'd told her the racing season started at the end of the month—it was the same time as Scarlett's baby was due, which was why she'd remembered it—but Noah's home-made calendar was finishing two weeks earlier. 'I thought you said the first race wasn't until the end of Feb?'

'It isn't but there's a test day in Sydney on the four-teenth. The teams get out on the race track to test the cars. That's my goal. I need to be fit for that weekend if I'm to have any chance of starting the season. I'll have to undergo a fitness test prior to that so that's what I'm aiming for.'

Ruby did a quick calculation. 'But that'll only be nine weeks since your accident.'

'I admit I might be pushing uphill to make it back but if I want to keep my spot on the team then that's my goal. I need to keep focused.'

'All right, then, what needs to go up here?'

'I've got a physio appointment tomorrow morning at ten-thirty. There'll be physio three times a week and you'll have to help me with daily exercises here. I have fortnightly specialist appointments, first one on the twenty-ninth of this month, and I'll have X-rays every four weeks. I'm hoping that after the next lot of X-rays I'll be allowed out of this chair and onto crutches. My elbow and collarbone should be able to take some weight by then.

'Can you make a note to remind me to speak to the physio to see if I can hire some Pilates equipment to use here? And hopefully I can get into the pool sooner rather than later for supported exercises.'

'Did the specialist tell you when you might expect to be able to weight-bear through your right leg?'

'No, that will depend on the X-rays, but as soon as I get the okay we can order an exercise bike or maybe I'll just use the gym here.'

'There's a gym?'

'Yes. A gym, an outdoor pool, an indoor pool, a spa, sauna, tennis court and a small cinema. We can go on a tour a bit later.'

Ruby couldn't imagine ever wanting to use the gym, she hated gyms with a passion, but she didn't mind swimming, although it sounded as though she'd have very little free time. Looking after Noah was sounding as though it was going to be the full-time job she had been employed for.

'So Pilates, pool exercises, cycling and gym work? How fit do you need to be?'

'It's not so much normal aerobic fitness. It's not sprint fitness, I need strength and endurance. The focus is on strengthening my core, back, legs, arms, but I also need endurance as the races can take up to three hours and my heart rate will sit between one seventy and two hundred beats per minute for the entire race.'

If her job was to help him to achieve his goals, she needed to pay attention. 'What do you need strength for?'

'It takes eighty kilograms of force to depress the brake pedal, twenty kilos to turn the steering-wheel and twenty-five kilograms to change gear. I might change gear twelve hundred times in a race. Core strength helps produce those forces and also helps me to absorb all the bumps and vibrations and cope with the G forces.'

Ruby couldn't believe he knew all these facts and figures off the top of his head. 'What is your normal exercise routine?'

'In pre-season, which is now, I'd train six days a week. Four gym sessions, two Pilates sessions and four endurance sessions, either a swim, a ride or a run. During the season I'll cut back. There'd be two rest days, usually Thursday and Monday, which are either side of an event, and then three race days, Friday, Saturday and Sunday, which only leaves a couple of days to fit in a gym session and then a Pilates session, followed with some cardio. I'm normally at home in Queensland for pre-season but obviously the accident has thrown a spanner in the works so I'll have to work extra hard to get fit in time for the first race.'

It was no wonder he looked as good as he did, she thought. He spent all his spare time exercising.

'There's only so much you can do,' Ruby told him. 'Your bones need time to heal.'

Noah shrugged. 'I was pretty fit before the accident, not quite peak fitness but close, so I'm hoping that will help to speed up my recovery. I just need to progress my rehab as quickly as I can. If I don't recover fast enough I'll be replaced, and I'm determined to give myself every chance to be back behind the wheel for the beginning of the season.'

Ruby wasn't about to argue about his fitness. He certainly looked like a man in peak physical condition—at least he did if you ignored his injuries. But her nursing training told her that he had a monumental task ahead of him but there was no denying he had the right attitude and even she was starting to believe that he might just pull this off. Although there was one thing he hadn't mentioned.

'What about driving practice?' she asked.

'None of us actually do that much driving in the

off season so I can really just focus on rehab. You can exercise with me,' he suggested. 'It's always nicer to have company.'

Ruby laughed. 'I refuse to exercise,' she told him. 'Unless it's dancing or swimming, and I enjoy those things so they don't count. Don't expect me to run.'

'I won't be running anywhere for the moment either. Have you tried Pilates? You might like that.'

She wasn't sure about Pilates either. She'd rather have sex, and lots of it, but now was probably not the time to tell Noah that. 'We'll see,' was all she said.

CHAPTER SIX

Tuesday, 23rd December

EVERYTHING WAS TAKING a bit longer than Ruby had anticipated this morning and she wasn't sure if it was because she was tired or whether she was just out of practice with this side of nursing. She'd been doing agency work in a teenage drug and alcohol counselling centre in Byron Bay but she hadn't told Noah that in case he'd decided she wasn't the right person for this job. And she'd desperately wanted this job.

But she had tossed and turned for the better part of the night—she couldn't blame her bed, it was made up with soft linens, plump pillows and it was huge and comfortable but with far too much room for one person—she hadn't been able to stop thinking about Noah asleep in his own huge bed across the hall. He'd fallen sleep in front of the television and she'd woken him to put him to bed still dressed in his shorts and T-shirt. If he hadn't been so exhausted from the transfer from the hospital and so badly injured she would have been tempted to climb into bed with him. It had been sexual frustration that had kept her awake until the early hours of the morning but there was nothing she could do about that yet. She'd just have to be patient.

Noah was waiting for a shower and it was her job to help him. That was what she was being paid for, not to fantasise about getting into bed with him, but undressing him did nothing to deter her imagination.

Ruby wheeled him into the main bathroom before carefully removing his shirt. It was the first time she'd seen him shirtless since the ICU and he looked every bit as good as she remembered. She tried not to stare but she did take her time pulling his T-shirt over his head, which gave her a chance to check him out unobserved.

He had no body fat and his torso was smooth and trim with well-defined pectorals and abdominal muscles, but his arms were to die for. She was desperate to run her hands from his shoulders down over his biceps and forearms all the way to his fingers.

She chatted away as she removed his boxer shorts and helped him to transfer to the shower chair. She tried telling herself he was just like any other patient and to stop feasting her eyes on him but it was difficult to do. Every part of him was oversized and glorious. His skin was smooth, and while his arms and legs were lightly covered with blond hair his trunk was hair-free except for a narrow trail of fair hair that ran south from his navel. Ruby averted her eyes, afraid she'd be caught out, as she settled him into the shower chair before removing his sling.

She ran the shower and adjusted the temperature then pushed the shower chair under the flow of water. Noah was able to take care of most of his ablutions using his left hand but Ruby needed to help him with his left side and his hair. But as she stood behind him to wash his hair she realised that the maxi-dress she'd thrown on that morning to combat the forecast heat of the day was not the most suitable attire. She hadn't considered the logistics of the bathroom when she'd dressed. It was spacious with ultramodern fittings.

That was good because the shower chair had rolled easily behind the floor-to-ceiling frameless glass shower screen but the shower head was enormous and the water poured from it like a waterfall. It was nothing like the hospital showers and there was no way she was going to be able to wash him and stay out of the spray.

Noah's hair was thick and long and it took ages just to get the water to penetrate the strands. She squeezed shampoo into the palm of her hand and worked it through his hair, massaging it into his scalp. Noah closed his eyes and she felt him relax under her touch. Ruby took that as an invitation to feast her eyes on his perfect proportions as she washed his hair. She tipped his head backwards to rinse the shampoo out. His eyes remained closed and she was tempted to run her fingers over the planes of his face. His lips were slightly parted, which made it look as if he was waiting to be kissed. She wondered what he'd taste like. Coffee, she suspected.

Rivulets of water were running down his chest, coursing between his pectoral muscles and gathering along his sternum. Ruby watched transfixed as the water made its way towards his stomach. He had dropped the washcloth in his lap, protecting his modesty, but Ruby's eyes didn't need to travel any further, she didn't need to see what lay beneath the cloth, she had the perfect image captured in her memory. By the time she had finished rinsing his hair she was soaking wet and more than slightly aroused. She needed to gather herself together.

'All done,' she said, as she flicked off the water and pushed him out of the shower. She exchanged the wet washcloth in his lap for a towel and used a second towel to dry him off. She stood behind him to dry his hair, squeezing the water from it before moving around to stand in front of him to dry his arms and chest. Her wet dress clung to her breasts, stomach and thighs, leaving little to the imagination, and she could see him looking at her as she leant over him. Her temperature rose steadily as he devoured her with his eyes.

She dropped her gaze and her hands. Her head dipped as she dried his stomach. Her head was aligned with his. He was close enough to kiss. All she needed to do was lean in a fraction more. She wanted him to close the gap. She wanted him to kiss her.

He lifted his head. She met his eyes. They had darkened considerably as his pupils dilated. He put his hand over hers, stilling her movements. She waited to feel his lips on hers but he moved no further.

'I can manage this bit,' he said. He took over, drying himself from the waist down.

She waited for him to finish before helping him to put his arm back into the sling. She leant over him, fiddling with the straps. She could feel his breath on her cheek. She lifted her eyes. His lips were millimetres away, tempting and teasing her.

She still wanted him to kiss her but instead she put her arms around him and helped him to stand.

They stood, hip to hip, chest to chest. Noah was locked in her embrace. They were as close as lovers.

Ruby's nipples were erect, reacting to the dampness

of her dress and the sensation of Noah's body pressed up against hers. She could feel her nipples brushing his chest. She was aroused and she could feel he was too.

She looked up at him and met his blue-eyed gaze and this time when their eyes met he didn't hesitate. He dipped his head and claimed her for himself.

Ruby met him halfway, opening her mouth under the pressure of his lips, giving in to desire. She held on to him a little tighter, wrapping her arms a little more firmly around his back, her hands pressed into his shoulder blades as she fought to maintain their balance as their kiss deepened.

He tasted just like she'd imagined. Soft, warm and sweet, with faint traces of his morning coffee. She pressed her hands a little harder into his shoulder blades, trying to bring him closer as he cupped her bottom with his left hand and locked them together. Her knees felt like jelly and she wasn't sure who was supporting who.

Noah broke first.

'I have to sit down.'

Five simple words were enough to jolt her back to reality. And the reality was that he was badly injured and needed all his concentration to keep his balance while standing on one leg.

While she knew the attraction was mutual, the bottom line was that he wasn't physically capable of taking this any further. Yet.

'Sorry.'

'Don't be sorry.' He grinned as he lowered himself into the wheelchair. 'You should be thankful. If I was fully fit you wouldn't be able to keep up. If you start exercising now, you might be able to handle me.'

Ruby raised an eyebrow as she dropped a towel into

his lap. The towel concealed his erection but Ruby was pleased to see from his reaction that she affected him as much as he did her. 'Is that a challenge?' she asked.

'If you want it to be. But it's only fair to warn you that I love a challenge.'

'Is that right?'

She was shivering now but she knew the goose bumps on her arms were more likely to be caused by the look in Noah's eyes than by her wet dress. But that didn't matter. If he wanted a challenge she'd give him one. She was eager to see how he coped with her next move.

She grabbed the skirt of her maxi-dress and turned her back to him as she pulled her dress over her head. She wasn't wearing a bra, she rarely did, but she kept her back turned towards him, giving him an eyeful of naked skin but with just a hint of the curve of her breast. She grabbed another towel from the rack and began to rub herself down, drying herself off. She held the towel across her chest as she dried one arm and then the other. She lifted one leg and propped her foot on the edge of the bath to rub that leg before swapping to the other.

'God, Ruby, that's not fair.' Noah's voice was a soft, deep groan.

'You're not the only one who likes a challenge,' she said, as she straightened up and wrapped the towel around her chest, tucking one end inside the other to hold it in place. 'We'll soon see who can keep up with whom, won't we?'

'I'm feeling better already,' he said, as he looked her up and down, and suddenly she wasn't sure that the towel offered enough protection against the force of his gaze.

'No, you're right. You need time to regain your strength. I don't want you falling apart on me. Besides, we haven't got all day,' she continued. 'I need to get you to your physio appointment.' Now that their intentions were clear Ruby knew there would be time later to act on their feelings. She just hoped she didn't have to wait too long.

Ruby and Noah spent the rest of that day and the next dancing around the issue of their attraction. She was being paid to take care of him and she was sure the rules would prevent her from having any sort of physical relationship with him. She wasn't having second thoughts about what she wanted, only about what was ethical. But it was a moot point really. He was still in a lot of pain, particularly by the end of the day, and she knew he wasn't ready for sex, despite what he thought.

Showering him in the morning was sweet torture—seeing him naked for all the wrong reasons was driving her crazy—but she wanted to make sure he could go the distance and she didn't want to risk any further injury.

Ruby had never been with anyone twenty-four seven before. Trying to do her job and ignore their chemistry was exhausting. And Noah wasn't the most compliant patient. He was finding it difficult being confined to a chair, and he was struggling with sitting still. Ruby suspected the problem was being compounded by sexual frustration but there was little she could do about that at the moment.

To pass the time and to distract them from their attraction they spent hours talking. They had a crash course in getting to know each other's likes and dislikes. Ruby loved green tea, strawberries and eggs Benedict.

Noah loved coffee and mangoes and bacon but, like her, he didn't drink alcohol. His favourite music was Aussie rock, hers was pop and dance music. He liked to exercise first thing in the morning, loved surfing and paddle boarding but hated running. Ruby preferred to sleep in but she would get out of bed early for Noah—after all, he was paying her to—but she refused to exercise. She liked foreign movies, especially French ones, while he liked thrillers.

She could handle all those differences. They just made things more interesting. What she wasn't so sure about were the differences in their lifestyles. She was surprised at how lucrative motor racing was and how expensive Noah's tastes were. He didn't seem pretentious but he certainly liked the finer things in life. From his clothes to his groceries, everything was a brand name.

She guessed she wouldn't mind expensive things but she had never been able to afford them. Most of her clothes came from second-hand shops or the occasional chain store. She'd never had large amounts of money to spend on her wardrobe and she didn't see the point. She moved so frequently that it was easier to leave behind things she'd grown tired of—including boyfriends and clothes. She could always find another boyfriend and she could always find something to wear in the local charity shop. Noah, on the other hand, had expensive tastes—designer clothes, designer watches and designer sunglasses.

He did argue that a lot of his things, including his watch and sunglasses, were sponsors' products and therefore hadn't cost him anything. Ruby could see his point but she could also see that he had grown very used to having the best that money could buy—whether or not that money was his wasn't the point. But, at the end of the day, it wasn't her problem and she wasn't going to let it interfere with the next few weeks. She was determined to enjoy herself despite any differences.

Thursday, 25th December

'Merry Christmas.'

Ruby had got into the habit of waking Noah with a glass of orange juice and a handful of vitamins, and today was no exception. Mornings were almost his favourite time of the day. He was slow to get moving and needed a shower to warm up his muscles but that meant a chance to see Ruby semi-naked. After the first morning she'd taken to wearing a bikini when she showered him. He kept hoping for a repeat of her striptease but seeing her in a bikini was a reasonable alternative.

She stood in front of him wrapped in a thick, white, towelling dressing gown but he knew that underneath that she would be wearing nothing but her bikini. He could re-create that picture without any effort. He already knew her body intimately. But only by sight. He could close his eyes and picture every curve, every angle, every freckle. He knew her left eye tooth was slightly crooked, he knew the exact colour of her green eyes and that her second toes on both feet were longer than her first. He knew she preferred not to wear a bra and that her legs were long and pale and gorgeous. He knew her lips were soft and she tasted of strawberries but he was desperate to know more.

He wanted to taste the hollow at the base of her throat, to feel the softness of the skin on the inside of her thigh and to trace the curve of her hip. He was longing to know if the spot where her neck joined her shoulder also smelt like berries and how her body felt under his. How she would respond to his touch, how she would sound.

He knew there was a promise of things to come. The touch of her fingers as she dried his skin, the moments when her hands remained on his chest just a little longer than necessary or when he saw her watching him in the reflection of the bathroom mirror all told him that she wanted him as badly as he wanted her. He knew that these things would happen but he wasn't sure how much longer he could wait.

'Merry Christmas,' he answered, as he ran one hand over the roughness of his beard and sat up, carefully swinging his legs out of bed. He was consciously attempting to make these movements seem as painless and as easy as possible in the hope that Ruby would think he was healing faster than expected. He was eager to speed up the process, eager to get to the carrot at the end of the stick. Ruby was that carrot. He had two goals. One was to have Ruby, the other was to get back behind the wheel of his racing car, and each goal was as enticing as the other, although at the moment he'd be happy just to have Ruby in his bed.

He reached for the handful of tablets and washed them down with the orange juice as he glanced at the bedside clock. 'How much time do we have?'

'Two hours,' she replied, as she drew back the curtains. The sun was shining and all Noah could see was a flawless blue sky. It looked like a perfect summer's day. 'We have to be at Jake's parents' by ten.'

Ruby was smiling and he could see that some of

the tension she'd been carrying in her shoulders had eased. He knew she was looking forward to today and he could understand why. She'd had a rough couple of weeks but he knew that today marked a turning point for her.

Rose was doing well and although she still wasn't fully recovered—and no one could tell them if and when that might happen—the doctors had considered her condition stable enough to allow her a leave pass from the hospital for a half day. With Rose's progress and the fact that Jake's five siblings and their partners were all gathered together for Christmas, Scarlett and Jake had decided that Christmas Day presented the perfect opportunity to get married.

The wedding would be a family affair at Jake's parents' home, followed by Christmas lunch, but when Scarlett had learned that Noah had no plans she'd insisted that Ruby bring him along too. He would be the only non-family member there but no one seemed to mind. Jake's family was large; one extra person would hardly be noticed.

'Do you think you'd have time to shave my beard this morning?' he asked. 'It's starting to get itchy and I look like a scruff but I can't shave left-handed.'

Ruby showered him and wrapped a towel around his waist and another around his bare shoulders in preparation for shaving his beard. She ran warm water into the basin and held the razor under it. She stood over his right shoulder and began with his left cheek.

She rested her fingers under his chin as she tilted his head towards her. The movement brought his eyes in line with her belly button and the soft swell of her stomach. She'd ditched the dressing gown when she'd showered him and hadn't put it back on. There were only three tiny triangles of bikini fabric between him and her bare flesh.

She drew the razor from his cheek down to his chin before rinsing it and repeating the movement. Her fingers were soft on his skin and when they brushed over his lips he felt her touch light a fire that burned from his mouth to his belly and beyond. He bit back a moan. He didn't think he could stand much more of this. It was pleasure and pain rolled into one.

She tipped his head back to shave beneath his chin and jaw, bringing their heads close together and their lips even closer. He was just about to reach for her, unable to resist much longer, when she stood up and patted his face dry with a towel.

'God, Ruby, how much longer are you going to make me wait?'

'Until I'm sure you're up to it.' She grinned and he knew she'd choreographed all her movements very carefully to drive him to distraction.

It had worked. 'I'm up to it now, believe me.'

'Not much longer, I promise,' she said, bent over in front of him and picked the wet towels up from the bathroom floor. She glanced back at him over her shoulder, catching him staring at the spot where the strip of bikini fabric disappeared between her thighs. One tug on the string at the side of her hip and he could put them both out of their misery.

'Merry Christmas,' she added with a wink, as she straightened up.

The vision of her bending over before him would stay with him all day. Merry Christmas indeed.

* * *

The wedding service was brief. Scarlett and Jake really only needed the formalities and Noah paid no attention anyway. He only had eyes for Ruby. She had arrived at Jake's parents' in her usual casual clothes but somehow in the time between arriving and the service she'd been transformed, with the help of one of Jake's sisters, into something magnificent.

He was pleased he hadn't been able to travel for Christmas. Normally he would spend Christmas on the farm with his parents and his younger brother, Sam, but his injuries had made that impossible. Instead he got to spend Christmas with Ruby, an outcome he was more than happy with.

He had always thought she was striking, interesting—noticeable without being traditionally beautiful—but today she looked amazing. She was such a bundle of contrasts. Her slight frame and husky voice, her round, youthful face and her wide sensual mouth but in the pale green silk bridesmaid's dress that matched her eyes she was stunning and he couldn't take his eyes off her.

She was relaxed and happy with no sign of the tension that enveloped her at times—either due to Rose's illness or to her relationship with her mother—and her relaxed demeanour only helped to further enhance her appearance.

She had dyed her hair back to her natural strawberry blonde, colouring over the pink, and the colour was a much better foil for the dress and her skin tone. She looked ethereal, like a Celtic fairy, and he spent the rest of the day watching her. He was also trying to work out how to convince her that he had recovered enough to stop dancing around the issue of their attraction and take their relationship to the next level. He wanted to get her out of that dress and into his bed. He'd never gone home with a bridesmaid before.

Just when he thought he was going to have to admit defeat, Ruby materialised in front of him.

'It's time to go,' she told him.

He'd been challenging Jake's eight-year-old nephew to a video game and his arm was starting to complain. The game had become a little competitive and he'd probably overdone it but he wasn't about to admit that to Ruby. But she must have picked up on it somehow and had decided it was time to take him home. He wasn't about to argue. He was ready to have her undivided attention. As selfish as it seemed, he wasn't used to sharing her like he'd had to do today.

Ruby had noticed the discomfort gradually creeping up on Noah after lunch and had kept a close eye on him until she'd decided he'd had enough activity for one day. He hadn't argued when she'd deemed it time to leave, which had confirmed her suspicions that he had done enough. But it did amaze her that she was able to read him so well after just a few days.

'Are you tired? Do you need to rest?' she asked, when they were back in the penthouse. She could see the pain etched on his face but he wasn't giving in anymore.

He shook his head. 'No, I have something for you. A Christmas present. I want to give it to you now.'

Ruby sat on the couch and waited as Noah took himself off to his room and returned with a large box made of glossy white cardboard and tied with a red-and-white ribbon. He handed her the package. 'Merry Christmas.'

Ruby rested the box on her lap as she untied the ribbon and took off the lid. She unfolded a layer of tissue paper and lifted the gift out.

'It's the dress we saw in the shop window.' She stood and held the dress in front of her. 'It's absolutely gorgeous. How did you get it?'

'I called the shop and had it delivered while you were visiting Rose.'

'That was very sneaky.' She was touched that he'd gone to that trouble for her but she wondered why. 'What's it for?' she asked. She couldn't imagine where she would wear it, as gorgeous as it was.

'For this,' he said, handing her an envelope.

The envelope had been opened. Ruby pulled out an invitation and read it. 'We're invited to a party at the home of Ron and Trudy Townsend? As in the media mogul Ron Townsend?'

'He's the team boss.'

'Team boss?'

'He owns the team I drive for.'

'He *owns* a racing team?'

'Someone has to,' Noah said. 'It takes a lot of money to race on the V8 circuit. And Ron is a huge motorsport fan,' he told her, as if that explained it. 'Every year he hosts a New Year's Eve party and as part of our contract he expects his drivers to attend. Luckily he puts on a good show, it's a lot of fun. We'll be his guests for two nights.

'I can't go.'

'Why not? Have you got other plans?'

'No, it's not that.' They both knew her plans revolved around him at present. 'But I can just imagine the type

of party and the type of people who will be there. I'll
be completely out of my depth.'

'Everyone will love you and I'll be there with you. I
promised to do something fun with you when I got out
of hospital. This is it. Have you ever spent New Year's
Eve in Sydney?'

She hadn't but that didn't matter. She shook her head.

'You'll enjoy it, I promise.'

Ruby was still shaking her head.

'Let me tell you how this works,' Noah said. 'When
someone offers to send their private jet to pick you up
and take you to an extravagant New Year's Eve party
at a house on Sydney Harbour to watch the fireworks
you say, "Thank you, that would be lovely."'

'A private plane?'

'Yep, and when someone gives you a gift you say,
"Thank you, I know just the occasion to wear this beautiful dress."'

Ruby looked down at the dress that was now lying in
its nest of tissue paper. It was superb but it just raised
more concerns. 'Thank you, it is a stunning dress but
what will I wear for the rest of the weekend?' She waved
a hand over Noah's gift. 'If this is any indication of
what people will be wearing, I have absolutely nothing
suitable. I brought one small bag with me and minimal
items of clothing.'

But Noah wasn't going to listen to her excuses. 'Borrow something of Scarlett's, go shopping with my credit
card, I don't care. You can wear your bikini all weekend,
I don't mind. In fact, I reckon I wouldn't mind that at
all.' He grinned and Ruby's heart raced a little faster in
her chest. 'But I need you there with me. I can't manage

without you. Now, are you going to argue or are you going to try on your present?'

She couldn't resist. Even if she intended to extricate herself from going to the party and therefore had no good reason to keep the dress, it couldn't hurt to try it on. She had to wear it at least once. She picked up the box and took it to her room.

She swapped her bridesmaid's dress for Noah's present then turned hesitantly to look at her reflection in the full-length mirror. She preferred not to look at herself but even she had to admit that the dress was gorgeous and suited her perfectly.

The design was simple but elegant. Sequins embellished a black, figure-hugging strapless dress that ended a few inches above her knees. The sequins had been applied to give the illusion of curves and the length of the dress showed off her favourite body part, her legs. It was a straightforward design but the embellishment turned it into something special.

Her hair and make-up were still in place from the wedding but she tucked the slick, side ponytail into a bun at the nape of her neck, streamlining her silhouette. This dress needed a simpler hairstyle, one that didn't distract from the perfect cut and fit.

The inky black of the dress highlighted and complemented her fair skin but she thought it would look better if her hair was a couple of shades darker. A deep, russet red might be more striking than strawberry blond. More sophisticated. That was the look she was after. She'd have to redye her hair before New Year's Eve. She loved the dress, she'd never owned anything so amazing, and she didn't think she could bring herself to return it. Which meant she'd have to go to Sydney with Noah.

Oh, well, some sacrifices were worth it. She grinned as she checked her reflection again. She adored it. She thought she looked elegant, which wasn't a look she normally felt she could carry off, but this was a confidence-building dress. She slipped her feet into the silver heels she'd worn with her bridesmaid dress and returned to the living area to thank Noah properly for his extremely generous gift.

He had transferred himself out of his wheelchair and was sitting on the modular leather couch. Ruby crossed the room and twirled in front of him.

'You look incredible.'

She felt incredible. She smiled at him. 'I've been practising my "Thank you". Would you like to hear it?'

'I'm kind of busy enjoying the view right now.'

'Oh, I think you'll want to make time for this,' she said, as she stretched one hand behind her and reached for the zip. 'Thank you for my present, I know just the right occasion to wear this beautiful dress but unfortunately this moment isn't it.' She pulled the zip down and the dress fell to the floor, pooling around her feet. She stepped out of the dress and stood in front of him wearing nothing but silver heels and a pair of tiny lace knickers.

CHAPTER SEVEN

HIS EYES WERE wide as he ran his gaze along the length of her body and Ruby smiled at his reaction. She could feel the heat in his gaze and it warmed and reassured her.

'You're right, you were totally overdressed for the occasion,' he said, as he reached out for her with his left hand and cupped her bottom. The swell of her buttock fitted perfectly into his palm and the heat of his hand seared through the lace of her knickers. He ran his hand slowly down the back of her thigh to the sensitive skin behind her knee, sending an intense bolt of desire through her.

He looked up at her, his pupils dark in his blue eyes, his expression hungry. 'You feel fantastic.'

His fingers rested momentarily over the pulse at the back of her knee before he ran his hand back up her leg. She could feel moisture pooling between her thighs and her legs were weak. He clasped her hand, intertwining her fingers with his, and pulled her towards him, settling her in his lap. She sat astride his hips, relieved not to have to stand any longer but careful not to sit too heavily on his right thigh. But he seemed oblivious to her weight.

She dipped her head and pressed her lips to his. She wound her fingers through his hair as they deepened their kiss. She opened her mouth and their tongues met and tasted. She could feel his erection pressing against the inside of her thigh. She shifted her hips a fraction, rubbing against him. Noah moaned.

Noah let go of her hand and moved his hand to her breast. Her nipple peaked under his touch and it was her turn to moan. His fingers trailed down between her breasts and over her stomach as he dipped his head and took her breast in his mouth. Ruby closed her eyes and arched her back as his lips closed around her and she was swamped by waves of desire.

'Wait.' She wanted to go slowly but she knew she wouldn't be able to hold back and she still needed to get him out of his clothes. This moment wasn't just about her. It was about both of them.

She opened her eyes and undid his shirt, one button at a time. She slid the shirt from his body, working around the sling. She ran her fingers over his chest and over the ridges of his abdominal muscles. She was familiar with the feel of him, she'd been running her hands over him all week as she'd showered him, but this time was different. This time she was allowed to revel in the touch of his body under hers. This time she was allowed to take a minute or two to enjoy the feel of his muscles beneath her fingers. This time the outcome was going to be different.

She slid her fingers under the waistband of his shorts and flicked the button open before unzipping the fly. She stood up to remove his knee brace and he lifted his hips to enable her to take off his shorts. They'd become very co-ordinated and worked in unison to get him undressed, but for the past few days it had been to get him ready for the shower. Her hands were shaking now.

'Are you sure you want to do this?' he asked.

'Yes.'

'You're not nervous?'

Ruby shook her head. 'No. I'm excited. Impatient, aroused, but not nervous. I've been waiting for this moment,' she said, as she stood back to admire him. She'd seen him naked before but this time he was glorious. She reached out to touch him. His skin was warm and every inch of his body was hard and firm.

'By the way,' she said as she ran her fingers along his erection, 'I quit.'

'You what?'

'I'll stay on as your housekeeper but if we're going to do this, I can't be your nurse anymore. Okay?'

'You know I'd agree to anything you said at this point in time,' Noah said, as he rested his head back on the couch.

Ruby smiled as she increased her pressure around his shaft. 'Do you accept my resignation?'

'There's a condom in the pocket of my shorts.'

She took that as a yes. She stood and retrieved the foil packet, holding it between her lips as she started to take off her knickers.

'Let me do that.' Noah's voice was thick and deep.

He reached for the lace with his left hand and slid the flimsy fabric down to her knees. Ruby stepped out of her underwear and was about to kick off her heels but Noah stopped her.

'Leave them on,' he said. His voice was so deep and quiet she could barely make out his words.

She left her shoes on as she tore the condom packaging. She knelt over him as she rolled the condom onto his shaft. Her knees were spread wide as she straddled him and Noah's fingers slid inside her, into her wetness. His thumb found the sensitive nub at her centre and she almost climaxed under the touch of his hand.

But that wasn't what she wanted. Not today.

She pushed his hand out of the way, taking control.

She wanted him inside her. She'd been waiting for this moment and she wanted to feel him. She wanted him to fill her.

She lifted her hips and lowered herself over him, taking him deep inside her.

She wanted to be gentle and she tried to be careful. She tried to be mindful of all his broken bits— his elbow, his collarbone, his ribs and his leg—but it was hard to hold back. She'd wanted this for so long, they'd been dancing around this moment all week, and now that they'd started she couldn't make herself take it slowly. She couldn't wait. If she had to wait any longer she would explode.

Noah thrust up into her. If he was in pain he wasn't showing any signs of it. He wasn't holding back and Ruby matched his rhythm. She put her hands on the back of the couch. Supporting her own weight was her only concession to his injuries as she lifted and lowered her hips and rode him towards satisfaction.

The peak came quickly, crashing over her, and she felt Noah shudder beneath her, joining her in the moment of release.

It might have been hurried but it was no less satisfying. Fast or slow, it wouldn't have mattered.

They had plenty of time to try all sorts of different

ways but Ruby thought it might be hard to beat their first time. In her opinion it had been close to perfect.

Over the next week they developed an easy routine. Ruby would make them breakfast then help Noah with his exercises and stretches, before taking him to his various appointments. He had a few sponsor engagements, mainly interviews, and he would schedule these for late morning, which gave him time for a sleep in the afternoon while she went to see Rose. When she got home she would climb into his bed and wake him in any number of imaginative ways and when they had finished making love he would tackle another exercise session.

Ruby had talked Noah out of hiring another nurse, having decided she was happy to still perform those duties but in an unpaid capacity. As a compromise she was being paid a very generous housekeeper's wage and it was an agreement that suited them both.

Their days were full and busy and Ruby was happy. She felt comfortable with Noah and for once she wasn't thinking about running away. They made love, they talked and he listened without judging, and Ruby could be herself.

She had seen Scarlett blossom under Jake's attention as she was free to be herself. Ruby had wanted that too, but she hadn't been sure if she liked herself enough to let someone else see the real her. But Noah seemed to like her so maybe she was worth something. Having his approval made her like herself a little bit more. But she didn't want to think of the power he seemed to hold over her. She hadn't resisted his job offer and she knew she wouldn't resist the chance now to get to know him even more intimately. That had been her objective all along. She'd just need to be careful. He had a knack of getting her to divulge personal information about herself and she couldn't imagine sharing her body and all her thoughts with someone. That was a recipe for disaster. In her mind that gave them the power and with that power came the possibility that they could hurt her.

New Year's Eve

'Ruby, the limo is here.'

Ruby shoved her floppy sunhat onto her head and grabbed her handbag and oversized sunglasses when Noah called to her. He was waiting in the hall. By the time Ruby got to him the chauffeur had already taken their bags, leaving them to follow when they were ready.

He put his hand on her arm, waylaying her before she could get into the lift. He pulled her down to him and kissed her.

'You look fantastic.' She was wearing her maxi-dress with flat sandals, and with the oversized glasses and large hat she looked like she'd stepped out of the nineteen seventies. She had dyed her hair a dark russet red that shone and would be a good contrast to the dress Noah had given her for Christmas. 'I remember this dress,' he said. 'It's the one you wore in the shower on that first morning here at the apartment.'

Ruby could remember how she'd flirted with him that morning with her striptease. How much had changed since then. She smiled to herself as she stepped into the lift, thinking about what she had in store for him today.

She almost had to pinch herself when the chauffeur delivered them to the waiting aircraft. She still couldn't believe that Ron Townsend had sent his private jet just to collect Noah for his New Year's Eve party.

The plane was sleek, white and much larger than she'd expected, and her heart plummeted as she wondered how many people were going to be aboard with them.

'Is there anyone else coming with us?' she asked.

'Not that I know of,' he replied. 'Why?'

'I don't want to share.'

'You want exclusive access? You haven't even got on board yet and you've already developed a celebrity attitude,' he teased.

'No, it's not that. I just assumed we'd have the plane to ourselves.'

It took a bit of organisation to get Noah on board. The plane wasn't really geared for passengers in wheelchairs, but that was the only negative. Once they were inside the aircraft, and alone—to Ruby's relief—she had no complaints. The interior of the plane was beautifully appointed with soft leather seats the colour of caramel that swivelled and reclined and small wooden side tables made of oak. Two flat-screen televisions were fitted into the walls and under their feet was plush cream carpet. It was all very modern, sleek and expensive.

'I can see why people get accustomed to the rich-and-famous lifestyle,' she said, as they settled into their seats and Carmelo, the male flight attendant, served them sparkling mineral water in crystal glasses.

'Our flight time today will be approximately two and a half hours,' Carmelo told them in a smooth Italian accent. 'Lunch will be served on the flight but please enjoy some light refreshments while we prepare for take-off.' He left a platter of hors d'oeuvres for them and disappeared into the front of the plane.

Ruby stifled a giggle. 'Do you think his accent is real?'

Noah smiled. 'I have no idea but it all adds to the experience, doesn't it?'

Ruby agreed and decided to settle in and enjoy it. It was likely to be a once-in-a-lifetime event for her and she intended to make the most of it.

As Carmelo cleared the remains of their lunch away, Ruby checked the time and excused herself to use the bathroom. When she re-emerged Carmelo was still in the lounge. Her excitement dissipated and her face fell.

'What's the matter?' Noah asked when he saw her expression.

Ruby sat on the arm of his chair and whispered in his ear. 'I didn't expect to have Carmelo hovering over us the whole time. I was hoping for a new experience, if you know what I mean?' Ruby didn't want to know if Noah had ever joined the mile-high club, it was enough to know that she hadn't and she wanted to and she wanted to do it with him. 'I wore this dress especially.' She opened her handbag and showed Noah a pair of tiny undies that she'd just removed in the bathroom.

His eyes lit up and he grinned and Ruby knew he was up for it. 'Are you going commando?' he asked.

'Yep.'

He laughed and told her, 'I'll take care of it.'

Ruby didn't know what he did but in the next moment Carmelo was beside them. 'Will there be anything else, Mr Christiansen?'

'No, thank you, Carmelo.'

'Very well. Enjoy the flight,' he said, before he disappeared into the cockpit, drawing the curtain closed between the lounge and the galley on his way.

'Are you sure he's gone?' Ruby asked.

'Positive.'

'Finally, we're alone.'

Ruby lifted her dress above her knees and straddled him. She bent her knees, tucking her feet under her bottom and sandwiching her thighs between Noah's and the armrests of the chair. She leant over and pushed back the lever on the side of his seat, lifting the footrest and reclining the seat.

Noah grinned. 'I'm beginning to see the attraction in flying in a private jet.'

Ruby bent her head and kissed him squarely on his mouth. She didn't know how long they had and she didn't intend to waste a minute.

Noah's fingers grazed her nipple through the thin fabric of her dress. As usual she wasn't wearing a bra and her nipple peaked in response to his touch and she moaned and parted her lips and took his tongue into her mouth.

She could feel the pressure of Noah's hand on the outside of her thigh as he slid it under her dress, loosening it and untucking it from behind her knees. She shifted her weight, lifting her bottom slightly so Noah could slide his hand between her legs and over the naked flesh between her thighs. She felt his fingers slide inside her; she knew she was wet, and she arched her hips, pushing against his hand.

She loosened his belt and undid the fly on his shorts. She pushed his clothes out of the way as much as possible and freed his erection. There wasn't time to get properly undressed. It wasn't important. It wasn't necessary. They had spent many hours over the past week exploring each other and getting to know each other intimately. Ruby could close her eyes and re-create Noah perfectly in her mind. Whether they'd been making love on the couch, in bed, on the daybed on the balcony or even on the baby grand piano, the sex had been fantastic. Sometimes urgent, sometimes slow but always satisfying.

His shaft was thick and warm in her palm and she could feel his pulse beating under her fingers.

His fingers were still inside her and his thumb was making little circles against her swollen clitoris. Ruby could feel her limbs starting to liquefy. She pushed her hips forward again, pushing herself against his thumb.

For Ruby today wasn't about taking it slow, it was all about the location and the experience.

But Noah had other ideas. 'Not yet,' he said. 'I don't have a condom.'

Her purse was lying on the seat beside them. She'd packed a condom in there deliberately. She emptied her purse and found the packet. She tore it open.

Noah withdrew his finger and watched her roll the condom onto his shaft. He lifted her hips and Ruby had to follow his lead, he wasn't able to lift her fully as he still only had one good arm to work with. He brought her down onto him, filling her, and Ruby breathed out as she took him inside her. Her breath came out in a sigh.

Noah moaned as he thrust into her and lifted her up and down.

Her breaths were coming faster now. She was breathing in time with his thrusts. There was no more sighing; she was getting progressively louder.

She arched her back as she took Noah into her time and time again.

Deeper. Harder. Faster.

Ruby could feel the waves of pleasure roll over her and she cried out as the orgasm swept her away. Noah shuddered as he came inside her and Ruby collapsed against his chest.

Her legs were like jelly. She couldn't feel her toes but she could feel her heart. It was racing so fast she could feel the blood pumping into her fingers. She loved this time with Noah—the afterwards—loved it almost as much as the sex. For a few minutes every day she could relax and just be. For a few minutes she could forget about everything else that was going on in her life.

Noah provided her with an escape, a very pleasant and satisfying escape.

While she rested against Noah the plane hit an air pocket and jolted her, bringing her attention back to her surroundings. She had forgotten all about Carmelo; she hadn't given a thought to how much noise she had made. She looked around, hoping he hadn't materialised unexpectedly.

'How noisy were we?' she asked Noah. 'You don't think Carmelo heard us, do you?'

'I wouldn't worry. Carmelo and the pilot would both have had headphones on.'

'Really?'

'Trust me.'

'I don't want to know how you know that.'

'They're very well trained,' Noah replied, with a laugh that made Ruby blush.

Thinking about Carmelo made her nervous about being caught in a compromising position. 'Do I need to make you decent?' She wasn't ready to move yet, she actually didn't think she could. She could feel Noah's heart beating under hers. It was a nice feeling.

'There's no hurry,' Noah said.

'What if Carmelo comes back?'

'He won't come out until I tell him we're ready.'

'And how do you do that?'

'I'll push the call button and then he'll know we're finished.'

'Oh, God,' Ruby said, as she buried her face in Noah's shoulder. 'He's going to know I'm a shameless wench.'

'Is there any other sort of wench?' he teased her. 'It's too late to be worrying about that now, don't you think?'

'Three, two, one! Happy New Year.'

The band began to play 'Auld Lang Syne' as fireworks exploded over Sydney Harbour. The display from the Harbour Bridge, the Opera House and from several barges moored on the water was magnificent but Ruby only had eyes for Noah.

In a room full of beautiful people he was by far the most handsome. His tuxedo fitted him like a glove, and so it should, having been made for him by one of his sponsors, a designer menswear label, and Ruby could see why they'd picked him. He wore a suit well. Until tonight she had only seen him in casual clothes—shorts and shirts—as they were the easiest things to get on over his sling and with the knee brace. She'd had to help him with his shirt buttons, his belt and his bow-tie. Tying his tie had almost made them late. Not because she couldn't do it but because it was such an intimate task and she'd been sidetracked by his proximity, they both had. But eventually they had both dressed and had made it to the party.

Ruby had been determined to have a night to remember. She doubted she'd ever have another chance to celebrate the start of a new year in a mansion overlooking one of the most spectacular harbours in the world, but she had made sure she was by Noah's side as the countdown had begun. She was going to make sure she was the one and only person he kissed when the clock struck midnight.

And when he kissed her she didn't care who saw them. She was happy for people to see they were together. Being with Noah gave her confidence she lacked. He'd seemed to genuinely enjoy introducing her to his friends and colleagues and having his attention was beginning to make her believe she was worthy of being loved.

'Happy New Year. Have you had fun?'

'I have.'

The party had been great fun. She had danced and met some interesting people but the best thing about the night was the fact that she was Noah's date. She'd been aware of the admiring looks from several of the male guests when she had accompanied Noah into the party and she'd loved the look of pride she'd seen in his eyes when he'd noticed it too. She hadn't cared about the other men but knowing that Noah thought she looked fabulous had been worth a thousand appreciative glances from strangers.

'I liked watching you dance.'

'You did?'

He nodded. 'You dance the same way you make love. As if you really enjoy it.'

'They *are* my two favourite activities.' Ruby laughed as Noah reached for her with his left hand. He cupped her bottom and pulled her in against him and kissed her again.

'In that case, are you ready for bed?'

Noah had insisted on being out of his wheelchair for the evening. He had propped himself on a bar stool and hadn't moved as the other guests had sought him out, but Ruby realised he was probably exhausted and needed to sit down properly.

'If you're coming with me, I am.'

Ruby lay curled against Noah's side, sated and happy but not at all tired. Even though they'd had a busy day, her mind was buzzing.

'Have you made a New Year's resolution?' she asked him.

'Not a New Year's one specifically. Just the same as before—to get back behind the wheel in time for the start of the season.'

'I heard you mention that to a few of the sponsors tonight. What will they say if you don't make it?'

'I'm going to make it. There's no prize for second best, as they say,' he said, reminding her how focussed and determined he was. 'What's your resolution?'

Ruby made the same one every year—to stay sober for another twelve months—but she wasn't ready to talk to Noah about that. She was sharing enough of herself already. 'I'm going to try to spend a bit more time in Adelaide.'

'You move a lot, don't you?' His voice was deep and

soft. It vibrated in his chest and rumbled through her. She could lie in the dark and listen to him all night.

'I guess so, compared to other people maybe.'

'Why?'

'I'm not sure. I'm looking for somewhere that fits me and I haven't found it yet. Then I get itchy feet and have to move.' She didn't admit that her feet usually started itching when people started getting to know her. If people got too close it could hurt her when they left so she preferred to leave first, before she could form strong attachments. 'I thought I might fit better there now that I'm ten years older and maybe wiser. I might even be able to get on better with Mum.'

'Are you closer to your father?'

'No. I don't have any sort of relationship with him. I don't have anything to do with him and he doesn't have anything to do with me.'

'What about with your sisters? He wasn't at Scarlett's wedding.'

Ruby could hear the frown in Noah's voice. This was why she avoided talking about her family. It was complicated and painful.

'That's because he isn't Scarlett's father. We're half-sisters.'

'Half-sisters? Why haven't you told me this before?'

'Is it important?' Ruby was nervous about telling him more. What if it changed how he saw her? Even though the logical part of her brain told her that her mother's choices had nothing to do with her, she knew those choices had affected how she was raised and she didn't want them to alter Noah's perceptions of her. 'Does it change anything?'

'No, but it might help me to understand you.'

'I doubt it. It's complicated. *I'm* complicated.'

'I prefer to call you interesting.'

'Really?'

'Really. So why wasn't Scarlett's father at her wedding?'

Ruby had opened Pandora's box now and she could tell Noah wasn't going to be fobbed off easily. She debated about distracting him, she found sex was a pretty good distraction, but she suspected it wasn't going to work on him tonight.

'Scarlett has never met her father and mine ran off when I was a baby. Rose's father…'

'Rose's father?'

'Yep, we're all half sisters. I warned you it was complicated.' *In for a penny, in for a pound,* she thought. She might as well tell him the truth about her parentage, that wasn't exactly a secret. 'Rose's father married Mum when I was four. We are all Andersons because he adopted Scarlett and me and he was the closest thing I've had to a real dad, but he died when I was thirteen.'

'Did you ever see your father?'

'For a little while when I was a teenager. I had nothing to do with him until after Rose's dad died. I didn't know anything about him until then, I'd never asked any questions and Mum had never volunteered anything. When I was sixteen Mum and I went through a difficult period and I ran off to Melbourne to live with my father.'

'That's where you went when you left Adelaide? You ran away from home at sixteen?'

'Mum knew where I was going. She tried to talk me out of it but I wouldn't listen. I thought I knew best. It turns out I didn't know anything. My father didn't want me there, I just made his life complicated, so he ignored me. I guess Mum knew what she was talking about after all. She made some bad choices in her time and he was one of them.'

'What happened between them?'

'He and Mum met when she worked in a nursing home and he was a rep for a medical-supply company—he was your typical travelling salesman. They had what Mum thought was a serious relationship but he neglected to tell her that he was already married *and* had a family who lived in Melbourne. That little bit of information didn't come out until Mum fell pregnant with me. That obviously wasn't part of his plan and he panicked and took off, back to his first family, leaving Mum with Scarlett and me. Mum had Scarlett when she was just eighteen. Scarlett's father never knew about her, it was Mum's decision to keep the baby against the father's family's wishes, so suddenly she found herself a single mother twice over.'

'So what happened when you went to Melbourne?'

'Dad was going through a divorce and I think having me there was like rubbing salt into the wound. I'm positive Mum wouldn't have been the only woman he'd had an affair with but she might have been the first one he had to admit to and I think he blamed me in a way. If Mum hadn't got pregnant with me, he might have got away with his infidelities. He didn't really want anything to do with me and I didn't like being there all that much either, but I'd made my bed when I'd run away from home and I refused to admit my mistake. I couldn't go back, not immediately, so I stuck it out in Melbourne and just made matters worse.'

Telling him about her parentage was one thing; confiding her complete family history was another thing altogether, and it was something she normally didn't share. There was too much that could hurt her.

It was one reason she kept her relationships short. If it was casual she wouldn't be expected to divulge her deepest, darkest secrets and thoughts. But she had surprised herself with the things she'd shared with Noah but she knew it was because she had a sense that he wouldn't hurt her. She hoped she was right.

'He blamed his estranged teenage daughter for his failings as a husband and father?' Noah asked. 'Didn't he take ownership of his mistakes?'

'Not really. I think he just moved on, leaving his messes behind.'

For the first time Ruby wondered if she had more of her father's traits in her than she'd realised. Did her tendency to run come from him? Was she less like her mother than she'd thought? Lucy was a fighter. She had fought to keep her children and Ruby was horrified to think that she might take after her father after all.

'I'm sorry, Ruby,' Noah said, as he hugged her a little closer. 'Everyone deserves to have parents who love them unconditionally.'

It was a good feeling to know that Noah had her back. Ruby had always depended on Scarlett for that but it would be nice to have more than one person in her corner. Lying in the dark tucked against Noah's chest with his arm around her, she felt as if nothing could hurt her. She felt as though this was where she belonged. Maybe the place she'd been searching for was beside Noah.

But was that a dangerous thought? Was she setting herself up for disappointment? The answer was probably yes but now that the thought had entered her head she found it hard to shift.

She put it to one side, choosing the path of least resistance. She'd deal with it later. For now she was going to enjoy the moment.

CHAPTER EIGHT

Wednesday, 11th February

JANUARY HAD FLOWN past and February seemed to be in just as much of a hurry. Noah's rehab had progressed well and Ruby was amazed at the speed of his recovery but, until today, she'd been successfully ignoring the fact that every step that he took towards a full recovery was taking him one more step away from needing her.

He had ditched his sling and the wheelchair and was now mobile on a pair of crutches. His big physical assessment was two days away and he was positive that he was on track to be back behind the wheel after that.

Ruby had been crossing the days off one by one on the makeshift calendar on the penthouse window. She was well aware of the date and of the fact that she'd known Noah for almost nine weeks.

Nine weeks. She'd let herself stay far longer than she'd intended to. Her relationships *never* lasted this long.

She tried to convince herself that this time was different, this time it was her job. Noah was paying her to be his housekeeper but she was free to walk away at any time.

But she knew that wasn't true.

The longevity had nothing to do with her employment and everything to do with their physical and emotional relationship. And that was the problem. Physical relationships she could handle but emotional relationships were a different matter altogether.

Ruby had become very comfortable with Noah and over the past weeks she'd gradually revealed more and more of her true self. She had never wanted to do that before and she hadn't really intended on sharing quite so much with Noah, but when they talked he listened and she found herself telling him things she would normally never reveal. She had worried that he'd judge her but that wasn't the case. He was allowing her to be herself and, even better, he seemed to like the real her. She had never been sure if she liked herself but knowing that Noah liked her made her feel as if she was worth something.

As the weeks passed Ruby had a growing sense that she belonged with Noah. This might not have been a problem except for the fact that she suspected her feelings for him ran deeper than his for her, and that wasn't something she was used to. Her relationships normally served a purpose—mutual satisfaction—and nothing more. Normally she could take or leave a partner; normally anyone could alleviate her loneliness. But Noah was different. She feared she had grown to need him but she suspected his need for her wasn't as compelling.

Was she just a convenience?

But despite these misgivings she couldn't make herself walk away. She enjoyed his company and she enjoyed sharing his bed. Even if he only needed her for convenience, that was enough. She'd worry about the implications of this relationship once he no longer needed her at all.

She dumped the shopping bags onto the kitchen counter. She'd been to the supermarket to buy the ingredients for the celebratory dinner she was planning. Tomorrow they were flying to Sydney for his physical test, which was scheduled for Friday—Friday the thirteenth. She hoped that wasn't a bad omen. If he passed he'd be allowed back behind the wheel for the test runs on Saturday the fourteenth. That was the date he'd been aiming for since day one. The big day was almost here.

Ruby knew she shouldn't be planning on celebrating tonight—he hadn't passed yet—but she was convinced he would. In her eyes he certainly seemed to have made a full recovery but his recovery was a double-edged sword. If Noah was allowed to drive, he wouldn't need her anymore.

She began unpacking the groceries, surprised he hadn't come to help her. Since he'd achieved the milestones he'd set himself and had become mobile, he was almost always on hand to help her. There wasn't much he couldn't do for himself now, except drive.

She went looking for him, there weren't too many places he could be, and found him on the balcony. There was a bottle of spirits on the table in front of him. Along with one glass. The bottle was open. She could smell the alcohol. She recognised the scent—rum.

Ruby frowned.

Why was he drinking? And especially why was he drinking when the driving test was imminent? He'd told her he didn't drink. He'd told her it didn't fit with his job description. She'd believed him, she'd had no reason not to, and she hadn't seen anything to contradict his words. Until now.

She stepped out onto the balcony. 'What are you doing?'

'Making a toast.'

'But you don't drink.' She didn't mention the obvious—that he was alone and it was kind of difficult to make a toast when you were the only one in the room.

'It's been ten years,' he said.

'I don't understand.' Who would choose to celebrate ten years of soberness by opening a bottle of rum?

He looked up at her and Ruby was shocked by the dullness of his eyes. It was more than alcohol, he looked exhausted. She'd never seen him look so defeated, not even in the early days when he'd been in significant pain. 'I'm drinking a toast to my brother. Grab a glass and join me.'

She remembered he had mentioned a brother who lived on the family farm. Sam. Something had obviously happened but it didn't look as though it was something Noah was happy about. So why a toast? She had no idea what he was talking about.

She chose to ignore his invitation to fetch a glass and instead pulled out a chair at the table and turned it to face him before sitting down. 'Your brother? Sam? Why?' Had he had bad news? No, bad news wouldn't warrant a toast.

'No. Adam.' Noah's eyes were dark, and all traces of the brilliant blue sparkle she'd grown to love had been erased. 'He died ten years ago today. This is the one day of the year when I have a drink. A toast to his memory.'

Ruby glanced at the bottle. It seemed to her that he

was doing more than toasting his brother's memory. He was halfway to obliterating it *and* the bottle.

She didn't really want to sit there and watch him drink. She always did her best to steer clear of temptation and avoided situations that revolved purely around drinking. But luckily rum had never been her choice of poison and she knew he needed her there. She could sit with him and perhaps if she got him talking about his brother he'd slow down on the rum. She'd only been at the shops for a short time, a little over an hour, but he'd made a serious dent in the level of the bottle. It was already half-empty.

Someone else might argue that it was half-full but Ruby had always seen a bottle of alcohol as half-empty and therefore it might as well be finished.

Where had it come from? She knew what was in the cupboards, she'd been doing all the shopping. He must have had it delivered, she realised. He'd organised other deliveries, her Christmas present included, but this wasn't such a nice surprise. Looking at the slightly glazed expression in his blue eyes and listening to the slight blurriness of his deep voice, she knew it had been full when he'd started so it must have been new. Had he deliberately waited until she'd gone before he'd opened it?

And why had he kept the significance of today a secret? Why hadn't he said anything to her?

Those questions just confirmed for her that her feelings towards him weren't reciprocated in the same way. She needed to start thinking about leaving. She needed to look for her own replacement or hope he passed the driving test tomorrow. Then she could be on her way. But she would not walk out on him tonight.

She wouldn't leave him to drown his sorrows alone. The least she could do was sit with him and listen if he wanted to talk, even if she wouldn't join him in a drink.

She hadn't had to make excuses to him for her own abstinence. He had never asked for more explanation than she'd originally given and she'd never volunteered any details about her vow of sobriety—that would have been divulging too much of herself. Giving him her body was easier than giving him her history. She hadn't wanted him to judge her so she wouldn't judge him now. How he chose to mourn or remember his brother was his business.

'How old was he?'

'Eighteen.'

Ruby knew that Noah was four years older than his brother, Sam. Ten years ago Noah would have been twenty so Adam would have also been younger than him. The middle brother.

Noah didn't seem to mind answering her question. He was obviously aware of her presence, not too caught up in his reminiscing, so she felt comfortable asking the next question. 'What happened?'

He swirled the rum around in his glass and the aroma made Ruby feel queasy. 'He'd been out in one of the paddocks, repairing a fence. He was a long way from the house.' Ruby wondered what distance had to do with anything but she didn't want to interrupt. 'I was on the other side of the farm, repairing a windmill,' he continued. 'When he wasn't home in time for dinner I said I'd go and look for him. It was a hot day and I thought maybe he hadn't been able to work as quickly as he wanted to. I thought I'd give him a hand to fin- ish off. I didn't want to think that he might have had an accident. All sorts of things can go wrong on a farm but nine out of ten times when people are late it's nothing. Just normal delay…'

Noah's voice trailed off as he remembered. Ruby waited, wondering if he was going to finish or if the memories were too painful.

'I found him.' His voice caught on the words. 'He was in his ute. The driver's door was open and I could see his feet sticking out. I thought he'd fallen asleep but when I got closer I saw the blood. His blood.' Noah rubbed his hand over his face. 'Splattered across the windscreen. Blood and brains and bits of bone.'

'He'd been killed?'

Noah shook his head. 'He killed himself.'

'Oh, Noah, I'm so sorry.' Ruby reached out and put her hand over his, connecting her to him. She had counselled teenagers before who had lost friends to suicide but it was so much harder when she was emotionally invested. She didn't know what else to say.

'In one hand was his rifle, we always carried a rifle with us, we never knew when we might have to put a sheep down. In his other hand was a letter. I thought maybe it was a suicide note but it wasn't. It was a letter from his girlfriend. Telling him she was moving to Sydney. She didn't want to live in the country. She was sorry but she couldn't imagine spending the rest of her life out in the middle of nowhere.

'That was all Adam wanted. To be a farmer. And I know they'd talked about getting married, even though they were young they had plans, he had plans and he'd wanted to make a life with her on the farm. The property was profitable and I was pleased one of us wanted to take it on. It meant I was free to pursue my dream.

But Annabel crushed Adam's dream so badly that he hadn't been able to see any other future.

'The letter was dated a month earlier. He hadn't said anything to any of us. He hadn't asked for help. He'd kept it all bottled up. None of us had any idea. And we hadn't been with him at the end. There was only Jessie.'

'Jessie?'

Noah hadn't touched his drink since she'd sat down with him but he was making less and less sense.

'His sheepdog.'

'Was she alive?'

'Yes. Adam would never hurt Jessie and she was always by his side. She wouldn't leave him.'

Now Noah's earlier comment about how far from the house Adam had been made sense. Ruby knew that Noah thought if Adam had been closer to the house maybe the dog would have come running back. Ruby knew it would have still been unlikely that they would have been able to save him but at least they might have known sooner what had happened and maybe had less guilt.

'It was almost more than Dad or I could bear when he had to put Jessie down too.'

'What had happened to her?'

'She was dying of a broken heart. The same as Adam. She refused to eat, she was wasting away. Dad had no choice but it was almost more than any of us could stand. And after that Dad and I drowned our sorrows. Night after night. And if I wasn't drinking with Dad I was drinking with my mates. I'd been offered a chance to drive with a racing team, I'd been given my big break, but I nearly blew it. My mother read me the Riot Act—she didn't want to lose two sons and if I insisted on drinking and driving fast cars there was a good chance she would lose me too.

'I decided I wanted to pursue the chance I'd been given. Killing myself wasn't going to bring Adam back so I decided to give up the booze and now I just drink a toast to him once a year.' He picked up his glass and asked, 'So, are you going to get a glass and join me?'

She could see the shadows in his blue eyes. Had he forgotten she didn't drink? Or didn't he care? Had the memories and the grief and the rum wiped everything else from his mind?

Ruby's hand shook as she reached for the bottle.

She didn't want to be rude or to ignore his brother's memory but she couldn't do it. It might be ten years since Noah had lost his brother but it was also ten years since she'd last had a drink and she wasn't going to break a decade of sobriety. Not for anyone. Not even Noah.

'I think you've had enough for both of us,' she said as she picked up the bottle and the lid and started to screw the cap on.

Noah's hand shot out and covered hers. The rum didn't appear to have dulled his reflexes.

'I'm a big boy. I can look after myself.'

Ruby had no intention of sitting there while he proceeded to finish off the contents of the bottle, and she suspected that was his plan. Surely that could kill a man.

'I'll make you a coffee and bring you a jug of water but I'm not going to join you. Drinking doesn't solve anything. It only makes things worse.'

'That's right. I almost forgot—you don't drink.' Noah looked at her properly for the first time since she'd walked onto the balcony. 'When are you going to tell me what that's all about?'

'When I think it's important for you to know,' she said. She doubted he'd remember anything they talked about in the morning but she wasn't willing to take that chance. Some things were better left unsaid.

'You know, you're an enigma. It's all very well to be mysterious but there comes a time in a relationship when you need to open up. That's what relationships are about.'

And that was what frightened her. She'd known this moment would come, it always did, which was why she usually had a self-imposed two-month time limit on relationships. She knew he would expect her to share at some point. But she couldn't do it. She wasn't ready to tell him why she didn't drink. Guilt and pain and sorrow made her go on the attack.

'That works both ways. Not once have you mentioned the significance of today to me. You've never mentioned Adam. The first time I hear about him is when I find you demolishing a bottle of rum and ruining your chances for the weekend. I don't think you get to lecture me about sharing.'

She stood up. 'I think you should get some sleep. We're flying to Sydney tomorrow. You've got your physical assessment and your simulator test in two days. You've done all the hard work at rehab. Don't let the past nine weeks be for nothing. You need to remember how much you wanted this chance all those years ago. Don't blow it now. Tomorrow is your only chance to get cleared to get back in a race car in time for round one of the championship. Ask yourself how badly do you want it? Do you want it more than you want that next drink?'

CHAPTER NINE

Thursday, 12th February

NOAH FELT AS if something had crawled into his mouth in the night and sucked all the moisture out of him. His head was pounding. He rolled over and groaned as his head threatened to explode and the events of the previous night gradually filtered through his foggy brain. The expression on Ruby's face was one of the first things that came to mind. Disappointment had been etched over it. She'd left him on the balcony but not before she'd lectured him on the error of his ways.

He had to admit she had a point. And he'd listened. He'd left the cap on the bottle and drunk the water and ignored the coffee, knowing it would only dehydrate him more, but he hadn't expected to feel quite so average this morning.

He was alone in his bed. He knew Ruby hadn't slept there last night. The pillow beside his had no indentation in it and her scent was absent. It seemed as though she'd kept her distance. He'd have to apologise for his behaviour. He suspected he'd been fairly antisocial.

He sat up gingerly, pleased to find the room wasn't spinning and his stomach wasn't heaving. He stood.

His leg was stiff but that was nothing new. After a hot shower and the stretches that had become part of his morning routine he knew most of the stiffness would abate. He checked the time. He needed to get into the shower. He needed as much time as possible to get his leg moving. It had to be better. His future depended on it. He had to prove he'd recovered enough to get back behind the wheel of a V8 racing car.

He couldn't believe he'd let his emotions get the better of him last night. What had he been thinking? The alcohol had knocked him around more than usual—he knew it was because he wasn't fully fit or fully recovered—but he'd hoped he was recovered enough to get through his physical. He couldn't believe he'd jeopardised his chances like that last night. Fortunately for him, Ruby had been there to talk some sense into him.

Snippets of their conversation slowly filtered into his consciousness. He had a suspicion he'd offered her a drink. He couldn't believe he'd done that. He knew she didn't drink—he didn't know why and he remembered now she'd refused to tell him, but he should never have offered her one. He knew he wouldn't have if he'd been even semi-sober. No wonder she'd avoided his bed. He'd been rude and unpleasant and he was mortified that he'd treated her that way. He needed to find her and apologise for his behaviour.

Ruby was in his room when he came out of the bathroom. She was dressed but she avoided eye contact. She handed him some paracetamol tablets and a glass of water and got ready to help him with his stretches, as she did every morning, but there was no accompanying banter, no smile, nothing. She was all business, no pleasure.

'I owe you an apology,' he said, as she stretched his calf. 'I think I offered you a drink. I'm sorry, I shouldn't have done that.'

'It doesn't matter. I make my own decisions.'

Her reply was short and sharp. She was obviously annoyed at him and he suspected she had good reason to be.

'I'm still sorry. I don't normally have such bad manners. I was poor company last night but I did listen to your suggestion and I did go to bed so I want to thank you for your cool head and wise words.'

'It's up to you how you choose to remember your brother but I hope you haven't screwed up your chances for your test tomorrow.'

Ruby noticed that he didn't apologise for his drinking, which was good, she didn't feel he owed her an apology for that. His drinking wasn't the issue. She did feel like he had let her down but she was the one who had put him on the pedestal. She'd thought he was perfect and she should have known better. No one was perfect. She realised her expectations of him had been unreasonable and it wasn't her place to judge him now. She was far from perfect herself.

But she was annoyed that he'd offered her a drink and she was annoyed that he hadn't told her about his brother. But she did have the good grace to realise she was being unfair. Although she had shared many personal stories with him, there were plenty more she had kept to herself, including the real reason why she didn't drink, and it was hypocritical of her to expect one kind of behaviour from him when she wasn't prepared to do the same.

But she did wonder why he hadn't shared the significance of the day with her until he'd been halfway to being drunk. Obviously the sharing wasn't an issue but the timing was, and Ruby felt it confirmed what she'd suspected—that his feelings towards her weren't as strong as hers were towards him.

She knew he was focused on achieving his goal of being cleared to drive by February fourteenth, but she couldn't believe he hadn't once mentioned the significance of the twelfth. He couldn't have forgotten about it, the dates were too close together for it to have slipped his mind, and judging by his behaviour last night there was no way he had forgotten, which meant he'd deliberately chosen not to tell her. He'd deliberately chosen to shut her out.

It was definitely time to start thinking about her exit strategy.

It had been nine weeks.

Nine weeks that they'd known each other, almost eight weeks that they'd been living together and seven that they'd been sleeping together. She'd got too involved too quickly, even by her standards.

It was time to go.

Friday, 13th February

It had been a tense twenty-four hours. The events of Wednesday night shadowed their movements and eavesdropped on their conversation and Ruby was well aware that she was more short-tempered and feistier than normal and it was almost with a sense of relief that she dropped Noah off for his battery of tests.

He was going to spend a full day undergoing a range

of assessments—reflex testing, mobility tests, strength, fitness and then into the simulator. There was no need for her to go with him, it would do her good to have some space and time to work out how she was feeling.

She had her day all mapped out. She was going to wander through the Rocks and take a ferry trip and find a market or two to browse. But her day didn't go according to plan.

Ruby was lonely.

She was used to being lonely, she didn't particularly like it but she was usually able to entertain herself, but she missed Noah. It was the longest they had spent apart in eight weeks. She told herself she would adjust, it wasn't as if they were going to be together for ever but it was the first time she'd ever missed a person.

She thought she'd always been wandering, looking for a place to belong, but perhaps it might not be a place she'd been searching for. Perhaps it was a person.

She was constantly thinking, *I wish Noah was here to see this,* or wanting to talk to him, but he wasn't there. They had spent so much time together over the past two months that it was going to take some adjusting to being without him, but she knew that soon, maybe even as soon as today, he wouldn't need her anymore.

She did some shopping at the Bondi markets. She bought a couple of things for herself and a T-shirt for Noah but when she got back to the hotel and saw all his designer clothes hanging in the wardrobe she realised he would never wear what she'd just bought him. It wasn't his style. It was just another reminder of how different they really were.

* * *

Ruby didn't need Noah to tell her the results of his test. She could see on his face that he'd passed. He was grinning from ear to ear when she arrived to collect him.

He wrapped his arms around her waist and picked her up and spun her around, as excited as a child. 'We did it!

'You passed.'

Ruby wasn't quite as excited as he was but his exuberance was infectious and it was hard not to be happy for him. She *was* happy for him, of course she was.

Noah took her out to celebrate and she tried to have a good time. She used to be so good at pretending to have fun. She needed to remember how to do that.

'What time do you need to be at the track for testing tomorrow?' she asked. Tomorrow was the testing day for the cars. Another day of wandering around, waiting for Noah, loomed in front of her.

'Eight o'clock. I'm not driving tomorrow, the team don't want to risk it, but I'll be out there, watching. You're welcome to come with me.'

She didn't want to spend the day sitting around, waiting for him. That wasn't where she wanted this relationship to go.

'And then I thought we could go and visit my parents,' he added. 'They're only a three-hour drive from here.'

Ruby had two options. She could go with him or she could leave. Both options frightened her.

If she went with him it would mean moving their relationship onto another stage. She didn't want to meet his parents. In her eyes that was taking a step deeper into the relationship when she should be extricating herself. A more committed stage would mean he would expect more from her and he already knew more about her than anyone else did. All that was left to tell him was what had really happened when she'd run away to Melbourne and she didn't think she could do that. Which only left the alternative—not having him in her life at all. And she knew, from the past twenty-four hours, how that felt and she hadn't liked it.

But when she got scared she had two choices. Fight or flight.

And she always chose flight.

'I'm not a "meet-the-parents" type,' she told him.

'What does that mean?'

'It's not my thing.'

'What? You've never met any of your boyfriends' parents?'

'Nope. Why would I need to?'

'Oh, I don't know. Maybe because that's what people do when they're in a relationship. They get to know the other important people in each other's lives.'

'We've been in a relationship for five minutes. It's not as if it's serious.'

'Isn't it?'

He sounded cross. She'd never heard him cross before and she didn't like it. She didn't want him to be cross, she wanted him to tell her how he felt. But of course he didn't.

'Why won't you let me close? You have put up so many barriers that whenever I get past one it's only to find another one in my way. What are you afraid of?'

'Nothing,' she lied.

'Is this like Ron's New Year's Eve party? Are you

worried about people judging you? My parents aren't like that, they will love you.'

But she was pretty sure his parents wouldn't be expecting someone like her. They'd only need one look at her to see how different she was from their son. She'd grown up in a single-parent house with no money. He had everything he could possibly want. They really didn't have anything in common.

'I've met your family,' he said. 'Can't you do the same for me?'

She couldn't. She didn't know what she'd do instead but she had all day tomorrow to figure it out.

Saturday, 21st February

Scarlett's daughter lay in Ruby's lap, looking up at her with her dark eyes. At one week of age Holly was the image of her mother and had totally captured Ruby's heart. Captured all of them. The whole family was enamoured of this tiny doll of a child.

She had left Noah in Sydney one week ago when Scarlett had gone into labour and given her the perfect excuse to flee. She had left him to visit his parents alone but she couldn't stop thinking about him.

They'd had their second argument in less than a week and she knew it was her fear that was heightening the tension between them and making her disagreeable. She was so afraid that he wouldn't want her that she was pushing him away. She knew she was doing it but she seemed powerless to stop herself. Just like she couldn't stop thinking about him.

Noah had offered her the use of the penthouse as it was being rented for the team until after the opening race of the season but Ruby couldn't bear to stay there without him. She had loved the penthouse before but returning to it now she realised that what she'd loved about it was that it had felt like their own private hideaway from the world and it wasn't the same without Noah in it. Nothing was the same without Noah. But she'd have to learn to live like that.

Scarlett had lost a lot of blood during the delivery and the baby wasn't feeding all that well so Ruby had moved in with Scarlett and Jake to lend a hand. It was good to be busy and she was finding Holly to be a useful distraction from her almost constant thoughts of Noah.

Ruby and Lucy were supposed to be working in shifts to lend Scarlett a hand but more often than not they found themselves just sitting and watching the baby, unable to tear themselves away to do the more useful things that could help Scarlett. Right now they should be wrapping Holly and getting her ready for a sleep while Scarlett was in the shower but Ruby couldn't bring herself to relinquish her just yet. She was so delicate and perfect and Ruby could sit and hold her all day.

'What are your plans?' Lucy asked.

'Mum, do you mind if, for once, we don't have this conversation?'

'What do you mean?

'You always end up asking what my plans are. Making it sound as though I need to be settled down or have some grand vision for my future. I don't know what I'm doing.'

'But you've finished working for Noah. You must have some idea about what you're going to do next?'

And that was the crux of the matter. Noah didn't need her anymore.

Ruby tried counting to ten. She had tried to keep her New Year's resolution of being less argumentative but sometimes it was proving difficult. She knew she was on edge—she was missing Noah and that was making her more short-tempered than normal—but that wasn't Lucy's fault and she shouldn't take it out on her, but she really didn't want to have this conversation. Again.

'I thought I might stay in Adelaide for a bit. I thought I'd stay to help Scarlett and to be here while Rose gets better.' Rose was recovering very slowly and at times Ruby felt as though she wasn't recovering at all. The infection had taken its toll on her kidneys and Rose now required dialysis. To add to that she needed surgery to amputate the tips of three of her toes. While it wasn't as bad as they had first feared, Ruby was still finding it confronting and staying for a while was an idea she'd had although she hadn't worked out the logistics. Things like where she would stay long term and how she would earn an income, all the things that Noah had worked out for her, were now her responsibility again.

'It would be lovely to have you home.'

Ruby wasn't sure if it was really what she wanted—in fact, she suspected it wasn't at all what she wanted—but she couldn't think of any other options right now. She heard the washing machine finish its final spin cycle and made her escape by offering to hang out the clothes.

The basket was half-empty when Scarlett joined her outside.

'Are you okay?'

'Why?'

'Mum thought she'd upset you.'

'Why can't she just accept that I don't have my life all mapped out?'

'I know you don't want to think you're like Mum but the truth is you are very similar—it's probably why you clash more with her than Rose or I do. But being like Mum isn't necessarily a bad thing. You are strong and independent—'

'I don't want to be independent,' Ruby said. 'I want Noah.'

'So what are you doing here? Why aren't you with him?'

'He doesn't need me anymore.'

'Has he said that?'

Ruby shook her head as she pegged a sock onto the line. 'No, but why would he? He's fine now. He'll be travelling around the country, doing what he does. I've got nowhere else I need to be so I thought I'd stay here.'

'What does he think you're doing here?'

'Helping you.'

'Did he ask you to go with him?'

'Yes.'

'But you chose to come here?'

'I didn't want to make the same mistakes Mum did.'

'What mistakes?'

'Falling for the wrong man.'

'Why is Noah the wrong man?'

Ruby had only intended to have some fun, as usual, but she was in over her head and afraid he would break her heart. 'Noah is in a completely different league from me. He flies around the country in private planes, stays in five-star penthouses and has a watch that is worth thousands of dollars.'

'None of those things are his. They're just perks of the job,' Scarlett pointed out.

'He still earns millions of dollars a year from his racing and sponsorships. He wears designer clothes and owns a beachfront house in Queensland. I shop at the markets or second-hand stores. When my things were packed up and sent over from Byron Bay they fitted into two moving boxes,' Ruby argued.

'So? Does that mean you don't deserve him?'

That was exactly how she felt. Because of her father's behaviour Ruby had never believed she was worthy of being loved. 'I was just the hired help.'

'Did he ever say that? Think of all the things Noah has done for you. He bought you a gorgeous dress that fitted you perfectly. I know he never asked for your size, he had paid enough attention to know. He has taken you to Sydney—twice. He has met all of us and even came to Christmas lunch when he could have insisted that you stay at the apartment with him. Does he even know you're not planning on coming back to him, that you're moving on from this relationship?'

'Not exactly.'

'You're doing it again, aren't you?'

'Doing what?'

'Running away. You need to ask yourself what you are running from.'

Ruby knew exactly why she was running.

'One day you have to stop running. You need to talk to Noah, you need to find out how he feels, you need to give him a chance. He should have a say in this. If you want what Jake and I have you can't keep pushing people away. One day you'll have to let someone in.'

But Ruby was terrified that once Noah knew all her

secrets he wouldn't like her anymore. It was better just to leave and not find out.

But Scarlett hadn't finished. 'I know you don't want to be like Mum, and I know you're not going to like what I'm about to say, but I think you're showing more traits of your father.'

'What is that supposed to mean?'

'Running away. Not telling people how you really feel. Mum has never hidden her feelings and she has faced up to her mistakes. She never did anything wrong except fall in love. It was our fathers who let her down. She has never let us down and neither have you. You can't be someone you're not and I'm sure Noah doesn't expect you to be, but don't you think he deserves to know who you are?'

Saturday, 28th February

He was back.

Ruby was by his side and her world felt infinitely better than it had three days ago.

She was standing on top of the pit building that had been erected for the V8 championship race. Noah stood behind her. His arms were wrapped around her waist and his lips brushed her ear and sent tingles through her as they surveyed the circuit. From the rooftop she could look across the park to the city.

The parklands and the streets on the eastern side of the city had been transformed. These were the same streets she'd been driving on, taking Noah to his appointments and visiting Rose in hospital but she wouldn't have recognised them. It looked like the circus had come to town, a massive, oversized circus.

Concrete barriers hemmed in the roads, turning them into a race track. Pedestrian bridges spanned the raceway and grandstands lined the circuit. Banners and flags waved in the breeze and added to the carnival atmosphere. There were vehicles everywhere—race cars, semi-trailers, news vans and food trucks. There was even a sideshow alley with showground rides and there were people everywhere.

Ruby couldn't believe the number of people who turned up to watch the races—hundreds of thousands over four days. Where had they all come from? It was busy and noisy and chaotic. Ruby's opinion had been that the race was for car fanatics but she suspected she would enjoy the spectacle too. It was crazy and colourful and loud and fun. And Noah was right there with her.

He'd been expecting to see her when he'd got back to Adelaide and she hadn't told him anything different. She had wanted to see him too. She hadn't even pretended to justify her behaviour to herself, she had run straight back to him as if her life depended on it. She had missed him and she had to admit that to herself, even if she wasn't prepared to admit it to anyone else. She had never felt like this about anyone.

She had been searching long and hard for her place to belong. She'd never expected to find it in the arms of a man. But she had to accept that she had found who and what she wanted in Noah. He was everything and all she wanted.

She had spent the past two days back in his arms and she never wanted to leave. She wondered if this was what being in love felt like.

'Come on,' he whispered. 'It's time to go.'

He needed to go and prepare for his race. Ruby had never watched a car race until today and she was extremely nervous when she thought of Noah out there among the action.

Noah left her with Ron Townsend, the team boss, in his corporate box. Ruby would have a good vantage point to watch the cars as they competed to see who could do the fastest lap and qualify for pole position on the grid for tomorrow's race.

The corporate box was in the pit building directly above the team's garages. Ruby kept her eyes peeled for car number twenty-two. There appeared to be no rigid system, it was all rather fluid. Cars would emerge from their garages and tear around the track in an attempt to post the fastest time before either retiring back into the garage or doing another lap. There was no lining up on the pit straight, no structure or fanfare. Rather the cars all seemed to do as they pleased.

Ruby held her breath when she saw Noah's car nose out of the garage. He merged into the traffic at the end of the pit lane.

'He'll have a lap to warm up his tyres first,' Ron explained, and Ruby relaxed and let out the breath.

Ron held a stopwatch in his hand. He turned his head to the left, waiting for Noah to reappear at the beginning of the pit straight.

Ruby saw Noah's car. He flew down the straight and in a matter of seconds had passed by them and was weaving through the chicane at the opposite end. Ron clicked his stopwatch as he went by.

'How fast do they go?' she asked.

'They can reach speeds of two hundred and sixty kilometres an hour.'

'What?' She had watched in the earlier races as cars had jostled for position, screaming around the circuit side by side, so close that several cars had had their side mirrors taken off by other competitors. Cars had spun or been shunted out of control and had collided with concrete walls, other cars and tyre barriers.

But the earlier races had just been a prelude for these cars. These were the cream of the crop and she could tell they were faster and would be more competitive. Being a spectator gave her quite an adrenalin rush and she could only imagine how Noah felt. She imagined it would be an addictive feeling. Battling to control the power of the engine in the hope of coming out victorious would surely put him on an adrenalin high.

Ron clicked the stopwatch as Noah came past again.

'Eighty-three seconds.'

'Is that good?'

'He'll need to shave a second or two off if he wants to qualify near the top of the list.'

'So they'll get their position on the grid and then come out tomorrow and do this for how many laps?'

'Seventy-eight.'

Ruby knew the race took about two hours to complete. She couldn't imagine keeping focused for that long at these sorts of speeds and especially not when there were twenty other cars on the track at the same time, all with the same goal—to cross the finish line in first place.

Watching the qualifying race clarified for her why he had spent so much time on his rehabilitation but she still found it difficult to comprehend that he'd made it back to the race track only eleven weeks after his accident. The G forces the drivers encountered, the effort required for the constant gear changes, not to mention the concentration required and the physical stress from the bumps from the track and the other cars, meant they needed to be super-fit.

The drivers' times were being displayed on the supersized television screens that were prominently positioned along the track. Ruby glanced up at Noah's time as he brought his car into the pit garage at the end of his third lap.

Jamie Winter in car number one had the time to beat. Eighty-one point six seconds.

Noah was currently tenth and Ruby wondered why he was coming in. Maybe he was happy with that position but qualifying didn't finish for another five minutes. What if someone else posted a faster time and pushed him down the rankings?

'Why isn't Noah out there?' she asked Ron.

'He'll wait until the last minute to try to post a faster lap. He'll be hoping that doesn't leave enough time for anyone else to catch him. This is a strategic competition. It's not just about who's the fastest, it's also about who plays the game the best.'

Ruby watched as the rankings on the screen were constantly updated as other cars finished and started their laps.

With three minutes to go, Noah came back onto the track. The first lap wasn't a complete lap, which meant he needed enough time to get around the circuit twice. Several other cars followed him out, including the current leader in car number one.

'Eighty-one point one seconds!' Ron clicked his stop-watch as Noah completed his final lap and Ruby waited for the time to be confirmed on the screen.

Noah had edged out Jamie Winter. He'd taken first place.

The clock counted down the seconds until the end of qualifying. With ten seconds remaining, Jamie's car crossed the start line.

'Damn.'

Ruby had one eye on the clock. 'He won't have time to finish his lap,' she said.

'It doesn't matter. As long as he starts it before the clock runs down he's allowed to finish.'

Ruby held her breath as she waited as one by one the last cars crossed the finish line.

Car number one turned the final corner.

Eighty-one point zero five seconds.

Noah had been squeezed out by the barest of margins.

Ron shrugged his shoulders. 'Can't complain about second fastest, it puts him on the front row,' was all he said, as he accompanied Ruby down to the pit garage.

Noah was out of the car. He had taken his helmet off and his hair was wet with perspiration. Ruby remembered him telling her the temperature in the cars could reach sixty degrees Celsius and she wondered how they tolerated that for an entire two-hour race.

Ruby hadn't seen him in his racing suit before. He looked fantastic—strong and capable.

It was red and white and fitted him like a second skin and she couldn't help but admire his bum as he bent over the engine to discuss something with one of the mechanics.

He straightened up, turned around and saw her. He was grinning from ear to ear. He pushed his hair off his forehead and tucked his helmet under his arm, reminding Ruby of her earliest fantasy involving Noah and a motorbike ride. She blushed just thinking about it.

He crossed the garage and scooped her up. 'I did it. I'm on the front row of the grid.'

Ruby knew how important it was to him to prove that he had made a full recovery and that the accident hadn't left him with any issues.

'What did you think?' he asked.

'It was incredible. Scary but incredible and you were amazing.'

He kissed her on the lips—she could taste the saltiness of his sweat but she wouldn't change a thing. He was pumped, on a massive high, and his enthusiasm was infectious. 'I'm going to get out of this suit. Come with me and you can tell me more about how amazing I was,' he said, still grinning widely as Ruby followed him out of the garage and into one of the team's semitrailers that was parked behind the pit building.

The trucks were used to transport the cars, tyres and all the necessary equipment between circuits but during events the front half of the trailer was converted into a lounge for the drivers and the back half became a nerve centre and computer lab. The trailer was abandoned. They had it to themselves.

'So you enjoyed it, then?' he asked, as he ripped open the top of his racing jumpsuit. He had several layers of fireproof clothing underneath and he stripped these off too, leaving him standing semi-naked in front of her. He had been working hard to control his car as he'd sped around the circuit and the blood was still coursing through the muscles in his chest and arms. They were all clearly defined and as Ruby ran her eyes over his torso she thought he had never looked better.

'It was brilliant,' she said in a husky voice. 'There's a lot to like about motorsport.'

Ruby didn't know where all the other team members had gone and she didn't care. All she cared about was the fact that Noah was standing before her in a state of undress and she was as horny as it was humanly possible to be.

She stepped closer to him. 'Does the trailer have a lock?' she asked.

Noah didn't need to be asked twice. He slid the bolt across the door in one swift movement as Ruby ran her hands down his chest and into the back of his jumpsuit, pulling him hard against her. She tipped her head up, offering her lips to him, and he kissed her hard on her mouth.

Ruby pulled his jumpsuit a little lower, enough to free his erection. Noah started to help her to take it off but she stopped him. 'I want you to leave it on,' she told him. He was seriously sexy in this outfit.

Noah grinned and lifted Ruby off her feet. She wrapped her legs around his waist as she let him take control. For several weeks she had been the one in charge of their lovemaking. She had been restrained and cautious, conscious of the fact that his body was still healing. Now there were no such concerns and she could feel that Noah was eager to dictate the terms.

To her left a bench ran along the side wall of the trailer. Noah spun around ninety degrees and rested Ruby's butt on the edge of the bench. He let the bench take her weight, freeing his hands, and pushed her dress up to her waist. He pulled her knickers to one side; there was no time to remove them. Ruby heard the fabric rip but she was beyond caring. All she wanted was to feel Noah inside her.

Ruby clamped her legs tighter around his waist as he thrust inside her. She arched her back, wanting to take him as deep as she could, and cried out as she rode him. The adrenalin pumped through her veins and heightened her senses. The sex was frantic and urgent but no less enjoyable.

But she wanted time to remember every moment. Time to commit every touch to memory. She wanted to be able to recall how he tasted, how he looked and how he felt as he filled her.

She needed to make memories to store away for later. For when he left. His job was going to take him away from her.

All she would have left would be her memories.

Friday, 6th March

Noah had left for Melbourne. Ruby wanted to be there too.

He had asked her to go with him but she couldn't be in two places at once. Rose and her family needed her here and she had made a choice, a responsible, grown-up adult choice, where she did the right thing by others, rather than just choosing whatever suited her. She knew she'd made the right choice but it was tough.

Rose needed a kidney transplant. The bacteria had irreparably damaged her kidneys and the dialysis wasn't going to be a long-term option.

Rose needed her family around her. Rose needed

her more than Noah did so Ruby had stayed. She was undergoing tests to see if she was a compatible donor. Her blood type was compatible but that was only step one. She had undergone several tests already and was waiting on the first lot of results.

The transplant team had done a skin cross-match, which had involved taking a small sample of skin from under her arm and incubating these cells in Rose's serum to see if they survived or were destroyed.

Noah knew she was expecting the first lot of test results. He phoned her before his race but unfortunately this was only minutes after the doctors had called her with the news that she was incompatible. Her skin cells had been destroyed. Her kidney was not an option for Rose.

She was devastated and felt lost.

She hadn't intended to watch the race. She needed to start putting some distance between her and Noah if she was going to be able to let go and move on, but she couldn't resist. She needed to see him. And seeing him on television was as close as she was going to get.

Ruby turned the television on just as the cars were lining up on the grid. Subconsciously she'd known exactly when the race was due to start.

It was only an exhibition race, there were no championship points being awarded, but that didn't stop the competitiveness of the drivers.

Noah was starting from third position. At the very first corner his car was clipped by the car behind. Ruby watched, horrified, as the impact turned Noah ninety degrees before the car behind slammed into his passenger door, pushing him sideways along the track. His car collided with the kerbing and rolled, doing a full somersault across the track.

Ruby's heart was pounding as she watched his car flip a second time and collide, midway through the flip, at high speed with the tyre wall. His car was tossed into the air and came to land with a sickening thud on its roof.

The windscreen exploded, sending fragments of safety glass across the track, and the front of the car was completely crushed.

Ruby was stunned. She couldn't bear to watch as the television network showed the crash over and over again but she couldn't make herself move. Her body and her brain had shut down, refusing to believe what she was seeing.

But she was seeing it again and again—in slow motion, in real time and from all different angles. She managed to mute the sound but she couldn't bring herself to change the channel or switch the television off. She needed to keep watching. She had to know what had happened to Noah.

Was he okay? Was he hurt? Was he still alive?

She eventually realised she needed to hear the commentary if she wanted to know anything. She turned the sound back on as the vision showed the safety car out on the track. An ambulance was pulling up on the other side of the concrete barrier and a tow truck was angled across the road.

And then she saw him.

He was climbing out of the car. Out through a window.

She let out the breath she hadn't been aware of holding as she saw him pull himself out through the side window. He was okay.

But just as she thought that his knees buckled and she watched helplessly as he collapsed onto the track. The paramedics were quick to get to him and the last thing Ruby saw was Noah being bundled into the back of the ambulance.

She turned the television off as the ambulance drove away with its lights flashing.

She didn't know what to do. She didn't know what she *could* do.

Her first instinct was to run to Noah. But he was close to eight hundred kilometres away in Melbourne and there were people here who needed her too. Rose's condition was worsening and baby Holly wasn't feeding properly because Scarlett was stressed. They need her too but who needed her most? All she could think about was Noah.

What if he wasn't okay? What would she do?

Ruby felt like she should now be in three places at once. With Rose, with Scarlett and with Noah. She wished someone would tell her where to go or what to do.

It was too much for her to handle and her first impulse was to run away, but she had promised Scarlett she'd try to resist that impulse.

But her promises mean nothing.

She still wanted to run. She just didn't know in which direction to go.

CHAPTER TEN

NOAH WAS IRRITABLE but it had nothing to do with the accident. Unfortunately for him, his out-of-character irritability was attributed to a suspected second concussion, which only served to increase his irritability as he was forced to follow routine medical procedure.

Despite what the medicos thought, he *knew* he didn't have concussion. He'd tried to tell the doctors at the track that but no one had been listening. He'd tried to talk his way out of a trip to the hospital but the medicos hadn't been prepared to take a chance—in their opinion, today's accident and possible repercussions were too close to his earlier crash and they weren't about to take his word for it. He'd been carted off to hospital and now he was cooling his heels, waiting for the results of a brain scan.

All the other tests had been normal and he was becoming increasingly frustrated as more time passed. He wasn't normally an impatient man but there were other things he wanted to be doing.

He kept one eye on the clock as the hospital staff kept one eye on him. He knew they were watching him like hawks—if they hadn't been paying such close attention he would have made a break for it. He needed to get to a phone.

Finally the doctor arrived with the verdict—all clear. No surprises there.

What a waste of time.

Noah didn't waste any more of it. He made a dash for a hospital phone. He dialled Ruby's number, knowing she would be worried about him. His phone was back at the race track—which was just as well. He could only imagine what the nurses would have said if he'd pulled his mobile phone out to make a call while he'd been in Emergency.

His call went straight to her message service.

He left a message, thinking she must be on the phone, and after signing his discharge papers he tried again.

And he tried a third time while he waited for a ride back to the circuit. But each time he got her message service.

That was odd. He'd assumed she'd be waiting for a call from him.

He wondered what was going on but he had no way of finding out. He could remember no other numbers. Maybe the accident had rattled him more than he'd thought.

He checked his phone the moment he got back to the track but there was no message from Ruby. No missed calls. Nothing. It had been almost three hours since his accident—why couldn't he contact her?

Scarlett's home number was in his phone. He had no other choice. He had to find Ruby. He dialled Scarlett.

'Scarlett, it's Noah—'

'Noah! Are you okay? Is everything all right?'

'Yes, I'm fine. I'm trying to get hold of Ruby but

she's not answering her phone. Do you know where she is?'

'She's not with you?'

'No. Should she be?' He frowned. Had he missed something? Forgotten something? He was starting to think he had suffered another bump to the head.

'She saw your accident on television. She told me she was flying to Melbourne to see you. You haven't heard from her?'

'No, her phone is switched off.'

'Maybe she's on the plane.'

He couldn't understand why she hadn't called and left him a message. Maybe she'd panicked. 'Did she tell you what airline she was going to fly with?'

'No. She was going to the airport to get on the next available flight.'

He could tell Scarlett was worried now. He was too. He took a deep breath as he tried to calm his nerves and settle Scarlett's at the same time. 'I'll call the airlines and get flight details, see if I can work out which flight she's on. I'll let you know as soon as I hear anything.'

He paced up and down inside the trailer while he made calls. The first two airlines he rang both had flights that Ruby could have been on but both had already landed in Melbourne and he still hadn't heard from her. He couldn't sit and wait, he was too restless, too worried. Something didn't feel right.

He called in a favour and got a lift to the airport. He'd wait for her there. He wanted to be on hand when she landed.

But two hours later he'd still heard nothing. Ruby was still out of contact. She hadn't miraculously appeared in Melbourne and Scarlett had heard nothing either.

Now he was really worried. He knew she was stressed about Rose. What had she done? Where was she?

Something was wrong. He could feel it in his gut. It was twisting and churning and making him feel quite nauseous. He'd waited long enough. He would have to go and find her.

His mind flashed back to the last time he'd waited.

Ten years ago he'd waited for his brother to come home. Ten years ago he'd waited too long. He wasn't going to make the same mistake twice.

He jumped on the next available flight to Adelaide and checked his phone the minute he was allowed to switch it on. Still nothing.

He hurried along the concourse with little idea of what he was going to do or where he was heading.

He called Scarlett. 'I'm here. Have you heard anything?'

'No.'

By now no one had seen or heard from Ruby for several hours. He knew she'd run away before—she'd run away to Melbourne when she was sixteen, she'd run away with him to be his carer rather than stay with her mother, and she'd run from him when he'd wanted to take her to meet his parents. It seemed whenever she was under stress she took flight. The difference this time was no one knew where she'd gone.

He had to find her.

'What do I do?' he asked Scarlett. He wasn't used to being uncertain. He was good at making decisions. In his job he often had to make quick, life-or-death decisions and he knew that wasting time in second-guessing himself was futile. But motor racing was different, he'd had experience in those situations. He'd had plenty of practice behind the wheel of a racing car but his feelings for Ruby were a whole different ballgame and he was terrified that something had happened. Something *must* have happened for her to disappear off the radar like this.

Despite all the time they'd spent together, there was still so much he had to learn about her. But he did know that this was out of character, even for her. He couldn't imagine her disappearing without telling Scarlett. She'd told her she was getting on a plane and maybe she had, but she hadn't flown to Melbourne. How on earth was he going to find her?

What did he know? Where might she go? And then it hit him and he knew exactly where Ruby would be. Her safe place.

The palm house.

He couldn't believe he hadn't thought of it before. He looked at his watch, the designer watch that Ruby had teased him about. What time did the gardens close? It was already five o'clock.

'Noah, are you there?'

Scarlett's voice interrupted his thoughts. He'd almost forgotten she was on the other end of the phone.

'Yes, I'm still here.'

'I said come to my house. Jake will be home soon, he can go with you to start looking.'

'No. I need to go to the botanic gardens,' Noah said.

'What on earth for?'

'She took me to a place there once. She might have gone back there.'

'I don't think that's where she'll be.'

There was a pause as Noah waited for Scarlett to elaborate but she didn't continue.

'Scarlett? You're worrying me. Do you know where to find her? You don't think she would have done anything silly, do you?' He'd already lost his brother and he refused to accept that he couldn't save Ruby. He couldn't lose her too.

'Nothing we shouldn't be able to undo.'

'What does that mean?'

'You need to start looking in bars, in hotels.'

'Bars? Why?' Nothing was making much sense. He was struggling to get things straight in his head. 'Ruby doesn't drink.'

'Has she told you why?'

'She told me she doesn't like the way it makes her feel.'

'It's a bit more complicated than that. It's really her story to tell but I'm worried that the stress of recent events—Rose's condition and now your accident—might have pushed her over the edge. We'll have to start looking somewhere and the bars and pubs is my guess. I'll meet you at my house and we can work out where to start.'

He couldn't imagine his life without Ruby in it. In a matter of weeks she had become a part of him, a part that he couldn't do without. He had fallen in love with her. He needed to find her and tell her.

He didn't care what she was doing as long as he found her, and he was positive Scarlett was wrong.

He was sure he knew where she'd be.

'I'm going to the botanic gardens. I'll call you when I find her.'

He disconnected the call and headed for the exit. His

path took him past one of the airport bars. He glanced inside, not expecting to see anyone he knew, but Scarlett's words were ringing in his head. A girl with red hair was sitting at the bar. He hesitated and took a second look. Did she resemble Ruby because he wanted her to?

The bar was dimly lit, making it difficult to see for sure. He walked in. He didn't want to find her in here. He didn't want Scarlett to be right.

'Ruby?'

The girl turned and lifted her head. She was a stranger.

Noah kept going, cursing himself for wasting time. He hailed a taxi and promised the driver he'd double his fare if he got him there in under half an hour. He couldn't risk the chance that the gardens would be closed.

He sprinted through the park, cutting across the lawn as he made a beeline for the palm house. The late afternoon sun was shining on the glass, turning it into one giant mirror. He held his hand up against the glare as he raced up the front steps, taking them three at a time and not stopping until he was in the centre of the building. He looked up and down the pathway as he called her name.

'Ruby?'

'Noah!' She was down the pathway to his right. 'You're all right!' She jumped up from the wall and ran towards him. Her eyes were red, she'd obviously been crying, but her face lit up and she managed a smile for him.

'I'm fine,' he said. 'What are you doing here?' he

asked as he wrapped her in his arms. She felt so good. This was where she belonged. With him.

'I had some things to think about.'

'I've been calling you for hours. Why didn't you answer?'

'I left my phone at Scarlett's. The battery was flat.'

'How long have you been here?'

'I have no idea.' She paused, thinking. 'I saw the accident on television,' she added. 'How long ago was that?'

'Almost seven hours ago.'

'I guess I've been here for a few hours, then.'

Ruby wasn't sure where that time had gone. Her first instinct when she'd seen the accident had been to run to Noah and she'd even told Scarlett that was what she planned to do, but she hadn't been able to make herself go through with it. She hadn't thought she could bear to be rejected. It had been a stressful day—finding out she was an incompatible donor for Rose and then seeing Noah's horrific accident had almost been too much for her to handle. She couldn't stand the thought of something happening to either Noah or Rose. She hadn't wanted to consider that one day they might not be around but that was the possibility she'd faced today. She couldn't afford to take them for granted. One day they might not be there.

She'd felt so helpless watching Noah's accident and she couldn't stand to think that she could lose him.

She would give anything to keep him safe.

She loved him.

She recognised the feeling now. She was in love.

It was time to stop being afraid of letting people into

her life. It was time to let people close but she didn't know how to do that.

She'd needed some space. She'd needed time to think about what this all meant and what she was going to do. And that had been when she'd headed to the palm house.

The palm house was her sanctuary. But it wasn't where she wanted to be. Not today.

She wanted to stop running but she didn't think she was brave enough. It had been a promise she'd made to herself twelve weeks ago but it was something she was struggling with.

The palm house had always given her hope that one day she'd find a place where she belonged. And she'd found it. Only it wasn't a place. It was Noah.

Noah was her palm house. She belonged with him.

'It's time to go.' Noah unwrapped her from his embrace and took her hand.

Ruby shook her head. 'I think I might stay.' She needed Noah to say he wanted her to go with him. If he didn't, she may as well stay put. She sat down on the retaining wall.

'You can't stay here,' Noah said. 'The park is closing soon and I'm not leaving here without you.'

'You'll have to leave eventually,' she replied. 'You'll have to go back to Melbourne. The races aren't over.'

'They're over for me.'

'You did get hurt!' Ruby ran her eyes over him, searching for injuries, but he looked unscathed.

He was shaking his head. 'I'm fine but you are far more important and you are coming with me. Let me look after you.'

She gave in because she was too tired to argue. And

because she'd wanted Noah to take charge of the situation and look after her.

He had booked them into a hotel on the beachfront at Glenelg. They had nowhere else to go but Ruby didn't care where she was as long as she was with him. He ordered room service while she had a shower. They were both exhausted.

Their corner suite overlooked the beach and Noah had turned the couch around so they were nestled into the bay window. Ruby was curled up into the curve of his side, watching a summer lightning storm light up the sky. There was no rain but the air sparked with electricity as the lightning forks hit the ocean.

Watching the lightning hit the water was reminiscent of the impact Noah had had on her. She was the water and his touch was the lightning that turned her to steam.

'You told Scarlett you were coming to me. Why didn't you?' His voice was deep in his chest, rumbling like the distant thunder.

'I couldn't decide if that was the right decision. I was scared.'

'Of what?'

'I have never run towards someone before. I've always run away.' Her first response had always been flight. She might have deliberated that point with Scarlett but she knew it was true.

'Why?'

'When the going gets tough,' Ruby said, 'the tough get going.'

'It doesn't mean they run away. It means they get ready to fight for what they want,' Noah told her. 'I'm in your corner. I will fight with you and for you.'

'You might not say that if you knew the real me. There are a lot of things you don't know.'

'If there are, it's only because you haven't told me. Why haven't you let me in?' he asked.

'I don't like it when people get too close.'

'Why not?'

'If they get close they can hurt me.'

'How?'

'By getting to know the real me,' she finally admitted. 'I've done some things I'm not proud of.'

'That's the beauty of life, though—if you're lucky you get a chance to fix your mistakes. You get a chance to make amends. I think you're special and I can't imagine there is anything you could tell me that would change my mind.'

'I'm not so sure about that.'

'Why don't you try me?'

Ruby closed her eyes and tucked herself closer against Noah's chest. It was time to stop being afraid. It was time to let him into her life, and if she was going to do that he needed to hear her story.

She felt safe with him, she'd felt like that since the day she'd met him, and she just hoped she was right in thinking she could trust him. To tell him her whole story would be like entrusting him with her soul.

She took a deep breath and began.

'I was a bit of a difficult teenager. Mum and I clashed constantly. Rose's dad had died and Mum was struggling to keep me under control. When I was sixteen I decided I'd had enough of Mum telling me what to do and I ran off to Melbourne to live with my father. A man who I'd never met and who I found out wanted nothing to do with me.

'The whole thing was an absolute disaster but I was too proud to admit my mistake and go home. I knew my "father" wouldn't tell Mum what was going on so I stayed in Melbourne, with a man who didn't want me around and who couldn't care less about what I got up to. So of course I got up to lots of things that no six-teen-year-old should.

'I dropped out of school and proceeded to get deeper and deeper into trouble. I was drinking a lot and one day I woke up in a strange bed. I had no idea where I was or what I'd been doing.'

'Where were your friends?

'I didn't have friends. Acquaintances maybe, for want of a better word, but no one who had the maturity or the empathy to watch out for another kid or to stop me from getting into trouble. If anything, they contributed to the problem.'

'What about your family? Your mum? Scarlett?'

'They were in Adelaide. They didn't know what I was up to.'

'A few weeks later I found out I was pregnant. I was terrified. I couldn't go home to Mum—I realise now that of course I could have, but at the time I didn't think it was an option. Mum had Scarlett when she was eigh-teen and one of the things Mum and I argued about was that I didn't want to be like her. And falling pregnant at seventeen was history repeating itself. I'd been drinking a lot and I was terrified I'd hurt the baby. I had no idea who the father was and I was not emotionally capable of being a mother. I didn't know what to do.'

'What happened?'

'I had a miscarriage. I think my body was in no con-dition to be pregnant and it was probably the best outcome but I've felt guilty ever since. But it had happened and I couldn't change it. All I could do was change my behaviour. I stopped drinking after that and I haven't had a drink since. I have never been good at dealing with conflict or resolving problems. I've always opted to run away to avoid dealing with anything unpleasant or stressful and back then I escaped by abusing alcohol.'

'You obviously survived and came through this. How did you do that?'

'Scarlett. She figured out something was wrong. She came to Melbourne and got me sorted. She got me to go back to school and got me out of trouble.'

'You must have some inner strength of your own too.'

'Why do you say that?' Ruby lifted her head and opened her eyes. She needed to see him.

'I imagine you've been under considerable pressure with Rose's illness and I assume today was stressful for you yet you got yourself through it. I think you are stronger than you give yourself credit for.'

'I barely got through today. I was just hoping that if I pretended everything was fine, maybe it would be. I've always done that. But today it wasn't working. There was too much to ignore. Rose's illness, Scarlett and the baby and you.'

'Me? What about me?'

'I'm a bit overwhelmed by how you make me feel. You make me feel like I did when I was drinking and that scares me.'

'I don't understand.'

'I liked the way I felt about the world, about myself, more after a few drinks. I wanted to feel better about myself and drinking helped me do that. Then it got to the point where I needed a drink. And then more than one.

'I felt the same way about you. I feel better about myself when I am with you but I don't want to be dependent on someone else for that. But I'm afraid that is what will happen. I'm afraid I won't be able to give you up.

'I'm not the same person I was ten years ago. But I'm still trying to find out who I am exactly and where I belong. Ten years ago I was searching for myself as much as I was looking for a place to belong. I didn't like the person I became when I was in Melbourne but without Scarlett's help I don't think I would have made it. Sometimes I still feel the same way. That I'm searching and searching but I haven't found what I'm looking for. I keep thinking that if I find somewhere I feel comfortable I'll be able to find the real me. But I've realised it's not a place I've been searching for.

'When I watched you in that accident today I felt as though it was me in that car. It felt like my heart was getting ripped apart but all I cared about was whether or not you were going to be okay. Nothing else mattered. Only you. I haven't been searching for a place, I've been searching for a person. I've been searching for you.'

'Why didn't you get on a plane and come to me?'

'Because I wasn't brave enough. I didn't know if you felt the same way and I wasn't sure if I was strong enough to cope if you didn't want me. You needed me when you were injured but you're not injured now and I don't know where that leaves me.'

'I want you with me. What will it take to get you to run to me instead of away?'

'I need to know you'll be there for me no matter what.'

'How can I prove that to you except with time?'

'You could tell me about your ex-wife.'

'Steph? Why?'

'I want to know what happened between you. I need to know that you tried to make it work. I need to know you're not going to give up on me.'

'Why would I give up on you?'

'Because I might not be what you expect.'

'No one expects you to be someone you're not. Being someone others expect you to be isn't sustainable. You have to be the person you are meant to be. I know because I tried to change for Steph. I wasn't coping at all with Adam's suicide. Getting married was Steph's idea, she thought it would fix me, make me happy again. I figured I didn't have anything to lose, things couldn't get worse, so I agreed.

'There were some parts of me that I wanted to change but I didn't want to give up my dream of racing cars. That was the only thing that made me feel better. So I kept my contract and got promoted up the ranks until I spent most of the year away, driving. That wasn't what Steph had had in mind. She didn't like travelling all the time and she didn't like being left alone. There was no easy solution to that dilemma so we split. But I liked being married. I liked the companionship, I believe in the commitment but we couldn't make it work. We didn't have the same dream and in the end I couldn't be the person she wanted me to be.

'And that's why I don't expect you to be someone you're not. I love you just the way you are.'

'You love me?'

'I do. You are kind, funny, considerate, adorable, sexy and strong and I'm not complete without you. I need you. All I could think about when I was being carted off to hospital was you. And when I couldn't find you I was going crazy. I was terrified that something had happened to you. I didn't know how I would survive that. I don't want to be in a world without you and I promise that if you'll have me, I will never leave you. I want to share my life with you. I didn't know you ten years ago but I know you now and I love you, just the way you are.' He paused then added, 'Except for maybe one small thing.'

'What is it?' she asked, not really sure if she wanted to hear the answer.

'I want you to have a husband.'

'A husband?'

Noah nodded as he unwrapped his arm from around her shoulders and got down on one knee. 'Ruby, will you marry me?'

'Yes,' she said, as she laughed and pulled him to his feet.

'Yes,' she repeated, as she stood up and stepped into his embrace.

'Yes,' she said, as she kissed him.

'I love you, too,' she said, as another lightning fork split the sky. But she was oblivious to the storm, she wasn't aware of anything other than Noah. She was in his arms. She was right where she belonged. She'd made it.

* * * * *

MILLS & BOON®

'Tis the season to be daring...

The perfect books for all your glamorous Christmas needs come complete with gorgeous billionaire bad-boy heroes and are overflowing with champagne!

These fantastic 3-in-1s are must-have reads for all Modern™, Desire™ and Modern Tempted™ fans.

**Get your copies today at
www.millsandboon.co.uk/Xmasmod**

MILLS & BOON®

Want to get more from Mills & Boon?

Here's what's available to you if you join the exclusive **Mills & Boon eBook Club** today:

✦ *Convenience – choose your books each month*
✦ *Exclusive – receive your books a month before anywhere else*
✦ *Flexibility – change your subscription at any time*
✦ *Variety – gain access to eBook-only series*
✦ *Value – subscriptions from just £1.99 a month*

So visit **www.millsandboon.co.uk/esubs** today to be a part of this exclusive eBook Club!